JANIS
AND THE
REAPER

NIKKI M. GRIGGS

Spellbound Publishing House, LLC © 2023
www.spellbound-publishing.com

Cover art by Anna Harmon
Copyright © 2023 Anna Harmon
Edited by Taylor Johnson

Spellbound Publishing House, LLC
Austin, TX | www.spellbound-publishing.com

First edition: October 2023

The publisher is not responsible for websites (or their content) that are not owned by the publisher.

Identifiers: LCCN 2023942900 | ISBN 9798891230064 (hardback)
ISBN 9798891230040 (paperback) | 9798891230057 (ebook)

To my grandmother, who always believed I would get here.
You would have loved this.

I miss you still.

ARIZONA

Fifteen and a Half Years Ago

A FOX SNUCK ALONG the exterior of the Oro Valley Hospital, bushy tail swishing through the desert air of a February afternoon. It was colder today than expected for Arizona even in the winter, and the animal shook itself from time to time, displeased. Rounding a corner of the building, the fox paused as he came across a garden.

What a boring landscape, he thought. *Human aesthetics. No reference whatsoever to any beauty.*

Large windows showed the inside of the hospital's cafeteria. Unseen, the fox sniffed at the seams in the glass. He was in the right place, but he wasn't sure if the parents—Mr. and Mrs. Pereda he had been told—would agree to the bargain. He didn't even know if he would make the offer. He sniffed again, dallying with his fickle thoughts.

If he completed the deal, his quota for the month would be satisfied, and it wasn't yet the full moon. The fox puffed out his chest. It would be a personal best.

There were only a few fae from the Hill with the responsibility of making deals with humans, and fewer still who were responsible for changeling bargains. Tensith, the fox sitting in the hospital garden, was one of those talented few. Though his was a conscripted vocation, it was important enough that he felt immense pride and satisfaction in the work.

If a faerie bairn, given willingly by their fae parents, was accepted by a human couple, Tensith returned sixteen years later to bring the changeling to bless the Hill. There was a strong magic from the love given by human parents that was soaked up by the changeling. No fae could replicate such an emotion asit was not in their nature to feel

1

unconditional love.

It wasn't easy to get mortal parents to agree to raise a changeling. Even under an ensorcellement, the caretakers had to truly, even desperately, want a child for the bargain to take. The enchantment was a simple one, meant only to aid in the decision-making process. If a mortal couple did not wish to enter into the contract, the glamour would be nothing more than a passing daydream.

Tensith was particularly good at these negotiations, though he tried to ignore a thought niggling at the back of his mind. The source of his hesitation was something he heard a few months back while in the lands of the fae, the Hill, when he traipsed through wild juniper bushes between Chain Lake and the bale fields.

"The deals are rotten."

Tensith had slipped into a better position for eavesdropping, but the pleasure of hearing gossip not meant for his ears faded the longer he listened to the words. They were two elves who spoke, two of the warrior class of fae that protected the Hill. They were off-duty and out of their armored uniforms, but Tensith could still scent the gritty smell of the training grounds and weapons.

"How can that be?" the second voice had said. "The contracts are steel-clad."

"The language has been changed," the first voice whispered back. "It's about the souls."

"Impossible! Someone would have noticed; someone would have said something," the second voice scoffed.

"Orders are usually followed, especially when accompanied by gold."

Ice had gripped Tensith's heart at the words. As a rule, he didn't mind such sour things, enjoying the lark of corruption as much as any fae, but this felt like something bigger. Corruption in either one of the courts, Seelie or Unseelie, was to be expected; it even bordered on tradition , but not in the contract business. Affairs having to do with human souls tended to attract the wrong kind of attention for the fae.

At the present, in the ugly little hospital garden, Tensith shifted on his feet. He scanned the surroundings, feeling exposed. This area of the mortal plane had never been fae territory and it was a risk to conduct operations this deep into the Southwest. Different things ruled here, things that wouldn't mind making his life very difficult for a while. Or making a quick snack of him, instead.

Tensith didn't much believe in conjecture or conspiracies, preferring instead to wait for firm, published evidence before deciding. How could he believe this overheard rumor without hard proof? Perhaps what the two had whispered about among the thicket of juniper berries was too large for him. Perhaps he should stick to what he was good at: closing deals and keeping his nose out of business that was not his own.

Besides, the couple sitting in the cafeteria on the other side of the glass would allow him to meet his quota. His job was more important than hearsay. The fox twitched his tail again, ruminating as he studied the hospital's interior.

There were a few occupants within the large room. A handful of bleary-eyed interns in pale blue scrubs sat at tables near coffee machines, looking astonished at their own exhaustion. A cafeteria worker wiped down a counter in lazy, unhurried movements. None of them were the parents.

Tensith craned his neck, searching, until he found a lone couple in the far back corner, secluded, uncomfortable, and upset. The woman's umber skin shone gray and wan in the cheap fluorescent lighting of the room. Sitting in a plastic chair beside her was a man with his head bent into her neck, seeking comfort. His long blue-black hair was tied in a ponytail that trailed down his back.

The fox focused on the couple, noting their tears. They were perfect; grief-stricken, at the end of their ropes, and without an extended family to get in the way. In a flash, he left to retrieve the bairn, shifting to his humanoid form to carry the basket. Rumors be damned.

The couple didn't notice anything, not the other people in the cafeteria and not the fox. They were too focused on clinging to each other. Two overnight bags stuffed full of toiletries, books, magazines, snacks, and fresh changes of clothing sagged on the linoleum tiles beneath their chairs. In the middle of the mess sat a colorful plaid baby bag packed with the best newborn diapers and the softest clothing. A pacifier, still in the plastic packaging from the store, lay abandoned on the small Formica table in front of them. Beneath it was a wrinkled pamphlet titled "Coping with the Loss of a Child".

"We have to go home soon, Kate," the man told his wife as he hugged her. His voice barely carried over her shoulder. "They won't let us stay another night."

Kate choked back a harsh sob at her husband's words. "I don't want to go. I have to stay with him, Robin. I have to."

Robin took a deep breath to collect himself. "He wasn't ours yet, cariño."

"He was supposed to be!" Kate wailed, pushing out of her husband's arms. Her outburst drew a few stares from the other cafeteria occupants. She set her jaw, refusing to care what others might think of her emotional display.

Even though an embarrassed blush crept across his copper complexion, Robin held firm. He reached over to wrap Kate's hands in his own, warming the cold tips of her fingers. A tear slipped over his cheek. "We said our goodbyes. She was kind enough to let us do that before the cremation." Kate looked away, focusing on the bright glow of a nearby soda machine. Robin gave her hands a squeeze. "We will be parents, I promise you."

"You've said that before. Multiple times."

"I still believe it's true, don't you?"

Kate bit her lip. Robin wasn't looking for an argument, but in her heartbreak, she needed to release the grief screaming inside her. "It's my fault we can't conceive."

"Kate," Robin frowned. "Please don't go there right now. You know that's never mattered to me."

"It matters to me!" Kate hissed, trying to prevent another loud outburst in front of the whole cafeteria. She shook her head, the decorative wooden beads at the ends of her shoulder-length braids clacking together. "Forget it, I'm sorry," she said with an audible swallow. "I don't think I can handle being let down again."

After the years of dismissive and bigoted doctors, IVF shots, and heartache, Kate had lost hope.

Robin gave a small smile, raising a hand to cup her cheek. "I love you," he told her in a quavering voice.

Movement through the window over her husband's shoulder caught Kate's gaze. "Holy shit," her eyes were wide, pupils dilated in fear.

Twisting, Robin squinted out beyond the glass. "What? What is it?"

An electric shiver of terror shot down Kate's spine. This wasn't something meant to be seen in broad daylight.

A small, skinny creature stood on the rim of rocks around the man-made pond in the hospital garden. He was naked and male, but not quite human. Black eyes, set at a slanted angle, flashed as he glanced between the couple.

"He's naked," Kate stated, words fluttering in her mouth.

"No, it's fur."

"Robin," Kate articulated with effort; it was impossible to turn away from the thing outside, "let's go home now, please. I want to go home."

"Yes, we should leave." Robin's voice was thick and confused.

The figure beckoned, causing them both to jump at the unsettlingly human gesture. The weak winter sunlight flickered over the creature's face through a break in the clouds and Robin gasped. "Did you see that? I thought he was a fox..."

"That's impossible," Kate whispered in a trembling voice, trying to rationalize the uncanny sight. "It had to be a trick of the light."

It is no trick, mortals. A voice penetrated through the glass windows and vibrated within the bone of their skulls. Kate clamped a hand over her mouth to keep her teeth from rattling and biting her tongue. Robin's hands flew to block his ears though it did nothing to dampen the sound. The noise was internal and unshakable.

I heard you want a child.

"Robin..." Kate's heart stopped. "Did he say...?"

That is what you want most, is it not?

The words pricked hard behind Kate's eyes, her vision blurring with tears. The creature's voice rang out again, this time with a harsher, more rapacious edge.

Tell me that is what you want.

5

Pain gathered in Kate's head. She felt her skull squeezing as if she were hundreds of feet underwater being crushed by the pressure. She heard Robin whimper next to her.

"Yes!" Kate cried out, breaking through the pain inside her mind. Her voice turned hoarse and soft, as if her first word had taken all her strength. "More than anything in the world."

At once, the pain dissolved.

Then come, and I shall give you what you desire.

The glass in the hospital cafeteria windows shimmered and waved. With a crack of ice breaking across a thin puddle and the smell of air before a lightning strike, the glass disappeared. Kate looked around, sure that someone would hear the clamor, but the cafeteria was now empty.

Come.

Kate stepped through first, followed by Robin. They shivered in the unnaturally cool air, blinking.

"Your names?" The fox-being now spoke to them out loud but in a voice so odd that the couple remained silent."Your names!" he boomed.

Kate and Robin stammered out their names before the fox continued.

"Your daughter is given to you on this twenty-sixth day in your month of February. You will care for her and provide for her and love her. On her sixteenth birthday, fifteen years and six months from today, she will be given back to us, whole, sound, and undamaged, to do with what we please. Do you agree to these terms?"

Kate hesitated. People weren't given babies out of thin air. There was protocol to follow, applications to fill out, and adoption processes to adhere. The normal things. The things that allow humans to go through life with the security of knowing there was nothing else out there, nothing like what stood before her now.

They shrank back as the strange man raised his hand in an arcing motion. A ripple of air passed over Kate and Robin, settling over them like a flute of champagne on an empty stomach. It warmed from within, fizzing in their throats and casting a delicate fog over their minds. As the two would-be-parents blinked, images materialized within their imaginations.

Kate saw herself holding a plump baby, the child cooing in her arms as Robin laughed from behind a video camera with a diaper bag slung over his shoulder. Next, a scene from a park with Robin catching a child before they could tumble off the bottom of a slide, Kate urging them to come join her on the swings. A vision of a birthday, a smashed cake on the table and sugary frosting smudged across paper plates, danced through their minds.

"These things and more are all possibilities for your future."

Robin and Kate sagged against each other as the magic dimmed its hold on them.

"Do you agree to the outlined terms?"

"Yes," Robin said, voice trembling.

"We agree," Kate added.

The creature smiled.

"It was a pleasure, Mr. and Mrs. Pereda," he gave a sardonic bow as the air around him shivered and warped, "and congratulations."

The creature disappeared, the smell of burnt plastic following his wake.

Wobbling on the rocky edge of the pond where the strange creature had stood was a portable baby bassinet. Before it could topple into the water, Robin lunged forward and grabbed the handle. He brought the basket close and they both peered in. Nestled in a tuck of blankets next to a thick sheaf of legal documents bound with a rough cord was a healthy, six-month-old baby girl, crying and red-cheeked and ferociously alive.

"Is this real?" Kate whispered with hesitant joy. The baby had warm brown skin and a full mouth with a cleft chin. Kate's heart began to melt and tears sprang to her eyes. "She looks like us," she said through joyous tears. "And her tiny, little curls; they're so cute." The infant began to squall in protest to cold air.

"Hello, Janis Lyn," Robin named her quickly, as if waiting a second longer would bring back the fox.

"People are really going to know how obsessed with classic rock we are now," Kate giggled, giddy with the wild turn of events.

Still wailing, the baby opened her eyes, taking the breath away from her new parents. Her eyes were slanted like the stranger's had been and pale green, the irises so large that the whites were barely visible. Janis Lyn Pereda closed her strange eyes, her cries continuing to pierce the afternoon air.

"Her eyes..." Kate began, trying to suppress the shudder of revulsion that rocked her system.

"She is ours," Robin interrupted. "And I love her."

Kate couldn't echo the sentiment. Not yet.

They left the hospital then, their own eyes shifting to and fro as they snuck back to their car and drove to their squat ranch house. The next day, a FOR SALE sign would be hammered into the front yard. It was Robin's idea, to move his family to a new place to hide their daughter away from whatever ills may come to them in sixteen years.

🦊

A fox slunk around the back corner of the Peredas' house on the day they left.

Tensith sat hidden in the bushes no one bothered to prune and watched their car drive away. He knew they would forget, the spell of the bargain smoothing out their memories like waves on rock. After a while, the Peredas wouldn't be able to remember anything about that fateful day or why they moved or even about the fox himself. It was written into the contracts through magic. Even the bairn's strange eyes were protected within the language of the bargain.

Some children of the contracts had pointed teeth or moss for hair or extra-long fingers with additional knuckles. There always was a physical sign betraying the changelings' strange origins; there was too much magic in them to hide completely. Humans could see when something was off, but if they took a critical look or wanted deeper answers from those they called doctors, their minds would be redirected.

With a satisfied swish of his tail, the fox found a nearby entrance to the Hill and vanished into the growing twilight.

ONE

T HE DAY JANIS LYN Pereda died she had been invited to a party.

The party's plans had been public online for weeks but her invitation came at the last minute and was very unexpected. She was lounging on the couch sifting through different bad television shows when a bell chimed on her laptop. Janis sat up, dragging the computer over her knees to peer at the screen. There it was, the little red box drawing her attention to a new notification. Had she been invited on purpose? Had all her classmates joined together to pull off some sort of elaborate prank? She clicked the icon taking her to the party's main page. Janis read through the details and told herself dumb shit like that only happened in movies.

The girl who had organized it wrote a simple three sentences for the main description of the event: "Last party of the summer before we start our sophomore year! This will give us a whole week to be hungover! See you Friday night!"

It doesn't sound like a trick, Janis decided, selecting the drop-down option saying she would attend. She wondered what her parents would think. Her mother, she knew, would announce that it was a bad idea, and her father would encourage her to go. She wished they were here to make the decision for her.

Decisions were always so hard to make. She never felt as if she were in control of her own thoughts. The worst was when people urged her to consider her gut feeling. She would always blink at them, wondering why her intestines would have an opinion on color schemes, types of pants, or breakfast cereal.

During Maddie Bronty's twelfth birthday party at the fanciest Italian restaurant in their small, Richmond-adjacent town, Janis was asked to choose between sorbet or a cannoli for dessert. With the waiter dallying behind her, Janis stared at the creamy white paper in the thick leather menu booklet. Her mind was a soft, dull blank. She had no preference or ability to choose. When the waiter leaned over and said that it was always better to take the cannoli, Janis heard one of the girls whisper to the rest of the party clustered around the restaurant table that it was like she didn't have a brain. Maddie's parents had shushed the giggling that followed but Janis ate her cannoli in contented silence. The dessert was sweet and good and she was pleased. That had been the last time Janis was invited to parties.

Janis scrolled through those who had been invited to this current party and saw most of her classmates. Her school was large enough for her not to recognize some of the names but once she saw the tiny profile pictures beside them, she could place them all. Everyone was familiar but none of them were friends. Maybe she wouldn't go after all. She closed her computer with a tight snap and settled back into the couch.

A commercial for cake mix danced across the television screen accompanied by a merry jingle and bright animations. Janis was reminded that it was her birthday on Sunday. Her sixteenth. It would be her first birthday without her parents. In the farthest back corner of her mind, she realized she should think this was strange, but the feeling slipped away as she tried to focus on the thought, a silvery fish in a dark pond. Something always stopped her from focusing too hard on her thoughts or feelings.

Her parents left Thursday evening after making the strange, spur of the moment decision to attend her mother's high school reunion in Seattle and leave Janis alone for the weekend. Janis wondered if she should have whined about wanting them home to bake her a cake and sing like they always did. She knew other girls who were about to be sixteen would have done so.

"Don't be upset," her father had said on the eve of their departure, though Janis wasn't upset at all. They were all in the kitchen, Janis sitting at the kitchen counter when they had told her. "Your mother and I haven't left Virginia in years, you know. We deserve a little fun, right?"

Her mother had then burst into tears, retreating upstairs to hide in her bedroom. "I don't even know why we want to go!" Her mother's words were muffled behind the closed door.

A text buzzed onto her phone four hours before the party was to begin. Disrupted from trying to take a nap, she peered at the message from a number not in her contacts.

You better be coming tonight!

She rubbed away the potential of sleep from her eyes with gentle fingers.

I'm sorry, I don't have this number saved. Who is this? Janis typed back with clumsy thumbs, unused to the exercise.

A laughing emoji was the simple reply before: *Bobby... Wright, in case you couldn't figure that out.*

She knew who it was even without the last name. There was one Bobby in her class and he was not the type to text girls like her. Then, as if to double down in her silence, he sent a picture of himself. Janis was pretty sure it was one of his stock selfies, reserved for occasions such as this. A business card. Above dark blue eyes in a face of pale skin was a mess of black hair, sweaty and tousled from his lacrosse helmet, which he held aloft, kissing the front grill in playful jest.

When she still didn't text back she watched him type: *You know...from chem.*

Janis put the phone down and rolled over in her bed. There was no way she'd be able to sleep now, she was too confused. This had to be a prank. Why the hell would Bobby be texting her? Her, who everyone called a "fucking weirdo" and "crazy eyes"? She was not party material.

Unable to nap, Janis decided to pass the time with a shower instead. She swiped over her skin with a warm washcloth laced with fragrant soap. Her mother had taught her the importance of cleanliness when she was very little, surrounding her in the bath with floating toys and firm instructions on how to wash her body and take special care of her hair. Janis used to squall during bath time, the experience awful enough for her to remember well into her teenage years, as shampoo stung her large, sensitive eyes every time. But there was something about the water that calmed her, once she figured out that if she stopped squirming, suds wouldn't drip down her brow.

The water was where Janis felt she could think. It was almost like the liquid washed away more than just dirt. Even if it was just a full basin when she cleaned her face at night, the water comforted her. It pushed away the strangeness covering her mind that kept her from connecting with her deepest thoughts. While her mother sought answers from online medical articles, Janis found solace in the water. She chased the feeling over the years, taking extra long baths or playing for hours on the sliding plastic sheet from the toy store hooked up to the hose in the summer. Now, Janis felt uncomfortable going just a day without a shower.

Even as the shower poured down, the mystery of her invitation to the party gnawed at her and no answers came to mind. With a sigh, she cut the shower short and wrapped herself in a towel, frustrated by the unfamiliarity of having a sudden interest in attending a party.

Water dripped from the baby hairs at the back of her neck and trickled over her shoulders. Was she pretty enough to go to a party? As the fog cleared from the mirror, Janis unwrapped her towel to dab around her hairline in places not protected by her shower cap. She fluffed out her hair and arranged her curls that were still clean from wash day earlier that week.

Did Bobby think she was pretty? She met the gaze of her reflection, framed by a vignette of condensation still clinging to the mirror. Startling green irises framed by warm brown skin. The contrast was arresting. Janis knew she was supposed to find her eyes ugly, that she was to hate them more than anyone else could so her deprecation would make others feel more comfortable. She closed one lid and then the other, trying to find contempt and failing.

Janis stood before the mirror until the air was clear from the steam and she was beginning to shiver. She liked her eyes. And she would go to the party because, if she were being honest, she was a bit bored with watching television.

Bobby found her as soon as she arrived.

"Your parents are chill," he commented, nodding toward a black car on the street driving away. "They dropped you off all the way in the city?"

"That was an Uber."

Bobby grinned and nodded toward the house. "Let's get you something to drink."

"Sure," Janis said, letting herself be drawn into the mess of high school bodies. At some point, a plastic cup was pressed into her hands and Janis sipped at it, then at another, then at a bottle, and then she stopped counting because it bored her. Bobby always noticed when her drink was finished and would lead her back to the coolers in the kitchen for a refill. Hours into the party they entered the kitchen to see Mark Beatty, a ruddy-faced blond boy from one of her classes, at the center island, pouring a line of shots.

"That's cool," Bobby pointed out. "Should we do some?"

Mark looked up from pouring and frowned. "How many has she had?"

Bobby considered Janis for a moment. "Uh, I don't know."

"She looks dazed. Is she wasted?"

Janis turned to Bobby waiting for him to answer for her. She couldn't tell if she was or not.

"No way, man. Just a little drunk."

"I'm a little drunk?" she echoed, halfway surprised.

Bobby snorted out a laugh. "Nah, you're just a nasty little bit of sheefrah trash."

"Bobby!" Mark yelped out, astonished. "What does that even mean?"

Janis focused on the row of shots dancing before her on the kitchen island instead of the strange word she had never heard before.

"I've never been in the garbage," she told the small army of glasses. If she was drunk she didn't feel any different than she otherwise did. Maybe a bit more off balance, like she was trying to walk one foot in front of the other on the sidewalk curb outside her house. She did know for sure that she wasn't trash. "Thank you for the libations," she hiccuped to Bobby with an unsteady curtsy. She didn't want another drink now. Her stomach was telling her this party was a prank after all. She needed space to breathe, to put fresh air into her body so she could

13

think. "I'm going to go outside now."

"Jesus," Mark muttered under his breath, watching Bobby follow an unsteady Janis out the sliding doors to the pool deck. "Someone go help her?" he called out to the general assembly. No one responded to his request. Instead, they noticed the shots and surrounded the table, all clamoring for a glass.

The night air felt good against Janis' skin. She sighed, looking up at the stars, wondering why people found meaningful answers in their distant, dotted patterns. To her they were cold and silent. Rough, pebbled concrete circled an in-ground pool that steamed at the surface, inviting swimmers who had yet to take up the offer.

Janis had an odd history with pools. The last time her parents talked about the past incident was the night before her first year in high school. It had been at dinner when her father spoke up.

"Janis," he said, clearing his throat and swiping a thumb through the condensation on his glass. "Are you ready for tomorrow?"

Janis nodded, pushing around some buttered peas with her fork. "Yes, Dad."

He shook his head, glass clinking as he set his iced tea down on the tabletop. "No, I mean, are you really ready? It's high school. You have the chance to start fresh."

"Fresh?"

Across the table, Kate was glaring at her husband though he kept on.

"Yes, brand new. You shouldn't let other people's opinions dictate who you are and how you live your life. What about starting the year by reconnecting with some people?"

Janis put her fork down, focusing on her father. "Which people?" She watched him swallow, something he did every time she looked into his eyes.

"I don't know." He paused to take a sip of tea, thinking. "How about Lauren Rayne? Wasn't she a friend once?"

"Robin, can I speak to you for a minute?" Her mother scraped back from the table, standing with abrupt force. She glanced at her daughter who had resumed eating. "In the kitchen?"

Janis trailed her parents' retreat with an unblinking gaze. Though

14

they moved to another room, she could still hear their words as they huddled behind the wall with the fridge.

"Stop trying to make her into someone she's not," Janis heard her mother hiss.

"She's fine, cariño. You and I both know she could do with some friends and maybe that Rayne kid would be perfect for her. She's mixed, too."

Janis' mother let out a low, harsh laugh. "If you think for one minute that Melody Rayne would let her precious little Lauren anywhere near Janis after what happened with Megan Becker, you're dreaming."

"What happened was an accident," Robin insisted.

"Janis told Megan there was gold at the bottom of the pool and the girl almost drowned looking for it. Gold coins, of all things. And Janis just stood there watching! She never called for help, not once!"

Her father snorted. "Not like it's the most scandalous thing that's happened here."

Her mother's answering voice was shrill. "We're lucky that girl didn't die! We're lucky there wasn't a fucking lawsuit!"

Janis took a big bite of peas and moved on to cutting a strip of chicken as her father said, "She told me it was from some poem she read in the school library."

She remembered that day. Her and a bunch of other twelve year olds had been at the public pool for a free summer swim session hosted by the town. It was glorified babysitting for parents who needed a break from their energetic tweens. When she heard that Megan's father had lost his job, all Janis had wanted to do was help. Gold was money and money helped people. Janis hadn't known the idiot girl couldn't hold her breath very well, otherwise she wouldn't have described the treasure in such an appealing way.

"They're scared of her, Robin!" her mother cried out before lowering her voice. "And it's not just the white kids and their racist bullshit. They all know she's different and don't understand why."

"Well," Robin muttered, at such a low volume Janis had to stop chewing her chicken to hear, "I don't think it's anything she does..." "I know," Kate murmured, voice soft. Janis had watched her parents come

15

back into the dining room, both blinking when they met her gaze. "Who wants seconds?" her mother had announced then.

At present, the water on the surface of the pool waved, as if it beckoned, but Janis had been told she should avoid pools.

"Do you want to go in?" Bobby's voice behind her asked.

"No," she said,.

Bobby moved to stand next to her. "Why not? It's hot tonight. It would be refreshing."

Janis shrugged. "I don't know. I don't care either way, I guess."

"That's always what you say, isn't it?" His voice had turned cutting but Janis didn't mind.

He was right, she never cared. In school, all she was concerned with was memorizing her lessons. She never understood the concepts but tucked them away as if storing them for later. In general, she was waiting for someone to come tell her what to care about, how to feel about this and that, what to do with her life. If anyone had bothered to ask, Janis would have likened her existence to a sluggish, strange dream over which she had no control but also no real desire to ask why.

She was about to tell him her thoughts when she realized she didn't care enough to open her mouth and form the words. Or was it that she couldn't open her mouth because her stomach might evacuate all the liquid it held? Janis' head started to spin.

Across the pool, hidden in the shrubbery, a fox sat watching the scene. His entire body was still except for a quivering at the very tip of his bottlebrush tail. He was attending to her now, sharing in her last twenty-four hours as was customary. Something about this particular child had always bothered him, though there was nothing he could change now. She didn't develop like the others he dealt out and checked in on over the years. She never smelled right, as if there was some barrier around her mind, holding it in place. But he could never be sure.

Greenish-black eyes flashed in the darkness as he focused on the boy. The fox scented the air. The boy smelled strange; metallic. He smelled of ash and fire and blood, but he was a human male, wasn't he? What was that smell? The fox remained still, waiting and watching. He was not to intervene.

16

Bobby's voice was rough and jagged as he repeated himself. "You say that a lot, right? That you don't care?"

Janis shrugged again, sensing he had a point but having no motivation to ask him to make it.

Ice rushed down Janis' spine as she felt Bobby's sweaty fingers brushing against the curls at the nape of her neck. The revulsion and outrage she felt at the invasion of her personal space cut through both the alcohol and film covering her mind. She jerked her head away.

"Don't touch my hair," she tried to say, but when she had turned her head, her vision became soupy and unfocused and her words never made it past her lips. Was she going to be sick?

"Look at me," Bobby commanded.

Janis tipped her chin away but he grabbed it, forcing her to turn and stare. Janis shuddered with...was that fear? She had never felt afraid before. This was all new.

"What ugly eyes," Bobby said. But there was fire in his own eyes, there, hidden behind the blue. Those were flames, unnatural flames that told Janis something else was inside Bobby, something that wore his skin. "At least it's an easy way to find your kind, right?"

"Sure," Janis agreed, marveling at the fact that she spoke without any negative repercussions from her stomach. Something was wrong. Very wrong.

"Cool," said Bobby. "So, I think this might hurt."

Janis felt a rushing of air and heard the yipping bark of some animal and she blinked.

She was in darkness. Not in a way where it was a counter to light, but that it simply existed. This was a nothing place: no before, no memories, no names. She was herself still, she knew that on some level, but she was after. She had nothing else but the understanding that she was unable to move.

A substance without form began to pour around the encasement of her. The sensation crashed in waves, coming again and again, a thick coating that held her fast. She was unable to shield herself, remaining under the deluge for hours, or maybe days. Perhaps it was mere seconds. She didn't cry out or squirm, she no longer had those instincts. Those had been left behind in the place before this one. And yet, as the substance continued to fall, something new began to happen.

The substance washed the nothingness away. Little by little, the pouring over her essence revealed first the memory of the feeling of water. This was some sort of liquid. More of the substance fell and she realized what it was flowing over was a body. Her body. She was no longer just a bit of self in this strange place, but she had a form. The torrent was unrelenting. As soon as she remembered she had a body, somewhere for herself to exist within, she also remembered pain.

There was no sound in this primordial setting and when she tried to open her mouth and shriek in agony, she had no voice. If she did cry out, it went as unheard and unfelt as it would in a dream. Her body remained, and more of her was becoming revealed. The onslaught of the lashing substance flayed her bit by excruciating bit. It peeled at her, demanding she remember, relearn, and refocus into something different than she once was. This was what the water had tried to do for her in the place before. It couldn't complete the task, not without this flood of revelation. Though it was torture, she became herself again, but sharper. She remained who she was before, but free.

She did not yet remember her name, but she remembered other things. Strange looks. Her mother and father. Isolation. The endless, stretching days of childhood bursting with possibility. Teasing and loneliness. The pain of something hitting her on the head and sending her from the before to the hereafter.

That was the real torture. The torrent cascading around her still had nothing on the pain of what she had lost, what she never had. The barrier holding her away from her true nature was sloughing off, a second skin cut free, and it left behind the feeling of rage. She never had control over her own thoughts or choices or life. That barricade had always been there, keeping her mind just out of reach of herself. It wasn't fair. It wasn't fair now that she wasn't back in the previous place to enjoy this new revelation for the first time.

She began to push back. She began to howl and pound her fists. She demanded it stop until she was sure her throat was raw and stripped of words. As fast as it had appeared, the substance left her, sucking with it the last vestiges of the slippery film coating her mind and trapping her from the inside out. No more.

Light was the first to return; the developing of a photograph. It wasn't yet a true sight back in her eyes, instead it was random moments of a lighter darkness than the rest of her surroundings. Then, there was sound. She tried to orient toward the noise. The sound came again. It was a metallic clicking noise, a bit of air moving, and then a sigh.

The sound of a person.

TWO

SUMMERTIME HAD LANDED HARD upon Richmond. It was late August, and the temperatures marked by local and national weather stations were record-breaking highs. Even when the sun settled back beyond the horizon for the night, the air remained thick and full with the heat from the day. This irked the man smoking out back of a single-story brick building. If he had his druthers, everything would be morgue-cold all the time.

His white lab coat lay in a crumpled heap behind him, fabric wrinkling in the humidity and creasing the blue embroidery on the left breast of the coat. It was a caduceus flanked by two scales of justice surrounded by a circle of words. The stitching read: *Jayan Mati, M.D. The City of Richmond, Office of the Chief Medical Examiner*. The man, Jayan, had liked how official it looked when he began his position. Now, when he looked at it, it just reminded him of Hermes and how humans' overuse of the symbol had gone to his head. Jay hadn't spoken to the god in almost a century but felt it safe to assume he was still an asshole.

Jay shifted his weight on the top step up at the back door landing. Without the aid of any wind, the best he could do was to fan himself with an idle flap of his hand between cigarette puffs. Beads of sweat clung to Jay's hairline and the small of his back. Soggy cotton stuck to his damp armpits. His stomach rolled as he felt the shirt sticking to his skin. The wet, the smell, the sticky salt of a mortal body—it all revolted him.

It is all so... He searched for the right sentiment, sighing out a large cloud of smoke as he flicked away the cigarette butt. *So human.*

Jay checked his watch. There was time for another cigarette before he had to go back. He fished for the half-crushed pack of Parliaments in his back pocket and shook one out. He brought it to his mouth, lit it, and re-pocketed the pack with the swift, practiced movements of a long-time chain smoker. He puffed, surveying the back parking lot stretching out before him, peppered with cars. Beyond the pavement, trees and buildings of the surrounding city sprouted up and were silhouetted against the lingering marks of the setting sun. Oh, the glory of sunsets. No matter where in the world, the sunsets were always beautiful.

"Nice night," Jay said up toward the stars just beginning to dot the light dusk sky. He knew They could hear him even if they hadn't answered in sixty-seven years. "But did You have to make it so hot?"

"Who are you talking to?"

Jay flinched, startled by a disembodied voice to his left. He peered into the shadows, dragging hard on the cigarette to calm his pounding heart. Ghosts formed close to their bodies after death. Some, however, were drawn to develop nearer to him. This one was doing just that. Her body had been brought into the morgue just before his Saturday afternoon shift began.

"Drunk teenager," the overnight pathologist had said to Jay by way of greeting. She had handed him a file. Jay flipped through it after glancing at the girl's head.

Her entire facial structure around the eyes looked crumpled, as if it had collapsed inward under some great weight. The cause of death in the paperwork was noted as asphyxiation by drowning with added blunt force trauma to the front of the skull. The police guessed she'd fallen, her balance lost from the large amount of alcohol in her system, and bashed her head on the hard lip of the pool before sinking to the bottom. There had been no trace of drugs, no signs of sexual assault. The photos in her file showed her as she had been found: skull coated in blood, oxidized scarlet drips trickling down her face and neck like long, decorative tears.

Jay had closed the file and looked up at his coworker. "You finished already?"

"Yeah, I wanted to treat her right, you know?" They both had looked at the body with solemn reverence then; the cadaver was naked on the exam slab post wash, dark brown skin pallid and glistening in the fluorescent light. "Kids always get me."

Now, sitting out back and smoking, Jay remembered what she looked like, but couldn't recall her name.

"You're..." Jay asked the darkness beside him in what he hoped was a leading manner.

"Where am I?" the voice asked. It sounded small and scared.

Jay scratched at the bridge of his nose. "You're standing out back of the Office of the Chief Medical Examiner. In Richmond, Virginia." He added the last as an afterthought in case she was from out of state. Another detail he couldn't recall from her file. "My name's Jayan. Jay. I'm a forensic pathologist and was assigned to your case. Do you remember your name?"

The space to his left rippled. "My case?"

"You died, I'm sorry." He smoked in and exhaled a cloud. The second Parliament was almost gone.

"Died?" the voice in the shadows choked out.

Jay remembered. "Oh! You're Janis right?"

"I'm dead?"

Jay nodded despite knowing she couldn't yet see him. "You're the spirit of your living body, an echo. You're a ghost."

"But I'm only fifteen. I mean, sixteen, I think. Is it Sunday?"

"Saturday. Around half past five." Jay pushed at the mess of dark brown hair hanging over his dripping forehead with the back of his wrist; skin slipping on skin. He had been outside too long and was overheating. "All life must come to an end. Someone will be along to collect you." He intoned the familiar words without ceremony as the anxiety of not being inside with cooled air crescendoed within him.

"What does that mean?"

The smoke of the cigarette burned in Jay's nose as he reached the filter and a cough built at the bottom of his lungs. He flicked away the finished butt, holding in a cough. Gathering his now very wrinkled lab coat, Jay stood, shaking out the fabric. "If you want to come inside and wait by your body you can."

22

"What?" the voice trembled.

"It's traditional. Besides, it makes it easier for the ferrymen to find you. They'll help you cross to the other side, if you so choose." He was hot, so hot. His vision swam and the building need to cough increased its demand.

"Find me?" Janis' voice slid upward into shrill panic. "I don't want to be found! I want to know what's happening!"

Standing, the air seemed to close in tighter. His breath shortened. He closed his eyes against the lightheadedness. He needed cool air. "I have to go inside, do you want to come?"

"I haven't even lived yet!"

Jay paused with his hand on the door handle, not looking into the darkness next to him. He needed a moment to think and then he could help. Just a moment in the cold.

"When you're ready, come find me."

"This can't be happening!"

Jay choked against another restrained cough.

"It's down the hall, left, second office on your right," was all he could say before pulling at the door and retreating inside. It was quiet in the vacant back hallway before the muffled voice of Janis began to howl.

"You have to listen to me!" she screamed out.

Jay was about to yank the door open and tell her if she kept up the noise, other things in the night would come find her before a ferryman did. Instead, his lungs rebelled. Doubling over, Jay submitted to a horrible hacking fit. The spasming was so deep his abdominal muscles clenched as if he would vomit. With one last great heave, Jay spat up a clump of thick black blood, entire body rippling in the effort. The mass landed on the floor with a sickening splat, wobbling in its mucus-like consistency.

Rubbing his chest, his gasping slowed to a normal rhythm and Jay tugged off his sweat soaked shirt. Standing for a moment in the dark of the back hallway, he faced a nearby vent and closed his eyes, inhaling the light chemical scent. The black hair upon his torso moved in the false wind, a soft, prickling feeling.

He was born of the coolness of death, the offspring of the frozen spaces between stars and the stillness of finished life. Air conditioning gave him the closest approximation to feeling like his normal self. He cracked open an eye as the vent shuddered and he could hear the protestations from outside cease. Jay wondered if she had stopped or if she had decided to make her way to her body. He supposed he should eventually meet her back there.

All too aware of his relative nakedness, Jay plucked his lab coat from off the ground and wrapped it around his body with a furtive glance down the hall. He stooped to clean the black mess of lung off the linoleum with his sweaty shirt and tried to look casual as he walked to his office. The way was deserted; a witching hour before another shift change. He darted around corners nevertheless, in case a coworker decided to go for a spontaneous walk. Shannon from the front desk had seen him without his shirt once. He had been changing in his office after another one of his frequent coughing incidents and she still giggled every time she saw him.

Jay knew what he looked like. Though he remained uninterested in utilizing his physical features to his advantage, humans still reacted to him like Shannon's giggles or slipping their phone numbers to him on the back of business cards. It had taken Jay a long time to comprehend the beauty standards of humanity, but this body fit within them.

He had a friendly, open face, with light, cool-toned brown skin that showed the wear of forty three years of life at the corners of his eyes, around his mouth, and at his forehead. Unruly, sable locks lay tousled on his head. Jay had no idea what to do with the thick waves and usually left them unstyled, but cut so they would just brush the lobes of his ears. Light gray and some strands of pure white dominated the hair at his temples and in patches in his close-cropped beard and mustache. A sturdy, straight nose sat centered below thick brows and dark brown eyes.

Jay ducked into a small room with no windows and deposited the ruined shirt into the trash can, plastic lining rustling as the waste dropped into the bottom of the bin. A clean shirt was draped over his desk chair for emergencies, which he pulled on fast enough to hear some stitching rip at a shoulder seam. He plunked down in the desk chair and nudged his mouse. The gray-white glow of Jay's computer screen flickered on and displayed a new email waiting for him in his inbox.

It was a group thread started by Laura from reception. The email contained a link to a video of a kitten falling asleep in the lap of a baby. Others in the chain already responded with statements such as "2 cute!!!" and "OMG the bessssst". After watching it a third time, Jay deleted the whole thread. Opening several documents from his shift that needed printing, Jay scooted in his chair to turn on the printer. As the machine warmed up, footsteps stopped at his open door.

"You're awake," Jay told the person lingering behind him. He wheeled his chair back to the computer to print several documents before swiveling in his seat to face his boss. "Why are you awake?"

An older man with wrinkled olive skin shuffled into the small room, yawning. Despite his apparent age, thick black hair covered the whole of his head, not a white strand among it. He wore ill-fitting baggy jeans with a blue and white bowling shirt tucked into the waistband under a protruding belly. Folded over his right arm was a white lab coat with a patch labeling the man as the Chief Medical Examiner.

The man, Anat, shrugged.

"It was hot, I woke up. Simple." He sank down into a creaky metal folding chair reserved for visitors Jay never had and scratched at his ear. "What are you still doing here? Overtime already?"

Jay shifted in the chair. "It's too hot at home."

Anat, too, was born of frost and cold endings. That icy being was tucked away behind glamour, hidden deep inside the mortal shell Anat wore, but wasn't bothered by high temperatures. Jay often wondered if Anat thought he was making up his sufferings, so opposite were their physical experiences. The difference was that Jay was in a human, instead of just wearing the glamour of one, and it couldn't be more different.

"You must get used to the weather, it's good for your body," Anat stated with a slight puffing of his chest. "You never listen to me, cousin."

Jay shuffled papers. "That's not true, you're my boss."

Anat chuckled in concession. "Did that ghost show up?"

"She did."

25

"And?"

"She threw a fit when I told her."

"They always do." Then, Anat squinted his brown eyes. "Are you alright? You seem not yourself."

"I'm fine." The final page printed and Jay tugged at it before the machine could finish, smearing the last lines of ink. "Like you said, it's hot out."

"That it is," Anat said, rising from the chair. He glanced down into the trash can and frowned. "This gets in the way of your work. Even most humans realize the dangers of smoking."

Jay shrugged. "It can't do me any damage."

"It still wears you thin. They will not take kindly to you burning through your bodies like this." Jay gave a lofty sniff. Anat leveled a look at him. "You enjoy the transition process that much?"

"You know it's more than painful."

"Then why speed up the inevitable?"

"Worry about someone else."

Jay turned away to end the conversation. He felt Anat's eyes on him a moment longer before the older man shuffled away down the hall. Jay never understood how Anat could muster up the energy to care. Jay had enough energy to worry about himself, his job, and the ghosts. Never anyone else.

He supposed he worried about when he would get his next cigarette but that was an easy concern. There were always packs available for purchase even if Jay forgot his own, which was a rarity. It seemed to him that in almost every shop window there were loud pronouncements claiming the sale of cigarettes within their establishments. Helpful, but loud. How humans could stand all the bright colors and wild shapes of advertising Jay didn't know. It was a constant onslaught that had gotten worse over the years. Still, he could always locate cigarettes in a store with just a glance at a window and something inside him appreciated that. He liked it best when the signs were shaped like stars.

Jay realized he had been staring at the same paper on top of his pile for several long minutes without moving. He shook himself out of the trance. He needed coffee. Or another cigarette.

Anat and Jay both loved the acrid drink. The muddier, the better, in Jay's opinion. He had let Anat drag him to upscale cafes but the coffee there tasted the same as the sludgy stuff at the gas station down the block. Anat had clutched his heart at the declaration but Jay wasn't swayed. As long as it was hot and had the electricity of caffeine, he was happy.

Even when he sipped the bitter liquid and it would scald his tongue he didn't mind. Coffee was always faultless, even if it hurt him. Cigarettes too. Anat's concern wormed its way to the front of his mind and Jay wrinkled his nose.

Jay rolled in his chair closer to his desk and gazed down at the stack of paperwork before him. He needed to complete the sorting of the printed pages into their correct file folders and then enter all the same information into the computer once the organization was done. Jay loved paperwork and when it came in triplicate, it was even better. Redundancies were calming. They soothed him as he moved from day to endless day, trapped in a diminutive human mind, scratching at the scab of his humanity that formed anew each morning. Getting lost in surplus filing systems that were so lamented by his coworkers was the best way Jay could see being able to stand the next four hundred years. He paused. *Four thirty-three.*

Another email announced its arrival with a ping and Jay moved his mouse to awaken the computer screen.

`From: JLP.70W91@T0300!!!!!!!!!!.com`
`Subject: WHATTHEFUCK.`

Jay frowned. This was not a usual email. The last time he clicked on something like this he got male enhancement pop-up spam for a month. He deleted the email without opening it and as soon as he did, the computer screen went dark. The lights flickered and the temperature in the room dropped from air conditioned to wintery.

Ghosts, Jay thought sourly. *They never can just appear. They always have to do something dramatic.*

The lights continued to flash.

"You were supposed to go to your body," Jay shouted at his computer. "Not induce a haunt!"

The screen flashed a blinding white, bathing the room, before static fell in horizontal lines over the screen. The printer whirred. Jay watched as a piece of paper shot out from the machine and floated to the floor, large black font on an otherwise empty page.

WHERE AM I?

Jay glanced upward looking for patience. "Please get out of my computer. I have sensitive documents in there."

The printer spun again.

WHO WOULD I TELL?

There were several emoticon frowning faces centered under the words.

Placing a hand on the top of the computer and one on the screen, Jay commanded, "Get out of the computer, Janis."

HOW?

The newest printed page fell onto the ground.

"Imagine yourself outside and in your own shape. Pull yourself apart from the object."

The lights blinked once more then remained on. The printer hummed to a stop, and the computer screen melted away from static back to a blue desktop with the OCME logo and a scattering of unorganized files. Jay removed his hands and waited.

The ghost appeared behind Jay. Her form was a skinny teenage Black girl wearing a denim skirt, light brown leather cowboy boots, and an oversized "The Clash" T-shirt with small gold hoops flashing at her ears. The cleft at her chin lent her an air of seriousness that was offset by the inviting friendliness in her full mouth. She had the barest shadow of dimples at the corners of her lips and high cheekbones on either side of a rounded nose. Her whole face was made for smiling, but Jay had the distinct feeling she didn't use the expression much. She was barely visible, her form wispy and desaturated. Jay could see the wall of his office through her. Dark hair stood out from her head in tight, natural curls. Without the heel of her boots and the poof of her afro, she would be about five foot eight.

"You," Janis growled out, pointing at Jay with a shaking, accusatory finger, "tell me what the fuck is going on."

THREE

J AY WAS PLANNING ON being kind. Despite his annoyance at the interruption from his work, he at least thought about aiming himself in
the general direction of politeness. He didn't get very far.

Seeing her face without the injuries to her body, Jay guessed mortals
would consider the arrangement of her features pretty. He knew human
standards changed constantly and quickly, but the girl's features hinted
at real, distinct beauty that would have taken shape had she lived into
adulthood. All but her eyes. Pale green filled their large, titled shape,
leaving almost no white showing. It wasn't how she should look at all.
Not if she were human.

"What are you?" Jay demanded.

"Tell me right—" Janis' words lost momentum at the abrupt turn of
conversation. Her finger drooped. "What do you mean?"

"Humans don't have eyes like yours."

"I don't know what you're talking about."

Jay shook his head. He hated when things weren't as they should be.
This was what Anat always complained about. Jay was still too rigid,
even after just over half a century. Even though ghosts no longer fell
under his authority, he couldn't help but press forward in his curiosity.

"Tell me what you are."

"You were the one who said I was a ghost!" Janis yelped as Jay moved
closer, towering over her. "Don't you remember?"

"Let me see your eyes," Jay ordered.

"No!" Janis cried, screwing her eyes shut. "Leave me alone! I know
you think they're ugly!"

"Ugly?" Jay pulled back, surprised at her admission. "No, you don't understand. If you're not human, you won't have a ferryman to shepherd you through the choice and instead... What's wrong?"

Janis stumbled sideways to keep her balance.

"I can't feel anything... My clothes...my body... What is happening to me?" she moaned.

"Are you okay?" Jay asked as the ghost swayed.

"Stay away," she mumbled, eyes still closed, voice tripping over the words. Janis lurched, throwing her arms out but unable to find any solid thing by touch. "Dead as a door-nail," she said in a sing-song voice. Janis tried to take a step but listed to one side and pitched to the ground where she remained unmoving.

"Shit," Jay stated.

Anat's voice interrupted from the hallway. "Cousin?"

"In here," Jay called back, hands on hips looking down at the ghost who sat squished between his desk and a filing cabinet.

"We just got a call," Anat said, walking into the room and stopping short, surveying the scene. "What is that?"

"That is a problem." Jay said, pinching the bridge of his nose. "She's out of order."

Anat snorted. "Everything in the human world is out of order. You must be used to it by now."

"This isn't my usual commentary about the chaos of mortality, this is different. Look at her eyes."

Anat squinted. The two fell into silence, studying Janis as she stared ahead with a blank look in her wide, glassy, green eyes.

"Can humans look like that?" Jay asked after a moment.

The older man shrugged. "If you insist on being so curious, look into her soul." He moved and took a seat again in the creaky metal chair by the door. "I'll wait."

Jay hesitated. "This isn't my problem. She'll be gone soon so there's no real sense in me getting invested."

"Couldn't have said it better myself."

"But," Jay dragged the word out as he thought, "there's no one else to help her."

"It will get sorted out in the end, it always does." Jay remained in hesitation and Anat shook his head. "I wish your kind wasn't so focused on the order of things. Takes up a lot of time."

"It may, but it's also what's right." Jay crouched down, mind made up. "Janis," Jay said, trying his best to sound comforting. "What's wrong?"

"She can't hear you. She's too far away."

"Come on back," Jay instructed the ghost.

"She's lost, cousin. Let her go."

"Come back. Come back to this place, Janis." While he waited, he allowed Janis' eyes to draw him in. He didn't know why she had called them ugly. For a human, perhaps they were off-putting and strange, but as a singularity they were magnificent. They were open pools that allowed a large window into the rings of her, a life story. Jay focused his gaze and looked deep into her eyes, squinting to move through to the heart of her.

"It's as if her soul is newborn," he described to Anat as he continued sifting through her. Jay heard the other man shift in the rickety chair. "In a way. The soul has the fifteen years her body does but in existence alone. There's no emotional experience. There used to be some sort of magical barrier around her spirit that kept her separated from her personality and feelings that wasn't built to continue through death. It was wiped away when she died."

He tried to look deeper but there were no more answers for him that could be read through her eyes. To dig deeper he would have to use his power, and he wouldn't inflict that uncomfortable experience upon a newly formed ghost just to satisfy his piqued interest. Jay stood, knees creaking. "Poor kid. She's meeting herself for the first time and experiencing everything all at once."

"Sheefrah," Anat breathed. "The only ones I know that have their emotions blocked in such a way."

The moment he spoke, Janis stirred, her body twitching.

"Síobhra?" Jay pronounced it with an Irish accent, thinking Anat had misspoken. "When was the last time you heard of a changeling switch taking place? The fae no longer care to host human children."

Anat shook his head. "Sheefrah is a derivative of that old Gaelic word. I think it changed when the fae came over across the ocean from the

Moor. She's a spirit child or an ogbanje, one who comes and goes. She's not human but not fae either, otherwise she wouldn't be a ghost."

Jay nodded. Nothing else took a ghostly form after death except the remnants of mortals. "They were born to be messengers or spies, right? When the fae came into the New World?"

"She was made, not born. A mixing of human and fae worlds. There hasn't been a spirit child in the human world for a very long time."

Jay frowned. "If she's part fae wouldn't they keep her under the Hill in their own lands?"

"Whatever bit of fae that resided within her in life is gone now. This is out of our hands."

"How can you say that?" Jay gestured around the empty office. "Where is her ferryman? If her humanity remains then it is tied to a ferryman and the choice. She should be afforded those rites."

"I don't know what happens when sheefrahs perish. You could be wrong."

Janis twitched on the floor again.

Jay glanced at Anat. "You might want to leave before she comes back to herself. You'll upset her."

The older man only settled further into his chair. Jay set his jaw against Anat's stubbornness and crouched down to Janis' level once more.

"That word," Janis coughed, "I've heard that word before. May I have some water, please?"

Jay glanced over to Anat, looking for help. Anat waved him off, encouraging Jay to keep going.

"No. I'm sorry, but ghosts can't drink," Jay told her.

"But I'm thirsty?"

"You're just remembering the feeling of being thirsty."

"I'd like to see my mom and dad," she rasped.

From his seat Anat said, "You can't, you're dead."

Janis took one look at him and gave a piercing scream. Behind the glamour, Anat's demigod form would be monstrous to the ghost's eyes. If Jay wished, using the bit of power still lingering inside himself, he could shift his vision to see past the glamour, but Anat without glamour was a fearsome sight to behold.

The demigod's head was a gathering of shadows arranged in a vague suggestion of a skull. The lower jaw was exposed bone with a pair of curved white tusks jutting upward, stained black at the tips. Two red eyes glowed deep within the darkness, the pinpricks of light moving back and forth as he studied Janis. Anat's true body was of a human male, but the torso of golden olive skin that started below the tusked jaw in a neck ended at the pectoral muscles. From there it turned into a dripping, blackened rib cage. A collection of sinew and ropes of night made up the middle of him, ending in folds of cloth at the hips that covered the rest of the demigod in a wrapped skirt of ancient fashion. Wings of inky velvet spread out behind and folded around his body like two cupped hands.

He was Thanatos, the embodiment of death. Well, one of them.

Jay jumped to throw a hand over Janis' mouth, forgetting her form was still insubstantial. His arm passed through the ghost, who turned to him wide-eyed, screaming at the fresh horror of something solid slicing through her body.

"I told you!" Jay admonished Anat over the noise of Janis screaming.

"What a racket," the demigod sighed and waved a hand and brought Janis' voice to silence. Her hands flew to her throat, the fear in her eyes deepening as she shrank further into her corner. "Anyway, you're needed at a crime scene. Forensics are already there processing but they're waiting for an official ruling."

"You're thinking about work? We have to fix this." He gestured a hand in Janis' general direction causing the ghost to flinch. "We have to wait for her ferryman."

"Yes, I'm thinking of work. The world goes on and people die, and we're expected to show up at crime scenes. Take her with you, if you're so worried. That way I don't have her lurking around here giving me a headache." He waved his hand over Janis again and she spluttered back into sound. "Dead body," Anat repeated. "38 Largos Street. And for your sake, cousin, you best hope to the high heavens the fae aren't going to come for her."

Jay closed the door with a tight snap after Anat exited.

Janis had begun to cry. Pale trails of iridescent tears made their way down her cheeks, disappearing into nothingness once they reached the edge of her chin. "I want to go home."

"I'm sorry, but until you're given your choice, returning home isn't advised."

More tears flowed. "What does that mean?"

"It means that I'm not great at explaining all this. You'll get better answers from someone else." Jay pushed a clump of hair that had fallen across his forehead out of his eyes. Feeling sorry for the ghost didn't mean he'd gained the skillset required to comfort her. Caring too much about humans and all their little woes was how he got into all this trouble in the first place. A jolt of realization ran through him. *I have learned nothing in my exile.* Jay gritted his teeth at his own idiocy.

Janis sniffed and took a long look up at the tall man. "I don't have anyone else."

This part wasn't his job. It never had been part of his job. *You wanted to open this door,* he chastised himself. *Walk through it.* He tried again. "I'm sure you didn't want to die but it happens to everyone sooner or later."

"Of course I didn't want to die! I was just about to have my 16th birthday!" The girl dissolved into fresh sobs as Jay waited for her to finish. "I can't be dead," she blubbered.

"Everyone says that."

"I'm not everyone!" Janis snapped. "I'm me! So do what you have to do and take me to whoever you talk to in situations like this!"

"Janis..."

"And who was that scary guy? I don't like his face."

Jay surprised the ghost with a short bark of laughter. "No one likes his face. That's why he wears a human one."

Janis wiped at her nose. "A human one? What is he?"

"A demigod of death." Janis' mouth dropped open, but Jay continued. "You're dead so you can see his true form."

"I can see death?" It came out as a whisper.

"No, Anat isn't Death itself, just one of the many beings associated with it. But, as a ghost, you *can* see through magical glamours. It's quite a useful skill." Jay paused to consider his own words. "I can see how it would be rather jarring for someone unused to such things."

"The world was not like this a day ago." Janis' voice cracked as she tried to hold back a sob.

"You were alive a day ago," he pointed out, though not without kindness. Jay took her silence as an opportunity to start packing up his things. "Can you stand?"

"Yes," Janis bit out with vitriol. On shaking legs, she managed to get to her feet. "I hope no one else meets you after they die because you're doing a terrible job."

Jay dragged his office door open. "I told you it's not my job."

The ghost took a few hesitant steps forward, concentrating on where she put her feet on the floor. "Then what is your job? Zombie patrol?"

"Ghosts aren't zombies and I'm a forensic pathologist. A doctor."

"Neat," Janis said with heavy sarcasm. "Must have been handy in med school to see ghosts."

Jay considered this as they walked. "I suppose it would be, but I never went to medical school."

"You're kidding," she said as she teetered a few paces behind him. "How did you get this job then?" Someone passed them walking the opposite direction in the lobby with a phone glued to their ear. "Hey! Hey, listen! This guy never went to medical school!" she called out to the person.

"They can't hear you," Jay muttered. As they walked through the OCME entryway, he noticed the ghost was crying again. "What's wrong now?"

"What if all of a sudden no one could hear or see you?" Janis said with a sniff.

"I guess I'd never thought of that before."

"Maybe you should."

Janis staggered across the parking lot bathed in the cool glow of fading twilight following Jay on rubbery legs.

Unfamiliar words spun around her head with an insistence to be heard and understood. *Dead...ferryman...ghost...ogbanje.* Echoes in her mind.

One that comes and goes. The threads of conversation reverberate all around her. *Sheefrah trash.* She had heard that word before, she was sure, but where? It clawed at Janis with a gathering urgency. Why couldn't she remember? Her thoughts were slow and plodding, like pushing through heavy and muddy terrain. *Sheefrah...*

"This is it," Jay said, gesturing to a van with OCME printed on the side in large, block letters.

In the dark glass of the van passenger window she saw the image of a reflected billboard. It was a low-budget advertisement for a local pizza chain. Whenever she had been asked to share her favorite food in an icebreaker exercise in school, she always picked pizza for lack of knowing what else to say. She had never cared before and now her heart was breaking over this small and silly thing. Shifting her weight, Janis was shocked to see Jay's reflection in the van window but not her own.

"Where am I?" she shrieked.

Jay flinched. "Your reflection?" he guessed.

There was nothing but the empty night air next to Jay in the curved glass. Where was she? Where was her face? Janis patted at her head with probing fingers. She knew she must be touching herself but there was no sensory feedback, no sensation of touch. She began to feel as if she were floating and dizzy at the same time. With a shaking hand, Janis reached out to the window, longing for something that never again would be.

"I'm gone," she choked out.

"Ghosts don't have reflections. I'm sorry," Jay added after a beat.

"I'm sorry," she echoed in a whisper. Another wave of disassociation spun through Janis. She reached out to touch the window. The pads of her fingers landed on the surface of the glass for a brief moment before passing through as if the window had turned to water. Her hand pushed forward, followed by her wrist, then her arm. The earth tipped beneath her feet and she was falling.

Janis had night terrors when she was younger. They were horrible things that trapped her in fear and darkness that she could never remember when awakened. Dreams of tearing flesh, repeating, organic holes, and falling without end. But this wasn't a dream. Janis was sinking into the space where her reflection should have been and there was no end.

She now knew, knew to the very center of her, she had been a sleeping prisoner all her life. Locked away in a tower to watch from afar without any control or any emotion. No love, joy, choice, opinion, anything at all. She felt the wretched sorrow pulse in her core, doubling the pain with every throb. It was too much. She hadn't lived her own life. She had been blocked from participating in the world around her. It had all been a performance she didn't even know she was giving.

It could have all been different. Her whole life, she could have been different. Someone...something...stole that from her. How could a life be stolen in this way?

Agony burst over her. It bloomed in a place deep inside instead of pulsing across her body like something physical. The torment felt of regret and the cruel loss of something she never knew she had.

"Are you stuck?" Jay asked, interrupting her inner turmoil. "I've been told it's odd passing through solids the first time. Ghosts are interesting because subconsciously, they instinctively remember the feeling of being solid, but it's at odds with how they experience their incorporeal form. For example, you don't even think about not sinking through the ground because that wasn't ever something you could do in life. Actually, it's fascinating, if I do say so myself. You'll have to learn to touch some things again and others you'll just naturally interact with. When you're completely solid, you'll be able to touch whatever you want. It takes several hours to fully solidify though..."

His rambling cut through her frenzied thoughts. In her mind's eye, she jerked away from the black void. Janis' body seized and her unsteady legs couldn't balance the sudden shift in weight. She was falling again but backward and it happened all at once. Janis once again found herself sitting on the ground looking up at Jay.

"Are you alright?"

Janis climbed to her feet and stared over his shoulder to the van window. "I don't know."

Jay opened the passenger side door for her. "Get in. Maybe the drive will help ease your mind."

"Doubtful," she muttered, climbing clumsily into the cab. "Very doubtful."

FOUR

T HE RIDE TO 38 Largos Street was quiet. Jay had no idea what to say to a teenage ghost, especially not one who kept weeping at random intervals. Everything seemed to set her off. At the start of the drive, Janis had asked if ghosts not having reflections had anything to do with vampires. When he informed her that vampires didn't exist as they had been hunted to extinction, her large, strange eyes had welled up with tears.

"Who killed them?" she had asked, voice wavering.

"Uh, everyone, sort of. They weren't especially good creatures. Besides, it was ages ago. The last vampire died in 1893, I think."

That set her into a fit of sobs that Jay endured in silence. The meeting of her emotional self with her logical self was proving straining on his nerves. He knew she wouldn't normally act like this and would settle after some time; considering her circumstances, he forgave her wild mood swings.

He wasn't overjoyed Anat ordered him to take Janis along, but he was grateful she wouldn't be causing any trouble without him to keep an eye on her. Jay resisted the urge to pull out a cigarette to ease his troubled mind. It was easier to survey a crime scene when his nose wasn't clogged with smoke.

Jay noticed the ghost was crying again and looked away.

She'll be gone soon enough, he promised himself. *We just have to wait for her ferryman to arrive, and then all will be set right. They will come, give her the choice, and then she will either stay as a ghost or leave for the next world.*

He quashed the little nagging voice in the back of his mind that asked the question why one had yet to show up and collect her.

A police cruiser sat idling in the driveway of the house at number 38, its flashing blue and red lights painted the side of the house in alternating colors. In the cul-de-sac flanking the driveway were two ambulances and a forensics van. Unlike most crime scenes Jay was called to, random bystanders or curious neighbors were not gathered about outside, though he noted the movements of curtains from houses on the street. Jay pulled up and stopped the medical examiner van at the bottom of the driveway. One of the ambulances, no longer needed, pulled around in the street and headed off to its next assignment. The driver raised his hand in a wave as he drove by.

"I shouldn't be too long," Jay told the ghost, watching the surplus ambulance retreat in the rearview mirror. Janis peered out the window at the house.

"No," she said in a rush. "I don't want to be alone again."

"That's fine, but I have to do my job." There was movement on the porch of number 38. An officer and a woman both looked in the direction of the van. "I'm not going to be able to talk to you with people around. They won't hear you but they can still hear me. Can you be quiet?" He reached over the middle console and fumbled with the glove compartment, looking for a pen and pad of paper.

"For how long?"

Hands closing on his tools, Jay shut the compartment and left Janis' question unanswered. "And don't touch any of them, either. I don't want you putting anyone off if your body glides through them."

"I have no plans to glide through people. I want answers!"

"And you'll get them!" Jay told her, sharper than he had meant. Drawing breath to calm his words, he added, "I'll take you to find your ferryman when I'm done here. Or maybe one will find us along the way."

"How do you know all this stuff?"

Jay sighed, not knowing how to tackle that question. Instead, he told Janis to exit the vehicle on the driver's side. "It would look odd if the passenger door opened of its own accord." He grabbed his medical kit from the floor behind his seat and got out of the van, leaving the door open for Janis. "Oh," he exclaimed.

"What?" she asked once outside.

The air wasn't full of summer heat; it was unnaturally cold. Jay zipped up his uniform jacket and shivered with delighted confusion. OCME was printed in large white letters upon the back of the fabric. "It's cold."

Janis waved a hand through the air. "I guess I wouldn't know."

A middle-aged white woman stood on the porch, leaning back against the front door of her house. She was half listening to the quiet words of reassurance the police officer murmured to her in a steady stream. Her straight, dyed orange hair clashed with a streaky fake tan. Her brown eyes were wide and disoriented. She blinked at Jay as he approached, eyelashes twitching when they collided with her long, damp bangs.

"This is Tessa Jennings. She found the body," the officer announced.

The woman drew her sweater tighter across her chest as she stepped away from the screen door, allowing Jay entrance.

"I don't know where he came from," Tessa blurted. Jay looked back at her, holding the screen door open. Janis snuck into the house under his outstretched arm. "I was just getting something to drink when it got all weird and cold and then the noise came. I didn't do nothing, I swear. I never'd seen him before in my life."

The mustached officer comforted Tessa as Jay slipped inside, letting the door close after him.

"Odd," he muttered.

"What?"

He hesitated in the middle of the hallway to the kitchen. "I can't smell anything." He spoke just above a whisper.

Janis answered at a normal volume. "Maybe that's just..."

He cut her off. "No. The house has no smells. No dog hair, no stale garbage, candles, nothing. It's an empty void."

"Creepy."

"This way." A different police officer standing at the threshold to the kitchen spotted Jay in the hall and waved him forward. "Hold onto your dinner," the officer warned, a grim smile on her face. Jay stepped into the room and stopped. Even without the aid of a thermometer, he was certain the air in the tiny room was thirty-two degrees Fahrenheit. He looked down and let loose a cold cloud of breath at what he saw.

On the cracked and faded tiles of Tessa's linoleum kitchen was a man dead on his back. He had sallow, milk colored skin and was wearing a green and gray tracksuit. Something had split his ribcage open, sliced from chin to groin, leaving his internal organs exposed to the cold air.

Jay expected to be able to smell a ruptured colon or stomach but there was nothing. The absence of smell left him with bumps rising over his skin. Blood surrounded the body as if whatever had opened the ribcage did so by exploding outward. The eggshell white walls and ceiling of the kitchen were splattered red.

Janis entered the room and yelped. "Holy shit! What is that thing?" She flinched backward and crashed into the stovetop, rattling a saucepan. Most of her sunk into the range and Janis looked down in shock at her half-disappeared body and screamed. "Jay! Jay, I'm in the stove! Help me!"

Jay resisted the urge to put his head in his hands. Those in the kitchen jumped at the crashing sound of metal, all looking around trying to see what made the cookware move.

"When did this happen?" Jay asked, trying to focus attention away from Janis' noises. "When did Ms. Jennings call 911?"

"Around 7:30 tonight," one of the paramedics answered. She had a faint outline of sunglasses circling her eyes and some red skin on her nose was peeling. Jay checked his watch. It was a quarter after eight.

"Are you ignoring me?" The indignant splutter came from the stove. "Jay," she hissed. "I will throw this pan at your head if you don't help me."

"I'm thinking it might've been a close-range shotgun blast?" the officer who had told Jay to watch his stomach guessed.

One of the forensic techs gathered in the small room let out an uneasy chuckle. "I'm more likely to believe it was a grenade."

No one else joined in with the laughter.

"I just don't know why it's so damn cold," shivered another one of the techs. "We already unplugged the fridge and checked the A/C unit."

Jay used to be that cold. Before he was forced into human bodies, before his punishment and exile. When he traveled from place to place he would leave behind pockets of chill that lasted hours. He could no longer remember the feeling, just knew it was once a mark of his essence. Jay ignored the small sounds of cast iron scraping on a burner behind him.

"Did any of you touch the body?"

Everyone shifted at the statement, uncomfortable and nervous. "No way," someone answered. Jay bent to examine the dead thing on the floor, still hoping against hope. The glamour the cadaver wore that he could sense showed a white human male, mid-sixties, with silver hair and a weathered face. Had his torso been intact, he would have had a beer belly.

"Well, he's definitely dead," Jay stated, drawing wary chuckles from the small crowd. He blinked, clearing his sight of the glamour covering the body's true form and held back a sharp gasp at what he saw.

Strips of mottled flesh twisted their way up a melted white skull. What little bone left of its face was frozen into an ever-lasting scream. One black raven feather stuck out of each eye socket. A mass of white, tubular creatures rooted in the open cavity of its torso stood about three inches high, giving a time of death. The parasites waved in an unfelt breeze, as if underwater. The rest of the body was burnt, singed into a ropey mess of flesh and bone and blood as dark as the night sky devoid of stars. Bone wings sprawled out from under its back in a messy skeletal tangle, they would span twelve feet across if opened in full. One of the forensic workers moved and his foot kicked at bones he couldn't see or feel, sending them all clacking. Jay's gut had been right.

It was a reaper.

"Brutal, right?" a paramedic with clear adult braces commented.

Jay stood up, knees creaking in protest.

"Yes," he agreed with the woman. Jay looked down at the reaper's face again, gaping mouth open in a silent plea for mercy.

It was wrong, all wrong.

My sibling, I'm sorry, he said in silent prayer.

Jay blinked and the vision faded from his eyes, replaced by the sight of a human male. He blinked again, holding back unshed tears. "Brutal."

"So," the officer ventured, "have you ever seen anything like this?"

"No," Jay said, his voice flat with two layers of truth. Reapers couldn't die. Jay had not known one to die, in any manner, until now. He swallowed hard. He didn't know this reaper but the loss of one of his brethren lingered in his chest, a heavy weight.

"What do you think, then? Close-range shotgun, right?"

Jay shook his head. "I don't know what this is. But I'm going to need some different tools."

The tech with the sunburn nodded and adjusted the elastic ankles of the clean booties she wore over her shoes. "We'll finish the photography."

Jay smiled tightly at the gathered team and turned to the stove. Janis, it seemed, had given up on throwing the frying pan.

"Jay!" she cried, her voice cracking. "I'm stuck."

Unable to give her verbal instructions, he passed closely by the stove before exiting the kitchen. Jay nodded at her, then his arm. When he was close enough, Janis reached out for his sleeve. With a great suction noise, she popped out of the stove. Janis tripped along behind him until finding her footing outside on the porch. When her ghostly body passed by the mustached officer and Tessa, they both shivered.

"Let me go!" Janis shouted at Jay as she stumbled down the porch steps, still gripping onto his jacket.

"You're holding onto me." Frost formed where her fingers clutched at the fabric. If he didn't think it would be so rude, Jay would have called the situation funny.

Spluttering her upset, Janis tried to let go and only succeeded in tugging the shoulder of Jay's jacket down under the strap of his bag.

"God damn it," she muttered.

Jay's mouth twitched. "You just don't know how to control yourself yet."

They continued to walk as an absurd pair back to the van and Jay opened the back door to shield himself from view. He lifted the bag strap up and over his head, the med kit passing through Janis' body and silencing her protestations at the abrupt strangeness of having an object flow through her. "Forget human physics. You're still thinking like you're alive. You can interact with materials in new ways. Like with the stove. Relax, and remember what it was once like to let go."

Scowling, Janis narrowed her eyes at where her hand remained clasped around Jay's sleeve. Her forehead wrinkled with the effort.

"It's not working," she informed the tall man through ground teeth.

"How did you sit in the car? How are you standing on the ground now? You're allowing yourself to remember what it's like to be human in your subconscious. When something new happens, it clashes with your understanding of the world around you. Close your eyes and integrate the two feelings, subconscious and conscious," Jay instructed. "Imagine your hand opening. Try to bring up any memories of you opening your hands. Releasing a blanket, a bunch of rope, anything."

After a few quiet seconds, Janis opened her hand and then her eyes.

"I did it!" she exclaimed, proud of herself.

Jay nodded once. "I have to go back in." He switched bags in the backseat of the van and shut the door.

"I'll stay here," Janis said loftily. "But, um, what was wrong with that thing?" she asked with a jerk of her head toward the house. "In there? Why would someone kill him like that?"

"Them," Jay corrected. "We don't have gender."

Janis stilled. "We?"

"I'm also a reaper." Jay paused. "Was a reaper," he amended.

Janis stared at him. "I can't see anything different about you like I could with that freaky guy in your office."

"I'm not wearing glamour. I'm actually in a body," was his simple, clipped answer. He checked the contents of the new bag and zipped it closed. "And I haven't just died in extreme agony. I assure you, we normally look much different."

Janis raised a brow. "Died? Or murdered? Because that didn't look like just dying."

Jay left her question hanging and stared at the house where his sibling lay deceased on a dirty linoleum floor. What in the known universe was powerful enough to slay a reaper? "I'm not sure. Reapers are just one extension of Death in the world, we serve the natural order of things by reaping souls ready for expiration."

Something in the air changed.

Jay bristled, feeling eyes on him. His gaze swept past the front porch to the surrounding woods. The sensation of being watched emanated from the gathering twilight between the trees. Something was there, something waiting for Jay to make the next move. He strained his eyes, searching.

What are you? he thought toward the silent darkness. Deep in the gloom the air flexed as if something had displaced the shadows to accommodate its bulk. Despite himself, Jay shivered. Without taking his eyes off the thing he couldn't see he said, "Hop in the car, Janis. I'll be right back."

"Okay," Janis said with hesitation, climbing awkwardly into the van.

Jay continued to watch the forest. "Don't open this door for anyone but me, alright?"

Janis' strange eyes rounded. "Who else knows I'm here?"

"No one," Jay said, distracted and shutting the door with a quick snap. Beyond the trees the shadows moved and rearranged themselves. With a blink, Jay felt himself relax. Whatever had been there was gone. He tried to give the ghost in the car a quick smile. "Just trying to take precautions. Nothing to worry about," he told Janis through the glass window. "I'll be back soon."

FIVE

Waiting for Jay to finish inside the house, Janis sat in the front seat of the van wary of the few people who walked past. She flinched if their eyes scanned the windows, forgetting they couldn't see her. Two of the techs from the kitchen came out to another parked van and changed into white body suits. Janis watched them carry large black bags into the house. She swallowed hard thinking of the dead body she had seen. It had been nothing like what she knew from television. The mustached police officer left his post at Tessa's side and surveyed the house and grounds after stopping by his cruiser to sip from a plastic bottle of soda. She loved soda.

Straightening, in her seat Janis felt breathless. That was a new feeling. She had a clear opinion about something, a welcome break from all the times in life she hadn't cared about anything.

In the dark moments before she had heard Jay smoking when he first told her she was dead, Janis remembered the freeing pain that washed over her, leaving her changed. Whatever happened in that place had taken away the barrier separating her mind from her feelings. She felt vindicated by it, to an extent. All those times playing in the water or taking long, hot showers she had known there was something strange. She felt sorrow as she replayed memories from her childhood, knowing now she had been prevented from connecting with her parents, with friends, all because she was different. Because she was a sheefrah, something not of the human world.

If she dove into her memory, she could recall having a wide range of feelings when she was alive. They had just been hidden from her, held back beneath a film that coated her like a thick fog. It wasn't fair, Janis sat in sullen silence. She never asked to be a...sheefrah or whatever it was called. She just wanted to be normal, to be herself. She wanted to do it all again.

The officer checking around the property stopped by one of the police cars and set his bottle of soda down on the roof. For years Janis had listened to her dad lecture about the dangers of soda and the enamel of her teeth. As a dentist, he never let the stuff inside the house. It had been with her mother that she shared the treat. Whenever Kate took Janis shopping for new school clothes, they stopped off for fast food and soda. Janis remembered her mother's giggling instructions to not tell Robin and the delicious taste of cheap meat and a sweet, effervescent drink. Janis' mood soured. She would never see either of them again.

"Oh, god," she said aloud, hugging herself around the middle. Janis was sure she'd never feel whole again. Tears began falling. It was so cruel, to know the love she felt in death was stronger than anything she felt while alive. She hugged herself tighter to keep from trembling.

Jay was taking forever. It was rude of him, leaving her alone for so long. She eyed the ignition where Jay had left his keys. Darting a look around, Janis reached out to touch them. On her first try, her fingers slipped right through. She closed her eyes, concentrating on what Jay had told her earlier about letting go, and imagined the feeling of her fingers touching objects when she was still alive. Her hand closed around the rubber coated metal key and she turned it away from her.

With a roar, the air-conditioning started up, though Janis couldn't tell if it was cold or not. Opening her eyes, she smiled in satisfaction. The car hadn't turned over but the battery was on and that was enough. Checking to see if Jay was still inside the house, she focused so her pointer finger successfully hit the button to turn the A/C off. Then, with a mischievous grin, she poked at a different button.

"...to buy this for our dishes?" a radio advertisement blared. Janis checked the radio channel but didn't recognize it. Jay probably listened to weird music. Tip of her tongue poking out the corner of her mouth, she pinched her thumb and forefinger around the dial and twisted, following the numbers out of memory from the stereo in her parent's garage.

"Welcome back to 96.5 WKLR Classic Rock all day, every day!" a heavily edited voice blared. A loud guitar screamed a random riff before the sound effect of a large crowd cheering out a chant in a stadium faded in. Janis beamed. "We've got all your classic rock needs covered like tight leather pants in the 80s! So, sit back, relax, and let the tunes of yesterday rock straight into your soul." The word "soul" echoed a few times before transitioning into a song.

Janis readjusted herself in the passenger seat, waiting. She recognized it immediately from the first double drum beat. It was Prince. It triggered a memory.

"There's nothing in the world better than Prince, baby girl," her mother had told her as she turned up the volume of the little radio unit they kept on the workbench in their garage. Her father was crouched on the dusty concrete floor with a wrench in his hand, sweating as he tried to take off the training wheels on her pink and yellow bike. It was around her eighth birthday and they were going to teach her how to ride without the training wheels. "You listen to this kind of music and it will fix anything wrong in your life. This music is for us." Her mother had then closed her eyes and swayed to the music streaming from the tiny speakers.

"Is he a real prince?" Janis had asked. In the present, a warmth blossomed inside her as she remembered her mother laughing at the comment.

"He should be. Robin, come here," her mother had held out her hands for her husband to join.

"These are welded on or something," Janis' father grunted in response, trying to turn the wrench around a nut and slipping, the tool clattering to the ground. "Morrita, go dance with your mother."

Her tentative steps forward had been from shyness, Janis now realized sitting in the OCME van. *And when her mother caught her hands and twisted her into the dance, the emotion had turned to joy. They had danced, her mother laughing and catching her father's eye a few times when he would wink and blow a kiss at his wife and daughter. Janis hadn't so much as cracked a smile but the music wormed its way deep enough that she remembered everything in the present.*

She remembered her mother's deep umber skin, just beginning to shine with sweat. She remembered the earthy smell of the oily butter she used in her hair. She remembered the feeling of the long braids her mother wore then, the way the strands passed over her bare arms when they twirled together as they danced.

Janis had been so happy, she just couldn't show it.

The song ended in the van, fading out along with the memory. With a sudden flare of anger, Janis pushed the power button to turn the radio off and twisted the van keys back to their original position. This was all bullshit. How could she be dead when she hadn't had a real chance to live? She felt everything now. Any memory she called up, Janis could feel what she felt then but now with an authentic clarity, without anything blocking her from accessing her emotions.

She couldn't go back to her old life and feel. She wanted to go running into her past, crying and shouting, telling her parents it was all okay now, that she was better. That she was finally normal.

Ghosts didn't have the sense of touch anymore, but Janis knew she still was crying. There was just no sensation of wetness trailing down her cheeks. She hugged herself again and closed her eyes, wishing everything would float away, even if just for a moment. She wanted to dive into a deep pool and never get out.

A pool. There had been a pool.

Janis remembered a pool. She wiped at her tears and fixated on the thought. A pool. And a boy. And a glowing set of eyes. And then blackness.

7

Jay yanked open his door, startling Janis out of her meditation.

"Damn it," Janis swore at him as he climbed in the SUV. "You interrupted me."

"Doing what?" Jay turned the keys in the ignition and pulled out of the cul-de-sac.

"I was murdered," Janis whispered. "I mean, I can't remember the details, but I was fucking murdered." She looked up at Jay, triumphant.

"You can't remember?" He shot her a quizzical look while paused at a stop sign. He cranked the A/C to the highest setting.

Her curls wobbled as she shook her head. "I remember something about a party and then looking at the stars. Then your office." Janis ran her tongue over her teeth. "Can I not remember anything because I was drunk?"

"You should remember by now, regardless of what you imbibed in your last moments. The police think it was an accident. You fell into the pool after falling and hitting your head."

"Or I was pushed," Janis pointed out.

"Do you remember who pushed you?"

"No, but..."

"Do you have any idea who might have wanted to harm you?"

"No! But I..."

"Then why do you think you were murdered?"

"It's just a feeling, okay? I don't have any proof yet because I'm a fucking ghost and can't collect clues or whatever!" Janis shouted.

They sat in silence for a while, Jay not knowing how to interact with her emotions, driving back to the OCME. He took a left turn into the parking lot and Janis cleared her throat.

"Sorry. I didn't mean to yell."

The engine rumbled to a quiet stop when Jay took out the keys. He took the opportunity to light a cigarette. "You're re-learning a lot at once, it makes sense that your emotions are going to be all over the place."

"Because I'm an sheeve..." Janis faltered over the unfamiliar word.

"Sheefrah." Jay pronounced the word slowly for her benefit. It came out accompanied by a cloud of smoke.

"And that's a type of ghost?"

"No, it's a type of changeling."

Janis' eyes went wide, giving them an even stranger appearance. "A what?"

"Changeling. A faerie child left in place of a stolen human."

Her mouth dropped open. "What the hell for?"

"Spite, mischief, love for the human child, no one knows. The Folk are strange creatures. At one point you were part faerie, that's my best guess. It's why you have such interesting eyes."

"So there is a reason! I can't wait to tell my..." Janis cut herself off with a slump of her shoulders.

Jay extinguished his Parliament in an ashtray nestled in a cup holder. "But you aren't a changeling. A changeling is simply a faerie baby left for humans to care for. And, you may find this interesting, but changelings were never left in the place of a human child. That's all a myth. I mean, what need would the Hill have for mortal children? Very interesting, I think."

"What the hell are you talking about?"

Jay coughed. "Nothing. Sheefrahs haven't existed in decades. It takes a lot of energy to draw up a human soul and mix it with the spirit of the fae. I'm not sure how it works. I know little to nothing about the Folk as they rarely die. When they do, reapers are not the ones who come for them."

"I'm assuming that means my parents aren't my real mom and dad?" Her voice was soft and thin.

Sweat began to bead on Jay's forehead without the A/C on in the van. "That's more a philosophical question. They were the ones to raise you so many would think of them as such."

"I don't want to think about theories right now."

"Then no. You were created into being by magic, not sexual reproduction." He paused for a moment. "It's possible their humanity was mixed with fae magic to beget you but that would mean they had to agree to such a process. I'm sorry, Janis. I just don't know."

She turned away to stare out the window. "It's fine. Tell me more."

He loosened the top few buttons on his shirt collar. "Well, I was able to look into your soul in my office through your eyes. You don't seem to have any trace of the fae left in you, but I'm also not certain. What remains as the ghost of you is human." Janis remained silent at this. Sweat dripped down Jay's temples. "Do you mind if we continue this inside? I'm dying for some A/C."

"*You're* dying?"

"It's hot."

Janis rolled her eyes but gestured for him to lead the way.

The halls of the OCME were quiet, even for this late in the evening. The yawning receptionist at the front desk waved Jay over as he crossed the lobby. "Moira just arrived," the man stated, naming the night pathologist. "You might be able to pass whatever's in that file off to her."

Once out of earshot, Jay turned to Janis. "We're screwed."

"What? Why?"

Jay opened his stride into a jog. "Because Dr. Blake is going to do the autopsy on the reaper body and might contaminate any non-human evidence before I can gather it." He rushed into his office and flung down his coat and bag. "Stay here."

"Why?"

"I'm going to do the exam."

"So?"

Jay sighed. "It's not the most delicate process."

Janis crossed her arms. "We dissected a baby pig in biology last year."

He closed his eyes. "Suit yourself. Don't move."

"Why?"

He cracked an eye open. "Because I need to bring us both into Sideways. Please don't move." Jay closed his eyes again and calmed the clutter from the human part of his mind. Thoughts slowed and were replaced by a pooling darkness. Inside him now was the waiting calm of a still lake, its surface not so much a color but a reflection of what hung above. In the surrounding emptiness, he bid his power to come.

It arrived in droplets, the slow and delicate start of a humid rainstorm; a dripping, inquisitive precursor before lightning. The rain fell faster, interrupting the still surface of his becalmed mind in a multitude of ringing ripples. In the distance, he heard it, and smiled.

From deep beyond came the heavy lowing of thunder and hidden behind it, the smell of something electric. There it was: his power, the essence of the reaper trapped within. He could still access his power, though it was much diminished, but only for a short time.

"Old friend," Jay said in greeting.

Old friend, the reaper power rumbled back.

A quickening of static currents danced closer as the preamble of his power rained down in sheets. It was tied to a pure primal nature and born of the very first darkness among the stars. No matter what body he occupied, the mortal coil could never dampen the trueness of him as a reaper.

The terms of his exile forbade the use of power to ease his toiling upon the earth, but there were always loopholes where Sideways, a place beyond Earth, was involved. His power trickled through his fingers, a comforting presence. Focusing, he gathered the thoughts of what he needed.

"We need some time," he instructed.

Some time, the power nodded in agreement.

The human muscles in Jay's arms strained as his power wound around his skin, forceful and demanding. It drew tighter like contracting springs. Jay gritted his teeth against the pain. He was rusty. It took so much energy to call his power in mortal bodies that he avoided it.

"Not that much!"

That much, it rumbled from within his mind.

Jay hissed a sharp inhale as uncontrolled power sizzled through his whole body. Gasping, he fell to one knee and heard a squeak of surprise. Jay opened his eyes to see Janis watching with a horrified expression. His gaze roved to the clock on the wall above her and he gathered his concentration. Grunting, he lifted his arms, pressure bearing down on them, making them shake, making him sweat, as he tried to point his hands toward the clock.

"Not that much," he repeated, growling in effort. The bones in his back cracked and popped, sounding dangerous even to his ears.

Yes, it said with a smile.

Jay's body started to seize. His arms rippled with power pulsing under the surface.

"Jay!" Janis yelled out as she moved toward him, concerned.

"Janis, don't!" Pain and the sting of drawn blood landed on Jay's tongue where his teeth had cut his bottom lip. With the metallic taste in his mouth, Jay thrust his hands toward the clock. Power burst across the air and collided with the target, cracking the glass and halting the hands in their progress around the circle of numbers. Then, the power faded.

What was left was a depth of silence not found on Earth. His office, the hallway, and the morgue of the OCME had been removed from the world with Jay and Janis as passengers. The rooms existed, for the meantime, suspended in a nothing place. If anyone had a sudden notion to visit the morgue back in the human world, they would not succeed.

Smoke curled up from Jay's arms as he fell forward onto his hands, still on one knee.

"Jay!" Janis yelped, running to his side, arms outstretched to help.

He jerked away. "Don't touch me, you'll explode!"

"Explode? Why explode?" Janis stopped mid-step, horrified by the statement.

The effort it took to shift a part of a building into Sideways was greater than Jay had anticipated. His body had overheated to the extreme. "If anyone touches me right now they would experience a quick but devastating end to their existence," he explained. "Even a ghost."

Janis made a face. "Why do you smell like burnt popcorn?"

Jay made sure to breathe through his mouth to avoid smelling the air, which stank of boiling blood. The last time he stepped Sideways was... He didn't know when. *The 1980s maybe?* Everyone he knew had been in Sideways for much of that decade. Cocaine made the journey easier. *Or if one is not trapped in mortal flesh.* Jay groaned, his muscles promising to be very sore tomorrow. The ghost made another move to help, but again he shook his head.

"I need to cool down," he croaked out to Janis, a puff of black smoke escaping from behind his lips followed by a small cough. He hauled himself to his feet with a grunt, forcing out another puff of black smoke with the squeeze to his diaphragm. Upright, the world started to swim and bile rose in his throat. Jay gripped a nearby table as he rode through the wave of dizziness. He looked up at Janis once his stomach settled with a dazed grin and fished in his back pocket for a cigarette. "That went better than I expected."

"You can smoke in here?" Janis asked with a snap in her voice, nodding toward a simple sign with a large X through an icon of a cigarette.

Jay blew on the tip, the lingering heat of his power on his breath igniting the tobacco. "I can smoke in Sideways. There will be no trace of it back on the other plane."

"Where are we?"

Puffing out smoke, Jay crossed to his office door. "Follow me."

With a nervous expression, Janis followed, poking her head out of the doorway. "It doesn't look sideways."

Jay waited in the hall, cigarette smoke hanging around his head like a halo. "No, the whole of Sideways sits sideways in relation to the direction of Earth. Your senses have already adjusted so it won't appear at an angle. It won't hurt you. In any case, we've just borrowed a piece of Sideways. We aren't all the way in."

"Yeah, that's what I was worried about." Janis adjusted the hem of her skirt. "Is this some alternate dimension?"

Jay shook his head as he walked in the direction of the morgue. "It's still the world, just a different copy layered on top. Many things like me, non-humans, don't like existing on this plane anymore. It's too..." Jay searched for the right word. "Loud. So, most of them live here. Here where we're hidden from humans and the passage of time."

"Is this Purgatory?" Janis asked, a flicker of fear passing over her face.

"No," Jay exhaled smoke. "Purgatory's next door."

Janis shivered. "How many dimensions or whatever you call them, copies of the world are there?"

"Not even I know that."

Jay pushed open one of the swinging doors to the morgue and held it for the ghost to walk through. He pointed at a stool for her to sit on while he prepped for the autopsy, instructions that she ignored. Instead, Janis picked her way around the room looking at various objects as if in a museum. She tried to grab at the handle of a bone saw to pick it up and failed.

"Which world do I belong in as half-human?"

Jay moved to the sink, snubbing out his cigarette in the stainless steel basin then washing his hands. He didn't know much about sheefrahs or the Folk but it couldn't hurt to tell her the basics. "You were almost all human and as such you were able to exist in the mortal realm. But, fae can walk between planes at will, which you could have done while you were alive had you been taught."

Janis gaped. "I have magic powers?"

"Had. And no, nothing like that. Just the ability to transition between places much easier than others."

"Sounds like magic to me."

Jay found himself smiling back. "I could see how it would." He snapped on a pair of latex gloves. "No one knows why the fae brought sheefrahs into existence. Creating specific creatures well-suited to spying I suppose makes a certain kind of sense, especially because the fae courts are...so very corrupt. They are always vying for controlling power, one over the other, so espionage is particularly important to them. But, seeing as you were never a spy, I can't think of a purpose for you."

"Are you kidding?" Janis choked out.

Jay turned in surprise. "What?"

She shook her head. "I can't begin to describe how rude that was."

"Would you rather I not tell you?"

"You've never heard of 'bedside manner' I'm assuming?"

"I have."

"Can't tell white lies, then?"

"I don't lie."

Janis scoffed. "Like in a 'I can't tell a lie' noble way or you actually can't?"

"I've never lied."

"In your whole life?" Janis let out a laugh.

"I never learned how. Reapers don't need to lie," Jay said, moving to the table and unzipping the body bag. The saccharine smell of rotting flowers filled the room as he pulled the material away from the dead reaper, making his eyes water. Huge bone wings framed the body, cradling its sides and back; a sinewy pyre.

"Gross," Janis mumbled. She flashed a look up at Jay. "No offense."

The bone wings clicked together as Jay zipped open the bag, the noise of the hollow bones sounding delicate, on the verge of breaking. The edges of the body bag held in the wings, keeping them in the shape of a bony cocoon.

"None taken," he said.

The harsh exam lights revealed to Jay just how excessive the damage was upon the reaper. Sideways cleared away whatever magics or glamour appeared in the human realm. To his great annoyance, his human form wasn't a glamour and couldn't be separated from the reaper within, even in Sideways.

With gentle movements, Jay reached for the eyes and removed the raven feathers, placing them on a nearby tray one at a time, the sweet stench of decomposing flowers wafting anew around the room.

A stool scraped as Janis walked over, her hip bumping past the seat. "What's with the feathers?" she asked, trying to manage the expression of disgust on her face.

Jay rubbed his forehead. "I'm not sure. It could be fae. It could also be Odin, so I don't know. I've never seen this before."

"Since when do killers leave a message in feathers?"

Jay blanched, running down a list of supernatural beings with an association with raven feathers. "A message?"

"On TV, the killers always leave a message, like a signature. It's what gets them caught."

"That's interesting, but the real world doesn't work like television shows."

Janis crossed her arms.

Grabbing tweezers, Jay searched for micro residuals. He found no dirt under the nails, no dried blood left between creases of skin, no foreign materials at all. Jay reached for a digital camera on a nearby table and readied the flash without taking off the lens cap. The bright light would show any lingering marks below the flesh, at the level of bone and marrow. Jay clicked the shutter button over and over, eyes watering as he kept them open when the flash illuminated the room in bursts. He saw nothing. Even when he used the handheld UV light, sweeping it over the body for a clue, there wasn't anything to be found. Aside from the massive, bloody hole in the chest of the reaper, they had been in perfect health.

A distant warning rumbled in Jay's ears; the thunder of a starting headache pounding to life between his temples. Visiting Sideways as a disgraced reaper was hard enough without a ghost in tow. The fraction of the true power he could still access while trapped in a mortal form wouldn't allow him to remain for long. The grip he held was slipping.

"We have to go," Jay told the ghost. "Hold onto me."

"No, you said I'd explode."

Jay exhaled a quick chuckle. "I won't get nearly as hot as before and proximity helps on the trip back."

With a moment of hesitation, Janis clutched Jay's elbow. The room shuddered and creaked, starting to vibrate as if in agitation. The structure of the morgue groaned, the air rippling with something unseen. Pressure mounted at his elbow as Janis leaned into him, shielding her eyes.

"Not long now!" he cried out over the noise of the magic, voice warbling with the heavy vibrations around them. At the last moment, he decided to reach out a hand and pat her on the back, his touch awkward.

The howling wind built around the room, circling the boundaries, pressing up against the walls like a wild thing scrabbling for escape. The sound crescendoed to a whining note of sustained discomfort and, in an instant, collapsed into a draining silence ending in a sucking pop as the OCME morgue slid back into existence. When Dr. Moira Blake walked into the morgue ten minutes later there was no sign of Jay or a ghost and she was none the wiser.

SIX

JANIS TROTTED TO KEEP up with Jay as he strode on long legs down the hall to his office. She didn't like any of this. Not the trip to Sideways, not learning about sheefrahs, and not being dead. Her stomach felt queasy from whatever magic Jay had worked. She wondered if she actually felt sick or if it was just a remembered feeling. In either case, it confused her.

"If someone is killing your friends do you have to tell the police?" Janis asked to distract herself from roundabout thoughts. "Or whatever your version of the police is?"

"I do need to speak to someone, yes." He paused in the middle of his office after grabbing car keys from a desk drawer. "Janis..."

She felt her stomach, or non-existent stomach, clench. "Why do you keep trying to leave me behind?"

Jay hesitated. "I'm going to see Anat."

"So?" she asked through a clenched jaw.

"That's the man from before with the...with the face."

"I'll stay in the car."

"It's better if you remain close to your body for your ferryman to find you this long after death. You'll be fully formed soon."

"Who is this person you keep mentioning? Are they supposed to just show up and tell me how to be dead?" She spoke with bravado, but Janis hoped whomever he was speaking of wouldn't whisk her away into a more permanent stage of death without even hearing her side of the story.

"No, not how to be dead. They're supposed to give you a choice."

"A choice?"

"To stay or go. When a human dies, their soul is reaped by a reaper or another purveyor of death. It depends on location, mostly. Then, a ferryman offers them the decision to move on to a new place of existence or to remain behind as a spirit."

"A new place of existence? Like heaven or hell?"

"I suppose."

"You suppose?" Janis shot back, incredulous. "Hell isn't something you can just 'suppose' about."

"You'd be surprised."

"You're not explaining anything." Janis rubbed at her temples. She needed to talk to a real authority and get it all straightened out. She still wasn't sure if this ferryman was such a figure but she didn't want to be left alone again.

"Not everything can be explained by human terminology. There are many places of rest. Some of which, I suppose, may be called heaven. There are also places of suffering."

Confusion buzzed around Janis' thoughts. This was a lot and it was all unfamiliar. Her mother had lapsed in her faith, but her father very much believed in his Catholic upbringing. He maintained a level of privacy around his religion, going by himself to church on Sundays. He always stated that he wanted Janis to be able to choose on her own if she wanted to join him. He never wanted to force her. Now, Janis thought, she would never get the chance to decide. With all of her recent strange experiences, she knew most likely her answer to her father would be no, but she resented that her choice had been removed without her consent.

"So, do you know what the right religion is?"

"They're all right. And wrong. But, I have to go. I can't waste time in a theological discussion."

"Please don't leave me here."

Jay studied her and Janis forced herself to meet his gaze, schooling her expression into something she hoped had a look of command.

Fine," he relented after Janis began squinting, "you can come with."

"I can?" she asked, not expecting him to have caved so easily. It must have been all her impressive staring.

61

"Have you changed your mind?"

"No, not at all," Janis said with haste. "Ready to go."

Jay waved at the entrance to his office, waiting for her to exit first before locking his door and leading her into the parking lot. The humidity of the summer night drew them in, wrapping around and pressing down on Jay. "It's this way," he instructed. Janis froze when she saw the battered blue Honda Jay aimed toward in the parking lot.

Weeks ago, her father had dragged Janis in front of his computer, scrolling through pages of used car listings, trying to tantalize her into signing up for Driver's Ed. She had no interest. Here she felt the lost opportunity, the missed desire that she could never remedy. Anguish plagued her as she stared into the passenger side window that held no reflection.

"Is everything alright?" Jay asked from his seat.

Janis ducked her head, not wanting Jay to see her crying. "I can't open the door," she said, even though she hadn't tried. How could she tell him she wanted things with a ferocity that startled her, a ferocity that she never had while living? Things like learning how to drive a car, going to college, and having a life at all.

Jay leaned over and opened it for her from the inside. "You'll get better," he offered in condolence as she slid into the seat.

"No," she promised with vehemence. "I'm not trying to get used to being like this."

Jay shrugged and pulled out a cigarette to light it.

"Those things kill people, you know," Janis noted, giving the cigarette a nod. She couldn't say she cared but she wanted to get a last shot in, lashing out to make herself feel better.

Jay shifted from park to drive and twisted in his seat, an arm resting on the passenger head rest as he backed out of the spot. He spoke around the cigarette clamped between his lips, "Here's hoping."

7

Anat lived in a small townhouse in a neighborhood called the Fan. It contained groupings of narrow homes denoting modest wealth and was a perfect place for new families, not aging bachelors. Anat, to Jay's amusement, lived in a house the same color as his ugly blue Honda. He parked inexpertly in Anat's driveway, blocking in Anat's car and not bothering to pull in farther, leaving his rear bumper to stick out onto the sidewalk.

"I'll be back in a minute," he explained to Janis' raised brow, quirked, he was certain, at his parking job. He could still see through most of Janis, but when her ghost hit the forty-four hour mark, she'd be solid. Then, she wouldn't have a choice. "Stay here."

"Why?"

"I'm going to call the City."

"Richmond?"

"No, it's where reapers come from. And Them."

Janis wrinkled her nose. "Who's Them?"

"I don't have time to explain now. Just, stay here."

"Can I have one of your cigarettes?" Janis asked, face full of mischief.

"I don't know, *can* you?"

Her tilted eyes widened. "Are you trying to have a sense of humor?"

Jay shut the driver's door. "I've always had a sense of humor," he told her as he walked away.

Anat's home was dark. A dog barked in the distance as Jay took the aging brick stairs to the front door two at a time. A little before eleven thirty at night, a knock was out of the ordinary. After rapping on the door, Jay fidgeted on the landing, keenly aware of this fact. Still smoking, he peered past the circle of light shining down from the streetlamp posted at the corner of Anat's drive and the sidewalk. There was nothing he could sense but Jay still couldn't help feel as if the knock had been too loud. He shivered and flicked away his finished cigarette onto Anat's stairs.

Jay noticed the heat more when he stopped smoking. The air settled around him like a humid, cloying blanket. He wiped at his forehead, drawn away from feeling overexposed. The stink of his perspiring human skin rose up to his nostrils and he choked on it. It was a repulsive musk of fleshy decay.

This is not what I am like, Jay thought in a wave of self-deprecation. *I am of coolness and routines and the space that exists between light.*

He raised an arm to knock again, wondering if Anat was taking a long time on purpose. Before he could knock once more, a light flicked on inside. The sound of Anat's shuffling gait approached the other side of the door before he wrenched it open, looking cranky in a plaid bathrobe.

"Cousin," he greeted Jay in a terse tone. "What are you doing here?" He peered around the taller man and stiffened when he glimpsed the ghost still in the car.

"I need to call the City."

Anat's eyebrows shot up. "You disturbed me at home for this nonsense? What about the sheefrah?"

Several beads of sweat dropped down from Jay's bangs into his eyes. "This takes precedence. I mean to contact Them tonight."

A muscle in Anat's jaw twitched. "No."

"Cousin," Jay pleaded, using the familiar nomenclature to elicit a reaction. They were not truly family, just related through death."It was a reaper, at the crime scene. Slain and with feathers where its eyes should be. Two black raven feathers." Jay darted a look over his shoulder. "We shouldn't talk about this out in the open, if you'll please..."

Cutting Jay off, Anat opened the door wider and disappeared down the hallway.

It wasn't much cooler inside the home, much to Jay's dismay. There was no window A/C unit or even a fan to move the air about. Jay trailed Anat into the living room, pausing at the threshold and watching as Anat bent to click on a lamp with a low-watt bulb. It filled the room with a weak yellow light that strained Jay's eyes.

Anat eased into a nearby recliner with creaks from both the wooden frame and his old bones. "Reaper," he stated, voice low, his body backlit. "I can see you tangled in a mess right now. Don't tie yourself into a worse knot."

Jay put his foot down. "Would you rather I not inform Them at all?"

"They don't want to talk to you. Remember last time?"

"This is different, this is important. Something was able to kill a reaper and I need to report it. The City has a right to know what's happening before they send out any more reapers."

"And halt the progression of death?" Anat snorted a laugh.

"No, of course not, but to warn them."

Anat put his head in his hand and rubbed his eyes, a very human gesture. "The City probably already knows."

"That is... The mere suggestion the City would know and not have prevented it is outright blasphemy!" Jay spluttered.

Anat sighed. "I'm just trying to protect you. Don't get involved. Keep your head down, let this problem solve itself."

"I won't stick my head in the sand while my siblings are being murdered!"

"It was one reaper, cousin. You've been gone awhile. You do not know if this is part of Their plan. Even if I called, what would you do then? The City doesn't care about you anymore."

A tightness settled in Jay's throat and he crossed his arms. Gathering low in his chest, a storm brewed. His coursing emotions were heavy and Jay felt righteous in his displeasure. "They will want to know about this."

"You'll embarrass yourself or get hurt," Anat said, raising his voice.

Jay thrust his arms out to the side, indicating nothing in particular. "What have I got to lose, Anat?" With the movement, another wave of his own human stench reached his nose. Jay wrinkled his face in disgust. He wanted to wipe away his body. He wanted to climb out of his skin, out of the meaty warmness of flesh and escape back into the darkness. He wanted reprieve from the constant onslaught of human senses, of the churning loneliness of a mortal life.

With a deep sigh Anat heaved himself out of his chair, crossing the room and placing a hand on one of Jay's shoulders. In the closeness, the particular blend of Anat's human body reached his nose. It was a mix of sour oil and decaying epidermis.

"Go home, get some rest. If you still feel the same way, we can discuss this further in the morning."

Heat seeped into Jay from the touch as if Anat's hand were flame itself. *Release me*, something inside Jay said. He couldn't think. He was being pressed down by Anat, pinned to the earth, an inescapable tether. Jay shook free of Anat's hand.

"That's not good enough!" he shouted. Jay knew he was being too loud for this time of night, too loud for Anat who he *knew* had most likely been drifting off to sleep while his favorite celebrity magazine slipped down over his belly. But Jay couldn't stop himself.

Anat glowered. "Calm yourself, cousin."

"Don't patronize me, Anat. Even in exile I could..." A deep laugh cut off Jay's threat.

"You could what? Harm me? Not from that cage you're in."

"Don't interrupt me." Jay's fists clenched at his sides and trembled with the rage pacing within him.

Let me out. It came again, another whispered command. Jay set his teeth against it.

Anat chuckled. "Arrogance doesn't suit you."

Jay slammed the side of his fist into a nearby wall, hard enough to chip the paint and dent the plaster. "I'm older and more powerful than you, demigod! I don't fail to remember this as you have."

"This had gone on long enough." The shadows behind Anat started to stretch, bubbling like hot tar. His body swelled in slow, undulating pulses that left his proportions distorted with each surging. "You know the rules. We lay low and assimilate."

Something inside Jay grinned. The muscles in his human face followed suit in a sloppy, mad smile.

"If we fight now, that will surely bring Their attention to us, is that what you want?"

Release.

"Wearing the glamour of an old man has made you weak." Jay's words echoed across the tight space of the living room in a clear challenge.

"All that is left of the reaper I once knew is weak and in an insignificant speck of a human body. You are a nuisance, cousin. You do not know to whom you speak and you must be taught a lesson."

The shadows behind Anat moved again, dripping off his body like molasses revealing a muscular warrior with deep, rich olive skin. The plaid bathrobe dissolved away into a long skirt made of faded rough-hewn fabric tied in a large knot at the waist. Inky voids in the loose shape of wings stretched out behind his back, the tips folding inward when they reached the boundaries of the room. The light in the floor lamp flickered in a wild dance. The furniture in the room slid across the wood floors away from the epicenter of Anat, driven by an invisible force. When he spoke, his voice was a deep rumble without a hint of human age, "Do not think for one moment that I am weak. Older you may be, but here, my dearest relation, but you have no power to match mine. I chose this life. You did not."

"Is that what you think?" Echoing thunder reverberated deep in Jay's chest. He would prove himself to this old man, to this nothing being. "Again," he called to his power.

Again. His power answered in a boiling, eager purpose.

It bubbled to the surface too fast. There was a whining downshift inside Jay, a stalling of his mechanisms. His power crunched and wheezed. Jay had no control. He had spent so much energy stepping Sideways in the morgue that he was exhausted now. Warnings clanged in his mind but he pushed them away. He forced his power to gather faster, like clouds before a hurricane.

"Reaper," Anat said, in shocked horror. "Your human body will not be able to contain this."

Wings pressed up from inside Jay, stretching the skin of their prison taut. Hollow bones clicked as they ground together in pulsing agony.

"*And now cousin?*" Reaper power spoke through Jay's mouth.

Anat curled in on himself. "What are you doing? You're pushing yourself too far."

"*I am doing what I have to.*" Jay pulled back to strike a blow upon Anat.

Then, he stopped.

Marrow and ligaments shifted inside him and he staggered, the skin of his human body forcing his pushing wings to snap back into their normal, hidden place. He lost his grip on the power. It screamed in frustration as it faded, sucked away over the horizon within him, leaving Jay to collapse upon the ground where his world went black.

7

Pain stung at Jay's face. Cracking open his eyes, he saw Anat leaning over him with a hand raised, human and old once more. His lips moved but no sound reached Jay's ears. The ringing silence started to fade. Anat slapped his face again.

"I'm awake, damn you!" Jay yelled, struggling to heave himself upright. Anat helped prop him against a nearby bookshelf.

"Good." Anat again wore his ugly plaid robe. There was no trace of his transformed self but his voice was razor sharp. "You dare bring a fight to me in my house? You would jeopardize my atonement over something so arbitrary? If this were the old days, I would have killed you."

"Reapers can't die," Jay croaked.

Anat straightened, looking down his nose. "It would seem they can." With a groan, Jay leaned his head back against the bookcase with a soft, defeated thump. "I told you, keep your head down. It's better this way. Go home, go to sleep, come to work tomorrow."

"You are old and fat. This place has made you soft." Jay squinted through a burgeoning headache. After a moment's hesitation, he accepted the hand Anat held out. The older man pulled him to his feet and Jay yelped in pain.

"Don't define me by what you yourself feel. I have chosen this life, I know what I've become." The old man shuffled past Jay to hold open the front door. "I'm not desperate enough to hurl my fists up against the inevitable. You're not in the club anymore and no one cares."

"I'm disappointed in you," Jay said with a sniff as he walked by, head held high with stubborn pride. In answer, the front door closed on his heels with a snap followed by the scraping sound of a deadbolt. Jay remained standing on the welcome mat for a few moments until the overhead porch light flicked off in a final dismissal.

"That went well," Jay mumbled out into the darkness of the warm, sticky night. He fished out a cigarette and eased his sore body down the steps back to the car, making heavy use of the wrought iron bannister. Jay yanked open Janis' door.

"What took you so long?" she asked, climbing out of the Honda. "What's wrong with you? You look like shit."

"We're going for a walk."

"You can't order me around. Also, you're double parked." Jay blew smoke in her face. She waved it away with some frustration, ghostly form doing little to dissipate the cloud. Most of it floated right through her. Janis scrunched her face. "Has anyone told you how nice you are?"

"Don't get used to it," he said, turning and walking down the sidewalk on legs of rubber. "You'll be through with me and this world soon enough."

SEVEN

TENSITH SHIFTED ON ITS feet. He had been observing the man, who smelled like something more than human, and the ghost for some time. In truth, he'd been keeping an eye on the girl for much longer, since she was still alive. Now, in the darkness of the summer night, he watched the ghost stomp behind the man while they traversed a community park. She was quiet until the man tumbled onto a bench and sat there, smoking, staring into space. After a short moment of silence, the man slumped over in unconsciousness. The ghost began to gesticulate wildly and shout words that came to the fox in snatches due to his distance from the scene. Most of what he could make out were curses.

Raising his hind leg to scratch at an itch behind his shoulder, Tensith sniffed at the pair. One of the scents they had brought with them was of a demigod of death. The fox gave a shake of his whole body to disguise a shiver of fear. He didn't make a habit of dallying with those types even in his younger, more daring years.

The night began to cool from the excruciating heat of the day and Tensith reached out two dark paws in a full body stretch. He fluffed out his tail and wandered closer to the girl who was now flopped beside the man sleeping on the bench. She looked miserable. She hugged her arms over her knees and rocked back and forth, less a motion of fear and more to self-soothe. Her semi-translucent form was picturesque in the gathering moonlight, shimmering and glinting in the soft night glow.

"Tensith," a low, cool voice came from his left causing the fox to almost jump out of his fur. He hadn't been paying attention to his surroundings and he cursed himself for that mistake now. "What are you doing in my park?"

Fur still puffed, Tensith looked at the new companion that stood next to him. It was a wood nymph, a spirit of the nature that still flourished despite all odds within a human city, and his half-sister. Tensith inclined his snout in a nod of acknowledgment.

Maeren, was the greeting he gave to his sibling. He spoke to her mind, unable to form words with his fox snout.

The dryad was tall, towering over Tensith in fox form with her elongated, willowy body. She was beautiful, as all nymphs were, in the way more of nature and less of humanity, though she did hold a form similar to mortals. Her long legs were streaked with moss and dirt and below her knees, her dark green skin morphed to a twisting mess of roots that held the shape of a calf, ankle, and foot and dug deep into the soil with each step. Her face was angular but delicate, and her ears were long, ending in the soft point of a veined leaf. She looked so similar to their mother that, though long dead, Tensith had no trouble recalling what she looked like.

Maeren settled herself onto a pile of moss, long cornsilk hair puddling around her body as she tucked her legs to the side and leaned close to him, balancing her weight on a slender arm. Leaves and tiny white blossoms fell around her as she sat and Tensith sneezed at the plume of pollen that swirled past his nose.

"How are you, little fox?" she asked, shaking a clump of hair that had fallen into her eyes over her shoulder with an easy flick of her head. Closer to her temple, her hair wasn't made up of individual follicles, but instead a crown of roots, yew green fading to white, grew from her brow and split into infinitesimal strands until it piled around her looking for the most part like hair. Tucked between the strands were leaves and small berries sprouting from brown twigs.

Tensith harrumphed at her nickname. *I am fine, sister. And I have asked you not to call me that.*

Berry-red eyes danced with amusement at his words but soon slipped to follow his gaze, resting upon the man and ghost.

"Are you watching them too?" Her voice was fluted and rich, the sound of wind rushing across hollow logs.

The fox hesitated. He supposed he could trust Maeren as she was a member of his family, if not his court. He still felt a tightness in his chest at divulging a secret such as this. He didn't want to involve her in case things turned dangerous.

Most of the fae, no matter to which court they belonged, cared not for the politics and governance of their council leaders. The majority of fae embarked on lives of frivolity, excess, and freedom from most responsibilities, save from what their courts asked of them. Servant or gentry, it was a good life, long-lived and full of many pleasures. Those on the fae council were driven by a desire to lead, perhaps a holdover from when they were a monarchy. Not all who dreamed of it could rise to the station, but those who did were powerful.

Their mother had been on the council before she died. When Tensith was young, he had adored her position in the court and how others respected her, bowing whenever she passed. His childhood had been spent enjoying the privileges and riches that came with his mother's position. When Maeren was born, they still wanted for nothing. Tensith yearned for that life again. Though he did not wish to lead, he desired the respect and comfort he had once known.

He gave an annoyed twitch of his tail, betraying the turmoil of his thoughts. Maeren tilted her head, the moonlight splashing across her deep green skin and yellow lashes. She looked good, for a city fae, he realized. Healthy and strong as the dogwood trees that surrounded them. Perhaps the iron and plastic weren't getting to her as much these days. He looked around the park and realized there was a lot less litter strewn about than when he last visited two years ago.

"What plagues you, my dear?" asked the dryad, dragging him from his reflections. Tensith pulled his eyes from the strange pair at the benches and looked to the nymph.

The Unseelie Court, of which Tensith was a member, had a long and venerable history of being a wrathful and reckless place. This was always how the Seelie court described the Unseelie. The Seelie, of course, championed themselves as the primary source of goodness and truth. There were two courts that divided the Fae with no third choice for those who wished for a more neutral existence. Though Tensith didn't often agree with the anarchy of the former, he much preferred that to the sanctimonious delusions of the latter. His tail swished again in agitation while he dithered. If he didn't have friends within his reclusive half-sister, he had no one at all. Even if she was a Seelie, as all nymphs were, he had to trust someone.

I know not of the man but the girl was a deal, he began, pointing his nose to the park bench and the ghost that sat on the ground beside it.

The smell of musky jasmine came to his nose as Maeren adjusted her seat upon the ground. With a start, Tensith saw four quail chicks tumble out of a wrapping of bark and mushroom leather across Maeren's torso. She wore the vest unbuttoned as if it was for the use of the pockets and not for clothing. Heavy green breasts with deep yellow nipples swung free as she dug into some inner compartment of her plant vest and drew out another chick, sleepy and fluffy. She put the chick on the ground before her and let them run around her legs, pecking at the ground between her root-like toes.

"You are good at bargains, are you not?" the nymph asked. "I remember this was your calling."

Tensith was glad his scent was downwind from the quail chicks, he didn't want to startle them. *I am good at my job, you remember well. But this girl...*

"I cannot sense her being a changeling," Maeren told him with confusion. "Was she a member of my court?"

She was of neither court. Tensith took a breath before barreling on. *She is a sheefrah.*

He expected more of a reaction, but Maeren simply raised a yellow eyebrow.

"Their kind was outlawed for the power they possessed," his sister said. "Mixing fae magic with the strength of human souls could not be controlled by either court. The sheefrahs became simple means to the end of magnifying fae power. But that was over five centuries ago."

They have made a resurgence of sorts, tucked in among my normal deals for wealth, power, and children. Instead of a changeling, every so often a family will receive a sheefrah instead, with me none the wiser.

Maeren was quiet for a long while as the quails began to cluster around her feet, settling down from their nighttime snack and romp. With gentle movements, she gathered the chicks together and hid them away in her vest again.

"I cannot think of what the point would be to that," was all she said.

At first, I was the same, Tensith admitted. *But, I began hearing gossip that the whole business was rotten, that something changed within the language of the contracts so these sheefrah bairn would not live the full sixteen years as the signing caregivers believe. Instead, they leave the world in a flare of power.*

Two flower buds poked out of her skin and bloomed at the apple of her cheeks in a floral flush of surprise. "Where does that power go?"

That was my thought.

"But the reapers, the ferrymen, they would know. How did you?" The new flowers separated from her cheeks and floated on the air on the late night breeze.

Tensith's eyes flicked from side to side as if he expected a representative of the fae to pop out and take him to the dungeons for divulging such traitorous musings. *I found out by chance.* He swallowed and if foxes could blush, he would have done so now. *I like to keep an eye on my changelings throughout the years, just for my own sake.*

Maeren smiled and her teeth were like little white pearls. "That is kind of you, brother."

The fox shook himself into a more dignified position. *Yes, well, I noticed this girl wasn't progressing as my others did and I grew confused by her behavior. She was so odd, distant and removed. Changelings are usually sociable and outgoing. They flourish under the loving care of their parents. This bairn was wholly opposite. Quiet, taciturn, and removed.*

The nymph pruned some leaves from her hair and nodded at Tensith to continue.

And then she was killed by a male.

Maeren raised and lowered a shoulder. "That is what humans do."

Tensith snapped his tail back and forth in frustration. *The male was a demon, Maeren. One inhabiting a mortal boy. And two days before her prescribed death date, as promised in the contract her parents signed.*

When Maeren shrugged again, the fox blinked in concession. *Yes, alone, none of these things merit a second glance. But together? With the fae gold I scented on the boy, the murder of a sheefrah before her time? I thought something was off. I could only surmise the boy demon had been paid by some fae to kill the sheefrah before her sixteenth birthday.*

A diminutive screech owl flew down from a tree and landed on Maeren's outstretched hand.

Tensith continued, *I followed them to a crime scene earlier. I scented the death, it was of a reaper.*

His sister kept the owl calm and scratched at the animal's head, but he noticed the stilling of her breath and the widening of her eyes.

"Reapers cannot die," she whispered, reverently.

Then, Tensith said, closing his eyes against what he knew would come next, *I snuck into the archives and discovered the change in the contracts that included sheefrahs alongside changelings.*

His sister sucked in a breath, startling the owl into flight. The nymph stood, thick, viscous tears of sap already threatening to fall from her eyes. "The penalty for that is death. I will not have my only family left die for something as frivolous as humans and murder!"

Tensith, not for the first time, wished that nymphs were not such emotional creatures, prone to fits of sudden weeping or great, unrestrained passion without so much as a reason. With a switch of his tail, Tensith drew a glamour around him, body shuddering and changing to something more humanoid. He stood on two legs and reached out to Maeren with his hands, not paws. He spoke now with a human mouth.

"Please, lower your voice." As it was, the night insects had paused in their chorus as if to listen in. Across the park, next to a wooden bench covered in flaking green paint, a ghost lifted her head with a frown. Maeren held still and Tensith released a breath when he heard the thrumming sounds of the park wildlife start up again. The ghost's attention wavered as well.

Maeren began to walk deeper into the small expanse of trees within the park. She shook free of her brother's grip. "This is foolish. Stay out of this business; it is not your own."

Tensith ran to catch up, his shorter legs working twice as hard. "But it is my business." Maeren made an angry noise and lengthened her strides. "Sister, do not worry so much. There are many other fae who work deals. Any one of them could have or might find out what I also know."

The nymph scoffed but stopped before a large dogwood tree near the center of the park. Her heart tree. "No one would be as foolish as you to go skimming through court archives."

"This cannot be kept a secret forever. It will get out. Someone is bound to notice. If not now, then soon. I must find the answer and bring it to the council. Fae were not meant to exchange gold with demons. Our kinds do not mix. Sheefrahs were not meant to be snuck into our bargains. Reapers were not meant to die." Tensith had the absurd thought that he would uncover this whole mystery and find himself at the center of veneration within the courts. Everything he wanted could be within reach.

Maeren had her hand on the dogwood trunk and already her green flesh was sinking into the bark, becoming one with the tree. "Perhaps, but we were not made to be heroes, either. We simply are." She pushed her back into the tree and half her body merged with the bark. "Be at peace, brother. Do not worry about such things that are beyond your grasp."

Tensith frowned but said nothing as Maeren's hair rose up around her as if with a will of its own and, like the crossing wired network of fungi beneath the soil, spread out across the bark of the dogwood tree and settled into the flesh of the tree, disappearing from view.

"Come see me again soon, little fox. I miss the exercise of talking." With those words, his sister vanished into the tree. With a little huff of a sigh, Tensith went back to his original spot near the park bench and settled down in his fox form, dropping the glamour.

He needed to think and watch.

EIGHT

A CACOPHONY OF VOICES and a prodding sensation at his shoulder woke Jay.

"Look, sir, this is a public park."

Morning? Jay blinked and squinted against the hot sun. The voice belonged to a police officer, a tall, dark skinned woman wearing a hijab under her officer's hat, poking at Jay with a nightstick.

"Get the fuck up!" another voice screamed at him. "I am so fucking mad at you it's not even funny!" Jay tried to sit and struggled so much the police officer bent to help. There was a ghost of a skinny teenager nearby, ranting at him. "You fell asleep! You passed out and left me alone!"

Her name is Janis, Jay remembered. His thoughts came in a thick sludge, making him feel as if he had forced his body to endure a very long, very alcoholic, bender. "What is it?" he asked, somnolent. Janis rolled her eyes, throwing up her hands and stomping away. The officer took a kinder approach.

"What time is it, you mean?" She checked her watch. "Almost nine."

Heat rolled over Jay in waves, the morning promising to be just as unbearable as the day before. "Fuck." The officer hummed in agreement.

"You alright, then? No trouble, just get on out of here, okay?"

Jay nodded, though the effort sent pain splintering through his head. The police officer moved off, assured he would do the same. Janis stomped back into his view.

"Know what I learned last night? Ghosts don't sleep! Know what else I learned? There are scary things out there that don't sleep either! And you left me alone to deal with them!" Sunlight glinted off her ghostly form. If Jay had enough energy he would have told Janis she looked like an angry disco ball. "I had to hide under your dumb bench all night."

"Ghosts can't be injured by other supernatural beings."

Janis kicked out with one of her cowboy boots clipping Jay in the shin. "Great to know that now! But that doesn't mean we can't still be scared out of our minds!"

"Ow, Janis!" Her kick had landed right on the bone.

"Good. I hope that hurt."

Jay rubbed his shin with a glower. "I don't remember what happened."

"Isn't that convenient?" Janis said, her tone clipped. "You said you wanted to smoke and think and you were mumbling about a city and you came and sat down on this bench and passed out. You didn't even put out your cigarette. It singed your fingers." At the mention, pain stung at his hand. A raw, pink burn lay between the pointer and middle finger of his left hand.

"I'm sorry, Janis." The ghost sniffed in haughty retort. "I mean it." Jay hadn't planned to fall asleep, he couldn't remember leaving Anat's house at all. The recoil from using his power so much in such a short span of time had knocked him out. He needed coffee and a cigarette. "I'm sorry."

"I accept your apology," she started. "But I don't forgive you."

That is as good as I am going to get. Jay roused himself from the park bench and stumbled. Cold pressed against his side as Janis caught and steadied him. "You're almost solid," he told her, too surprised at her help to thank her. "And have all your color again."

"Hooray for me."

With Janis helping to support his weight, they made the short walk back from the bench to Jay's car.

We must look a sight, Jay realized passing another human who stared. *Me leaning on something they cannot see.*

He kept his eyes down and away from people passing on the sidewalk. Janis' coolness was a welcome balm against Jay's already overheating body and her nearness kept his headache to a dull roar.

Anat's car was gone from his driveway, long left for work. There was a dent in Jay's front fender from where Anat had scraped past the Honda.

It sat askance, half on the sidewalk, half off. Jay stood staring at his car and Janis untangled herself out from under him when he didn't move.

"You got a ticket," Janis said, pointing at the windshield. A neon colored slip of paper was stuck under one of the wipers.

Jay sighed. If Anat wasn't going to help he was going to have to resort to a more rudimentary method of contacting the City.

"Alright, come on. I've got at least one other friend in this area. I think you might like her."

It didn't take them long to drive through Richmond even with the lingering rush hour morning traffic. Janis stared out the window while Jay chain smoked and drove downtown.

Spending the night alone had been terrifying. For hours, Janis watched formless things move in the night as Jay slept on the bench. She kept watch, eyeing the things that moved around the edges of the park. Dark as pitch, flashing with a discordant rainbow at their edges as if made of ink, they moved languidly in no direction yet the meaningless ebb and flow of their shapes had been all the more menacing to Janis. She hadn't been able to see more to them than just unctuous black, some monstrously huge and some dangerous and small, but she knew without a doubt they were supernatural.

Jay parallel parked in front of an interesting shop on a side street Janis had never seen before even from her few travels into Richmond. A faded wood sign proclaiming the store's name as "The Cottage" was nailed up above the lintel. Janis couldn't see through the window but the large grass pentacle wreath hanging from the front door felt promising to the ghost.

Hollow wood blocks tied together with twine and attached to the door clacked against each other as they entered the shop. The space was small but comfortably cramped. Flowers and vines bedecked the crown molding and a bundle of blue sage was burning in an iridescent half shell on a bed of moss. An oversized oval table laden with herbs sat almost too close to the entrance. The dried plants were packaged in various sized plastic baggies and lay underneath bundles of herbs drying from the ceiling. Some more of the pre-made packets were nestled in hanging wicker baskets that moved back and forth as customers passed by.

Pinecones, smudge sticks, and clumps of ribbon-tied lavender were stored, overflowing, in wooden milk crates beneath the table, out of sight until someone stubbed a toe on one of their corners. Adorning the walls between shelves stuffed with dusty new age books hung carvings, reliefs, and splotchy folk art displaying a variety of spiritual scenes and symbols.

In a brief glance, Janis realized all religions she had ever heard of, and some she hadn't, were represented in the iconography. To her surprise there was even a wooden cross on one wall, above a display of sealing wax and vials with the label "Witch Hazel" taped to their rounded sides.

A tall, free-standing mantle around a defunct wood burning stove bisected the store, keeping the large table on one side and a gathering of crude silver jewelry behind a smudged glass display case on the other. Stuffed onto the top of the mantle were objects unfamiliar to Janis though after reading a small museum like placard she discovered the paraphernalia was on something called an altar and was for a holiday known as Lammas. Daring, she reached a hand out and poked at a loaf of bread that looked very stale. She snatched her hand back when her finger disappeared into the hard crust.

"What is this place?" she asked.

"Siroun owns this shop."

Janis circled around, balancing back on the heel of her cowboy boots. "It's so cool here! I wish I had known about it before." The shop *was* cool. She loved that everything was jumbled together. It felt exactly how the magical world really was, or as much of it as she'd seen so far. Everything was all mixed up. Her eyes ran over the labels on a display for talismans. One little tag read: *to ward off the vampiric*. "Jay!" she called over to him. "Jay, look at this. It's wrong, right?"

He peered at what she pointed to and nodded once.

"No one else is in the store," she complained. "You can speak to me."

"I just didn't want Leanna to overhear. She's Siroun's employee," he added when Janis opened her mouth to ask.

She shrugged and tried to pick up a ceramic mushroom statuette. "I'm just excited we're going to meet someone else. Are they a faerie? Will they know what's going on? More than you, I mean. Because, honestly, Jay, you haven't been helpful."

He spluttered in protest. "I haven't been... I don't know everything, especially not about the fae, I told you that!" he argued. "And Leanna is just a human. Siroun is the witch."

Janis grinned at his upset as she examined the bottom of the mushroom and raised her eyebrows at the price. The sound of muffled conversation filtered in through the back of the store, behind another glass display case serving as both a counter and another display case. Jay snatched the ceramic out of her hands and plunked it back on the table.

"Don't let Leanna..."

"I know, I know," Janis interrupted with a roll of her eyes. "Don't let anyone see the ghost of Christmas Past, I get it."

Jay approached the display case counter and Janis peered past the glass at the contents. It held more silver pendants and some knives made of both bone and holographic coated metal.

"Those are ugly," Janis told Jay, though she knew he wasn't listening. He dinged a bell on the counter near the register that was shaped to look like a dragon. A woman came around the corner, appearing from the back of the store. She stood at the door frame set back from the main counter.

"I'm not saying it's anyone's fault, you know, Mark? I'm just trying to explain the circumstances as I see them." She was blonde, pale, and very plump. A large assortment of barrettes were clipped in her hair, both tortoiseshell and purple glitter, though they did nothing for the frizzy flyaways. She wore an oversized purple-and-teal-swirl dress that fell over her rotund shape and dragged against the floor, catching on the backs of her thick orthopedic sandals. Wide set eyes blinked from behind thin, frameless glasses. "Hold please," the woman said into the air before pressing her ear.

"A Bluetooth? I didn't think they still made those," Janis said.

"Hi, Jayan," the woman said, stepping up to the counter and beaming at Jay. "It's been such a long time. What, a few months? How are you?"

"I'm fine, Leanna. Is Siroun in?"

Leanna shook her head. "Just stepped out, but you're welcome to wait. I could make you some tea?" She held up a black electric kettle from one of the shelves behind her. "I was just about to make myself some."

"No, thank you."

"You sure? It's oolong." Jay shook his head and Leanna grinned. "Always the same, huh? No tea, no nothing. Well, I could read your cards to pass the time?"

"No, I'm fine. I don't want to interrupt your call anymore than I already have."

"Who, Mark? Oh, goddess no, don't worry about him. He calls every week. Fucking debt collectors." She leaned forward over the counter to whisper to Jay, the glass edge pushing into her stomach. "But I looked him up on his social media the other day and he's cute. And my moon is in the right house this week so, you know..." she trailed off with a waggle of her eyebrows and Janis giggled, deciding she liked her. "Well, anyway, if I can't tempt you with tea and Tarot, come on back."

Leanna lifted up the partition on the counter. Jay and Janis followed through the doorway and into a back office space with a staircase tucked into the far wall leading upstairs. In the room were boxes of supplies the main part of the store couldn't hold along with a microwave, a rickety folding table, and a plastic covered maroon couch with embroidered paisley motifs.

"Go, sit. She'll come get you when she's done." Leanna went back to crushing herbs in a mortar on the wobbly table and pressed the Bluetooth in her ear to continue her call.

With a loud squish, Jay sat on the couch.

Janis looked at him and crossed her arms. No way she was letting him take a break when she still had a mystery to solve. "You're just going to sit there? Who the hell knows when she'll be back. She could be out shopping for hours or something."

"Siroun isn't physically gone from upstairs." Jay whispered.

Janis peered at the ceiling. "She's up there?"

Jay nodded. "She's astral projecting. Best human witch I know who can do it."

Without a sound, Janis perched next to Jay on the ugly couch. "Like a real witch or like in the movies?"

"I don't know what that means."

"Like, is she hot or does she have green skin and warts?"

Jay gave the ghost a level look. "She looks like a human, Janis."

"Oh my god, you're so annoying," she told him, shaking her head. "How do you not know about *The Wizard of Oz* and shit?"

"I don't have a television in my current home."

"What do you do after work?" This was crazy. Who didn't have a TV?

"I go to sleep."

Janis burst out laughing. "You are so weird."

Jay watched Leanna pace around the other end of the room, talking on her Bluetooth. "How is that weird?"

"You'd know if you watched TV," Janis quipped, still giggling. "So, how do you know her?"

"Leanna? I don't."

"No, the witch."

"Siroun." Jay heaved a sigh. "I'm not sure I know her either. She used to come into the police station every once in a while, trying to speak to the dead. We've kept in touch ever since."

Janis nodded, knowing several TV shows with similar premises. She didn't even try to explain that to Jay. "Like a psychic?"

"If you like."

"Can she tell the future?"

Jay shook his head. "No one can."

"What?" Janis was astonished. That couldn't be true, not after everything she'd seen. "Why not?"

Jay itched at the underside of his chin. "No one can tell the future, Janis. It's an ever-changing thing."

"Then why is she in business?" Janis asked, jerking a thumb over at Leanna who had just burned her hand with some hot tea and was yelling into her Bluetooth that she'd call Mark back.

"Because it's nice to believe there is a way to read what's ahead. You're the human—you tell me."

Janis thought back, sifting through her memories. "This girl in my class, Camilla, was obsessed with that kind of stuff. She and a bunch of her friends would always be going on and on about the zodiac. I was never much concerned." She paused. "Because I wasn't concerned with anything." Janis heaved a loud sigh and lapsed into silence.

Jay rested a hand on her shoulder. "Life isn't very fair, is it?"

She looked up at him. "No, it's not. If no one can see the future, why are we here?"

"Because," Jay said, standing up from the couch as footsteps sounded above them, "Siroun is a great place to start if you want to contact someone and go unnoticed."

The stairs creaked and protested as a fawn-skinned woman came tumbling down the steps, pausing halfway and bending at the waist to peer through the balusters. Her long, silky black hair fell past her shoulders in a dark curtain, brown eyes sparkling with exuberance. "Jay! I thought that was your energy. Wow, I haven't seen you since the OCME holiday party."

"You crashed that party."

Laughter greeted Jay's words. "True enough. Come on up and I'll meet you in my office. I just have to run to the restroom real quick." Pivoting on bare feet, the woman disappeared, though her accented voice rang out above her retreating footsteps. "And who did you bring with you?"

Janis froze. "Holy shit." She stared at Jay, her eyes huge.

"I did say she was good." He ducked halfway up the stairs to avoid bumping his head on the low overhang.

"Wait, Jay. Jay!" Janis hissed at his retreating back. "Does that mean she can see me?" He was gone. "Fuck," she muttered before leaving the small back room to take the stairs. She hadn't encountered this many stairs since dying and was hoping it wouldn't be too hard to walk up a large flight of them as a ghost.

Concentrating, she took the stairs one at a time, worried for the first few steps. By the time she hit the middle of the staircase, she was confident she wouldn't slip through the wood and fall to the first floor. When she reached the top of the landing, she heard a toilet flush and spied Jay hovering in a room to her left. Someone brushed through her and Janis squeaked, leaping sideways and disappearing half into a wall. Too late did she realize it was Siroun who had walked by. Pulling herself out of the wall, Janis ran into the room. "Jay!" she yelled, still shocked. "She walked right through me!"

Jay flinched at the volume. "That's the ghost who's with me," he explained.

Siroun's hand was on the base of her throat and she looked around in helpless empathy. "My goddess, her fear is coming through loud and clear. What's her name?"

"I'm Janis Lynn."

Siroun turned to face Janis' general direction. She spoke to her, eyes fixed on a spot above her head, as if Siroun thought she was taller. "Janis," she said and at her tone, Janis felt herself start to calm. "Are you alright?"

Janis' eyebrows shot up. This was the first time someone had asked her how she was since she was alive. "No!" she snapped. "I'm not alright."

Siroun nodded, eyes roving around empty space trying to see what she never could. "Would you like to sit down?" She pointed to an empty easy chair. Janis wondered if Siroun knew ghosts didn't need to sit, as they never grew tired, though the humanity in the gesture was appreciated.

"Thank you," Janis said, trying to keep the quiver out of her voice. Maybe she had just needed to speak to another woman. Jay was no help. Janis peered up at Siroun as she sat, arranging herself in a cross-legged position on the chair, knees disappearing into the arms.

The woman whom Jay had labeled a witch was wide and spread out in a pleasant way with full hips and strong shoulders. She wore no shoes, and her dark jeans were ripped in strategic places. Her top was plain, a dark olive that complimented her light brown complexion with smokey, adult makeup on her face. Her shiny black hair was wavy and full of volume even as it hung down almost to her waist. Biting down on her jealousy, Janis tried not to think about how she would never get her own chance to look womanly and grown.

"Definitely like in the movies," she decided aloud with a little sigh.

Siroun smiled. "Thanks."

Janis wondered if ghosts could blush, because she felt heat rush to her cheeks even without blood circulating through her. "I'm not used to people being able to hear me."

"I can't hear your exact words, but I feel the meaning. And it's a compliment, right?" She winked at the air next to Janis' left ear before looking up at Jay. "She doesn't sound older than sixteen."

"Yeah, I'm technically still fifteen," Janis supplied and Siroun extended her hand to further underline the point.

"Is that why you want to contact the City, Jay?"

"No," Jay said with a short shake of his head. "We found a reaper, dead, at a house not too far from here."

Janis nodded vigorously, feeling included. "Dead on the floor of a kitchen. Totally exploded. It was so gross."

Siroun frowned at the space Janis occupied, distracted and appearing unbothered by the gruesome news. "Her aura is so strange. How did she die?"

"It's not the oddness of her death you're sensing. She's a sheefrah."

Outside the room on the staircase, almost to the top of the landing with an extra mug of tea in hand, Leanna froze when she heard that word. Every inch of her body locked in painful rigor while fog rolled into her mind as if it were a forest on a damp night.

A message had come to Leanna in a dream a night ago. She had walked into a beautiful forest grove filled with a quorum of witches in long, flowing robes. At the front of the gathering stood a shadowed, non-figure who had greeted everyone in the crowd one at a time before addressing the group.

They might say sheefrah or changeling, or misbegotten child. When you hear it, you must tell us as soon as possible. You must tell us. It hadn't felt real until now. Leanna retraced her steps and went to find her obsidian mirror. She had a spell to cast.

Back inside the room, Siroun was shaking her head. "I'm not familiar with sheefrahs."

"Jay says I'm not one anymore," Janis informed Siroun, more than pleased to see the woman concentrating on her words. It felt so satisfying to be treated with consideration. "Death wiped the part away. It kept me sedated or something when I was alive so I didn't have like a personality or anything. Crazy, right?"

Siroun was looking at Jay. "What does Janis have to do with a dead reaper?"

"Nothing, I don't think. But I'm not sure. Too many things in this world are coincidences when they shouldn't be. I don't want to take a chance."

"What about your friend, Anat? Can he not make the call?"

Janis quirked an eyebrow at the flush that crossed Jay's cheeks.

"He would not help in this matter. But," he said, returning to his original plan. "All paths start with the City and I must alert them."

Siroun quirked an eyebrow. "I won't have the path origins argument with you again, Jayan."

He rubbed at the bridge of his nose. "I'm telling you the truth. The City is where They reside. They are the origins of all life, of everything. They are above everything, every religion, even your goddess."

"I don't care about the truth, I care that you're respectful in my house."

"I'm sorry," Jay said with an incline of his head.

"Thank you. Now, what do you want your message to say?"

Janis' wide eyes bounced between Siroun and Jay, impressed. She wondered if she could ever command such a presence, or would have if she had remained alive to grow up. Forlornly, Janis adjusted the hem of her shirt, plucking at the fabric and letting it drop. She wasn't even grown up enough to choose her own clothing. Her mother had picked out this outfit before they left for Seattle on Thursday night.

"I know you don't like to choose outfits, baby girl," her mother had said while digging through her closet. Janis had been sitting at the foot of her bed, watching. "And don't like anything that's too itchy or uncomfortable, but I think this would look nice together." Kate had pulled out a shirt and a denim skirt and wiggled them in the air in presentation.

It wasn't that Janis minded picking out clothing and putting them together into a cohesive ensemble, it was that she couldn't. Each time she approached her dresser or closet, an overwhelming feeling of exhaustion flowed over her, often making her sit or lie down on the floor until her mother came in to warn her about the time and that she'd be late for school. Eventually, they fell into an unwavering routine where Janis sat on the foot of her bed while her mother went through her clothes until she found something satisfactory to collect together on a hanger and place on a hook behind Janis' door. The next morning, Janis would simply dress in whatever was on the hanger.

This continued even when Janis didn't have school in the summer months. "I don't mind doing it," her mother would say when asked by her dad. Janis overheard that conversation multiple times. "It makes me feel like I'm helping."

Part of the outfit chosen for Friday included her mother's vintage shirt. It was too small for Kate and became a favorite of Janis' because it was so soft and worn. Not one to miss a detail for her daughter, she had also set out a pair of small hoops on the top of Janis' dresser. The night she picked it all out, Kate had said, "I do suggest wearing your cowboy boots, baby, but your sneakers would also be fine." The night of the party, Janis had selected the boots.

Pushing uncomfortable thoughts of her mother from her mind, Janis sat back into the recline of the chair. Siroun would make this call for Jay, then she would answer all of Janis' questions. After that, Janis was confident she would see her parents again. The room was comfortable, bedecked with items Janis thought most witches would own along with some that confused her.

A sleek flat screen television and entertainment center occupied most of one wall right next to a rug with a rolled smudge stick. On a low table was a box of watercolor paint squares, brushes, and a huge sheaf of watercolor paper with unfinished symbols lined up to look like an alphabet, but Janis wasn't sure. All the letters were made out of birds and they weren't from the ABCs Janis knew.

"What's that?" Janis asked, pointing and interrupting the witch and reaper.

"*Trchnakir*," Siroun answered distractedly. "Armenian bird letters." Janis nodded, still unsure of what that meant but unwilling to let her ignorance be known. She went back to her study of the room.

On the wall opposite the tv was a huge oil painting of a nude woman that was graphic enough to make Janis' eyes flick away. The bottom of the golden frame was inscribed with the name "Taralyn". Next to the painting was a lucite shadowbox with red velvet cradling a ribbon tied bunch of grayish brown fur. Janis had a feeling she shouldn't ask who Taralyn was, it felt far too intimate.

Turning her head, Janis realized she could see into the hallway from where she sat. With a jolt, she noticed Leanna. The large woman's pale face was peeking up from the staircase. She was staring into the room. Leanna's face, from what little Janis could make out, was dripping with sweat.

"Uh," Janis said, feeling stupid. "Your, um, friend is spying on us?" Janis' words swooped upward at the end with her uncertainty.

"Leanna?" Siroun asked with a frown.

Janis nodded. "And, um, not to be rude but, she looks...sick or something."

Siroun's frown deepened. "Lea?" she called out, getting to her feet. "You alright?"

"It hurts me," came the awful, wailing response from the hallway. The words were laced with a sinister growl, as if two people spoke at once. Deep black muck spilled from Leanna's open mouth and dribbled over her chin, smoking when it landed on the floor. Janis shrieked and rushed to cower behind Jay.

Siroun dashed across the room and slammed the door shut upon the unctuous malice hovering at the top of the stairs. "Can you feel it?" she called out to Jay leaning her back against the door in a blockade

"No, what is it?"

The witch wasn't one to waste time. "Fire escape," she ordered Jay, who hesitated. Siroun shook her head. "You have other responsibilities now," she said with a significant glance in Janis' direction. The door shook with a deep rattle as whatever held Leanna used her body to pound against the wood.

"Help me, Siroun," the wretched voice cried. "Open the door, it's just me, and us."

"Fuck you!" Siroun shouted over her shoulder, heels digging in on the floor for purchase. "Get out of my friend!" A wet howl and another bang sounded on the door.

"Siroun, I can help," Jay said, taking a step forward.

Siroun slashed a hand in his direction. "Don't you dare open your power here. You would do more harm than good."

"But..."

"I don't need a sledgehammer for a thumbtack, Jay. It's just a posses-sion. Get yourself and the little ghost out of here." When Jay remained hesitating, fury blazed in Siroun's eyes. "Now!" she growled. Jay jumped to open a window. Halfway out onto the landing of the fire escape, he looked back over his shoulder.

"My message?" He locked eyes with Siroun who nodded.

"I'll get it out to the right people. Now, go."

"Thank you." Jay ducked outside and began to clatter down the squeaking metal stairs.

"I don't know who you are, little ghost." Siroun addressed the air before her. "But you stick with Jay. He'll protect you." Janis' face fell. She liked the witch, liked how considerate she was, how she wasn't weird like Jay. "I know," Siroun said, as if sensing her thoughts. "Don't let him boss you around."

Janis smiled. "I won't."

The door banged with the full weight of a person being thrown against it. "Go!" Siroun yelled and Janis exited through the window hearing chanted words in another language fade as she descended the stairs and caught up to Jay.

NINE

J AY'S PHONE RANG AS soon as he and Janis were in his car driving away
from The Cottage.

"It's me," came Siroun's voice on the other end when Jay picked up,
"Leanna's fine."

"Turn up the volume," Janis said, poking Jay's arm.

"Does she remember what happened?"

"Not a thing. Doesn't even remember how she got upstairs. She's very
upset."

Jay hummed. "What was it? Does Leanna carry a trace?"

"No." Siroun tapped her nails in the background as she thought.
"Whatever it was, it wanted your little ghost and it wanted her badly.
I've never felt a presence like that except one time in Yerevan, years
ago. And Jay," she added after a pause, "it was evil."

"What do I do?" he asked in a low voice, eyeing Janis as she fiddled
with her skirt hem in the passenger seat.

"Keep her safe, Jay!" Siroun chided. "I don't know why I have to tell
you that. She's just a kid." The phone line crackled a bit as she sighed
into the receiver. "I'm going to do some digging on what happened
before I make your call. I want to make sure my ass is covered."

"Thanks, Siroun, I appreciate it."

"Maybe after all this you can finally come clean to me about who you
really are."

"You know I can't."

"Take care of Janis," Siroun repeated before she clicked off the line.

"What do we do now?" Janis asked.

Jay had no idea how to answer Janis' question. Siroun had told him

91

to keep her safe. Anat had told him everything would shake out in the morning. No one was giving him answers. He was sure something had gone wrong in his world and, while he didn't know how, it needed to be righted. He itched for a cigarette.

Siroun's words echoed in his mind. *Safe, keep her safe.* He needed a safe space for himself to think. Not his awful apartment but someplace cold, quiet, and with dead bodies. "Now, we go to work."

"You work on Sundays?"

Jay pressed the gas pedal, confident with having a purposeful destination. "I come and go as I please."

"Are you leaving me in the dark about what happened with Siroun on purpose?"

"Janis, I don't even know what happened." Jay was busy lighting a cigarette and spoke in a mumble around it in his mouth. He darted a look over to her in the passenger seat. The summer sun was reflected at the edges of her, sparkling with iridescence as if she were a prism of glass. "Still think you were murdered?"

"Yes," Janis said, exasperated. "Help me find proof. Siroun told me to tell you that."

To both their surprise, Jay let out a laugh. "Did she?"

Janis gave a tiny smile. "Yes, and she said for you to be nicer to me. And that a tad bit of groveling might be in order."

Jay grinned, shaking his head as he navigated them back to the OCME.

👻

Jay stuck Janis in his office once they arrived, promising to return as soon as he had cleaned up in the locker room. While she waited, she tried to play solitaire on his computer. Her hand kept disappearing through the mouse when she tried to move the cards, though when she concentrated, her palm and fingers remained solid. The office door snapped shut when Jay came back, but Janis was trying to move the mouse and she didn't turn when he spoke.

"I have something to tell you." Jay tugged on his lab coat. "Janis? Are you listening?"

"Hmm?" She moved a five of hearts to a large pile of cards.

"I just saw Layla."

"Who's that?"

"A liaison. The point is, um, at this stage, well, this is when..." He cleared his throat and began again. "Your parents are here to collect your body."

Janis stiffened and turned in the swivel chair. "Mom?" Her voice cracked and she stood, making to rush out the door. Jay blocked her.

"This is important, Janis. They won't be able to see or hear you." She glared at Jay and tried to push around him. He grabbed her now-solid shoulders. "If you make noise by influencing human objects you will only frighten them. It isn't fair, I know. Normally, ghosts are gone before they see their families."

"I'm just some special case, then?" Janis croaked behind a sob. Tears dropped from her large eyes.

Jay released his grip from her shoulders. "I don't know what you are."

"Besides dead," she pointed out. Jay hesitated, glancing toward the door. "Fine." She wiped at her cheeks. "I'll behave."

They walked together to the morgue and waited for her parents. "Are you ready?" Jay asked when a knock sounded outside the room. She shook her head but locked her jaw as the doors swung open.

Her parents entered looking like ghosts themselves, ashen and despondent, in the cold atmosphere of the medical viewing room.

"This is Doctor Jayan Mati, the forensic pathologist assigned to your daughter's case." A woman, Layla, Janis guessed, made the introductions. Kate and Robin, for the most part, ignored Jay, focusing instead on the wall of closed compartments across from them.

Janis ran to her parents, pacing before them, trying her hardest not to interact. It was as if she had never seen them before. She reached out and was about to caress her mother's cheek when Jay cleared his throat, startling the ghost into snatching her hand back, cradling it like it was burned.

"My condolences for your loss, Mrs. Pereda, Mr. Pereda."

Janis' father looked at Jay then. His eyes were bloodshot with dark circles beneath.

"We were told she was drinking?" Robin said by way of greeting.

"No!" Janis wailed. "Dad, I'm sorry!"

Jay flipped open the file in his hands and consulted his notes. "Her blood alcohol content was a 0.17 and in someone of her height, weight, and age, it impaired her gross motor functions." Janis sobbed, the sound echoing off the walls. "The cause of death was asphyxiation. Blood was found on rocks by the pool at the party she was attending. It was hers. She fell and stumbled into the water."

"What are you doing?" Janis protested. "Tell them I was murdered!"

"Please," Janis's mother, Kate, spoke. "Can we see her?" Robin draped an arm around his wife's shoulders.

"Tell them, Jay! Tell them what happened to me!" Janis was furious. Here was her chance, to prove once and for all she wasn't supposed to be dead. She could reconnect with her parents, show them how much she had changed. She could be the daughter they deserved, she could make them happy. Jay was ruining that chance. "You asshole!"

"This way." Jay led the small party in a short walk to a large glass window built into an interior wall. With a quick rap of his knuckles on the glass, the unhappy party watched as the curtains on the other side were opened, revealing the main room of the morgue and a body, covered by a sheet, resting on a stainless steel gurney.

"Oh, god," Janis said in a soft voice, distracted from her anger.

In her whole life, she had never known anyone who had died. Her parents had no close relatives and when her mother's father died around the time Janis was eight, there hadn't been an open casket. She'd seen made-up murder victims on reruns of crime shows, but knew that wasn't the same.

"Oh god, okay, I'm ready, just do it," she muttered in a string of words.

Jay nodded and the assistant behind the glass pulled back the sheet revealing the body. The covering was tucked in around Janis' torso, exposing her from the collarbones up. A wide strip of cloth had been placed across her eyes, to block the violence of her wounds. Robin and Kate Pereda burst into fresh tears. Janis hissed in a sharp breath and stepped back, recoiling from the sight.

"Jesus, fuck," she swore. It was an exquisitely awful experience. Empty warmth fogged into her mind, attempting to reduce the strangeness of the situation into something she could process. "I can't do this," were the words that slipped past her lips.

A curious sort of dysmorphia rippled through her as she stared at the girl on the table.

Is that me? Janis' mind fluttered.

Looking at herself in mirrors and pictures was nothing like seeing her whole body all at once. Her features looked mutant, different. Her rich, brown skin was bloodless and washed out. Her hands were so small, thin fingers with fragile looking nails while her face looked large and bloated. And her... Janis looked to the top of her head and yelped.

"My hair looks like shit! Who the hell touched my hair?" Janis' perfectly teased afro had been flattened and left to dry without moisture, causing the curl structure to look frizzy and undefined.

Memories rushed at her then, remembered quiet moments between her and her mother standing before the mirror and sink in the bathroom or Janis sitting on a stool at the kitchen counter, while they did her hair together. Janis would yelp if the movements were anything but gentle and Kate complied, tenderly tugging her hair into bunches or braids and patiently teaching Janis how to lay her edges down with a thick goop that smelled of peaches.

Hours were spent between Janis, her hair, and her mother. She remembered the soothing voice her mother used when sharing tricks on how to best care for her natural curls. She liked copying whatever style her mother wore, it was easy to make choices when she could see an example. While Janis didn't like sitting for hours to achieve the same long braids her mother came back with from the salon, she preferred when the crown of her head was covered in rows of braids that ended in a poof of one or two buns.

"There is so much beauty here," her mother would tell her as she detangled her curls on wash day when Janis was younger, before she had the coordination to do it herself. "Never forget that, baby girl. You are beautiful."

Now, in the morgue, Janis was overwhelmed with the desire to fall into her mother's arms to be comforted. She wanted to tell her mother that she had worn the outfit she chose, that she had used the new pink hair pick her mother bought when her last one broke, that she had listened to everything her mother said and was sorry she was gone without saying goodbye.

"That's her," Kate said, her voice constricted. Layla, watching from behind the parents, made a mark on her clipboard.

Janis remained staring at her body. The skin on her face looked like it was carved from a wax block. Her limbs were still, like she'd never inhabited them, moved them, bumped them up against walls, snuggled them under blankets. "I don't feel good."

Kate rounded on Jay, tear tracks down her cheeks. "You're sure she was drinking? Janis is a smart girl, she wouldn't do something like that."

"I'm sorry, Mrs. Pereda, the test was accurate."

"And you ran it more than once accounting for any errors?" Robin asked, eyes remaining on Janis's face. Jay assured Robin the test was correct, that he had run it twice. Robin slapped his hand on the plexiglass, startling everyone in the room. "This isn't fair!" he cried. "We left her alone for one weekend, the first time she's been alone..." Robin trailed off into a whisper and more tears. Layla moved in, uttering soothing words.

Kate leaned into her husband's shoulder, crying without sound. Robin covered his eyes while his other hand curled into a fist with white knuckles. The ghost of Janis stood next to them, overwhelmed.

7

Jay darted a glance to Layla who was blinking back her own tears at the scene. He wondered if he should try and force himself to cry. He didn't even know if he could. In his first human body, Jay had been expecting, and was halfway excited, to feel the wide array of passions boasted by humankind. But when he settled into a mortal life, past the shock of the transition, there had been nothing.

He supposed he shouldn't discount the mild sensations of amusement, disappointment, or polite interest that passed through him, but those he had already felt as a reaper. There was nothing else new for him to experience in a human body except for the awful jumpy feeling of surprise. That one, he hated. It had roots in fear, which he knew ran deep in mortals. When, in his second body as Olga, he had been startled by the sound of a car backfiring on the cold winter streets of Moscow, he thought he had been on the brink of death.

Love, joy, sorrow, even true fear were all foreign to Jay. Especially sorrow. For a reaper to do their job they must never know grief or sadness; it was forbidden. Even dumped in a human body he still wasn't allowed to feel any deeper emotions. Jay studied Robin and Kate as they wept.

It couldn't be as awful as it looked, he mused. *Not if mortals kept writing all those poems and songs. It might be beautiful. Profound, even.* He wished he could try it for the experience, as if sampling an exotic food. Perhaps it would be good for him or he might like it.

With the Peredas' fifteen minutes complete, and at a nod from Layla, Jay indicated to the assistant through the glass to shut the curtains. Once the business with the parents concluded, the OCME truck idling at the loading dock would transport the body to wherever the parents wished. Layla ushered the couple out of the morgue trying to soothe with platitudes.

"Janis, I'm sorry, that must have been hard, but you were..." Jay turned from the window to an empty room. The ghost was gone. "Fuck," he grumbled. "This is why the ferrymen are supposed to do their jobs!" He let his voice rise in annoyance, speaking to the air. The dead on the other side of the glass, or anything else that might be listening, did not reply.

Jay left the morgue, sneaking down the hallway to peer around a corner, looking through the glass of Layla's office at the front of the building. She was just gesturing for Janis' parents to take a seat. A shimmer of a ghost winked through the glass, already in the office. He would wait here, Jay decided, until he could make a good enough excuse to collect Janis from her mother and father.

After a few more minutes, the Peredas reemerged from Layla's office, a packet of information in their hands and fresh tears in their eyes. After shaking Layla's hands, Kate and Robin turned to leave and Jay twitched. Janis was walking backward next to her parents flipping him off with both her hands. He pointed to his feet, ordering her to return to his side. "I'm not a fucking dog, you unhelpful dick! I'll figure out my murder alone!"

Jay was grateful no one else could hear the ghost.

"Cousin," said a voice from behind him, causing Jay to jump. "Is that your ghost?" There was no smile on Anat's face but Jay heard light amusement in his deep voice.

"Yes," he said with a clenched jaw.

Anat heaved a sigh. "It's for the best, Jay. She made her choice. Get back to work, you're not paid to stand around."

Jay felt a snap of frustration reverberate through him. "She didn't get to choose!" he cried, startling several people in the lobby. Jay's phone rang, a cheerful jingle from inside his lab coat pocket interrupting his self-pitying thoughts. It was Siroun again.

"Jay," she said, the sound crackling and skipping like it came from far away.

He plugged his other ear to try and hear better. "Siroun?"

"It's Leanna," Siroun said, as best Jay could make out. "She's saying she remembers...before when you were here."

Jay moved around in a tight circle, trying to catch better reception. "The connection is bad, I can't hear you."

"It was..." Siroun's voice faded out.

"What? It was what?"

"I'm scared," Siroun's voice wavered back in through a mesh of static. "I don't think...call for you. Don't come here again." The line went dead and Jay realized his heart was racing.

"What's happening?" Anat asked, meeting Jay's wide eyes with a worried frown. "Who was that on the phone?"

"Siroun," Jay said, panting though he hadn't moved a muscle in exercise.

Anat drew back, confused. "The witch? What does she want?"

Jay was dazed. "I have no idea what's happening," he said. "This is wrong. Everything is all wrong."

"Oh," Anat waved a hand in dismissal. "It's just living among humans."

Jay wanted to slap the older man. "Do you not see it? Feel it?" he spat out. "We have a part fae girl who is now a ghost with no ferryman and a dead reaper. How do you not think something is amiss?"

Anat's eyes flicked around the lobby to where a few people were still eyeing the pair with curiosity. "Not here, cousin."

"Then where, Anat? When? I'm tired of being left in the dark." He turned and sprinted across the lobby, almost crashing into Layla's door-frame, his human body unused to even the shortest amount of exercise. She looked up wide-eyed at Jay hanging off the handle, sweaty and gasping.

"Goodness, Doctor Mati. What's going on?"

Sweat beaded at his hairline and he swallowed against the nausea from the perspiration. He was hot, always so hot. "Where is that girl's body going? Janis Lyn Pereda?"

Layla frowned. "Why?"

He couldn't tell her it was because reapers were built from things like order and due process and seeing a ghost without a ferryman was so abnormal, so outside of standard procedure, that it strained at his very essence. "Please, Layla, tell me. Where did the parents send the body?" He didn't bother trying to disguise the thick desperation in his voice. He gulped against his heavy breathing, trying to regain control.

Layla shuffled some papers on her desk before pushing one toward Jay. "Hall and Hill," she said. "I already called it down to the morgue. The body's on its way. It's right here on... Doctor Mati?" Jay had already run out of Layla's office, leaving her, and Anat who was still standing across the lobby, baffled.

TEN

L ATE AFTERNOON SHOPPERS STROLLED the city streets for a good weekend bargain, clogging the sidewalks. Jay had illegally parked in a back alley and walked around the block to get to the main entrance of The Cottage. Navigating through the crowd, Jay felt he was the only one in a hurry.

Get to Siroun and then to Janis, he told himself over and over again in a silent chant. Siroun's voice over the phone had been so full of fear that Jay needed to check in on her, despite her warning him not to come. And Janis... Jay didn't know what to do about her but he couldn't just abandon the ghost without a ferryman.

With his body being so tall, it was maddening to see several steps ahead and not be able to arrive there until a group of slow moving tourists moved out of his way. He resisted the urge to pick one old man up by the shoulders and remove him from his path. Jay ran the last few feet to the front door of Siroun's shop and froze when he saw the door ajar. It bumped against the frame, holding on with one hinge left at the top. There was a spell covering the doorway, one that pushed mortals away and helped the door to appear undamaged.

Jay pushed open the broken door.

"Siroun?" He hissed in a sharp breath. The interior of The Cottage was ruined. He crunched over dried herbs scattered on the wooden floor. "Siroun!" he called again, louder. The heavy wooden table in the middle of the shop was upended, leaning on its side against one of the walls as if it had just taken a light breeze to blow it over. Cracked glass bottles and ripped books littered the floor. Jay saw a streaky black burn mark upon the wall above the candle display but there was no live fire. Everything was coated in a damp film of drying water; the sprinkler system having done its job.

The pungent mix of herbs, wet wood, and spilled tinctures began to give Jay a headache and he pushed his way to the back of the shop. The partition to the back rooms from the counter lay broken into pieces on the floor. The glass cases displaying jewelry and athames were destroyed and the little dragon bell that sat in front of the cash register had rolled off somewhere under one of the now listing bookshelves.

"Leanna?" he tried as he made his way back to the break room and storage area behind the shop. He drew up short. The blonde woman was half draped over the plastic couch, legs resting on the ground as her top half reclined upon the cushions as if in repose. Leanna had been eviscerated from her head down to her chest. Long, deep claw marks penetrated into her eye sockets, ripping downward to expose muscle and bone from her neck to her ribcage. Jay saw her heart was missing. His own began to pound in earnest.

A creak of wood came from upstairs and Jay froze, peering up the staircase trying to discern if the danger still lurked around the corner. After a moment of continuous silence, Jay whispered, "Siroun?" A faint moan met his words. Taking the stairs two at a time, Jay pounded up to the second floor and rushed into Siroun's rooms.

The witch was huddled in the far corner, curled around herself in a shallow pool of dark liquid. Her shirt was in tatters along with the skin beneath. She lifted her head weakly as Jay peeked at the room's hidden corners. "Jay?" she croaked. "Is that you?"

Abandoning his caution he moved to her side. "What did this?"

Siroun coughed, a blood bubble forming and bursting at the corner of her mouth. "They're back, Jay. They came back, I always knew they would." Her voice was thick with the blood pooling in her throat.

"Who?"

Siroun reached out to him in a great effort, and he helped her out of the corner to lay in a more comfortable position on the rug. "Did you keep her safe, Jay? Your little ghost?"

Jay wished he could lie in this moment, wished he had all the answers. "Don't worry, Siroun. Tell me what happened."

She coughed again, her gaze troubled as she looked up at Jay who cradled her head. "They knew you had been here."

"Me?" Jay was shocked. "Why?"

"You've seen them," Siroun's words came out in a wet wheeze. Jay knew blood was making its way into her lungs. "The raven feathers."

"Who are they? Siroun?" Jay watched as the woman dipped into unconsciousness. He fumbled in his pocket for his antiquated flip phone. Smearing blood over the buttons his thumb slipped before he got to the speed dial. He could hear the rushing sounds of his own breathing in the speaker between dial tones. The line clicked.

"What is it?"

Relief flooded into Jay. "Anat! Can you get to The Cottage?"

"The witch shop? Why?"

"I need your help. Please, cousin." Jay heard a long sigh on the other end of the line.

"It will take me a moment but I will get there." The line went dead before Jay was able to voice his thanks. While he waited, he ripped up a blanket from the couch and bound Siroun's torso against the steady flow of blood. Gently, he moved a thin pillow under her head and smoothed back her head from her forehead, hoping he'd done enough.

The body of Jayan Mati may have been to medical school, but the reaper occupying his flesh had not, and neither had much experience in helping patients who were still alive. There was nothing Jay could do but wait for help to come. He arranged himself on the ground in a nervous position.

Jay heard sounds of crunching glass beneath footsteps in the store below. He held still in case whatever it was who had done this was back. "Reaper?" Jay heard Anat's voice call up from the bottom of the staircase.

"I'm upstairs!"

Shock and wariness were splashed across Anat's face as he entered the upstairs room. He looked at Jay who shook his head.

"I don't know what happened." Jay let out a sigh, trying to release the tension strung so tightly within him. "All Siroun managed to say was that this attack is connected to the dead reaper."

"And the ghost, I imagine," Anat said, rubbing his tired eyes.

Jay hummed in a non-answer. "I'm not sure, but I have to find her. I need to make sure there isn't something I missed when reviewing the autopsy." Not that he enjoyed admitting it, he might have made a mistake. The human body of Jayan Mati obscured his immortal senses on the best of days.

Anat bent to a crouch and placed two large fingers against Siroun's blood splattered neck. "Her pulse is strong, at least. There might be hope."

"She needs to get to the hospital, Anat." Jay stared across Siroun's prone body until Anat met his gaze. "Will you take her?"

"Are you crazy? I can't just show up with a half-dead mortal in my arms to an ER." Anat sat back and crossed his arms over his large belly. "No, I refuse to sit through hours of questions."

"What, then?" he snapped out. "When will you wipe whatever caul is over your eyes and see that this is bigger than your job, bigger than the OCME?"

Anat gave Jay a heavy look. "The trials of mortals are not more important than my life."

"They used to be." Something sour began turning in Jay's stomach he had never felt before.

"Cousin, I am no longer who I once was. You know this. I am trying to become one of them and I cannot do anything to jeopardize the probationary period."

"Damn your probation," Jay cursed. "Our friends are in danger."

Anat's lip curled. "We do not have mortal friends, reaper. Humans live and die in mere moments for us. Any connection created is gone ere long."

Surprising himself, Jay murmured, "Their ephemerality doesn't mean connections can't still be meaningful." He imagined the eye roll Janis would give him at that sentiment.

The muscles in Anat's jaw clenched as he worked through the decision. "Fine. I will take her. Help me wrap her in that blanket." Jay grabbed another blanket from the couch and tossed it to Anat. They worked to tuck the fabric around Siroun's body, mindful of the slashing wounds. Jay helped to bundle her into Anat's arms. Anat stood, strong arms protecting the unconscious witch, and looked up at the tall reaper.

"What of you and the ghost?"

Jay strode toward the staircase. "I have to go to the funeral home where they took Janis' body."

Anat followed, slowed by the weight of his burden. Once downstairs, Jay directed Anat to follow him to the back exit. He held the door open for Anat and they moved into the alley behind the shop. They tucked Siroun into the backseat of Anat's car. The older man closed the door and stretched his back. Carrying the woman hadn't been an easy task, his body was folding more and more into a mortal one and his muscles were a mere shadow of his former self. Still, Anat relished the feeling of aches and pains and cracks. He had chosen this for himself, unlike the reaper who was busy unlocking his own car.

"Why go to find the ghost at all? Why not let this unfold without you?"

"A ghost must have a ferryman to make their choice. I have to help Janis before I can figure out what happened here."

Anat shook his head. "That love for procedure will be the death of you, reaper."

Jay stood and looked down the alley. In the very distance he could see where it met up with the busy streets as the crowds for the dinner rush began to take over the sidewalks. All those individual lives. It was so intricate and chaotic. Jay understood there was beauty there, but he could never figure out why.

7

The parking lot of Hall and Hill Funeral Home was almost empty. Jay maneuvered around the few parked cars there were and came to a stop at the back under a scraggly tree. Shutting off the Honda's engine, Jay squinted into the late afternoon sun, shading his eyes against the glare. Something flickered in an upstairs window. He waited, searching. A half minute later, the flicker came again, this time to the front porch before puffing away into thin air. Jay's eyebrows rose. She was already jumping. She was traveling between places in a single instant, a power only afforded to fully formed ghosts.

Janis, as a full ghost, was a rarity. Fewer amounts of people wished to remain behind once dead these days. There was no desire to stay in a world that did little to support them in life. Most who did stay were very vindictive or overly stubborn. There were still ghosts in existence, multitudes of them from over the centuries, but they didn't wander as they once did. Instead, they hide away from the world, congregating in places of isolation away from the increased noise of modern life. Even if Janis had decided to stay as one such spirit, it was an egregious oversight she was not asked her preference.

Jay waited another long minute before movement blinked outside the funeral home, off to the side, near the outdoor A/C unit. The apparition lingered long enough for him to glimpse the form of Janis, looking confused as her head turned this way and that.

"Janis!" Jay called through the window glass, hurrying to exit the car. The ghost turned her head toward his voice but disappeared just as she opened her mouth to speak. Jay hurried to cross the parking lot, skirting along the edge of the building, and came to a back garden where there was space for the bereaved to come and get some fresh air. Somewhat hidden among the shrubbery, Jay waited, nervous and jittery, with sweat dripping down the small of his back.

Jay whirled, hearing Janis gasping behind him, doubled over.

"What's happening to me?" she asked between gulps of air she no longer needed.

"You're jumping."

"Jumping?"

Jay nodded. "It's what ghosts do."

Before she could reply, she flickered away again, leaving Jay to wait several more minutes before she appeared behind him, looking frantic. "How do I stop?"

"Focus on this spot as where you want to be." He retrieved and lit a cigarette and she disappeared and reappeared again. "Calm your mind, and you'll stop," he told her when she flickered but held firm.

With a deep breath, Janis remained. "When were you going to tell me I could do that?"

"You can do lots of things." He checked the watch on his wrist.

"What kind of things?"

He spoke fast, in clipped tones. "As a full ghost, you're strong, you can pass through solid objects and manipulate them, and you can jump. It means you can disappear and reappear when you want, within reason and range, of course."

"Oh, of course," Janis echoed, voice distant. She looked down at her hands, palms up, her form now opaque and in full color.

"Janis," Jay said with urgency, thinking of Siroun, "we have to leave."

"I couldn't go home with them." Janis dropped her hands, looking at Jay with a pathetic expression. Her voice cracked as she explained. "And then I didn't know how to get back to you and I broke a vase and scared a family and then I kept bumping in and out of rooms and I didn't know what was happening."

"Jumping," Jay corrected her. "You were overwhelmed and couldn't control it."

She wrapped her arms around herself. "I don't want to be here any-more. It..." she trailed off, searching for the right word. Her shoulders slumped when she was unable to find an eloquent description. "Sucks."

"That's why I'm here," Jay said. He stood and crushed the cigarette butt under the heel of his shoe. "I'm going to find you a ferryman and sort out this peculiar situation." He started in the direction of the car. "Come on," he ordered when he realized Janis wasn't on his heels.

"Why won't you help me?"

He returned to the garden, eyes flicking over to the funeral home windows. "I am helping you."

"Are you? Because I still don't remember anything about the day I died and you said that I would."

"Nothing more from before your death?" Jay didn't like this. She should have recovered her memories by now as a full ghost. Even with her level of intoxication, death wiped away the fog of any substance and left a clear path for the deceased to follow. It allowed them to reflect on their last moments to help them make the right choice.

Janis shook her head, her springy hair moving. "I still don't remember ever falling down. I swear someone hit me."

"Hit you?" Jay echoed.

"Or pushed me, or whatever. The point is there's a murderer on the loose!"

He glanced at the time on his watch. There were still a few more hours before sunset and the idea that he might have missed something in an autopsy set a thorn in his side. "I can take a look at your body one more time. But then we have to leave." With one finger, Jay pressed it to Janis' forehead. A black, thick dot appeared on her brown skin. "I need to see if there's anything supernatural lingering around you. I should've done this before, but I didn't know to look. It will have to be you, though, I can't walk around the funeral home without a good explanation. Jump inside and take a look at yourself. Blink a few times and look for anything out of the ordinary. Signs, symbols, something that could be moving across your skin."

Janis rubbed her forehead. "Is that permanent?"

"No. Hurry up, I don't want someone to see me and start asking questions." Janis crouched and screwed up her face. "What are you doing?"

"Trying to jump."

"Don't think too hard. All you have to do is..." Jay stopped as the ghost blinked out of existence. Minutes ticked by and Jay waited, trying not to fidget. He checked his phone but there were no new messages. He rang Anat a few times, the calls all ending at his voicemail until they stopped going through. Either he turned his phone off or blocked his number. Jay lit another cigarette. A dead reaper, raven feathers, something that used Leanna's body, and a ghost without a ferryman. None of it added up or made sense enough for him.

Janis jumped back to the garden, flickering with her lack of mastery over the action like a verbal stutter come to life.

"Nothing," she reported. "And it still sucks looking at your own body, by the way."

"There's nothing left to do but to go to a cemetery." Jay looked at the sky then double-checked his watch. "We'll be a little early."

Janis took a step back in alarm. "Why a cemetery?"

"Because they are conduits to other sides and it's either a cemetery or a church and I don't feel like going to one of those sanctimonious clubhouses right now."

"Maybe I don't want to go to a cemetery."

"You were just saying how much it sucks to be a ghost. Crass, but poignant."

"It sounds very permanent."

Jay tossed his second cigarette to the ground. "We need answers and a cemetery is where we'll get them. If a ferryman won't come to you, we will force one to talk to us." In one of the windows above them, a curtain fluttered.

Was someone watching? He took a desperate gamble to get her to go with him without argument. *Or,* he conceded to himself. *Much more argument.*

"Janis, you're not supposed to be dead." The statement came out flat and strained, though Janis didn't seem to notice.

"Oh, now you get it," she remarked with a huff.

"So, if you come with me to the cemetery to look for answers you might be able to see your parents again." This wasn't a full lie, but it was too far from the truth to be well-meaning. At his words, Janis smiled up at him with complete trust in her large green eyes, twisting Jay's stomach into a knot. He swallowed hard to try and clear the lump. "We'll take my car," he announced, distracting himself.

When Janis got to the car, she was able to open the passenger side car door alone and looked to Jay with an excited expression from her small achievement. Still feeling off, Jay said nothing as he climbed in and started the engine.

Janis shut her door with a huff at his dismissal. "You need to work on being nicer."

Jay moved the transmission into reverse and circled the car around toward the exit. "I'll think about it." He looked over at the ghost to see if he had made her smile. Janis gasped, causing Jay to slam on the breaks. "What? What's wrong?"

Her eyes were wide. "What is that?" Jay followed the ghost's pointing finger and let out a whimper at what he saw. Jamming the gear shift into park and wrenching out the keys, Jay fumbled with the door, trying to extract himself from the vehicle in a desperate rush.

At a small intersection a short way down the street standing in the bed of a red pickup truck was a reaper. Jay stood open mouthed, holding onto the open car door for support. The reaper noticed the movement and looked over to the funeral home parking lot, nodding in greeting. They turned back to do their job before Jay could wave back. Bending down, the reaper's body disappeared into the cab of the truck, save for their wings. The huge, bone things remained outside the truck, stretched out over the car like an umbrella. They clacked when the reaper moved.

"Holy shit," Janis whispered from inside the Honda, trembling.

Jay knew what she saw, it was how he looked when he was a reaper. Able to peer through the glamour, Janis would see an expanse of shadows, the sound of whispers, the smell of lavender. Reapers were beauty and finality and transition. They were neither a thing nor a non-thing, they simply were.

The reaper wrapped their arms around the driver in the truck cab, an older man in his sixties. They set two hands on the man's chest and pressed in a gentle motion, initiating a heart attack. Placing a delicate kiss on the side of the man's cheek, the reaper stood in the truck bed. They hopped down, wings beating once to let the reaper float to the street. They crossed over to where the Honda with two astonished passengers was idling as the man in the truck began to die.

"Hello, my love," the reaper said over the delicate snap-clack sound of their wings folding away. Their voice was beautiful, designed as if to sing, not speak. Jay's breath left him in a rush. His skin felt clammy, sweat from the heat of the day evaporated in the shock of seeing the reaper. Like at the crime scene, Jay didn't recognize this one.

"You're allowed to talk to me?" The sweetness of acknowledgement was overwhelming. Jay hadn't seen another of his direct kin alive since he fell to Earth.

The reaper shrugged. Their glamoured form was of a short, bald human, neither male nor female, with yellowish skin. They wore a well-tailored pencil skirt and matching blazer, shirtless underneath. The button on the blazer clasped together at the belly, revealing a flat chest without nipples. "I should not but there is something I must tell you."

"I'm listening," Jay said, hand on his chest. "And I'm honored. Thank you for speaking to me, you've no idea how long it's been."

The reaper smiled, narrow eyes crinkling. "You speak like them, my love." Jay swallowed, waiting. They drew close and cupped both sides of Jay's face. "You are so tall here." They forced his head down and pressed their forehead to his in a long moment of stillness. Jay breathed in the reaper's scent of calm water and cool air. The muscles in his shoulders released their tension. The reaper kissed Jay's forehead before stepping back. "Beautiful. How much longer must you stay in exile?"

He ignored the urge to glance over at Janis whom he had heard make a strangled noise when they had bowed their heads together. "Four hundred and thirty three years, five months, seventeen days, and thirty-seven minutes."

The reaper smiled with sympathy. "My love, I am so sorry."

He shrugged the apology away, not wanting to focus on his plight. "It's my burden. What did you wish to tell me?"

A darkness passed over the reaper's face. Their bone wings clicked in agitation. "Someone is hurting us."

"Yes," Jay interjected. "I've seen one, back in my morgue."

"My love, my love, much more than one." Jay closed his eyes until he felt hands upon his face once more. "With raven feathers in their eyes."

Jay nodded, unable to speak.

"We haven't known for long but there is a pattern. There have been souls of humans mixed with fae magic who pass before their time. They are left to wander without a ferryman because of the early departure. Their souls disappear before we can help them find their way."

"Who is doing this?" Jay whispered.

"We don't know who began it, but demons paid with fae gold slay the souls and let the fae collect them to siphon off the magic. When a reaper is called to the human, their ferryman is missing because these mixed souls have died before their time. A ferryman does not know to appear. And when we ask questions, my love, we are slain upon the Earth, scattered, alone, and far from home."

"But how? I thought we couldn't die."

The reaper gave a sad smile. "We may all be extensions of Four, but we can indeed perish. With enough power... The marker of such a heinous act is in the raven feathers left behind. It is the fae who murder us, fae with bursts of power unnatural for even their kind that leave the mark behind in the wake of the killings."

Janis moved in her seat, the flash of her ghostly form drawing the reaper's attention. "Hi," Janis said, voice muffled by the car.

"Mixed souls are powerful, my love," the reaper said by way of a hello before leveling a look at Jay. "Killed before their time, they hold even more power. She should not be here."

"Yes!" Janis blurted out. "I knew it! And I told him so, I..." she trailed off, aware of both Jay and the thing of darkness staring at her. She slumped down in her seat and remained quiet.

Jay restarted the conversation. "What does the City know of this?" His heart sank when he watched the reaper's expression shift in response to the question. They looked disgusted.

"The City knows and has done nothing. It must be part of Their plan." Dark eyes flashed and the reaper stopped and tilted their head, listening to something in the distance. Their face paled. Looking back into Jay's eyes the reaper reached up, dragging him close to kiss him on both cheeks.

"It is my time," they said, releasing him. "They come for me as I led a mixed soul to the ferryman Archer and the soul chose to pass on. I have cost the fae their precious power and I will pay for it now."

"No," Jay protested in dismay. "Come with us, I'll protect you."

The reaper unfurled its wings. "I will die having given you all I know. I go with pride."

Jay felt desperation knead at his stomach. "You don't have to. Come with us instead." The reaper shook their head and backed away, gaining space to spread their wings. Jay clenched his fists. "Please," he tried one last time.

"Goodbye, my love." They leapt into the air with the cacophonous racket of bone moving against bone. "Go now! I will lead them away from you!" the reaper cried out before turning over and pumping their wings, gaining speed. Jay stood frozen watching his sibling fly until he couldn't see them anymore.

"Jay?" Janis questioned in a small voice. "Are you alright?"

At the small scene of frenzy surrounding the idling red pickup truck at the intersection, someone was on the phone with 911. Jay could hear their scared voice from across the street. Warmth blossomed in his heart, the lasting connection flaring as the reaper's life was snuffed out somewhere in the distance. The worst part—the thought came to him with unexpected clarity—was that he didn't even have the proper emotions to mourn the sacrifice of his sibling.

"No, Janis," Jay answered, climbing into the car. "No, I'm not."

The fae are killing reapers.

A shudder passed through Jay at the unnaturalness of the thought. Maybe the reaper had been misinformed. And, the mere thought Four would let crimes such as this take place was so unfathomable it bordered on revulsion. There were too many little loose threads unspooling around Jay and it set him on edge.

A touch of cold spread out from a place on his arm. Janis had reached out with her fingers. "I'm sorry. Have you been dating for long?" Jay stared at Janis in surprise. Her face was so earnest he burst out into laughter, releasing the anxiety within. "What's so funny?" Janis demanded, snatching her hand back from Jay's arm. "You were the ones doing all that forehead touching."

"That's how we greet each other," he told Janis. "It's a handshake or, more accurately, a hug."

Janis puffed out an embarrassed laugh through her lips. "Oh." She shifted in her seat. "I'm still sorry, though."

Jay didn't have the emotion of sorrow to let overwhelm him, but he felt a heavy disappointment at the waste of life. "Thanks," he said and navigated the car onto the freeway in silence.

ELEVEN

T HE IRON AND STONE fence marking the entrance to West View Cemetery loomed in an archway over the entrance. All the moss and crumbling stone made Janis feel like it deserved to be a graveyard. She looked around as Jay drove into the sprawling grounds. Loose bits of gravel and small pebbles bounced around the wheels and pinged up against the undercarriage. He stopped the Honda at a back corner and let the engine idle so the A/C could continue.

In a plot of land some distance away, gravediggers were at work. Jay lit a cigarette and cracked the window. While he smoked, Janis watched the light of the setting sun turn rich and golden. She wished she'd had more of these kinds of days, lingering and lazy. Janis wondered if anyone listened to the wishes of ghosts. *If someone is listening,* she thought, *I'm sorry I wasn't a better daughter.* Janis cleared her throat, coughing around unshed tears. "It was a nice day out today, wasn't it?"

"Bit hot for me," Jay told her.

Janis gave a little hum in response, tracing a finger on the window glass, leaving no smudges. She needed a distraction from her thoughts. "What do we do now?"

Jay shifted his hips. "We wait."

"For how long?"

"Until after sunset. Ferryman prefer the dark."

Waiting wasn't what she had in mind. Janis flipped down the visor above her seat to look into the mirror before remembering she no longer had a reflection. With an angry grunt, she slammed the visor back up and crossed her arms.

"I should have never gone to that stupid party," she announced. She knocked her head back on the seat rest and glared up at nothing in particular. "I thought it was a joke, you know. That anyone would want me there." She heard Jay light a new cigarette. "Bobby Wright invited me and that would really mean something to you if you knew our school. But if you look like me you don't get invited anywhere and certainly not by *Bobby Wright*. I guess I should have known something bad would have come of it."

"I don't understand," Jay said around the cigarette. "Why would it be a joke if you were extended an invitation?"

Janis fixed him with her wide, glassy stare then looked away. "People are cruel," she stated.

More smoke curled within the car. "That, I understand."

"Does it have to do with my eyes that I can't remember anything?" She asked the question louder than she intended, masking her nerves with a bravado of words.

"Maybe. I really don't know much about sheefrahs. But I can say that your eyes are fae. In fact, fae don't always look human, they have many distinct forms, even animal ones. I should have grabbed some coffee for this stakeout," he added.

Picking an invisible piece of dust from the hem of her shirt, Janis asked, "What happens after all this? Like, where do these ferry guys take people?"

Jay shook his head. "I can't tell you, even if I wanted to. Reapers are forbidden from answering those kinds of questions."

Janis pulled a face. "But you're not a reaper; you're just a coroner guy."

"I'm a forensic pathologist and I'm still a reaper even if in the body of a mortal."

"A male mortal," Janis pointed out. "I thought you said reapers don't have gender?"

Jay looked at his body and sighed. "We don't. This body does. I was just put into this body. I don't associate with the gender or use the male parts for human copulation."

"How wonderful for you," she told him, wrinkling her nose. He didn't look as if he minded but Janis was mortified at the turn in conversation. She had yet to talk about sex in detail with her own parents let alone a complete stranger. She hadn't even decided on her feelings toward the whole matter. After a mandatory health unit in sixth grade, she had put the whole subject out of her mind. Janis realized with a start that she had died before kissing anyone. *I'm so pathetic*, she thought, miserable.

7

Almost twenty minutes passed before the ringing of a cell phone interrupted the quiet car. Jay fumbled with the phone for a moment before flipping it open and answering.

"Anat?" Jay asked, anxious. "Is she alright?"

Janis sat forward in her seat. "Is who alright?"

"She is stable for now," said Anat's voice through the phone. "I was able to do some maneuvering with my OCME status and pretended there was a misunderstanding in paperwork to get the information."

"Just put it on speakerphone," Janis whined. Distracted, Jay complied with her request.

"What was that noise?" Anat's voice filled the car.

"I put you on speakerphone," Jay said.

There was a pause. "Why?"

"So I can hear," Janis answered.

"Reaper," Anat said through a clenched jaw. "What are you doing?"

Before Jay could answer, Janis jumped in.

"I am just as much part of this investigation as you are," she protested. Jay shot her a look and she mouthed "what" to him laden with attitude.

"I very much wish to be excluded from all this going forward," Anat stated. "I helped you with the witch and now I'm done. I cannot jeopardize my standing."

Janis frowned at Jay. "The witch? Did he mean Siroun? What happened? Is she okay?"

Ignoring the mutters of complaint coming from Anat, Jay pinched the bridge of his nose. "She was attacked..." he started to say.

"Attacked?" Janis interjected with a yelp.

"...but she's fine," Jay continued with a firm note to his voice. "We got to her in time." He refrained from mentioning Leanna to avoid upsetting Janis further.

"What the fuck? When were you going to tell me?"

Jay shook his head and focused back on the phone call. "Anat, I have to stay here for a little while."

"Where is 'here', reaper?"

"West View. I need to remain with the ghost but, Anat, I spoke to a reaper. The raven feathers are from the fae killing my kind. I have no doubt it was also the fae who hurt Siroun. They are in league with demons. I don't know how far this treachery runs within the fae courts but if it has to do with gaining power, I can only assume they've kept the truth from all but a small few."

After a beat of silence, Anat sighed into the speaker, the noise distorted and static. "I'm done. I'm out of this. I will tell you to be safe though I don't think you will heed such a request."

"I'll keep him safe," Janis said with a look on her face that told Jay she knew just how much her words would annoy Anat. As it was, in the moments that followed, Jay was certain he heard Anat's blood pressure rise.

"If you find out which fae did this to Siroun, call me back," Jay ordered.

The demigod of death hung up without another word. Jay pocketed the phone and tipped his head to rest on the seat back and closed his eyes.

"I don't know why you insist on leaving me out of this process," Janis told him while fiddling with the window crank on her side of the car. "I can help. Now that I can jump, I can help figure out what happened to me and..."

"You can't, Janis!" Jay snapped, louder than he'd meant to. He took a moment to draw a long breath and calm himself. The ghost was glowering at him so he inclined his head. "I meant that we need to check in with a ferryman first, and then we decide what to do next."

"What happened to Siroun? Were there any more raven feathers?"

Jay closed his eyes and tipped his head back again. "No, thankfully. But the fae are formidable foes."

"Faeries? Why would they be formidable?"

"They aren't like how they are portrayed in human media."

"How would you know? You don't watch any TV, you said."

"I never said I didn't read." Jay debated lighting another cigarette. "The fae are powerful beings. While they keep to themselves and their courts only govern the Hill, their magic is the most powerful in the world." He glanced at the clock. It had been three hours since they arrived at the graveyard. The late summer sun was beginning to set. The gravediggers were long gone, and the dirt was fresh, the upturned earth a screaming target for a ferryman. "Looks like we won't be here much longer." Jay eyed the setting sun. "We'll have to leave before the scavengers arrive in any case."

"Scavengers? That doesn't sound...good."

"It's not, but it feels like this man," Jay nodded, indicating the gravesite some ways off, "was a bad person in life. If a ferryman doesn't show up, like with you, all manner of unpleasant things will arrive."

"They didn't arrive for me though," Janis said, trying to sound brave.

"You weren't a bad person when you were alive."

Jay heard her gulp. "I cheated on a math test once."

Despite his darkening mood, Jay chuckled at her admission. "You needn't worry," he assured her.

The toe of her cowboy boot disappeared into the dashboard as she crossed her legs. "Don't laugh at me." The shadow of a faint smile tugged at the corners of her mouth.

There was movement by the fresh grave. "Be quiet," Jay hushed his companion.

Janis was indignant. "I didn't say anything!" Jay peered through the last streaks of sunlight visible above the distant tree line at the far end of the cemetery. He felt the pull of the soul in the grave, even from the car. Janis was unnerved by his silence. "Jay, what's going on?"

He threw his arm out across her chest, pinning her back against the seat.

"Hey!"

"Janis," Jay repeated, watching the light in the sky turn from a dirty yellow to gray. "Be very quiet. I hate this part," Jay muttered, removing his arm from Janis' body, confident she would remain still.

The sun set in a final wash of yellow-gray light, leaving the world in dusk. A chorus of night insects started their symphony. Jay squinted into the twilight. A firefly or two blinked in the gloaming. There it was again, movement behind the freshly dug grave. A passing truck on the highway beyond illuminated the cemetery and a figure was caught for a moment in the headlights. Jay groaned.

"Why did you make that noise? Jay? Who is that?"

Keeping his gaze on the figure, Jay moved to unbuckle his seatbelt. "That is Tick. Don't get out of the car, all right? I'll talk to him."

"What's the tick?" Her voice was small and quivering.

Jay hesitated getting out of the car and looked at her wide eyes.

"No 'the'. He's a ferryman of the damned."

Janis licked her lips. "Is he...nice?"

"Does he look nice?" She didn't answer and Jay left the car. Trepidation curled low in his belly as he stood, his sense of heightened dread surprising him. The emotion was strong, stronger than the worry and guilt he felt before. Something to worry about later.

The sound of the door shutting attracted the ferryman's gaze. Jay hurried toward him, drawing attention away from the car and the ghost within.

"Evening, Tick," Jay called out to the thing by the new grave, forcing his thoughts away from ones of unease.

Tick was tall, far taller than the body of Jayan Mati, standing around seven and a half feet. He was a naked, gray, skeletal thing with skin wrinkled and parched like a mummy. His legs took up most of his body, his shrunken torso disproportionate to the lanky legs and long arms. Each hand ended in three spindly fingers clad with several glittering rings of gold and jewels. Between his legs dangled sickly looking genitalia. Jay tried to keep his eyes off the repellent sight, a difficult task as they were so close to eye level.

"Reaper," Tick replied, voice sounding as if it came laced with a sinister smile. His face was made of shadow, even in broad daylight it would still show darkness. "I have not seen you in ages and ages and ages." Tick's words were drawn out, as if extracting vowels was hard work.

Jay stopped before he would smell him. "Indeed."

Tick paced in a short line before Jay, enjoying the warm night air. He

118

had two knee joints on each leg and two elbows for each arm, forcing his movements to be fluid and twitchy all at once. "You've been busy...or not." In the silence that followed Jay assumed Tick was laughing, though he couldn't hear it. "Or not...so, I am here for this squeaker but look, look, look at that. There's a girl, a ghost, a dead thing in your car."

Jay shifted his weight. "She's been deceased for over a day and not one ferryman has come to give her the choice. Do you know anything about that?"

"Ah, yes, the choice. So sacred, so traditional." Tick swiveled his shadowy head and spoke into the fresh grave. "That reminds me. Stay or go, my little squeaker, which is it to be?" Tick listened a moment before bending to thrust a hand deep into the dirt. "Come, come, come now little squeaker," Tick told the new ghost. "Don't run, don't hide, don't leave poor old Tick to pine."

With three fingers clasped around the neck, Tick held the dead man aloft, shaking the ghost free of grave dirt. The ghost struggled, translucent fingers scrabbling at Tick's hand. The solid parts of the man succeeded in nothing but twisting a few rings on Tick's long fingers. The ferryman shook the ghost some more until the protests ceased. Jay almost felt bad for the man but the assault he could see tainting his heart stilled any further feelings of goodwill.

"You're going down, down, down," Tick told the ghost before humming an eerie rendition of a 1950's ballad. He sucked the dead man toward the black chasm of his face with the accompanying sound of thick liquid drawn up by a straw. Screaming and wailing the whole way, the ghost of the rapist took some time about leaving this world, although Jay guessed Tick dragged out the process on purpose. With a slurp and a pop, the ghost was gone and Tick turned to Jay. "Second course."

He took a step back. "No, she's not supposed to go with you, we are waiting for Khara or River or..."

Tick interrupted. "Or Archer, yes, but busy, busy, busy. They will not come. You have me. Give me the girl, the ghost, the dead thing. I will take care of her. Everyone is so busy, we missed one. Not our fault, not our fault, a slight error. I am here now, give her to me, reaper. Give her to me."

Jay glanced back at the car. The top of Janis' hair was visible as she crouched on the floor of the front seat, trying to hide. "She's not damned, Tick, she's not for you. We'll wait." Jay took a staggering step back as Tick rushed him. Long fingers gripping Jay's shoulder and waist holding him in place. The smell of rotten marrow meat and dried organs hit Jay's nose and he choked on the foul stench.

"Too late, Reaper. I'm all you've got. They are busy, busy, busy. And it is my turn."

Jay breathed through his mouth. "You promise not to take her down? She's not damned."

Tick let him go and he brushed at his shirt sleeves. If Tick's fingerprints lingered too long they would eat away at any material he touched.

"Rules, rules, always with the rules, reaper rules. Yes, I say I will not take her downtown, I will not take her down to town." Tick held up a long arm, three fingers on his left hand pointing up. His other hand rested upon his chest. "I cross my heart. Stick a needle in my eye." The words sounded again as if they came with a sinister grin.

Jay considered this as he stared into the empty blackness of Tick's face. "You don't have a heart."

He dropped his arms. "True enough. So, the girl, the ghost, the dead thing."

"Janis?" Jay called over his shoulder, turning as much as he could while keeping Tick in sight. "Get out of the car." There was no answering movement. "It's alright, I promise."

"Beautiful promises," Tick mocked.

"Shut up," Jay snapped.

The car door opened and closed followed by Janis' approaching footsteps. When she stopped at Jay's elbow, Tick sucked in a breath and bent close to her. "So you're the girl, the ghost, the dead thing no one came to collect?"

Janis stared at the Ferryman with wide eyes.

"Silent thing?" Tick asked, straightening.

"Not usually." Jay gave Janis a brief smile. She looked up and something in his chest clenched. Her gaze was heavy with a human emotion unfamiliar to Jay. "What?"

"Smell it, Reaper. I frighten her. Don't worry, I'll take you to where you need to go."

Jay dug into his front pocket, turning away from Janis. This was how it always was to end.

"Here, for your trouble. Make sure she gets to the right place." Jay handed over two gold coins, which Tick snatched up and brought to his shadowed face. There was a clinking sound as unseen teeth bit the money before the coins disappeared into the blackness.

He made a sound like he was licking his lips. "Good, good payment. Tasty." Tick turned his blank face to Janis. "Tasty. Time to go." He held out a hand to Janis who remained standing frozen.

"Take his hand," Jay prompted.

She turned her face to glower at Jay.

"I hate you," she spat through clenched teeth before extending her hand. "You told me I'd see my parents again."

How could he explain in an instant that this was the correct way of things? "Oh, Janis." The words caught in his throat. Jay blinked and swallowed at the unfamiliar pain. He rubbed at his neck, wondering why he felt as if his body was going to crack open.

Tick made an odd noise. "Feisty, feisty, tasty one you are," he crooned, fingers closing around Janis' hand. He tugged her close to him and with his other hand he patted her head. Her tight curls sprang back after they were flattened. "What power your soul must hold, much gold, much gold."

Jay blinked. "Gold? I already paid you."

Tick's blank face turned to Jay. "The harvest moon burns bright this month."

"What does that mean?" Janis asked in a small voice.

A softness rang in Jay's ears. Whatever mortal exhaustion and strange feelings lingered within him faded and his mind was quiet. This was wrong. Of course the fae and demons working together to control the sheefrahs would have a few ferrymen on their side. He chided himself for not realizing it sooner.

"Give her back," Jay's voice was low.

"Reaper, that is not the way things work. She is mine now, mine, you paid in gold, gold, gold."

"No. This is not the way. You have no power over her." Jay shook his head, thoughts plodding and slow.

He remembered the other reaper's touch upon his brow, its words, the death he felt in his heart. His voice was thick, it was difficult to speak. Something rumbled in the distance. Was it a summer storm on the horizon? It sounded like his power.

"Janis," Jay stated, fingers twitching as if he wanted to reach for her. This was all wrong.

"You cannot break the payment," Tick said jerking Janis backward. "You were the one who gave me the gold, golden gold."

"Jay!" Janis screamed from a tightening grasp, pleading. "You promised!" She squirmed against Tick's hold and stretched out her hands towards Jay.

His fingers flexed again. He felt split in two, as if it was his human body telling him to reach out and grab her hand, not his own mind. Thunder rumbled within him coming from that split.

"No," Tick growled at the girl. "You are dead and you are mine."

The world slowed around Jay. The ghost was not for the ferryman. The ghost needed the choice.

"Please!"

Her voice rang out to him from far away and he looked into her strange eyes. They were wide, pupils dilated with fear. Jay felt something new take root deep inside him. It came from that divide of self around where his power now swirled. It pushed out of that split and crawled into the depth of him, something altered, something strong. Whatever the thing was, it directed his body to shift, having him take a wide stance. It then told him to raise his right arm and point his index and middle finger at the center of Tick's shadowed face.

In a wave of air smelling of moldy ostrich feathers, Tick breathed, "You wouldn't dare."

"Janis, close your eyes."

Yes, the eyes, Jay's power roared to life. *Take the eyes*.

Bright white light burst from Jay's arm and shot into Tick. The ferryman released Janis and howled in fury, the beam disintegrating his eyes and scattering him away into the night. The rush of bright light rippled back up Jay's arm and knocked him onto his back. The last thing he saw were the stars swirling above him.

I need to stop passing out so much, Jay thought, dizzy. *It is getting tiresome.*

TWELVE

T ENSITH BROKE INTO A flat sprint. He darted out of the cemetery as fast as his fox legs could take him and he ran into the brush of the nearby undergrowth that was peppered with youthful or underdeveloped trees. He hastened across roads, under fences, dodging cars and pet dogs as he raced toward the nearest entrance to the Hill. There wasn't even time enough to rush to Maeren's heart tree to warn his precious nymph sister. He had to get word to the council.

The man he had been following the past few days while he kept an eye on the ghost wasn't a human male after all. Tensith chided himself for missing such a detail. He was an exiled reaper, of all things, and that reaper had just stolen the eyes of a ferryman of the damned. If Tensith had time to delay, he would have shaken his head in frustration. It was a stupid thing to do, even for a reaper. The ferryman would send hellhounds in furious, awful revenge.

Tensith skirted around some human's car backing into a driveway and dug down into a blueberry bush planted into the unkempt empty lot next to the house, zoned for construction. Another entrance that would have to be relocated. No time to dwell on that thought now, Tensith wriggled into the rough hewn tunnel, dirt falling over his coat.

A tumble of darkness pressed in around him and squeezed his body from snout to tail tip. The portal brought him into a wide tunnel dotted with the bioluminescence of mushrooms and gemstones embedded into the passage walls. The cave opened onto a forest clearing where several pixies exploded into flight, surprised by Tensith's entrance. They chittered their anger down at him as they buzzed in the tree branches overhead on gossamer wings.

He was in the Hill.

Tensith kept running. Past the moonlight dappled Pellanian Meadows, past the waving, twisted spires of reeds within the southern salt marsh, and past the Great Augury where the haruspex with their gruesome knives divined the will of the lost spirits from the past. Tensith moved with the preternatural grace of the fae, drawing upon the strength and will of his magic that flowed from the very Hill all around and moved through his veins. It pulsed there now, bright as a spring day and deep as October rain.

Fae dwellings blurred around him as he swept by the greenwood nabes on his way to the Hallow, where all business of the fae, Unseelie and Seelie, was conducted. This is when he slowed, on the cut stone pathway of the main road leading to the Hallow, a wild and sprawling holt beneath a breathtaking stronghold made of ancient, crumbling stone fused with the architecture of massive trees.

Aware now of others viewing his progress, the fox drew to a stop, quivering and panting as the journey caught up to him. Tensith approached the main entrance and slipped inside, hoping no one would want to stop him for a quick chat, not until he could make his report. Fae of all kinds idled amongst the rock and vegetation, between freestanding pillars and lounging on various daises made both of stone and carved into trees. Fae lights danced beneath archways and nestled into walls, winking merrily. Laughter ebbed and flowed as did the easy conversations of the lackadaisical fae occupying the fragmented ruins of the former palace. Somewhere out of sight, a fountain splashed.

Nose down, signaling he had no time for frivolities, Tensith wended his way through the groupings of fae and worked his way deeper into the Hallow, what used to be the seat of power for the elder fae of the past on this new continent. Now, the castle was covered in an overgrowth of nature and the large slabs of rock making up countless courtyards and arching cloisters were crumbling into dust, as they would all do one day.

"Tensith!" a faerie with drooping red moth wings and blushing blue skin called out to him, her long, slender hand outstretched in invitation. She was smoking a long pipe stuffed full of catnip and bayberries. As she smiled, she blew out several smoke rings that earned her adoring claps from the aristocratic group circled around her. They were clustered around blackberry brambles at the foot of an arcade of pillars. The entire party was seated on a blanket of silk stained with dandelion wine. He trotted over to the gathering and nodded his greeting. A cluster of fae lights floated above them, casting those below in a gentle, flattering, evening glow.

I cannot dally, Heartsworn, he told the blue faerie woman who, in answer, tossed her silken sheet of black hair over a shoulder and resumed smoking.

Another faerie with skin like an oyster shell grinned at him with wood teeth. "Too busy with your bargaining, foxy fox?" the faerie taunted. The group tittered with amusement.

I work so you don't have to, Tensith growled.

The oyster shell-skinned faerie waved this away with a flap of his black and gray mottled skin. "No, the council works so we don't have to," was all he said before settling onto the silk blanket and falling asleep.

Tensith bared his fox teeth but said nothing else as he moved on through the Hallow's grounds. There was no arguing with fae, him included. His kind were circuitous at best and brought an inane amount of disorder to anything requiring logic. The Folk were capricious and contrary and violent. Tensith couldn't help his nature and that of his people, but sometimes it was something he loathed.

In order to reach the offices of the council, Tensith had to traverse almost the whole expanse of the grounds. The further he went, the less ruinous the castle was, the inner structure still somewhat intact. The living quarters for both the council members, staff, and servants remained along with the kitchens, receiving halls, libraries, and the grand chamber. Tensith dashed into one of the informal entries and hurried to where the head of fae bargains sat in a large office.

Between one moment and the next, Tensith shifted to his upright form and knocked on the closed door.

"Enter," a voice said from the other side.

The office within was well-appointed with polished wooden walls and carved oak corbels at the seam of the painted ceiling. Shelves lined the wall behind a large desk that was an unfinished cross section of a stump. Instead of books there were sheaves of rolled parchment tied with strings of spider silk.

"Tensith," the fae sitting at the desk said without preamble. Stacks of the curling parchment balanced on his desktop and ink stains splotched like raindrops on the surface.

"Hello, Ocimum," Tensith said, inviting himself to sit on a stolen human chair beneath a tower of pillows. He did his best to perch upon the cushions.

"What do you want?" The other fae was a hobgoblin and was younger than Tensith, a fact the fox fae resented. The hob had risen to his station early in his career, when Tensith was still out in the human world organizing ley lines. In either case, Tensith had to remind himself to put aside his jealousy for a moment and focus on the task at hand. He looked at the hob's squashed pinkish face, wrinkled around a small wet nose, and chose his words with care.

"I have just come from the human world," Tensith began, leaning into formality. "Where a sheefrah was given as a deal but died before the correct time designated in her contract. She is at this moment a ghost in the company of a reaper who has discovered a trail of dead reapers."

Ocimum remained silent. He scratched at a small, piggish ear with black tipped fingernails while he considered Tensith's words.

"Following that, this reaper seemed to see fit to attack Tick and take the ferryman's eyes."

At that, Ocimum stilled. "I cannot say that was a very smart decision, but is that all?"

Tensith clenched his jaw at the condescension.

"No," he tried not to snarl the words, "that is not all. The sheefrah was written into one of my contracts, Ocimum. The creation of their kind was outlawed centuries ago and their magic has wormed its way into my contracts without my knowledge. I will not be blamed for the illegal act."

The hob was quiet for a long moment, surveying Tensith with yellow coin eyes with goat-like pupils. Then, he smiled, showing a mouth crowded with two rows of pearl-white baby teeth.

"I heard you snuck into the archives," Ocimum said.

"You knew about the contracts?" Tensith whispered, heart sinking in dread. If Ocimum knew, the council knew. And if the council knew... "They're doing it on purpose, aren't they? Why does the council need sheefrahs written into deals?"

Ocimum was shaking his head. "You were always too curious for your own good. Always prying into things that are not his own, our Tensith."

"Why are they doing this? What need does the council have for more magic? The Folk already have a powerful sovereignty and we retain that status despite changing human beliefs. We are still strong still, are we not?"

The hob stood and came around his desk. Stunned, Tensith remained sitting in the chair, staring at the other fae.

"I hate to do this to you, my dear friend," Ocimum said with a wide sinister smile. "But if this got out to the greater population, we would have a riot on our hands. Not to mention if this secret left the borders of our land."

"It already has left," Tensith growled. "You have involved demonkind in this scheme of yours."

Ocimum had the audacity to look insulted. "It is not *my* scheme, dear Tensith. It is not for me to decide what is best for our people, that is the job of the council."

"What do you get out of this, worm?"

"Oh, don't debase yourself with cheap insults, it's gauche. Besides, this isn't about me, it's about the greater good of the Folk. The Seelie must remain in power, you of all people should understand this best. Now, if you will remain still..."

Tensith trembled. "You cannot bind me without a trial!" he yelled, jumping up from his seat. The door to Ocimum's office was locked.

"Oh, but my orders are from on high." Ocimum clapped his hands together above his head. "Tensith of the Fox Hole, you are henceforth banned from the Hill forever more."

A white light flared from hob's joined hands and a sharp swirling of air wrapped itself around Tensith, urging him to flee.

"Run, fox," Ocimum said, unable to contain the satisfied glee in his voice. "Run and stay gone."

Tensith ran. He ran to find the only demon with whom he would ever wish to speak. He turned his nose south, heading toward Atlanta.

Friend was taking part in one of her favorite pastimes—admiring herself in a floor-length mirror—when she heard a frantic scratching at her front door. She frowned. Her house was a gorgeous two-story ranch in a gated community in Brookhaven. If whatever was at her front door marred the bottle-green painted wood, she would be livid.

The house was a new construction, as all of the houses in the neighborhood were. Friend luxuriated in the fact that the homes in the community were built without any regard for reducing waste. She lived in much the same way as the house was built, watering her lawn during droughts, leaving lights on at night, and turning the air conditioning as low as was possible and leaving it running while fires roared in every room in gas fireplaces to balance out the temperature. She was a daughter of Lilith, one of the Forsaken, a cat-shifting demon of the pit. She did as she pleased and wouldn't change her behavior for anyone. She ignored the noise and went back to studying her reflection.

To say that Friend loved the way she looked was an understatement. She worshiped herself. Her body was her own distinct possession and she treated it well. Each day, she submerged into a tub of holy anointing oil, indulging in the restorative properties for her earthly flesh, the wastefulness, and the subversion to the popular religions of man. Each night, she covered her hair and body in wrappings spun from spider's silk, procured from a fae weaver who was not finicky in his dealing with demons.

Friend's daily self-care was ritualistic, a prayer of adoration to her own appearance. None of her fellow demons noticed, but, when she chose to walk among them, humans did. They saw the smooth, glistening softness of her dark skin with its contrasting white patches and were drawn to her like tides to the moon. Friend basked in the visual praise and found it felt similar to when she reclined beneath the sun in her feline form.

Today she wore a sleeveless jumpsuit in a buttery cream color that complimented both the cedar brown and the pinkish white vitiligo of her skin. After she was born, Friend spent most of her childhood, if it could even be called that, as a kitten. All demons chose when they wanted to shift into their demonic bodies and claim their power, most after their first 50 years had passed. Friend avoided it as long as possible. She saw how her legion of siblings appeared and hated their rotten flesh and stringy tendons. She much preferred the softness of her fur to decaying ligaments.

Yet, that was how she had to appear when she was presented to the Morningstar. He had kissed both of her necrose cheeks and welcomed her into the fold, blessing her crooked magic and sending her on her way. The missive was always to use their free will and use it with abandon, so Friend found herself in the business of running demon dens, places where the multitude of the Fallen or the Turned could gather in relative peace from places of good and light.

She loved her chosen vocation, but she loved herself more and mostly remained either as a cat or in human shape. Her neighbors saw her as a Black woman or as a tortoiseshell cat, though none of them were the wiser when she conducted business as a feline.

The scratching continued. Friend paused, angling her head toward the noise. It didn't sound like one of her rescues. When it came again, she knew she would have to open the door to satisfy her curiosity. Friend sighed and abandoned the mirror, tossing long locs over her shoulder and padding down her carpeted stairs in bare feet.

Outside, on her front stoop, sat a fox.

Friend squinted at what her security camera feed showed in the app on her phone. Stray cats found their way to her residence where they sniffed out food in the kitchen accessible by a rubber flap cut into the back door. At the moment, there were about twenty of the animals lounging around her home in various places. She never got an accurate count because it was forever in flux. Once they were sheltered and comfortable, she spayed and neutered the animals before sending them on their way. It wasn't the most demon-like behavior, but Friend felt satisfied by her work.

Now, however, neither a cat nor a true fox sat outside her house.

Instead, she was sure it had to be Tensith, a fox fae she had not spoken to in decades. She pressed a button on her phone, wanting to see him squirm.

"Hi, Tenny," she purred, grinning at the expression that crossed the fox's face at the sound of her voice on the speaker outside. "Fun isn't it, this human technology?"

She chuckled as Tensith bristled in surprise. While demons were adaptable, the fae were not. Despite some supernatural creatures adopting human inventions, the fae couldn't even be taught to use any of it, their minds unable to adjust to such equipment.

We must speak, demon, he said.

"You didn't say the magic word."

Tensith swished his tail. *I do not know your password. Let me enter.*

"Find the way and we'll talk." Friend clicked out of her phone app and padded to find her tablet. With a few quick taps and swipes she brought up four camera feeds that split her screen. She smirked as she watched Tensith slink off the porch into the decorative plants and bushes covering the skirt of the house and melt back into the shadows.

On the top left security feed, a lone tuxedo cat streaked by at a run. The feline darted around the back of the house and into the next camera feed. On a corner of the tablet, stepping across mulched wood between azalea bushes, the fox fae followed the path of the cat and pushed, snout first, through the swinging cat flap.

He was greeted by a bright flash of light and a loud clicking noise. "That was so cute," Friend said, holding out a human phone away from her body and studying the picture. In lieu of an answer, he drew a glamour around himself and shifted into his two legged form. Several cats, who had been perched on the counters in the kitchen, scrambled to vacate the space a fae now occupied.

"I request your aid, demon," Tensith said once his glamour settled.

Friend looked up from her phone. The fox in this form looked boyish, owing to his small stature. He remained covered in fox-patterned fur and male genitalia hung between his legs. Friend sighed. The fae were always running around naked, the perverse little nature lovers.

"Come sit, Tenny." She moved to a sitting room off the kitchen that had plush gray carpeting and an oversized sectional couch in a bottle green color that Friend thought set off her long, bleached-blonde locs very well. She was experimenting with the color and hairstyle and found she enjoyed it very much. Friend swung several thick bunches of her long hair over her shoulder before settling onto the couch. "What has got you so riled up?" She grinned at him, flashing canines that were a shade longer than a human's.

Tensith took a seat on the L section of the couch at the opposite end from the demon.

"I require help," he said with a cough to clear his throat. "I would not ask this of you unless it was of the most dire need."

Friend squinted at the little fox fae. His glamour showed a human-like face shaped like a heart with deep russet hair that grew thick and long, sprouting from his hairline that began almost at his eyebrows and flowed up and back over his head like a mane. He had deep black eyes, tinged with green that flashed in the dim, mood lighting of her living room. Tensith's stare was plaintive and worried.

Despite both their kinds embracing the many forms of chaos, fae and demonkind did not get along. At their core, demons didn't care about the natural world around them and the fae were beings of the earth. Despite any possible similarities, this essential difference was where any fellowship failed even in the rare instance in which it began. Nature, it seemed, could not be swayed here.

Demons had always been in this country, demons were everywhere. It mattered little to them the differences in human cultures or religions. They had no such rules or compunctions pinning down their actions and tying them to a specific faith. The one uniting front was that their leader was Lucifer Morningstar. Demons across the Earth had watched when he fell, impressed by the ultimate act of rebellion.

They had flocked to the crater where Lucifer lay, broken and burning, their dark forms illuminated by his shattered wings. He was what they had been waiting for, a leader, a chosen one to unite their scattered factions and bring them from chaos into one hoard. Now, they were ruled over lovingly by their dark angel.

Fae, much like demonkind, had long since existed, though their race was older, tied to the first forming of nature upon the world. Unlike demons, however, the fae did not come together under one common leader. They gravitated instead toward distinct clusters of jurisdiction centered around a court system unique to each region. They did not mix, not in the old country, and not in the new.

Some of the more enterprising or idealistic fae had slunk over from the old world hidden among supplies on the ships that made it across the Atlantic. The vessels would limp into port and as the passengers were distracted at first by exploration and native inhabitants and then by their own self-important business, the fae began to take root. Unlike the sprawling Moor where the fae first lived, the Hill they created in the new country was much more contained, created around the allowances given to them by the spirits already in residence. At some point they had intermixed, though only on the eastern side of the newly named America. The west remained indigenous. It was through one of those fae and spirit unions that Tensith and his sister had been born.

The first time Friend met Tensith was in the late 1800s, when she was still living along the border in Juarez, Texas. It was hot there and Friend liked it scorching. Tensith and his ilk were running interference with her first demon den. It hadn't been on purpose; the land she had chosen was on the border between warring factions of two of the last vampire covens. It should have been neutral territory.

Unfortunately for Friend, Tensith had been tasked with creating a new entrance to the Hill right where she had begun to build. They had argued over who should own the rights to the ley line before the spirits of the desert had intervened, chasing everyone out. In the exodus, Friend and Tensith had grown somewhat close as they traveled northeast to convalesce and plan their next move. From there, the faerie council had ordered Tensith to return and transition into changeling deals. Wandering alone one night after he left, Friend had met a reaper and became quite distracted.

"Tenny, darling, out with it already. I don't like spending my days off waiting for your other furry foot to drop."

Tensith drew a deep breath, looking around the room as if someone else besides Friend or the cats would appear. "I just watched a reaper take the eyes of Tick."

"And?" Friend smirked, imagining the scene.

"And," Tensith added with annoyance, "there was a ghost of a sheefrah in tow."

Friend toyed with the end of one of her locs, inspecting the twist. "Again, and?".

"The reaper was in the body of a human male. A reaper in exile."

"Why would I care for a reaper in exile?" Friend asked, picking at an invisible bit of lint on her pants. She looked down her nose at the fox fae. "Why did you come here tonight?"

"I have been banned from the Hill. Our contracts have changed. Someone has tampered with the writing within them and now there are sheefrah's running about and dying before their deals have completed. It happens a few hours or a few days before their proper end so no one notices."

"The reapers would notice."

Delicate strands of fox fur fell from Tensith and landed on Friend's couch as he shook his head. "They are being killed."

At this, Friend drew back with wide eyes. A foreign feeling clenched her stomach as she thought of the one reaper she would do anything to spare from that fate. "I didn't know they could be hurt," she said, her voice quiet.

"We all can," Tensith said, just as quiet.

Friend hummed out a purr of contemplation.

"So this reaper..." she said with a rolled R, sounding as casual and at ease as anyone. Tensith adjusted his short legs on the couch.

"To be trapped within the body of a human... I have not heard of Them doing such a thing. Whatever the reaper did must have been dreadful."

It was; Friend knew this. The action they took, or rather didn't take, wasn't *that* bad but according to Them it was. The reaper had rushed to her after their last mistake, defeated and worried. She had been so angry at them, not for making the mistake, but for them having only superficial feelings in reaction to the blunder. The fact that the reaper could never delve deeper into emotions such as she felt was the reason she turned them away all those years ago. *That's what I get for falling for a fucking reaper,* she chastised herself.

"I'm sure," she demurred to Tensith.

"Yes, well, in either case, I find myself in a bit of unpleasantness about all this." Tensith folded his hands.

Friend's ruby-red painted lips parted in a sinister smile. "This is why you Folk should leave the bargaining to us."

A gray short-haired cat jumped up to sit beside Friend on the couch and she stroked it, distracted. Content, the cat settled down beside the demon to nap.

"What is done is done. Now, however, I am unable to go back to the Hill. I do not think I was supposed to find out about the modifications to the contract or to report it."

The demon gave a hearty laugh. The cat next to Friend cracked open one eye at the noise. "No, I imagine you have just ousted yourself as a potential loose end."

"But it does not make sense," Tensith pressed with irritation in his voice. "What would be the point of bringing sheefrahs back now, hiding them in our contracts, just to kill them early?"

Friend shrugged. "What are you going to do now?"

"Ask you to stand with me, as we did together many years ago."

"I don't want to get involved with the fae," she said, noting when his shoulders slumped. "But I will keep an eye out. And offer you shelter in my den if you need it."

"Thank you, Friend," Tensith said.

The demon held out a hand to inspect her nails. "My advice? Track down the reaper, follow the breadcrumbs. When you find them, send them my way."

"Agreed," Tensith stated before removing his glamour and shifting back into a fox. *I hope to see you again soon, demon,* he told her, leaping off the couch and shaking out his back legs.

Friend said no goodbyes. She watched Tensith leave in his fox form. Lost in thought for a long time, she stared at the bush he had slipped under and wondered about the reaper.

THIRTEEN

J ANIS WAS ON ALL fours, shaking.

"Is he gone? Can I open my eyes?"

Wind stirred the tops of the faraway trees and in the tufts of grass, crickets chirped.

"Jay?"

There was no answer. Breathing hard, Janis cracked open one eye and then the other. She sat back on her heels and scanned the empty field before her. Janis twisted around and gasped when she saw a body sprawled some yards away and rushed to kneel at his side.

Jay lay as if sleeping. His black hair was mussed across his forehead, his skin slick with sweat. Janis couldn't tell if he was breathing and she knew she wouldn't be able to feel a heartbeat. She wanted to scream she was so frustrated. When Jay had fallen asleep on the park bench, Janis had curled up in the space beneath him and cried. She had never felt so alone, her existence so easily dismissed. She felt the same now, alone and without help and, if she were pressed to admit it, frightened. But most of all she was furious.

Passed out on the ground before her was the only person able to help her with her problems and he was useless. She ground her teeth together. And he had been about to give her up to that...that *thing*. Janis shivered and glanced around for any sign of the gangly creature. They were alone in the graveyard.

He looked dead. Janis' stomach lurched at the thought. She would be well and truly alone in this new world if he were. Hesitating, Janis placed a hand on his chest trying to see if it was moving up and down.

"Don't be dead," she pleaded.

"Not dead," he croaked.

Janis jerked in surprise. She was relieved for a moment before anger took her.

"You asshole!" she yelled down at him, thumping him on his shoulder in punctuation. "You betrayed me!"

Jay groaned. "What happened?"

The ghost beside him sat back on her heels and folded her arms across her chest. "To start, you double crossed me and then changed your stupid mind at the last fucking second and killed him."

"What?" Jay repeated.

"What do you mean, 'what'? You pointed at the tick thing and then you killed him or whatever." Janis glared at him hoping to communicate just how pissed off she was and that she was the one allowing the conversation to continue with civility.

"Oh."

"That's all you can say?" She watched him struggle for a moment before standing to grasp his hand and tug with a hard jerk, lifting Jay onto his feet with tremendous strength. "Not even 'sorry for giving you away to a disgusting monster'? Nothing like that?" She watched him sway on his feet.

"We have to leave." Jay's voice was froggy.

Janis rolled her eyes, shaking her head in irritation. "Yes, great, I agree. Let's get in the car."

Jay blanched. Grabbing his phone, he tossed it hard onto the ground, the cheap thing breaking in two. "Get in the car, now!" Jay yelled, stuffing himself into the driver's seat, slamming the door, and rushing to turn the ignition.

Janis jumped into the front passenger seat as Jay shifted to drive and pulled away from the cemetery at a tearing pace. He pushed the Honda to sixty before clearing the cemetery grounds.

"Not that I don't appreciate the urgency," she said in a trim voice as they tore onto the main road," but why are you freaking out? I think I should be the one to—"

"I didn't kill him."

"What?"

137

"Tick, I didn't kill him, I just pissed him off." Jay floored it through a yellow light and somewhere to the left a truck honked. "You can't kill a ferryman."

"But you can kill a reaper?"

"It would seem so."

"Your rules don't make sense." She eyed her companion as he sat in tight-lipped silence, careening the Honda around a corner and making her shoulder slam into the side of the car.

"I'm sorry," he told her. After a long pause, he added, "For everything."

Janis' eyebrows shot up. "You should be," she snapped at him.

"This is so strange," Jay muttered, more to himself than to Janis. "I think I feel guilty."

"You. Should. Be," she repeated herself, punctuating the echo with attitude.

"Reapers don't have emotions."

"You are not a reaper anymore, remember?" Janis said her words with a staccato rhythm, trying to get them to sink into Jay's thick skull one at a time. It was like talking to a brick wall. "You told me you're in the body of a human, not just pretending to be one with magic. And humans, newsflash, have emotions."

She sat back in her seat, content to have taken the role of a wise woman doling out sage advice in this conversation. Of course, she hadn't experienced many emotions when she had been alive, but she knew others had. She watched classmates cry over poor grades or a lost soccer match, even TV shows. Her own parents had laughed, sobbed, and been emotionally moved by movies they watched as a family every Friday night. In death, however, Janis had more than her fair share of emotions.

"Regardless, I am very sorry, Janis. I thought I was doing the right thing. I will fix this for you, okay?" Still speeding, Jay passed a slow moving minivan at a double light before it merged back to a one lane road.

"Not like I have anyone else, do I?" Jay remained silent at her statement, which satisfied her for the moment.

Janis watched as they found their way onto the main road, hovering around ninety and passing cars across a double yellow line. There was no one else but this sorry excuse for an ally. Janis didn't know how much longer they'd have to endure each other's company but her intense curiosity was overwhelming her desire to remain taciturn.

"So, you made Tick mad. Which is bad." She turned her questions into flat statements in case she came off too eager to strike up conversation thereby forgiving Jay. A car's horn whined and faded as they flew past.

"Which is very bad."

Janis considered that for a moment. "Can you tell me where we're going?"

Jay yanked the car onto the highway. "We make for Atlanta." He pushed the car past a hundred now that they were on the freeway. The engine whined and the car shook in protest. "I used to know someone there. If we can find him he will shelter and help us."

"What about me?" Janis yelped in shock. "And my family? I don't want to leave, my funeral is tomorrow!"

"What would you do there? Ghosts can't speak to the living. You would have driven yourself mad trying to talk to your parents. Don't you want them to be able to grieve? Why would you keep them trapped in thoughts of your death?"

Janis stamped a foot on the car floor, fed up. "You agreed that I'm not supposed to be dead! You were the one that said that if I went with you to that stupid cemetery and did what you asked I would be able to see my parents again!"

"We needed answers, Janis!" Jay knocked his head against the head-rest in frustration. "I couldn't have just left you at the funeral home to fend for yourself."

"Of course not! You had to drag me to a naked mummy to be eaten!"

"He wasn't going to eat y—"

Janis sliced a hand out in the air to cut him off. "You're my only fucking option right now! Don't you get it? I wake up dead and no one else but you and your creepy friend can see or hear me. And despite being the one person who can help me, you proceed to tell me nothing about anything."

She paused as a city limits sign came up before them, illuminated by the headlights, and Janis followed it with her eyes until they were past. A heavy stone turned in her gut. She hadn't always lived in Virginia, her parents had mentioned Arizona a few times, but this was the only home she could remember. Janis never knew why they had moved and she had never thought to ask. She felt the sadness of another missed opportunity grip her. Now she'd never know why. What other invaluable details about her family had she missed out on by being so lackadaisical? By not being more interested in her mothers photo albums, her fathers meandering tales? Janis wished, not for the last time, she had never gone to that party

"Oh! And then you fucking betrayed me. Don't forget about that." Her words filled the space between them.

"I know," Jay said at last. "I know."

7

The car remained silent for many long, dragging minutes. There was still some needling pain behind Jay's eyes from when he used his power on Tick. There also was a knot twisting within him, as if something cold and wet had settled deep in his stomach. He felt queasy and his heart thumped low and heavy in his chest. How could he have been so stupid to have walked right into Tick's trap? The cold feeling trickled up to his shoulders, hunching them downward in an unseen yoke.

Guilt. No reaper should be able to experience such a human emotion. He mulled over this uncomfortable idea. *Janis has to be wrong*.

Of course he was inside a human but he had never felt anything like this in his other bodies. Jay glanced at the ghost and oily guilt slid around his heart and squeezed. He decided to break the quiet, though he was sure any words of apology were more than inadequate for the situation.

"I'm sorry, Janis. And I can't figure out what's happened to you. This form..." he gestured to his body with choppy, frustrated movements. "It dulls me. I'm as trapped here as you are. But it's all connected. I will figure this out and help you, I promise."

"Like you thought you could help me by giving me to that guy?" Janis scoffed.

"He was not supposed to go back on his word, a ferryman should know better."

Janis barked a humorless laugh. "Jay, he looks like he goes back on his word all the time. Why did you think he would listen to you?"

"I paid him and I'm a reaper, he should have obeyed me."

"*Were* a reaper," she reminded him again.

They drove in the quiet of the night for several miles, stress and tension hanging heavy in the air. Jay slowed the car to eighty to stop the vehicle from wobbling, ignoring the hot smell of the overworked engine. When Janis spoke, she startled Jay into dropping his lighter after igniting a cigarette. "Why did that thing want me? Am I special or something?"

He looked down at the lighter on the ground. He'd have to retrieve it later, maybe at a rest stop. Jay breathed out a cloud of smoke. "He didn't want you, per se, he wanted your soul."

"Why?"

"I've no idea. All souls have value but you haven't done anything to draw attention to yourself." Jay scratched the bridge of his nose. "Despite what you may have heard, trafficking in human souls of any kind is outlawed."

"Mm, yes I have heard otherwise," Janis said with heavy sarcasm.

"It's a dangerous business, though many have made it theirs, such as demons. It goes against all natural order and is forbidden. Souls move on into mist and shadow to rest or they are sunk into pits to be punished," Jay inclined his head at Janis. "Or they decide to stay as ghosts. That's how it is."

"Pits? He would have taken me to hell?"

"No, you don't belong there. I have no idea where he would have taken your soul." Jay drummed the steering wheel and frowned. "No idea at all..." he trailed off into thoughts of dead reapers and human souls. Nothing fit. Even if he weren't in the body of a human, reapers didn't know everything.

The welcome sign for North Carolina came and went. Janis wriggled in her seat. The clock on the dashboard read out that it was almost midnight and most cars that they passed were few and far between.

"Since you're kidnapping me all the way to Atlanta, can I at least put on some music?" Janis reached for the power button.

"What? No, don't!" The radio buzzed on in a fit of static before it focused on a song. It had a rousing country melody surrounded by the sounds of several fiddles whining at high speed.

Jay slammed the power button. It was too late, Tick would be able to track them through the radio waves they had let into the car. He had to get off the road, and fast. "Hold on!"

Jay yanked on the steering wheel and accelerated onto the shoulder of the highway. Janis screamed as the car bounced and jerked across the uneven earth. Dust and sparks flew up from the front bumper obstructing the windshield. The Honda dipped and rocketed into a ditch and Jay twisted the steering wheel too late. One of the wheels hit a rock and the car tilted to the right, threatening to tip. Jay stepped both feet on the brakes, a useless gesture, as the car thumped over to its side and rolled over onto the roof. It skidded along the grass for several yards and crashed up against a tree. The metal squealed as it crumpled around the sturdy chestnut.

Janis jumped out of the car before it slammed into the tree. The metal crunched around the wood with wicked sounds.

"Jay!" she cried.

The wheels were still spinning. The glass in the driver's side window had shattered, leaving a gaping hole in the door. She could see Jay hanging upside down, suspended from his seatbelt. A small trickle of blood dripped out his ears and into his hair, mixing with the estuary of blood flowing over his forehead from a giant gash at his brow line. Janis reached in through the broken window and tried to grab him. Her hands slipped on his shoulders, not because she couldn't stay solid, but because of the blood.

Jay's vision was empty. When he blinked it was a daze of darkness and purple spots. The harsh taste of copper stung in his mouth. Blood. His throat was clogged with it and his ears chugged with the slow sound of it.

"You're bleeding," he heard Janis say through the red sounds blocking his hearing. Spots of cold fluttered at his shoulders. It was her hands trying to pull at his clothes. "You're bleeding a lot."

Pain ripped into his shoulder as he tried to move his arm to swat her cold hands away. Something was wrong. The world felt too heavy. Jay blinked several more times and his vision returned. Peering through a film of blood upon his lashes Jay saw grass through the spiderwebbed cracked windshield. Grass growing out of the sky.

No, he thought. *That is not right.*

Shaking with the effort like he was cold, Jay tucked his chin to look down. The seat belt wrapped around his torso, holding him to the car seat as he dangled upside down. "Janis," he croaked, the smell of burnt rubber replacing the words in his mouth.

"Jay, thank god!"

"Janis," he rasped again. "I'm sorry, I lost control of the car. Are you alright?"

"I'm already dead. Can you get out?"

With jerky movements, Jay looked around, taking stock of his other body parts, wondering how to answer her question. One arm dragged along the car ceiling, knuckles grazing the plastic, wrist at a disgusting angle. Both his knees were shattered and the wheezing from his chest hinted at a punctured lung. The shoulder of the other arm was dislocated from its socket.

"No," he said. "You're going to have to remove the door from the car."

Janis took a step back. "Jay, I..."

"Ghosts are very strong without the boundaries of their physical bodies." Doubt flickered across her face. "You've shown your strength before. You can do it."

She scrunched up her nose at the sentiment but moved to wrap her hands around the seal of the broken window, where glass used to be. Janis closed her eyes. The metal of the car groaned and cracked. Janis' eyes flew open and she let go of the car. She shook her head.

"I can't."

Jay struggled against bloody vomit. "Yes, you can, you almost had it."

Sucking in a breath, Janis gripped the door again. The car groaned once more, metal and plastic parts protesting until the door gave out and was ripped away and Janis tossed it on the ground.

"Holy shit, I did it," she breathed, staring at the car door. "I'm the fucking Hulk."

Jay worked to detangle himself from the seat belt using his better arm with no luck. "Can the Hulk spare another moment?" he gurgled, a bubble of blood bursting on his upper lip and trailing into his nose. He coughed, pain shooting out from his punctured lung. *Shock*, he told himself. *Do not go into shock.*

"Hold on a second." Janis reached out toward the seatbelt buckle. He landed hard on the roof of the car once she released the mechanism. Struggling, Janis twisted to get a better grip before pulling the tall man out of the smashed up opening. Inch by inch, Janis managed to tug Jay onto the grass beside the car. She sat next to him. "Can you walk?"

"Not yet."

"What do you mean not yet?"

"I wish we were under some cover for this." At least they crashed out of view of the highway. No one had seen them hurtle off road and no one would find the car for hours yet. *The stars are beautiful here*, Jay dreamily thought.

"For what?"

"My body needs to heal. It takes a while." Jay twisted his mouth in a sardonic smile. "For They won't let me rest, even when injured."

"Why can't you ever just say what you mean?"

He gave a weak cough. "I must live out my exile in human bodies. The binding magic shields the bodies from harm so when I am injured, they heal. I'm sure there's a limit to how much damage they can sustain, but I haven't reached it yet."

Janis said nothing and they remained prone on the grass, silence broken by the pops and grinding squeaks of Jay's bones clicking back into place. The rest of his body knitted together internally in a chorus of slimy noises Jay was thankful Janis couldn't hear.

The stars whirled above him as he burned with a fever fighting off any infection in his bones. Hercules danced, bent legs shimmering. The stars were brighter here, away from the city of Richmond, but still dull. As dull as he was in a human body.

Jay had once spent a long year with early pioneers journeying west across the Rocky Mountains and between killing the settlers off one by one, he spent his time star gazing. The constellations twinkling above him now reminded him of those open skies, of when he was free.

Tendrils of the coming dawn hovered in wait on the horizon by the time Jay finished piecing himself back together. Sitting up, he rotated his dislocated shoulder and the joint fell back into place with a loud clunk. Janis screwed up her face in disgust.

"I'm dizzy and my healing isn't yet complete," Jay announced. "We have to find a place where I can rest. Someplace with water." He staggered to his feet, steadied by Janis moving to support his weight, a crush of cold pressed up against his side. Surprised at her help, Jay looked at the top of her head, studying the intricate coils of her natural hair, and felt another stab of guilt pass through his heart. "Thank you, Janis," he told her, stumbling over some rocks.

They made their way deeper into the woods off the highway, wandering in no particular direction. Janis had enough grace not to comment when Jay started to shake and drip with sweat, occasionally stating, "almost there," and "just a little farther". Jay clutched at the ghost, giving her most of his weight. He not so much walked as was dragged through the forest.

Sunrise trickled over the earth, blinding the pair as they walked in the direction of the growing light, pushing through golden grass and around trees silhouetted in the morning sun. Janis stopped and caught Jay with a hand upon his heaving chest, the coolness of her touch comforting.

"Look! A building!"

Squinting, Jay saw a speck of something in the distance. Then he turned to one side and vomited on the ground.

"I'm sorry, my concussion hasn't quite dissipated."

"We're almost there."

The building was a squat, run-down apartment complex with three stories. There was a pool in the back that was a bit dirty. The gate squeaked open when Janis pushed it and with a series of blundering and stiff movements, Jay splashed belly-first into the water. Floating to the surface, Jay turned onto his back, ignoring the taste of rotted plant life behind the mask of chlorine. Water, even dirty water, was the best conduit for magic, a way to make it stronger. The rest of his injuries healed and his exhaustion was washed away in the pool.

"Jay?" Janis' voice came through muffled by the water lapping around his ears. Before Janis could finish her question, something hard struck Jay on the side of his head, new pain blooming at his temple.

Spluttering, he thrashed in the water until he found footing on the slippery pool tiles. He hissed as his sore muscles screamed in protest of his jolting movements. Steadying himself, he wiped his eyes and spit out pool water, glaring at the offending object. A half empty plastic water bottle bobbed at the surface and Janis was staring wide-eyed at something at the far end of the pool deck.

FOURTEEN

F OLLOWING JANIS' GAZE, JAY drew a quick breath of surprise when he
saw why the ghost was staring. Holding a magazine, rolled up like
an absurd weapon, was a pale, plump white woman in her late thirties
sitting on a chaise lounge wearing a blue bikini top and high waisted jean
shorts. A ruddy pink flush was spreading over her cheeks and down her
neck as she grew more afraid. Her dark red hair was thrown back into a
ponytail and her straight cut bangs hung over her eyebrows. Before Jay
could come up with a halfway clever story, the woman spoke.

"What the fuck are y'all doing? This is private property." The woman
twitched her wrist, moving the rolled magazine to point first to Jay, then
Janis. They both looked at the woman with their mouths agape.

"You can see her?" Jay asked, caution thrown to the wind.

The woman cocked her head, brown eyes flashing over the Janis to
confirm. She gripped her magazine afresh and jumped her gaze back to
Jay. "Yes?"

"Your weapon was a water bottle?" Janis said in a high pitched voice,
strangled with stifled amusement.

"Who the hell are y'all?" She had no real accent but the idiosyncrasies
and speed of Southern speech still invaded her words. Janis and Jay
looked at each other, unsure how to answer. Janis with her wrinkled
party clothes and smudged makeup. Jay in the pool, ripped slacks and
a bloody shirt. The woman swung her legs over to the side of her chair,
ready to stand, her suspicious look changing to a deep frown. "You know
what? I'm just going to call security."

"Okay," Jay said in what he thought was a soothing tone. He pulled
his hands out of the water and raised them above his head. The woman

147

narrowed her eyes and followed his slow progress to the ladder on the side of the pool. "Ma'am, is there somewhere quiet we can go to talk?"

"Ma'am?" The woman pulled her head back. "I'm not that old."

"I'm sorry for the interruption," Jay hoisted himself out at the ladder, leaning forward against the weight of his wet clothes. Out of the pool and dripping all over the concrete deck, he moved to fish in his back pants pocket. "I can show you my credentials, I work for the state of Virginia and I have my identification in my wallet."

Unfolding the sopping leather of his wallet, he extracted a laminated license and held it out to the woman who did not move closer to get a better look.

"The state of Virginia? You're in North Carolina."

Jay felt pleased they had made so much headway on their journey. He refolded his wallet.

"Would you like to go somewhere inside to talk?"

"No, right here is fine." The woman blew at her bangs, trying to move them out of her eyes. She stood from the chaise lounge. She was short, just over five feet. A large, metal necklace in the shape of a Celtic knot swung low across her chest.

Jay smiled afresh at her, all business. "Please, my friend and I have been in a terrible car accident and we need a place to recuperate. We came to the pool to rest." The words sounded stupid even as he said them.

The woman held her rolled magazine up higher. "I feel like you're lying."

"No, we did get in an accident, it's true," Janis said as she looked the woman over.

"Yeah? Who goes for a swim after a car accident?"

"How can she see me?" Janis asked out of the corner of her mouth.

Jay was pulling at his wet trousers that were stuck to the backs of his legs. "I have no idea." It didn't work. He grimaced as he adjusted his stance.

"I'm not kidding about calling security. Did you kidnap her or something?" The woman gave Janis a concerned look. "If he kidnapped you I will take him out."

Janis barked a laugh. "No, he didn't kidnap me."

"Are you sure?" The woman sounded doubtful.

"I haven't been kidnapped," Janis said. "We got lost in the woods. Do you have a phone we can use?"

The woman shook her head. "I left it upstairs. I suppose y'all can borrow it."

Janis shot Jay a quick look. The woman couldn't call security as she had promised. "Thank you so much. What's your name? I'm Janis."

"I'm Sylvie. Your eyes are...interesting."

"Nice to meet you." Janis smiled, ignoring the comment. The ghost stuck out her hand and shook Sylvie's. The woman gave a tiny shiver when she touched Janis but there was no further indication Sylvie noticed anything odd. "It's been so long since I've been able to talk to anyone but Jay over there so thank goodness for you."

Confusion laced Sylvie's brow. "What do you mean?"

"Jay, come here, be polite."

Uncomfortable in his wet pants, Jay moved toward Sylvie with a friendly look on his face. She took a step back and Jay stopped a proper distance away, holding out his hand. Sylvie's eyes flicked back and forth from his hand to his face and over to Janis. She dropped the magazine down on the lounge chair behind her and extended a reluctant hand. Their fingers met and an electric crack of power shot out of Jay.

Hello.

Sylvie screamed. Jay saw himself, his true form, reflected in the depths of her eyes and he snatched his hand away in horror.

"I'm sorry! I'm so sorry!"

Sylvie fell backward and was on the ground, devolved into sobs.

"What the fuck, Jay! What did you do?" Janis knelt down next to Sylvie and held the woman, arms around her shoulders.

"She saw what I look like, my true form. I had no idea that would happen," he raised his voice above the racket.

Janis glared at Jay and muttered soothing words to Sylvie. The woman struggled to stand with the help of Janis and in the shuffle the triangle top of her bikini caught and tugged down, exposing her breasts.

"Janis!" he called out a warning before turning his back to be polite.

"Look away, you pervert!" Janis chided him.

He waved his hands, looking out over the pool. "What do you think I'm doing?"

"I'm so sorry, come on, let's go, let's go inside," Janis soothed the hysterical woman, talking the whole time as her voice faded away and a click of a door cut them off.

Jay was alone on the pool deck.

He stood near the doors, anxious for Janis' return. This was a mess. Involving other humans was already dangerous but he hadn't met one who had been able to see ghosts before. Minutes passed before Jay gave up on waiting by the entrance and moved to sit on one of the chaise lounges. He watched the morning sun rise and dry out his clothes. Jay fumbled around in his pockets for his cigarettes, remembering too late they were soaked. He dropped the package on the ground next to him on the chair. As soon as they were able, Jay would need to stop to buy new ones. Even if he could have a cigarette, Jay remembered his lighter was back in the wreckage of the car. Gloomy, he stared out over the water.

This is a disaster, he thought.

Healing from the car wreck had taken up too much of their precious time. They were losing their head start. Jay looked out the pool gate and into the woods, in the direction from which he and Janis had come. Closing his eyes he breathed in and out through his nose, steadying his nerves and focusing his mind. His stomach rumbled. Jay shoved the thought of his hungry belly away and concentrated. He called down into himself, reaching for the smallest thread of power. It was hard work, he felt it resist, drained from the massive round of healing. Frowning, he pulled harder until it yielded, sweat beading at his hairline.

"Work, damn you," he grunted in effort.

Yes, it conceded.

Jay opened his eyes to look through his power. He squinted and blinked, adjusting to his enhanced vision. The sun clung in golden droplets to every surface. The world glittered back to him with history woven into every atom where Jay could read the lifecycle of a single leaf on a tree. He hadn't used this sight for a long time, it took too much energy, but it was intoxicating to see as he used to.

He first discovered that he could see as reapers did through human eyes without using a drop of his power in his second body, Olga. The body had come with a preexisting condition of seizures that were untreated as she lived, homeless, on the streets of St. Petersburg. She was scooped up once by the police during a sweep and was escorted to the psych ward where she earned a huge shot of phenobarbital. The drug induced the same kind of sight, but only in the brief moments before her human body shut down. That didn't stop Olga from being labeled "junkie" by the emergency room doctors once they figured out she was faking the number of seizures she had in order to score the medicine.

Jay tore his eyes away from the entrancing fluorescent chemical whorls on the surface of the pool and looked in the direction of the gate.

Two trails twisted out in a line away from Jay, disappearing into the line of narrow trees. One was Janis', made of golden light. It was delicate, a mere shimmer of collected particles hanging three feet high in the air; the trail of a mortal soul. The other was a line of wing bones. The tiny bleached things were stuck into the dirt on the ground like a dotted line. Jay felt the jittery weight of fear press down onto his shoulders. The trail would come to fade, the bones disintegrating into ash and the golden shimmer dissipating into the air, but not fast enough.

The scent of their trail would attract anything sent after them, Tick or his lackeys. Jay had stolen Tick's eyes and that was not something he would ever be forgiven for, even if they had grown back by now. He shivered as another wave of fear washed over him. Tick stalking them was bad enough, but what he would send in his stead...

I would rather Tick, Jay admitted to himself.

Turning his head toward the apartment building and looking at the glass door of the back entrance he saw the ghost's golden trail next to another one, Sylvie's. Her human essence was a line of white light. That was normal enough but, Jay squinted, the edges of her trail were tinged with iron. Odd. Perhaps she was taking too many iron supplements. His throat tightened with a new thought.Their scent would lead Tick straight here, straight to Sylvie.They still had some time, but not much.

And when the sun set, all bets would be off.

"Why did you show yourself to the woman?"Jay addressed his power.

It shivered as if in a shrug, distracted by how the world looked now that it was let out to observe.

"Why?" Jay pressed.

She is different, was all it said before shivering again.

With a sigh, Jay settled into his breathing, diving deep into himself to find the answer on his own. "Where are you?" he mumbled, seeking out his power, instead of just borrowing a moment of it to adjust his eyesight. He approached it with caution, unsure if it would be wild and without control as it was when he met Sylvie. Down he went, darkness wrapping around his mind.

When tunneling down into his own blackness, there was a certain sense of familiarity and homecoming. Now, Jay was a tourist in foreign territory. The landscape of his power was alien, a twisted vista he didn't recognize.

I am here.

Worried, Jay pinched at a bit of the power, forming a body within the deepness of his mind, a representation of his true self: tall, made of shadows, and with bone wings. He opened his inner eyes and took a shocked step back in his imagined form. A strange, warped vista greeted him. The inner world was painted in sickly neons and dripping, greasy blacks. Jay brushed a hand against the space around him and his form buzzed, vibrating with the unfamiliar. The colors shifted to pulse a shade of nasty yellow behind the blacks and neons.

Jay's breath came out faster than he could pull it, leaving him gasping and with the feeling that it was never going to end. "What is this?" he asked.

Human, his power rumbled in retort to Jay's stupefaction.

"That is impossible. This place has always been apart from the one who is Jayan Mati, from all of the bodies we have been inside."

This is what a human sees of a reaper.

"But I am not human, I am in the body of one."

Not anymore.

He looked around once more and shuddered. The yellow mutated into a shade of unnatural pink and then morphed into the color of polluted water. This place was no longer reaper. Where his body sat in the lounge chair of the pool deck, his stomach heaved.

"How? How is this possible?"

The child.

A sharp stab of shock cut through him at the revelation. This was the splitting within himself he experienced in the graveyard. The bifurcation he had felt then was a breaking of his power, making room for something human to take root.

Jay felt sick.

He thought back to Janis reaching out to him from Tick's grasp. He had felt a need to protect her: an empathy that was so deep he understood her emotions of fear, abandonment, and panic. Jay blanched. This was where it came from, the roots of human emotion spreading out and tainting his inner world, changing it.

None of his other bodies had made a connection with another human. No singular event ever before had made him question the world around him and his position in it. The strength of the mortal feelings had, unbeknownst to him, drawn out the reaper power to merge this body with the immortal essence within.

"Can I remedy this?" Silence greeted his question. With a manic snarl, Jay reached out and ripped back a chunk of power and squeezed, forcing an answer. "Can I fix this?"

We cannot.

Jay slumped, both inside himself and on the poolside chair. "Ow!" he exclaimed, squeezing his eyes shut against a sudden spasm of pain shooting from behind his eyes.

Done, his power said, retreating with pain in its wake.

Jay jumped at a rapping on the glass door and turned to see Janis making frantic motions from inside the building. He took his drying wallet from the chair and shoved it into his back pocket, fabric now damp instead of soaking wet. Janis opened the door when he approached.

"She thinks we're crazy cult people here to murder her."

"You did tell her we're not, right?"

The ghost rolled her eyes. From somewhere above they heard the sound of a window sliding open. Jay took a few steps backward, tilting his head up and Janis jumped to stand beside him, head also craned upward.

"What is that?" she asked, hand over forehead, squinting at a large black shape several floors up.

"Leave...me..." the words were grunted out as the object was pushed further out onto the ledge, "alone!"

The thing dropped.

"Janis!" Jay cried out in warning as he tripped backward to avoid the falling object. It passed through the ghost and crashed into the concrete. It used to be a large decorative black vase with garish red decorations painted onto the surface.

"Dead, remember?" Janis looked at Jay on the ground and held out a hand. Cold seeped into the skin of Jay's hand as Janis helped haul him to his feet. He twisted around to try and look at the seat of his pants, brushing at dirt.

"What are you doing?" Janis yelled.

A straining grunt answered her as what looked like a long wooden folding screen appeared out the window. After a sliding push, it came tumbling down toward the pair. Jay dodged the crashing debris, hopping out of the way before any of the wood splinters could spear him.

"Stop throwing your ugly Pier 1 shit at us!" Janis shrieked up to Sylvie who was hanging out the window checking to see if her latest round of ammunition hit its mark.

"I've called security!" Sylvie screamed back.

"Janis, we can't leave her here."

"Why not?"

"We've left a trail. Whatever is coming for us will see we dallied around the woman and will likely hurt her."

A plastic carton of strawberries collided with his head, the package bursting open and the fruit spilling out over his shoulders. To her credit, Janis tried not to laugh.

"How likely?" Janis asked, still struggling against a smile. The juice of one of the berries ran down Jay's shoulder. He shook off the rest of the fruit.

"Very. She comes with us or dies."

"Dies?" Janis exclaimed. "Why dies?"

"It's what they do."

"Fucking cult psychos!" Sylvie screamed from the window. She was now holding a stack of very large books.

"Will everyone back at your job die?"

Jay shook his head. "They started tracking us after the graveyard, when the car crashed. They'll torture her, Janis. Human tortures are but a tribute to a shadow of what awaits her and anyone else who helps us along our escape. The closer we get to sunset, the more danger we are in." Jay sidestepped a falling book that slammed into the concrete. "The longer we stay here in general."

"Security will be here any minute!"

Janis' strange green gaze was piercing and full of fear. "What's after me? What did I do?"

Jay stepped forward and put a hand on her cool shoulder. It was like palming a block of ice. Another large book slammed to the ground in the space where he had just stood. "You have done nothing, Janis. This is bigger than you, than the both of us. We're just stuck in the middle."

"Lucky us," Janis huffed as Jay gave her a half smile and squeezed her shoulder. She jerked a thumb upward. "What are we going to do about Bananas up there?"

Jay glanced up to see Sylvie's head dart inside, no doubt to search for more things to throw. "We can't leave her."

Janis grumbled. "Why not?"

"We can't leave her like this," Jay amended. "Let's go up there so I can try and cleanse our presence."

A small potted succulent sailed through Janis' body and crashed into bits, the plant bouncing around spilling dirt beneath their feet.

"After you, Cult Psycho."

FIFTEEN

"**I** DIDN'T MEAN TO frighten her," Jay told Janis as the elevator dinged open on the third floor.

The ghost said nothing but led the way down the hall to an apartment door with a welcome mat that said "The house was clean last week, sorry you missed it". A rustic looking wooden sign hanging from the handle read "She who laughs, lasts".

"It's worse inside," Janis assured him. "She's got one of those 'live like no one's watching' things as an actual wall sticker above her living room couch.

"I don't think that's the original saying."

"I'm paraphrasing." Janis put a hand through the door and glared at Jay. The lock clicked from inside and Janis reached up to undo the chain before extracting her hand. "Après vous."

"You're getting good at that, you know."

"I know." Her tone was dismissive but Jay could have sworn he saw a flicker of a smile across her lips.

Jay opened the door and they stepped through, greeted by a piercing shriek from Sylvie and a very distastefully decorated apartment. The furnishings were all pieces that had been made to appear vaguely East Asian in origin. The designs started at kitsch and moved on to insulting. Sylvie had put on a sweatshirt over her bathing suit top and floral robe and was sitting on her floor barefoot beneath the window clutching a bottle of cheap whiskey as a throwing weapon.

"Oh, dear," was all Jay managed to get out.

"Yeah," Janis said in a bland voice. "It's a lot of woven shit."

"No, not that. Your scent is everywhere. They'll know she spent time

156

with you."

"Your smell is here too now."

He snapped the door shut behind him. The bottle of whiskey smashed on the wall next to Jay, thrown in a clumsy, wide arc. The liquor inside sprayed out and Jay was sprinkled in alcohol.

"Breaking and entering!" Sylvie screamed at the top of her lungs. "They're here to kill me! Someone help!"

"There's no one else in this whole complex." Janis spoke from the small table to the left of the door, complete with a rustic carved wooden bowl in the shape of a fish and a keychain that proclaimed "Normal people scare me". Janis held up the top envelope from a small pile with a large red stamp on the front and several sheets of paper with official seals at the top. "They're about to tear this place down. She's squatting."

They rounded on Sylvie who gave a sheepish smile as her hand crept toward a shoe on the ground behind her. Janis was unimpressed when the brown sandal sailed through her body and bounced against the wall behind her.

"We can't leave her," he stated.

"No," Janis said, shaking her head. "I'm dead, you have magic, we can defend ourselves. This one over here," she jerked a finger, "can't. Look at her. She'll be dead weight."

"I have powers, not magic," Jay clarified.

"Magic begone!" yelled Sylvie cowering from her spot on the ground. She held two engraved wooden chopsticks in the shape of a cross, hands shaking as she held the symbol out, assuming it would ward off evil.

"That never works, you know," Jay told her. A chopstick flew past his head.

"And she has terrible aim," Janis whispered. Jay took a firm step forward, halting when Sylvie squeaked, then took another step.

"We're not going to hurt you, but I do need you to listen to me. Can I sit?"

The woman eyed him, the second chopstick clutched in a balled up fist like a spear. She nodded once. Folding his legs, Jay sat, trying to ignore the feeling of his trousers, which were still on the wetter side of damp, sticking to his legs. Jay gritted his teeth against the awareness of

157

his skin. He grasped for the right words with which to begin.

"Things are not what you might have previously imagined."

"Jay, come on." Janis punctuated her sentence, he imagined, with an eye roll.

"What I meant was, I am not human. I think you have guessed as much. And Janis, she has passed on from her mortal life and her soul is now represented on this plane in a spectral form."

A noise of exasperation came from behind Jay. "He means there's real magic in the world and all of the terrible things exist except vampires since we killed them and I'm a ghost."

Jay slapped his hand down on the floor causing Sylvie to flinch. "Damn it, Janis! I'm trying to explain this piece by piece so she gets it. Understand?" It was Sylvie who answered.

"I mean, I get it," the woman said in a slow voice. "You're, like, a crazy person."

"No, I'm not." Jay tried to gather together his patience. "I have to tell her everything," he said, more to Janis than to Sylvie.

"Don't, Jay!" Janis rushed to his side and pulled at his arm. "You'll break her mind or something." He peeled the ghost's hand away.

"She'll be okay, Janis, I'm under control now. I'll just tell her the whole story in one easy step." *Then she can decide for herself,* he added in his mind. "Do I have your permission?"

Sylvie eyed his outstretched hand. "Permission to do what? Murder me?"

"Oh, my God," Janis swore.

"No one's going to murder you, Sylvie. I'm just trying to show you something."

"Show me something through your hand?"

"Yes."

"And you'll leave me alone if I hold your hand?"

"Sure, Sylvie," Jay huffed, "yes."

"You promise?"

"We promise," Janis answered.

Sylvie glanced first at Janis then to Jay with a sulky, wide-eyed expression. Resignation shone in her brown eyes when she lifted her hand, the one not holding the chopstick like a weapon, and placed her palm atop Jay's. His heart leapt at the contact, excited to use his power again.

Now? his power asked as he gathered it to him. Jay clenched his jaw, forcing it to be gentle.

He pushed into the woman's mind, easing in like a body entering scalding bath water. Sylvie's mind threw up subconscious defenses, a wall of fear and anxiety that shielded Jay from her mind. He waited in an atrium-like space in the forefront of her consciousness until she relaxed. It was a bland white lobby with a large gray table with a matching chair. A rubber desk plant stood in one corner. Jay looked around wondering what kind of human mind hers was. Though, how many human minds had he ever entered? Not enough to draw average comparisons to this quiet landscape. The back of his neck prickled and Jay whirled around, expecting something to be standing behind him. He felt like he had on Anat's porch, that he was being watched. Not by Sylvie, though her focus poured over him, but by an additional someone who shouldn't be there.

An electric crackle came from above him and Jay looked up to see a circular speaker built into the ceiling of wherever this place was.

"Get out, get out, get out." It was Sylvie's voice, distorted by the strange PA system. The command became a chant as Jay tried to reason with something he could not see.

"Calm down," he said.

"Get out, get out, get out..."

She was too scared. Jay conjured up a memory for her to see. In this place, it took the form of a fax memo, a moving picture on a piece of paper. It was a memory Jay had of Janis, crying the morgue with her parents. The memory flickered, then reset to the beginning, showing Janis crying next to her parents.

"Get out."

Jay submitted it onto the empty gray table, pushing the paper across the stainless steel surface and waited, watching the memory play upside down. The chanting stopped, speaker above Jay crackling in the silence. The screeching sound of a mic being turned off blared through the speaker grate and a door slid open behind the unoccupied desk. The feeling of being watch subsided and Jay crossed the threshold of the door. Back in the apartment, Sylvie's body twitched as Jay merged with her subconscious.

It was dark in this new place. Snatches of songs and jumbled lines of conversations darted around him. The entire German language floated by intermingling with scenes from movies and plays and embarrassing public mishaps. Memories came in flashes; a childhood bike with plastic noisemakers on the wheels, summers around a lake with sunburnt and freckled shoulders, a naked woman tangled up in bedsheets, a rolled diploma received on a blue stage, a student crying in an office over a test, a kiss. The flashes rotated through cycles, showing different pieces each round from her birth to the present. Lining the outer edges of Sylvie's mind was a film of iron from the Celtic knot she wore around her neck.

That was out of order. Everything about this woman was strange, annoyingly so. The metal was pure, made of iron, but there was something else lingering about its essence. Jay sifted through Sylvie's memories to find its origin. It had been a gift when she was born, the one constant in her ever-changing mortal existence.

Back in the apartment, Jay heard Janis tap her foot. He took a breath, ready to press his own thoughts into Sylvie. He told her of Janis appearing behind the morgue, of the dead reapers, the corruption of the fae, and of the altercation with the ferryman at the graveyard. Sylvie pushed back. The unusual elements of Jay's story were too strange, too frightening, and too... Familiar? In the apartment, Jay frowned.

You know this world? he asked Sylvie in her mind.

I know it. She sounded like air blowing through cobwebs.

How?

I've always known it. A picture formed before Jay, a tree in a grassy yard, perfect for climbing. The image flickered and Jay found him looking out from the perspective of being in the tree. It was dark and menacing shapes lurked around the shadowy edges of the yard. *I couldn't tell at first, when I was younger, that they were separate things from the darkness.* One of the beasts opened its mouth and roared without sound but the vibrations in the memory rocked Jay. *But I figured it out that night.*

The scene shifted. Muted daylight streamed down and Jay was looking up from the grass.

How did you know where to look? How did you know where to find them? Resistance pressed against Jay.

No. The scene faded and Jay was left alone in gray darkness. *You cannot know.*

More. A crackle of lightning zagged down into the space between Jay and Sylvie.

There was more, an ice Jay sensed deep within her, a counterpart to his lightning power, darting here and there, never landing in the same place twice. When it did land, it left behind a kiss of cold iron. He chased after it, moving deeper and deeper into the depths until he forgot who he was.

They were furious that their deepest secret had been told. Why had they done that? To a stranger in the darkness they had laid their heart bare. They dragged themselves downward, wanting to bury it, to hide it away, for it never to see the light again.

"Jay!"

The sound was far away, shouted through an expanse of water. Who was that? The girl from before? It must be the girl with cold hands and strange eyes. The world shook again.

"Jay! Wake up!"

Jay opened his eyes. Bile rose in his throat. He looked around, dazed. Janis was shaking his shoulder so vigorously he bit his tongue. Sitting across from Jay was Sylvie looking confused and like she was also on the verge of throwing up.

"Janis," Jay said in a flat voice, though he remained looking at Sylvie. "Sylvie."

He tilted his head one way, then the other. In sync with him, Sylvie tilted her head. His gaze was cloudy, as if cobwebs coated his eyes. Jay wiped at his face with the back of his hand and Sylvie did the same, a perfect mirror image. A slap hit him on the back of his head rocking Jay back to focus.

"Janis!"

"Sorry, your eyes got all white and scary."

Rubbing the back of his head, Jay considered Sylvie with a heavy gaze. "If I didn't know any better I'd say she was a psychic. That's why she pulled my power out of me earlier. Help me up." Jay extended a hand to Janis who helped him to his feet. In turn, Jay offered his hand to Sylvie. After a moment, she took it.

"You told me they don't exist," Janis said.

"I am not a psychic. I'm a, well, I'm unemployed now, but I was a German Language and Culture professor. I'm a normal person." Sylvie glared at the two.

Jay wasn't sure how to process this information. People like Sylvie just didn't exist. "I saw it in your mind, Sylvie."

She held up a finger at him. "No. You do not get to talk to me like we're friends. I'm not some forest moon priestess, okay? If I were psychic how'd I not know I was going to get fired?" Sylvie moved to the couch, giving Jay and Janis a wide berth, and mumbling about crazy people under her breath. She sat before she remembered her manners. "Do you guys want something to drink? I have coffee. Do you want some coffee?"

They didn't have time for coffee, but Janis was answering. "I can't drink anymore."

"Oh, I'm sorry."

Janis waved the apology away. Jay crossed over to the open window and peered down the six stories to the pool glinting in the sunlight. "We have to go. All of us."

"I also can't eat anymore," Janis had said over Jay's words. "I would literally kill for a pickle."

Sylvie glanced from Janis, who had a wistful look on her face, to Jay. "'We' as in you two, right?"

Jay remained scouting out the window. They were safe this close to noon, the hot summer sun protecting them from most of the tracking creatures under Tick's employ. He liked to stick to the darker beings, which made it hard to track during daylight hours , but he more than made up for it once the sun lost its strength. Jay shuddered. "No. 'We' as in all of us."

Sylvie let out a hollow laugh, slapping her thighs once with her hands.

"Well! This has been a fun morning, meeting new people and touching minds and shit. But there is no fucking way I'm going with y'all on your weird little road trip."

Janis sighed. "Can't you just zap her and make her come with us?" Sylvie rounded on Janis who quickly backtracked. "Or just, I don't know, clear her memory that we were here?"

"You know we left a trail; they'll kill her even if I make her forget."

Sylvie sat back hard on the couch, making the dark wicker backing creak. "Whoa, wait. What the fuck? Kill? You brought someone here to kill me?"

Jay shut the window and drew closed the tacky, embroidered curtains. "You can't stay here. If you come with us, you'll be protected."

She let out another incredulous laugh. "Protected from whom? You haven't told me anything!"

Janis picked at a cuticle. "I think you're wrong about the psychic thing, Jay."

"Yes, very wrong." Sylvie pointed to her chest, nodding emphatically. "Normal person; wants to be left alone to live a life of peace."

Jay's eyes darted around her apartment, taking in the signs of life amongst the horrid decor. Surfaces were littered with papers, either bills or old textbooks and other files belonging to a world of academia. From inside her mind, Jay knew she hadn't had gainful employment for some time. Laundry, clean or not, slumped in piles around the corners of the apartment or under pieces of her cheap furniture. In the bookshelves were dusty pictures of old friends and on the walls hung framed merits of great academic achievement. She caught him looking.

"Don't judge me."

Jay shook his head.

"No, you were. You were thinking how anyone could wish to stay here in this apartment, in this life. It's not like your life is roses."

"No doubt," Janis added dryly. Jay glared.

"I don't like this," Sylvie announced from the couch, looking glum. After a moment, she heaved a heavy sigh. "At least tell me where we're going?"

Jay's brow creased in a frown. Something nagged at him. "We make for Atlanta," he told her in an even voice, trying to work out what was wrong.

"Atlanta! Damn, you're serious." She waited for a moment before her eyes widened. "And you want to drive there?"

"Planes are too risky."

"People, real human people, don't just up and abandon their lives," Sylvie argued.

"This place isn't safe. It's no longer about if the deadbolts on your door have been locked. The things hunting us are bad, very bad, and will not hesitate to tear into you to get the information they want."

The small apartment was thick with the scent of a ghost and reaper, it would be all but too easy for the trackers to pick up their trail. If Tick meant business, and he always did, he would send the hounds.

"But my life, it's all here." Sylvie swept an arm around the tiny space. "My books and my clothes and, and all my friends know I live here. What would I tell them? There's a lot of red tape tied to being a human."

"Cut it all," Jay said. "You staying alive is worth more than remembering to collect your mail."

Sylvie cast her eyes around again. "As soon as I step foot off this property, I'll be evicted."

Jay moved in the direction of the door. "I don't suspect we will be gone for long, if it helps. Maybe a month."

"A month?" Her hand flew to her throat where she fiddled with the chain holding the iron Celtic knot around her neck.

"They will kill you," Janis enunciated, as if speaking to a very small child. "What part of that don't you get? Do you want to die?"

"No," said the woman, looking angry at Janis' tone. "But I don't want to run off with two complete strangers who might be making this whole thing up!"

Jay crossed his arms, patience worn. "Then stay and die. But don't pretend to think we're lying. You've seen what I said to be true."

Even as he said it, he knew he would never let her remain in the apartment. Jay and Sylvie locked eyes as she considered his words. He refused to look away and she was first to break eye contact, sliding down her couch in a slump.

"I hate you both."

"That I can live with. Get up. We need a car," he told the ghost as Sylvie stood and poked at one of the piles of laundry with her shoeless foot. Jay hoped as they got on the road, whatever was nagging at him now would come to him.

"I'm not stealing a car," Sylvie said, picking out a shirt from the heap and inspecting it. She nodded toward the side table at the door where keys dangled. "We'll take mine. Best thing I got in my divorce."

Jay could see the symbol from where he stood.

Porsche.

SIXTEEN

"**Y**OU MIGHT HAVE ENOUGH money to move to a new place if you sold this car."

Janis was in the small backseat of the Porsche, next to Sylvie's duffle, legs disappearing into the bag so she could spread out in the close quarters. Sylvie had packed the bag in a hurry, with Janis helping and Jay surveying for followers through a crack in the curtains, and lugged it down the hall to the elevator, insisting the whole way that she would be the one to drive.

"I don't care if you're a supernatural being from another dimension, you're not going to ding my Porsche. If you want me to come, I drive," she had called out from where she was changing clothes in her bedroom when Jay had asked her for the third time if she was sure. She came out of the bedroom wearing tapered jeans and a loose and baggy gray shirt. She had strapped her feet into brown leather sandals that tied at the back and had settled into a tetchy silence with Jay, one that Janis now broke.

"Seriously, why'd you keep it?" Janis persisted in her line of questioning from the backseat.

"When you divorce someone and end up getting the super nice car you bought together for the second anniversary, you keep it." Sylvie steered the car in the direction of Jay's pointing finger and took a left to get closer to the highway.

Jay fiddled with the armrest on the passenger side door, running a finger over the leather stitching and poking at the lock and window buttons.

"What is wrong with you?" Sylvie said with annoyance after his fidgeting didn't cease.

"He probably wants a cigarette," Janis piped from the back.

Sylvie gave a quick laugh in disbelief. "A reaper is addicted to cigarettes?" she asked, astonished when silence followed her laughter.

"I'll get over it," Jay said, sounding long-suffering. "Take a right."

"I know," Sylvie snapped. "I live here."

"I'm just making sure you know," Jay spat back.

"Smoke these." Sylvie reached across to the glove compartment and dug around inside. She tossed a lighter and a crushed box of Marlboros onto Jay's lap and snapped the compartment closed. With fumbling motions, Jay tore into the package, ripping the flip top clean off.

"Thank you," he said in a mumble, a cigarette already in his mouth. He flicked the lighter and the sooty, sour smell of burning tobacco filled the Porsche. "You're sure you don't mind?"

"They aren't mine."

It wasn't an answer but Jay was too overwhelmed with relief to question her further.

The trio sat in silence as Sylvie directed the sports car onto the highway due south, merging at a zipping pace into the left lane.

"So..." Sylvie said after they drove through Raleigh. "Can you tell me why people are after us? We could go to the police and get protection."

Janis snorted. "They wouldn't be able to handle this guy. Trust me," she added with a shudder.

"That gross-looking guy?" Sylvie asked. "Why is he after you? You didn't tell me that in...in my head."

Jay heaved a sigh. "I don't know the reason why, but Tick is a hired lackey working for the fae."

"What do you mean 'you don't know the reason'?" Sylvie shifted into second gear.

"There is an order to the world, a particular way things lay when they fall."

"Sure, like a balance," Sylvie said with a nod. "I've heard that, rules of the universe and stuff. I just didn't think it was true."

"No, there is no balance. There is only the way things are. I don't think I can explain it better but there it is. A balance denotes that there must be equal good to equal evil, for example. That is not the case in this world. Things are here as they are meant to be. If there is to be more evil than so be it."

"Well that sucks," Janis quipped after a brief moment of silence.

Jay shrugged. "It's just the order of things. The way things always have been."

"What does this have to do with us?" Sylvie asked.

"When things begin to happen out of order, the rest of it begins to fall apart. There can't be too much of one way."

"So, like a balance." Janis quipped.

Jay pushed at the hair flopping into his eyes. "Reapers reap souls. Ferrymen take them onto the next life. That is the way in this instance. I'm just giving you examples; we don't have time for me to explain everything."

"We get it. Move on," Sylvie said.

"If fae are using the power of sheefrah souls to kill reapers that means the order has been corrupted. While I'd prefer not to reduce it to such terms, the murders of my kin is a symptom, indicative of some greater issue."

"What if the order now is for reapers to be killed?" Sylvie questioned.

Jay fiddled with the box of cigarettes. "I do not think it is in the right order for a human not to be given a choice. And who would wish to murder death? For all that it's seen by your kind as something frightening and terrible, isn't something to be avoided. There is a set way to follow. Our duties, more like our natures, are preordained and we may not deviate from the path."

Janis leaned forward. "That sounds kind of boring."

"Would you prefer a world ruled by chaos?"

"No."

"Then be thankful the order hasn't been overturned. I'm hoping this deviation is but a small flaw that won't grow into a destructive domino effect."

"What if that's the order for it to do that?" Janis asked, a childish tone entering her voice.

"Who determines this order, then? God?" asked the older woman, interrupting the conversation from devolving.

Jay sniffed. "Not even close."

Sylvie flashed him a sideways glance. "A different god? Brahma?"

"No. They are beyond even his powers. They are beyond all else. They set the order by which we all must abide."

"Who?" Sylvie asked with a frown.

"They."

"You said that already. Who are they?" Janis said.

Jay shrugged. "They have no name. They are the order. They simply are."

Janis gave an unimpressed snort. "That is so stupid."

Jay just shrugged again. He wasn't sure he was explaining it well, but it felt nice to confide in the two. With Janis, telling her these secrets help lessen the feeling of guilt still churning in his heart. Including her by sharing these details gave her further agency within this new world she was exploring. He felt it absolved him a little that he was helping to make her into a willing accomplice rather than an unhappy passenger. With Sylvie... He didn't know what to do with her. He felt awful for dragging her into this. He shifted in his seat as he felt another stab of guilt shoot through him. It was different from the guilt he felt when he dragged Janis to the graveyard under false pretenses. How complex were human feelings that they could have different shades of the same emotions?

"Is your name really Janis?" Sylvie asked the ghost, eyeing her in the rearview mirror.

"Yeah." Janis squinted at Sylvie, confused. "Why?"

The older woman pointed in Jay's direction. "Well, his name isn't his real name so I was wondering if when you become a ghost you get to choose a new name or something."

"Jay! That's not your real name?" Janis shrieked.

He looked around, distracted from the tumult of his inner thoughts and worries. "What? My name?"

"Is it like Mr. Death or something dumb?" The smile slipped from her face when she saw Jay's expression. He was gaping at her. "What?"

"That's not my name. Don't ever call me that again." His heart was pounding and he felt an electric jolt of energy sizzle under his skin. It was the most uncomfortable emotion he had felt so far, worse than guilt. Was it fear? It felt similar but it was laced with a heavy, nauseous feeling of worry.

"It was just a joke. You kind of are though, aren't you?"

Jay shook his head. "No, and it would be perverse of me to let you assume so."

"Assume what?" Sylvie asked.

"That I am Four."

"Who's Four?"

"Its name. *The* Death; the ending of all things."

Janis leaned forward. "You're not?"

Jay shook his head again. "No, I am death, or I was, but I am not The Death. There are many reapers, many deaths, all working under The Death."

"Uh-huh," Janice said after a moment. "You're just one of the workers? Just a regular old reaper?"

"All reapers share the same title, the same duties, we have the same powers, and we are all responsible for the dead. But to let either of you assume I am more than who I am is blasphemy for my kind."

"What would happen if you were to, um, blaspheme?" Sylvie asked.

"Four would pay me a very uncomfortable and unpleasant visit."

Sylvie said nothing but merged into the middle lane to avoid a slow car in front of them. Janis settled back into her seat.

"So do you have a number for your name?" Sylvie picked up the thread of her original question.

"No."

"So, you're Jay?"

"Reapers are nameless. This body's name is Doctor Jayan Mati," Jay gestured to all of him then felt self-conscious. Another human emotion he could do without ever feeling again. He closed his eyes, lamenting the merging of his reaper essence with humanity, when he heard Sylvie ask him a question. "What?"

"I said, you stole a body?"

"This man, Jayan Mati, was already dead when I was given the shell. I am placed in bodies in the exact moment after brain death and before true death. This is part of my sentencing. This is my third one. In a long line of many to come. I seem to burn them out."

"Sentencing?" asked Janis in a strained voice.

Sylvie tensed up behind the wheel. "I knew I was in a car with criminals."

Jay tipped his head back with a groan. "I'm not a criminal. In the mortal sense of the word. I don't think."

"You don't think?" she squeaked.

"Then why are you in a human body, Jay? You never told me," Janis spoke over Sylvie's disconcertion, poking him with a cold digit when he didn't answer fast enough for her.

"I disobeyed my orders. Twice. Although, I suppose the first time wasn't me flouting authority, more a simple mistake. Still, there were consequences." Jay blathered in his nervousness. Another emotion with new depth to it. As a reaper he'd felt apprehension, but this was different. This worry seemed to have a social link. He realized they were both staring at him. Jay took a deep breath and barreled on, "I killed someone. It was an accident. I understand this sounds strange knowing what I am, but my kind don't deviate from the prescribed deaths we are to administer. I was in Brazil to reap a family and I..." he faltered, "I couldn't let him get away with it, with all the foul things he was doing to his children. I was so upset that he wouldn't see justice, I lost control over my powers and killed him."

It was silent in the car for a long while until Janis poked her head back up between the front seats.

"What was the second time?"

Jay fidgeted as he fought the truth, debating if telling them would lose the regard of his friends. He had never had friends before, not even as a reaper. The duties of reapers not leaving much time for casual relationships. He glanced at Sylvie and Janis. Not that these two were so much his friends, since he didn't think they would call him one, but they were companions. Companions whose safety he wanted ensured and whose opinions he valued, even their opinions of him. That was a new feeling, and a strong one.

"I let someone live." Jay waited for their judgements.

"Who?"

He didn't know which one of them spoke, the voice was too low.

"It doesn't matter who, just the act instead. She was a brilliant mathematician and I didn't see the point in taking her away; her mind was too singular and the world needed her, I felt."

Sylvie caught his eye before looking back to the road. "I'm sorry, but how could someone punish you for that? It seems like a good thing, right? To let someone so smart live?"

"There will always be smart people in the world, before and after her. The point is I disobeyed my orders and the price for that is humanity," Jay swallowed. "If I longed so much to experience the free will of humans then I would have it in full."

"I still don't think not killing someone couldn't be a bad thing," she told him.

"Is being human so bad that it's considered punishment?" Janis asked.

Jay considered her words. "No, but it's lonely. That can be punishment enough."

They drove on, the occupants of the car sitting in contemplative silence for the time being. Janis sat back and twisted around in the seat, leaning up against the window. Jay took out another cigarette to smoke and Sylvie drove, her wrinkled brow the only sign that she was thinking and not just daydreaming as she navigated the Porsche down the highway.

"So!" Sylvie stated brightly, trying to bring up the mood. "What else can you do?"

"Do?" Jay coughed around the sour smoke in his nose.

"You know, mind control and all that. What other magic shit can you do?"

Before Jay could answer, Janis did so for him. "He can heal himself and do this weird thing with light to send bad guys away and he can stop time."

"You can stop time?" Sylvie downshifted to circumvent another slower car.

"Time means nothing to me, as it's measured by humans. Most non-human beings exhibit a modicum of control over the phenomenon."

"Whatever that means. So, I'm assuming you're not in your, what, mid-forties?"

"No."

Janis stirred in the back, shifting in position. "How old are you?"

Jay blew smoke out the window before answering. "Old. Older than Earth. Older than you can understand." The human mind had interesting limits when it came to conceptualizing things like time and large numbers. "Older than time."

Sylvie hummed, as if in agreement. Then added, "Wait, so if you're so old, you must have been around famous people, right?"

Janis sat up from the back. "Was Jesus real?"

The car was silent save from the wind whipping in from the open sliver at Jay's window. He wasn't supposed to talk about this. He heard the humanity within him say "fuck it". He pushed the finished cigarette out the window and closed it. "Yes."

Sylvie and Janis had been holding their breath and released it at the same time. "Are you going to elaborate on that?" Sylvie asked.

"He is real and so is his Father." They both held themselves still, Sylvie as much as she could driving a car. "They are just one of the many gods in existence. That's all I'm going to say."

Janis gave a little gasp. "They're all real? All gods from all religions?"

"That's all I'm going to say."

Sylvie accelerated around a large shipping truck as they crossed the state border of South Carolina.

"That's... I'm not sure if that's more or less comforting to know."

"I agree. Can we use the radio yet?" Janis asked.

Jay threw out a hand to cover the stereo. "No! No music, no radio, no electronics. Most non-humans can use electronic signals to track quarries, like through the radio or phones."

"Phone-phones or cell phones?" Sylvie asked, digging into her pocket and producing a smartphone. "I brought this along and it hasn't been a problem." Jay stared at the device in her hand. She turned her head back and forth from the road to watch him. "If you keep making that face it will freeze that way."

"They're tracking us," Jay said in a low voice. "This whole time, they'll have been watching our progress. Why didn't I remember to tell you to leave your phone behind?" He smacked the dashboard hard with a fist.

"Hey!" Sylvie cried out. "Watch it!"

"What is the point of allocating a space in the brain for memory if humans never use it!" He yelled to no one in particular.

"You're scaring me." Sylvie gripped the wheel tight and started to slow the car in her confusion.

Janis echoed from the back, "You're scaring me, too. Is it Tick?"

Jay's heart pounded in fear. Is that what it was? He had never felt it before. Trepidation and unease, yes, but this was something more, something that curled in the pit of his stomach and shortened his breath. Sweat beaded at his brow despite the air conditioning.

"Sorry, Sylvie," he told her, closing his eyes and pulling at his power. "I know you wanted to drive."

"What?"

Drive.

Jay opened his eyes with a small popping sound and found himself in the driver's seat with Sylvie on the passenger side.

"Fuck me!" she screamed. "Do not do that again!"

Jay took the wheel and found the pedal and gear shift. "We need more speed and I can't argue with you about why right now."

Cars in front of them decided to change lanes and move out of their way on a whim. The drivers remembered nothing but the passing fancy to move to a new spot. The power inside Jay chuckled with the dark joy of total control as more vehicles parted.

Sylvie's hand was at her mouth. "I'm going to be sick."

"Ew," Janis said.

Jay pressed hard on the gas pedal, coaxing everything out of the Porsche.

"Ditch the phone," he told the psychic.

"It's worth twelve hundred dollars, Jay. I'm on a twenty-four-month payment plan."

Jay pushed a button on his door and it rolled down the window on Sylvie's side.

"Throw that damn phone out the window!" he yelled over the sound of Janis complaining about his manners and the rushing wind of the highway. Sylvie continued to stare at him. "Throw it away!" he screamed, making her jump and toss the phone out of the car. He shut the window into deafening silence.

"I want to go home," Sylvie said in a shaky voice.

"Why are you such an asshole?" Janis asked.

"We're almost to Columbia, I think. We'll have to stop there and try to lose them in the city." They passed a sign on the side of the road, solar powered, an LED display set up for highway construction.

"Did that just say my name?" Janis asked.

Jay twisted to look but it was too late. "Did it?"

"I thought it said 'Janis Lyn Pereda'."

More solar powered signs had been set up on the highway shoulder for construction and Jay squinted at the next one they passed. The digital orange block text shook and morphed before Jay's eyes.

SAFETY FIRST

WE WANT THE GIRL, THE GHOST, THE DEAD

BUCKLE UP, REAPER

"I don't feel well," Sylvie said with her eyes closed, white knuckling the sides of her seat. "Something's coming."

Janis made a choking noise. "Jay?"

"It'll be alright, Janis." He tried to make his voice sound unafraid. "I won't let them take you."

A loud crash banged into the right side of the car and the Porsche jerked to the left. Jay hugged at the steering wheel, dragging on it with his weight to get the car back under control. Janis was screaming. Heavy running footsteps beat around them. The car swerved again from a large object bumping into the car on the other side. The sound of barking dogs filled their ears. Above it all, Sylvie was praying.

"Please, don't let me die. I don't want to die."

"That's not going to help!" Jay yelled at the woman. He pulled again at the steering wheel in response to another hit.

The attackers began to howl. Jay risked a look out the window. It was a hound. Impossibly large, the huge, dark thing was made of shadows and bone, its skin that of a hairless rat dipped in black ink. Yellowish foam flecked off dirty and stained teeth, disappearing into the wind. A blue-black tongue lolled in anticipation while green eyes flashed with malice.

"Hellhounds don't have green eyes," Jay said before yanking the Porsche to the left, avoiding a head-butt from the giant beast. The stunted, flat ears made the hound look like an aqueous creature.

"Who gives a crap about their eyes?" Janis screamed.

The tires of the Porsche screeched against the pavement of the highway as he pushed the car around a minivan and dodged into another lane to avoid the attackers. A third hound bounded up behind them, cackling with gleeful malice.

"How is this possible?" He stared at the thing in the rearview mirror. Sunlight glinted off its sleek, seal-like skin, the black color oily. It laughed.

Hellhounds don't laugh. "These are fae direwolves under a glamour, not hellhounds! Tick called to the fae for help."

"Drive faster!" Janis demanded.

Why wouldn't Tick call the hounds? Jay thought, confused. *Unless, he didn't want the pits to know about his mistake letting Janis escape. That would mean some demons didn't know about the sheefrahs...*

"Jay, look out!" Sylvie shrieked, tearing his gaze away from the beast.

At the last moment, Jay turned the car away from rear-ending a massive eighteen wheeler. The truck's horn blared as they sped past. Jay gripped the wheel tighter, concentrating again. The other drivers would only see a Porsche driving recklessly past them at a furious speed, nothing else.

"Go away!" Janis yelled from the back seat. One of the disguised direwolves nipped at her window, jaws clacking, and she shrank back. "Jay, use your magic!"

"I am!" he yelled back. "I'm using it to keep us from crashing into other cars!"

Jay maneuvered the Porsche around a pickup truck and slammed on the clutch, grabbing the gear shift hard. The car's engine roared.

"It's me they want, I'll just jump outside!" Janis sobbed.

"No!" Jay cried out over the loud crash as the Porsche sustained another hit from one of the creatures. "Don't you dare! Stay in this car, Janis, do you understand?"

Without waiting for an answer, Jay hit the breaks. The engine ripped out a stuttered growl. The Porsche slowed and the pursuers ran past, not anticipating the sudden change in speed. There were three of the hulking black beasts. Their powerful muscles rippled beneath their hairless skin, shifting in their movements as expert pack hunters.

Jay pushed at the gas pedal again and the engine groaned out a loud protest as he drove the Porsche in reverse. Horns sounded as the other cars on the highway moved to avoid collision. The glamoured wolves collected themselves, huge claws skittering on the pavement, ripping up sections of the road. They turned to bound after the car's new direction, baying as they pursued. Sylvie screamed in fresh terror.

"Janis," Jay told the ghost in an even voice, keeping his eyes on the gaining creatures. The biggest was barking commands to the other two, fanning its companions to flank the Porsche. "Remember what you did with the car door when I was stuck?"

"Yes," she replied with uncertainty.

"I need you to use that same strength to jump with all of us. I need you to jump us and the car to safety."

Janis spluttered, "I can't do that!"

"Yes, you can, you have to try. Hold onto my shoulders and take my power. Imagine a quiet alley in Atlanta, someplace large enough to fit a car." The engined whined, protesting the reverse gear.

One of the dogs was fifty yards away. It snarled, jaws biting the air.

"Janis, do it now!" Cold settled onto him as the ghost placed her hands on him.

Twenty yards.

"Close your eyes, can you picture the alley?"

The other animals were catching up to their leader. One of the pack howled and the sound turned into a hyena-like cackle at the end.

"I think so," Janis said with hesitation.

Ten yards.

Ghost, Jay's power said with a grin.

Five yards.

He nodded and drew a deep breath, pushing his power into Janis.

"Jump! Now!"

Jay saw the open jaws of the camouflaged direwolf and heard Sylvie's lasting scream ringing in the air before the word fell to blackness.

SEVENTEEN

J AY'S EYES OPENED TO a world of blue. There was something cold swirling around his ankles. He jerked his head to look down and his neck spasmed in response. He brought his head back to rest against the seat, neck muscles on fire.

I am in a car. The sound of someone retching came from his right. A woman bent over in the passenger seat vomiting between her knees, the sound ending in a wet splash.

"Sylvie?" *Was that her name?* "What are you doing here?"

The woman sat up, gasping, brushing her hair back from her face. She looked out the window and screamed. A faint gurgling noise came from the bottom of the car. A spray of something cold and wet hit Jay's cheek, clearing his mind.

The Porsche was sinking nose first into water.

"Everybody out!" Jay yelled. He grappled with his seatbelt and kicked at the door, trying to force it open before the car submerged and the pressure became too great. Water surged in through the open door, flooding the entire bottom of the Porsche in seconds. The car tipped toward the passenger side, the water throwing off the balance. Spitting, Sylvie struggled with her seatbelt.

"Jay!" she cried out, terror in her eyes. "I can't get it!" He reached across and popped it open. She tried for a moment to open her door before Jay grabbed her arm and hauled her across his lap. He pushed her out the driver's door ahead of him.

He twisted around to look for the ghost. "Janis?" The back of the Porsche was empty except for Sylvie's duffle. His heart sank. "Janis!"

The water was at his chest and he had started to float, his head pressing up against the ceiling. Twisting to kick against the side of the passenger seat, he pushed out the door and tread at the water's surface, watching as the rest of the car bubbled under. Sylvie was splashing up ahead, swimming in short, desperate strokes toward the shoreline. Jay followed in her wake, kicking hard against the water in his shoes and heavy clothes, struggling until he could touch the bottom.

Coughing and spluttering, they dragged themselves onto the grassy shore, rolling onto their backs and heaving. Jay closed his eyes against the bright afternoon sun, gasping and hoping that when he opened them again, he would see Janis.

"You sank my fucking Porsche!" Sylvie's voice was an angry rasp.

"We're alive, that's all that matters." Jay sat up and shook his hair out of his eyes, watching Sylvie's face darken to a glower. "It is, you know, just a material object..." he trailed off.

Jutting a finger out at him, she illustrated her point with sharp jabs. "You're not human, you don't get it, and that's not the fucking point."

"I don't care what the point is!" he bellowed, the effect of his cry lessened by him sitting on the bank of a river, sopping wet. Jay's intense human emotions of worry for Janis caught up with him. "We're alive, you're not being tortured, and that's all that should matter. Now, we find Janis, we fix this, and we all go home in one piece, okay?"

"You owe me a new car," she muttered.

Jay decided not to answer and checked their surroundings. Across the water to the left some distance from where they sat was a power plant. Behind them was a mess of tall grasses and short, twisting shrubs leading to a narrow cut of trees framing the river. Extending his hand to Sylvie, he leaned back against her weight and pulled her upright.

They picked their way along the water. They drew close to a large bend, stopping to gaze up at a bridge passing over the water. The sound of cars driving by overhead filled their ears as the pair stopped to collect their bearings.

"I think this is Marietta Boulevard," Jay said, walking up next to Sylvie and looking up, hands on his hips. "It runs northwest and if we follow it, it will lead us into the city."

"We can't take a cab?"

Jay shook his head. "Not until I know we're not being watched."

They walked on in silence, traversing the landscape of outer Atlanta. It was much hotter in Georgia than it was in Virginia. It had been a long time since Jay visited and he had been a reaper then. Now, he was covered in so much sweat he appeared feverish. Hours passed before they began to see the high-rises and skyscrapers of the city appear closer.

"I can't go any farther," Sylvie said, stumbling to sit on a curb next to a tall backyard fence. "I'm not in shape for this."

Jay put his hands on his thighs, bending over and breathing hard, grateful for the rest. Smoke collected at the bottom of his lungs, lurking behind his gasping breaths. All the exercise triggered the need to clear his lungs sooner than he would have without the urban hike. "Shit, don't look." He managed to get the words out before his abdomen rippled in preparation of a cough. Jay stumbled, arm reaching out and grabbing onto the corner of the wooden fence.

"Are you okay?" Sylvie cried out when she heard the deep, wet noise coming from his lungs.

His breath hitched as body expelled up a small, black glob. Jay spit it out onto the ground, it was much smaller than it had been a few days ago. "Sorry," he apologized in a hoarse voice. One of his eyes was squinted in his pain as he watched her.

"What the fuck was that?" she demanded in a shaky voice.

Jay cleared his throat several times and spit out the residual phlegm from inside his lungs. He glowered at the black mass on the ground.

"Smoke. Cancer. At least it would be if I were human. My power prevents this body from becoming sick." Jay gave a wretched smile. "I must live out my full sentence."

"Yes, you've said. How long?" Sylvie asked, trying to avoid looking at the stuff on the ground.

"Five centuries."

Her eyes grew round. "Five hundred years for letting someone live?" Jay nodded.

"Well, shit." Sylvie climbed to her feet, an emotion on her face Jay didn't recognize. "Don't do that again. Are we close?"

Jay shook his head. "We make for the city center. To the business district. Evil things like to gather in places of affluence and influence."

"Evil things? I thought you had a friend down here?"

"Two friends, to be exact, and I have to talk to the one in a place I dislike first. If anyone has heard of a strange ghost showing up in Atlanta, it will be the Turned."

"Turned?"

Jay studied a street sign before taking a left. "Not like me. Bad things."

"I wish I hadn't come."

He caught her severe expression. "You would have been killed."

"I could still be killed. In fact, I already escaped death once today in the river. You know, when you sank my car?" Sylvie shook her head and her bangs fluffed across her forehead at the movement. "So how are we getting to this evil business place where I won't die?"

Jay squinted up at another street sign. "We'll take MARTA."

"Who the hell is..." Sylvie trailed off when she spotted the sign for the Atlanta subway system. "Oh."

They made their way down the steps to the Bankhead stop and fumbled at a ticket kiosk like tourists. After a transfer at Five Points, they exited the subway at the Civic Center stop and blinked when they emerged from underground. It was still bright out, the southern August sun was strong, even with it close to setting. Jay led their way down the city blocks, stopping only for cigarettes at a sidewalk kiosk.

"This is just annoying," Sylvie commented when Jay pulled a cigarette out of the new package and lit the tobacco.

"It's a habit," he explained after a long drag.

She rolled her eyes. "You can heal yourself from cancer. I'm pretty sure you can stop being addicted to cigarettes."

"Perhaps I don't want to stop being addicted to cigarettes."

"Exactly."

Jay beckoned her to stand beside him on the sidewalk out of the way of the foot traffic that bustled around them, the workday coming to an end. They were standing on a corner at the end of a block next to a small used bookstore tucked underneath the bottom level of a tall building. In the retail space next to it, at street level, was a coffee shop attached to a bank.

"That's where I'm going." Jay stated. He pointed to the lower level. The steps to their right descended down from the sidewalk and ended at a door painted an unnamable shade of blue. Next to the door was a large square of dirty glass with a few dusty books strewn about for a window display. Behind the glass was a sun-faded black curtain, blocking the view of the interior from the outside. Gold, peeling plastic letters were stuck onto the glass in an arc proclaiming: *District Books: Used Paperbacks and Hardcovers, Rare Manuscripts.*

Sylvie frowned. "A bookstore? I didn't notice it."

People hurried by on the street, ignoring the wrought iron stairs that led down to the shop situated at basement level. Most would never notice this place, as was meant, unless it was pointed out to them. The glamour also forced humans to avoid the spot, urging them to take care of sudden business or pressing matters elsewhere.

"It's not a bookstore. There's a cafe attached to the bank. Go, and stay there until I come get you. Don't talk to anyone or anything."

Sylvie was taken aback at the mention of "anything" but Jay puffed hard on his cigarette, threw it down to step on the butt, and left Sylvie as he walked down the steps.

The darkness inside the building seemed to grab Jay when he opened the door, an invisible force pulling him in and snapping the door shut close on his heels, giving a pressurized hiss as it sealed shut. Dim lights shone above him, recessed into the ceiling, glowing in gray and yellow hues, coloring the interior like a sickness. When the door latched, music started, or maybe it had always been playing and he hadn't heard it until the noise of the Atlanta street corner had ceased. The song was atonal, a relentless horrible grinding melody with a soprano harmony that sounded like the wailing of young children. The short, dark wood paneled hallway Jay stood in ended with a black curtain that had a red arrow painted on the waving folds.

Come forward, it said.

Jay felt ill. The whole place smelled of decay so noxious his stomach rolled. Hit bit down on the inside of his cheeks to keep from heaving. This wasn't the first time Jay had been in a demon's den, but he had never visited one as a human. It called to his mortal shell, eager to corrupt it.

"Tickets?" a helpful voice chirped to Jay's left. A demon stood in a small but ornate box office, her body visible from the waist up. Glass was built into the wall serving as the window to her workstation with a round metal grate used as a two-way speaker in the middle of the divider. A smoothed divot had been scooped out of the center of the wooden countertop to better pass tickets and money through. The whole structure looked as if it belonged to an antique carnival. Flaking gold leaf revealing ancient black wood carved into intricate baroque designs framed the opening and the expanse of dark wood beneath the glass window was painted with vertical red and gold stripes. "Would you like to buy a ticket?"

Jay stumbled forward and leaned on the counter. The air of the demon den pressed in on him from all sides like he was in deep water. He had to swallow several times to get his ears to pop and adjust to the pressure. His human senses were assailed by the cloying smell and evil that lay all around, laced into the very molecules of the den. He opened his mouth to speak and coughed around the taste of sour brine that coated his tongue. The demon behind the counter was studying his suffering with an even stare. She was short, standing just over five and a half feet.

"Tickets?" she trilled again, as if she didn't recognize him. "You may not enter the den without a ticket."

"How are you, Friend?" Jay gritted his teeth against the strong smell of the den assailing his human nostrils. This human body was making him rude.

Feigning innocence, and doing a good job of it considering what she was, the demon gazed up at him through fluttering black lashes.

"Long time no see, reaper," Friend purred. Her golden-green eyes flashed over his appearance, vertical pupils dilating from a tight line. "You look like shit."

She adjusted her dress. The fabric was cut from some kind of fur, the clothing clinging to her body in a silhouette that would have been stylish if not for the bald spots of organic rot in the material. Skin showed through the twisting ropes of her clothing, mostly a dark shade of brown but in some places it was splotched with vitiligo in light pink, like the nose of a cat or the petals of a delicate flower.

"I'm in the body of a human, of course I look like shit."

Friend, on the other hand, was perfect. Jay's entire body paused at the thought, falling still as a very new emotion slammed into him. He tried not to choke as he looked at the demon again, really looked.

Friend's body was exquisite. Her frame was small, slender, and cat-like, but she had ample curves built on top of the graceful structure that hid a lethal strength in the soft corners of her body. She changed her hair since the last time he had seen her. Her hair now was bleached white-blonde with jet black roots and twisted into locs of various sizes piled into a large bun at the top of her head. Her hairline had been shaved back several inches, making her forehead appear much larger than it was. Jay supposed it must be some sort of beauty trend among demons. He raked his eyes across her body, peering through the glass and feeling dizzy from the feelings surging through him. It felt as if his blood was slowing to a steady chugging pace and enough oxygen wasn't reaching his brain. He supposed he ought to say something and forced his eyes back to her handsome face.

"Friend, you look..." Words failed him. He angled his head as his gaze swept over her body once more. As the sallow lights caught different planes of her face and body, some of her form shifted to show thin strips of flesh clinging onto a skeletal structure that resembled a mutated cat. She was perfection. The music changed to a pounding bass rhythm without any melody. The pulsing notes marched in Jay's ears, urging him to say something, do something, something, something. "I came to ask you..."

"Yes?" she asked with another long purr at the end of her question. Friend leaned forward at the hungry look in his eyes, her gaze trapped within his.

"I'm looking for someone, a ghost. Have you heard anything?"

The music throbbed through Jay and his entire body felt tight, more than just from the squeezing of air pressure. He couldn't stop his eyes from drawing down to the low neckline of the demon's dress, the cut revealing rounded breasts pushed together.

Jay had never seen another living woman's body before. The only women he saw naked were either his own body as Delilah or Olga or the cadavers on his exam table. But now his human emotions weren't tucked away and inaccessible. Jay's eyes lingered on the tightness of her dress and the curving of her breasts that rose and fell in time to her shallow breaths. The movement caused a new sensation to grip his body. Ice poured through him in a rush and it set every hair on his body rising, pricking up as if he were in danger, but it was a wonderful kind of danger that was heady and felt as addicting as one of his cigarettes. To his utter dismay, something tightened within him at his core, a drawing together of something, and it coalesced around his groin.

Jay abruptly stood when he realized what was happening, the sudden movement causing his ears to pop again in the thick air. He tried to clear his head from the onslaught of attraction and lust. *How do humans ever get anything done?* he thought as he tried to shift his pants into a more comfortable position around his erection. This was not how he expected his day to go.

This was not the way Friend had expected her day to go, but it was thrilling.

"What an odd question," she answered in a voice that matched the sparkling darkness behind her eyes. "What do you want with a ghost?"

"If you don't know anything just say so."

Friend smiled, the slash of a grin spreading across her lips. "You always were so dramatic," she *tsk*-ed, going back to moving groupings of tickets this way and that on her counter behind the glass. "If you can go around asking questions, so can I."

"Please, Friend, I will owe you when I am restored." Jay raked his hands through his hair, the roots damp with sweat.

The demon could not stop the purr that began deep within her, though she tried to massage her throat to get it to subside. When the fox had turned up at her door, she hadn't dared to hope that she would get to see the reaper again or anytime soon. Friend smacked her lips, painted in black, glossy lipstick, putting on a show of being unamused. "And how long will that be? Four hundred years? Five hundred? I don't like being owed when I can't collect right away."

Jay slammed a hand on the counter, "You know I'm good for it. Charge me your damn demon's interest, I don't care, just tell me what you know!"

Friend tapped her poisonous yellow painted nails on the counter, one at a time.

"I'm sorry," he said with a crack in his voice and she nodded.

Something had changed about the reaper who stood before her. The body was handsome, the human face had a countenance that pleased her. Of course, the reaper had been beautiful before, otherworldly and all dark death, but now... Friend couldn't help but let her eyes rove up and down the mortal body. Now this was something she could sink her teeth into. His inky hair had a bit of salt to it at his temples and the unkempt waves flopped over his forehead, charming her. Wonderful, grave dirt colored eyes were soft as he looked at her and she found herself wanting to lick all over his coffin-wood brown skin. To her, he was hauntingly beautiful, even in this human shell.

"What is your name in this form?" His throat bobbed as he swallowed and her purring kicked up a notch.

"Jay," he said, voice catching again as he spoke. She flicked her eyes up to his, away from the delicious column of his throat, and raised an eyebrow. She wanted to swallow that name.

"It suits you," Friend said.

Jay dropped his hand from the glass. She debated telling him about Tensith but decided it would be more fun to let the two of them circle each other for a little longer. The demon shook her head in amusement.

"Alright," she conceded. "I might know something. But," she held up a finger in warning to Jay's grateful sigh. "But you will owe me." She moved the finger to point at him. "You'll owe me big time. A favor for a favor, we'll say."

Crooking the finger she reached toward the glass, tapping the material four times counterclockwise with her knuckle creating a square out of the four touch points. The partition disappeared when she completed the shape.

"Come here, big boy," she purred, leaning over the wooden counter, breasts threatening to fall out of her dress. She half hoped they would.

Jay tensed, his eyes darkening. His gaze lingered on her mouth and her lips flickered from plump human skin, to fibrous strips of dying flesh.

"Friend, I-I haven't..." he trailed off.

"I've got you," Friend purred. "Close your eyes, I'll show you what to do."

The demon tucked her finger under Jay's chin, dragging him closer across the wooden counter. With a pinch of her own magic, she fixed her lipstick in place so it wouldn't smudge. Friend balanced on her toes to meet him and was thankful she had decided to wear platform heels.

Their lips eased together in an unhurried meeting and rested there, on the precipice of ecstasy, each ready but not yet wanting to tumble further. It was a beautiful torment and neither wished to experience the end.

From far within, she heard the reaper's power rumble in deep satisfaction. As a reaper, they had never felt the desire to even try to kiss, though Friend had wanted to. Loud purring reverberated from her chest. Her lips were soft, pliant, and she knew he was enjoying the sensation. When she pressed her lips harder into his, he echoed her enthusiasm.

Friend would not let herself stop. It was not in her nature to be wary or accommodating. She needed more of him, deserved more for all that stupid pining she had done and even the few tears she wouldn't admit to shedding even under pain of torture. She grazed her tongue along the seam of his lips and smiled as he drew back, eyes opening wide in shock. For just a moment, Friend thought she had lost him and anger began to boil low in her stomach, warring with the desire already simmering there. Much to her delight, the reaper instead cupped his hands on her cheeks and pulled her back to him.

"Teach me," he demanded in a husky growl before their lips met once more.

Friend shivered at his low voice coated in a thick wash of need. She would give everything to him if he asked like that.

This time, he darted out his tongue experimentally and Friend was delighted that it wasn't a shy movement, but a bold sweeping gesture that belied confidence behind the inexperience. She opened her lips and coaxed him to do the same and as they deepened the kiss into something passionate and raw, Friend showed him the steps he followed and mastered.

When they broke for air, Jay was panting and Friend's dress had bunched from where it rubbed up against the ticket booth counter.

"You still need the information," she said with a grin. Her smile grew as she watched a genuine blush creep up Jay's cheeks. Friend leaned forward once more and pecked Jay on the lips, lest she get lost in another deep kiss. She pushed the information into him through the kiss with an electric jolt but was given a shock of her own in return. She pulled away, uncertainty filling her gaze.

"You have too much power." Her voice was low with frightened awe, her pupils had dilated so much her eyes were almost black.

"What did you taste?"

"The real question is, what did you?" Friend darted her arms out to hook behind his neck and pull him close toward her again. With hands on either side of his face, she studied him.

"Human emotion?" she exclaimed in a harsh whisper, eyes wide. She pulled away and wiped her hands on her dress as if it were catching.

Jay stood clear of the ticket counter and the partition reappeared without warning, filling the air with the smell of hot glass. Friend gave him a heavy look.

"You did not. Oh, that's bad, even for you."

Jay looked down at himself. "What do you mean, 'bad'?"

Friend shook her head, her bun wavering with the motion. "What were you thinking?"

Jay scowled. "Tell me what you felt."

"You broke the barrier. That human body you're in comes with human emotions. You broke the separation between your reaper self and the humanity in that body. But something tells me you already knew that." Friend licked her lips in thought, looking Jay up and down with concern. She shook her head and grinned up at him, mischievous once more. "I don't think it can be undone. Does your big kahuna number Four know yet? And They can't be happy about what you did."

"They don't care," Jay sniffed. "And don't call Four that, it doesn't like it."

"Your emotions are too strong and your power is burning bright. Someone might see the flame." Friend shook her head at her poor reaper. This predicament with the human emotions was more than intriguing but she had to admit she was worried.

"It's good to see you again," Jay said after a moment in a gentle voice.

Friend turned away, a pink tinge to the apples of her cheeks. "Yes, yes," she said.

"Thank you for the information."

She turned to a pile of tickets needing shuffling. "Don't thank me," she said, her narrow, yellow-green eyes flicking up past him and down the hall. "Really, don't mention it."

"I won't."

She looked him up and down then. The reaper's shirt was well past ratty and his pants were caked in mud and grass.

"What happened to you?"

"Long story."

Friend grinned, "I'll bet. You can change it here. I give you permission."

Jay rubbed his hands together before taking a rocking stop back. "I have too much power," he stated with awe.

"That's what happens when you mess with human feelings. You start acting like one of them." Friend fiddled with one of her locs that had fallen from the tie at the back of her head.

The door to the den banged open.

"Don't say a word," Friend hissed at Jay between her teeth as a threesome of demons tumbled in through the front entrance, rowdy and laughing.

One of them pushed Jay aside and rested his elbows upon the counter. They were all dressed in expensive looking suits but the one smiling at Friend over the ticket counter seemed to be the leader. His suit was a deep indigo, almost black, and trimmed with a black leather piping on the lapels.

"My, what a pretty kitty," he said by way of greeting. His friends guffawed behind him. They looked like young, white human males, though Friend knew these weren't their true forms; they had found viable men to possess.

Demons preferred this more modern practice of corrupting souls by possession over the "long con, hands off" way of whispering in their ears or haunting a house to slowly drive the human insane, though that method was considered to be more traditional. With a possession, the demon could let the human go about his day, enhancing the ill will already in their hearts, and take over the body when they saw fit to have their own fun. It was faster, easier, and more entertaining.

The leader of this pack tossed Jay a demeaning look. "He bothering you?" he asked Friend.

"It's just a reaper. How many tickets?"

After a long look, the demon tore his eyes off Jay and turned back to Friend with an easy smile.

"Three. I'm paying today."

He put down heavy gold coins and something dark and small that tried to wriggle away. Friend collected the coins before darting a hand out to snatch at the escaping thing. Bending behind her counter, she deposited it into a container that was out of sight. One of the demons leaned in to try and peer down the front of Friend's dress while she was crouched. She stood up, startling the demon.

"If you like what you see I can take your sight," Friend said, raising a knuckle. She tapped on the glass and it vanished. Her smile was saccharine. "We could make the trade right now?"

The demon stood, eyes darting back to the trio waiting behind him. "What? I was just looking."

Friend's face darkened. "Don't forget your rank," she spat out, fury painting her words, face morphing into the bone structure of a feral cat with sunken eyes and rotting strips of flesh before flickering back to her human face.

"I...I..." the demon spluttered.

Friend darted a hand out and snatched at him, dragging him close with her hands, scratching deep into his cheeks. Red lines of blood appeared in the demon's face from where her nails dug into his flesh. Friend snarled, enunciating her words shaking with deep ferocity, "I own this den. And when you're here, I own you."

"I'm sorry," the demon whimpered. "I didn't know."

"Now you do." She released her grip on the demon and shoved him back, watching as he stumbled until he regained his footing, adjusting his suit. Blood trickled down his face and landed on the chest of his white shirt. He wiped at his face with his pocket square, smearing the blood around. His companions stood behind him as Friend doled out three tickets, keeping Jay in her sight through lowered lashes the whole time.

"Enjoy your show," said Friend with the sweetest of smiles, sliding the tickets through the small opening in the bottom of the now reappeared glass. The group of demons moved off toward the curtain, the last of whom threw a furtive glance at Jay before disappearing behind the fabric.

"That was impressive," Jay told her, soft admiration in his voice.

"Fix your clothing and leave," said Friend in an even tone.

"Right." Jay closed his eyes and placed his palms on his stomach, tips of his fingers touching at the center. A ruffle of clean, cool air fluffed at his ruined shirt and pants. When the fabric settled, the cloth was good as new, color restored and tears mended. "Thanks again."

"Be careful, reaper," Friend warned, refusing to lift her eyes from the tickets. "You are being watched."

EIGHTEEN

J AY WALKED INTO THE bank's cafe, searching for Sylvie. She was in a far corner, sitting in a leather chair glaring at anyone who came too close. She waved when she spotted him. "Did you get what you needed?"

"Yes."

"Good. Buy me some food."

"What?" Jay was taken aback.

"You dragged me out here and dumped me in a river and sank my car. I'm hungry, buy me lunch. Also, I lost my wallet in the Porsche."

His heart sank at the mention of the car, heavy guilt coloring his thoughts. Jay let his mind drift for a moment, trying to calculate how much overtime it would take him to buy her a new Porsche. In his wallet was only a handful of change. Abandoning the prospect of counting coins and small bills, he drew out a credit card from the damp interior.

"You have a credit card?" Sylvie asked, dubious.

He shook the plastic card at her until she took it and went to order at the counter. Jay slumped into the other chair across from Sylvie's and put his feet up on the low wooden table between the two.

Jay was exhausted. His body was beginning to stiffen and grow sore from all the walking earlier in the day. More than that, his mind felt weary as if it too had traveled for miles. Strange sensations drifted through him, thoughts mingled with feelings that were either new or had a new depth to them he wouldn't believe possible if not for his current experience. Worry was no longer a mild bunching at the back of his neck when he was fretting about work. Now, it was a rough anxiety over the safety of Janis and the confusion at her predicament.

It had all come from the graveyard when he reached for her. He would never forget that awful look in her eyes when she realized he was abandoning her to Tick. Jay felt ashamed.

Sylvie returned with two coffees and a line up of baked goods in crinkly paper pouches clutched close to her chest. He grabbed for a pouch, peeked inside, and pinched out a part of a cinnamon roll.

"So what now?"

Jay swallowed a bite of the pastry. "I can't tell you."

"You're too old for secrets."

He grabbed a paper napkin and crumpled it in his hand, wiping his fingers and extracting the rest of the cinnamon roll from the bag.

"It's silent information." He popped the pastry into his mouth and his eyes flew open in shock. "This is good," he said.

"It's okay, yeah," she halfway agreed as she made her way through a slice of lemon poppy cake.

Jay shook his head. "No, this is really good," he emphasized.

In truth, it was better than anything he had ever tasted. Somewhere in the back of his mind, some lingering part of the human that was once Jayan Mati, found comfort in this food. Jay ripped off another piece of the roll and stuffed it into his mouth where he held it for a moment before chewing, savoring the flavor and unique texture. Perhaps this is what Anat had meant all those times he had urged Jay to try more food besides his usual coffee and meal replacement bars.

Syvlie distracted him from his thoughts turning too poetic about a simple pastry. "So, it is a secret."

"No, well, it just has no words. The information can only be conveyed through a, um, a certain way."

She sipped at her coffee, clear brown eyes staring. "In what way?"

Jay stuffed his mouth full of the last bit of cinnamon roll. Chewing fast, he tried to think of a better answer than the truth. He swallowed the bite without coming up with anything.

"I would have to kiss you to tell you what I know." He wiped his mouth clean of sugar crumbs.

Sylvie sat back in her seat. "No, thanks."

Jay reached for a package of sweet potato chips from the table of cafe food. "It's just a transfer of facts, the act itself is not romantic."

"I don't want to talk about this. Eat and then we leave to find Janis." Sylvie disappeared behind her coffee.

Outside, Sylvie gestured for Jay to take point. Jay followed the directions Friend gave to his lips, the information stored in his head leading him on.

"We're close," he said over his shoulder. Then, he stopped.

Sylvie wasn't behind him. Panic swallowed Jay as he searched the crowd.

"Sylvie!" he cried out, frantic.

A large man with patchy, silver hair and a thick mustache stepped off the sidewalk to cross the street revealing Sylvie walking behind him, hidden by his girth. His breath rushed out of his lungs.

"I thought I lost you, too."

"I was behind you the whole time."

Jay felt his concern mount. "I can't keep you safe and find Janis, you have to stay near me."

"I never asked to be kept safe did I?" she yelled at him, causing passerby to turn and stare. "You were the one who came into my life and dragged me into all your shit without my permission!"

More than irritated, he stamped his foot, unable to help himself. People were watching them as they passed, curiosity clashing with their Southern politeness. Sweat trickled down his back and stained his fresh shirt, the cotton sticking to his skin. And there, on the nape of his neck, came again the tickling feeling of him being watched. Jay whirled, scanning the crowds. There was no one. Maybe the feeling was that he needed a cigarette. He didn't know. All the new human emotions were cluttering his mind. He spun back around to Sylvie and wiped at the sweat on his upper lip.

"Well, we're here now, like it or not, and I will take you back once I settle this matter and you will be safe but I need to keep you that way until then. That means staying close to me and not getting lost in a crowd."

"I wasn't lost," Sylvie grumbled.

Jay scoffed in vexation and the woman pursed her lips.

"Fine, I'm sorry."

"Proximity is for safety."

Sylvie gave a tight-lipped nod and the pair walked on.

It was a beautiful day, but the blueness of the sky and the crisp quality to the breeze were wasted on Jay. Sweat coated his body and his legs chaffed together through his pants. The map in his mind directed him down certain streets, connecting to narrow back alleys.

The smell of a city in summer winnowed into Jay's nose and he coughed at the heavy scent. Sylvie watched him in alarm. He waved her off. The pair walked for another minute before the taste of the summer air turned acrid in Jay's mouth, burning his tongue. He spat on the ground and wiped at his lips. They tingled with the growing sour taste and the information Friend gave to Jay came to the forefront of his mind.

"What are you doing?"

Sylvie moved out of the way of a mother with a baby stroller, joining Jay where he had stopped, off to the side at the mouth of an alley, peering down the back street. It was out of view of prying eyes and appeared wide enough to be able to fit a sports car. The memory of the kiss disappeared into the hot air, taking with it the trace of information but leaving behind the disgusting taste.

"This is it," he told Sylvie, touching the concrete walls. "This is where Janis ended up after jumping."

The woman circled around, looking up at the alley walls, doubtful.

"She must have lost control and dropped us in the river. It's impressive she got us as far as she did."

A scraping noise came from Sylvie's direction as she kicked at a discarded piece of sheet metal on the ground. "But she's not here now."

"No," Jay said, peeking behind a dumpster to make sure. "This is where we pick up her trail."

"Ghosts have a trail?"

"Most beings do." Jay closed his eyes, searching for his power.

Ghost? it asked.

Jay was still shocked to find such an immense well of power, it was almost back to how much he had as a reaper. Perturbed, Jay shook his head to clear it. He had no time to worry about himself.

"Yes, the ghost," he replied to his growing power.

He fixed his thoughts on Janis, on her smile, her thick, fluffy hair, her large green eyes, and knitted them together forming a shadow of a shadow. Holding his arms out to the side, he brought his hands together before him, pushing against an unseen pressure in the air. His task was difficult with him trying to hold back any extra power from slipping out and ruining his work. His power wanted to be released, wanted to charge out to be as it once was and Jay had to control it and was unused to the exercise. The closer his hands came and more sweat poured from his brow.

Done.

Jay's hands touched and he opened his eyes, breathing hard through his nose.

"There," he told Sylvie, panting. "Can you see it?"

Where Janis had been, a slight flicker of gold lingered in the air, like shifting sunlight behind closed eyelids. Sylvie shook her head.

"It's a soul trail, very faint, very difficult to see," Jay added.

"But you can see it?"

"Yes, and I made sure it will stay around long enough for us to follow it before it fades."

"Then, by all means," Sylvie gestured with one hand for Jay to take the lead.

Janis was alone.

She had imagined a nondescript alley before placing her hands on Jay's shoulders in Sylvies' Porsche. Something wide enough for a sports car to fit into, just like he said. She was there now, in a shaded alley with wet cardboard at one end and graffiti on cracked brick walls, but alone.

"Jay?" she called out, hopeful. "Sylvie?"

The dripping sound of water falling from an overflowing A/C tray in one of the windows above her plopped into a puddle on the paved ground.

"Anybody?"

Janis crouched and hugged her arms over her knees, making herself as small as possible. She studied the stitching on the toes of her cowboy boots and tried not to cry. She felt more hopeless now, in this moment, than she had when Jay first told her she was dead.

Dead.

She shook her head as if trying to clear the word from her mind. Despite everything that had happened, Janis still couldn't think of herself as dead. Logically, she knew she was deceased and now was a ghost, but she couldn't bring herself to keep that knowledge at the forefront of her mind. Each time she was reminded, it was a hot needle piercing through her.

Light shone bright at the end of the alley. It was the middle of the afternoon and people strolled or walked quickly by on the sidewalk. Couples, groups, people on their own, all striding past the alley mouth busy living. Janis approached the sidewalk cautiously, not because she was afraid someone would see her, but because it hurt too much to be reminded of being a person.

A tumble of kids around Janis' age walked past the alley, calling to each other and laughing loudly in the easy alacrity of adolescence. Janis froze, her eyes tracking the happy procession. One of the boys yelled out a joke to another at the front of the group and Janis found herself smiling along with the laughter. Two girls bent over a single phone, sharing secret moment. A third girl flipped and flicked her long, brown hair, trying to get the attention of a tall redheaded boy who was blushing under his freckles, refusing to meet the girl's eye. Before she could stop herself, Janis found herself following the party.

The chatter turned from friendly ribbing to a more serious debate about the most recent summer blockbuster and Janis listened intently to their opinions and critiques. It was a movie that had come out the previous Friday, on the day of the party where she was murdered. Janis had been looking forward to seeing the film after seeing the trailers for it constantly on TV the past week. In fact, she planned to go by herself that Saturday, a way to pass the time of her parents' absence. Now, she would never see the movie.

What a silly thing, she told herself as the upset of the missed opportunity rushed through her. It was just a movie, it didn't mean anything. Missing out on her life, missing her parents should feel worse than missing a two hour film. But, it didn't. For some reason, the pain felt equal. None of it was fair. From movies to her family, she had been denied it all.

The tone of the group's conversation shifted, snagging Janis' attention away from her morbid thoughts.

"It's not true, is it Owen?"

It was the brunette who asked the redheaded boy the question. He blushed further under her attention but nodded and addressed the whole group.

"My cousin Brady told me that his friend Susan from summer camp heard about a wild bear in the city."

A few of the boys guffawed and the girls bending over the phone looked up from the screen with disbelief etching their features.

"No way," one of the phone girls said, pocketing the device. "Bears don't come into cities."

Owen shook his head. "Not this one. And Susan said her older brother even saw it. They said it was all mutated or some shit. Like had weird, diseased skin."

"Bullshit," a boy with brown skin said, nudging his companion.

They collapsed into giggles.

"Yeah, I call bullshit, too," said the other phone girl, her arms crossed in front of her chest in a way that suggested she was trying to get the boy who spoke to notice the deep cut of her shirt collar.

"Believe what you want," Owen said with as much apathy as the four words could carry.

"I believe you," the brunette told him, placing a pale hand on his freckled arm.

He grinned and turned red at her touch.

Janis halted, allowing the group to walk on without her. That didn't sound right to her. Hesitating on the sidewalk, Janis wished Jay were with her. She could at least bug him until he gave her some semblance of an answer. Not a satisfying one, none of his answers were satisfying, but an answer nonetheless.

But she was alone.

Janis made up her mind. If she was alone and dead the best thing she could do for herself was to find Jay again. She wondered if the big idiot was looking for her right now, but she couldn't be sure. He wasn't the most trustworthy person.

"Not even a person at all," Janis snorted to herself, amused despite her circumstances.

She blinked a few times and cast about her surroundings. Jay had told her she could see past glamours. So far, that skill had been more terrifying than useful. But, true to form, what he *hadn't* told her was that she could also see the auras surrounding people and creatures and the trails these auras left behind. She made a mental note to chide him for it later.

Sparkling, golden light danced everywhere on the streets and sidewalks. Janis assumed that color marked humans. She peered through the glittering metallic color and tried to decipher different trails. There weren't many. The bright human auras hung suspended in the air. Beneath, slipping into the cracks and the potholes on the street and sidewalk, was a rust colored substance that looked too much like dried blood for Janis' comfort. Something about that particular trail clinging to the shadowed fractures in the concrete told her at a primal level to stay away.

Janis searched for another aura resembling a reaper stuffed into a human body but she couldn't see anything else besides the gold and the rust-red. She sat down at a bus stop bench and sighed. Remembering survival TV shows she had watched with her dad, Janis decided the best option for her was to stay put. As lost as she was, there was no reason to get even more lost. Jay would find her here. He had to.

An old Black man with a wooden cane and round frame sunglasses shuffled into the bus stop shelter and moved to sit on the bench where Janis was. She jumped to the other side of the bench, flickering in and out of view for a brief moment. Another few minutes passed before a bus arrived and left, without the man joining as a passenger. Janis glanced sidelong at the man when a second bus came and went without him moving.

He wore a nut brown suit with a black shirt and dusty black dress shoes. The clothing had seen better days, especially the hat he wore. It was woven from straw and looked homemade and anachronistic, as if it had been made in a different age. Every so often, he would reach into an inner pocket of his suit jacket and produce a small flask that flashed silver in the light of the sun that slowly crept lower in the sky. Janis shrugged at the strange behavior and dismissed her bench companion.

Boredom began to chafe against the logic of staying in one place. Janis tapped her foot, then experimented with pushing the toe of her boot into the concrete and back out as if the solid material was nothing more than a pool of water. She stood from the bench.

"This is ridiculous," she announced to no one.

"You're a long way from home, ghost," the old man at the end of the bench said in a raspy, accented voice.

With a squeak, Janis jumped a few feet to the left out of surprise. The old man capped the flask from his latest drink and tucked it back into the folds of his suit.

"Sit down, child. I'd like to chat a while."

He didn't have an aura that left a trail, at least, not one Janis could recognize. And, if he wanted to attack her, she reasoned, he would have done so by now. Feeling brave, she put a hand on her hip. "How do you know *this* isn't my home? I could be from here."

The man chuckled. "I recognize a fellow traveler when I see one."

"Yeah? Where are you from?"

"New Orleans," the man said, drawing out the word long and slow in his accent.

Janis hesitated, but when he wasn't forthcoming with any more information, she decided to sit like the man had asked. "Then what are you doing in Atlanta?"

The man pulled out a yellow candy from one of his pockets and undid the crinkly wrapper.

"Stretching my legs," he said before popping the sweet into his mouth.

He smiled at Janis who didn't return the expression. For some reason, she was afraid. Not in expectation of him doing something to her, but in a way of deep deference one feels around those of great importance and influence. He was dangerous, of this Janis was sure, but that danger was not directed at her. For now.

"Uh huh," said Janis. "So, what did you want to talk about?"

"Where are you headed, child?"

"I...I'm waiting for someone." She felt tongue-tied beneath his stare. She couldn't see past the dark lenses of his sunglasses. They had strange leather caps at the sides that hid the profile of his eyes from view.

"Interesting. And you're waiting here for them?"

"Well...um, yes?"

"Hmm..." he said, rolling the hard candy in his mouth. It knocked against his teeth. "I thought you were a traveler, like me."

"I couldn't—"

"Find the right trail?" he finished for her.

"Yes."

"At a bit of a crossroads?"

A soft warning rang in Janis' ears at this statement. She couldn't put her finger on it. It must have come from a story she read in school or a book read to her by her parents. Whatever it was, the warning told her not to talk to this stranger any longer.

"I think I should go," she said, standing from the bench again.

The old man nodded.

"Don't forget, Janis, you're the only person who has a say on how you get to live your life. And I'd follow the moss."

Already backing away, Janis tilted her head. She hadn't told him her name.

"Okay, thanks. I'll...I'll remember that. Thank you," she repeated herself before turning and hurrying away. When she dared to look back over her shoulder several moments later, the bus stop was empty and the old man was gone.

It took her another few moments to feel calm enough to stop walking and look around. She wasn't sure if she trusted the dangerous stranger, but she was curious enough to look for a trail of moss. It wasn't easy to find. It wasn't a trail like the other auras that collected into a continuous line. When she finally noticed it, it became hard to miss. Bits of moss clung to the outer edges of buildings in a haphazard pattern, like droplets of water splashed from a great height.

The sun began to set as she walked through the city following the splotches of moss. Janis darted around stores and restaurants and high-rises with empty rooms. The green and brown patches grew bigger as the night drew around the city and settled onto it. Lights began to twinkle on in the apartment buildings she passed. On the lower floors, she could see people moving about, making dinner or watching TV or talking and laughing with one another. It was all very normal. Janis felt her non-existent heart ache.

As she walked, Janis wondered at the stranger's words. What had he meant about living her own life? She'd never been in charge of her own life, not even when she was alive. She certainly didn't choose to die and now that she was a ghost, there was nothing she could do about it.

"Being the only one who gets a say on how to live my life," she scoffed, still mystified. She shook her head, annoyed that she couldn't figure it out. She passed another apartment building and paused. Through the gauzy linen curtains, she could just make out a man picking a little girl up from the couch and hugging her close.

"There's nothing more powerful than you, morrita," her father's voice echoed in her mind.

"Yeah right," she muttered to the memory.

Janis lowered her eyes from the view of the apartment and trudged on. She didn't feel powerful and she didn't feel in charge. The only thing she felt was hopeless.

The trail of moss bloomed into the largest patch yet around the next corner, settling into the mouth of an alley. Janis stopped when the ground became spongy and soft beneath her feet. Cautiously, Janis walked to the mouth and squinted into the darkness. None of those weird blob shapes she had seen during that night at the park were visible. She took another step and, when nothing happened, she relaxed.

"Jay?" she called out in a shaking whisper. The strange man at the bus stop had told her to follow the moss. He must have known it would lead her to someplace she needed to be for Jay to find her.

The ground vibrated. Janis frowned. That was odd. She peeked over the top of a nearby puddle and saw ripples run through the water as the ground shook again. Even without the years of movies preparing her for this moment, Janis knew it was a bad sign. She looked up from the puddle and let out a gasping scream.

Some sort of monster stood before her. It was a huge beast with strange, gray pebbled skin covered in a patchy, fuzzy layer of green that looked like mold. How anyone could mistake this hulking creature for a bear, even a mutated one, was beyond Janis. Small black eyes shifted as it studied her before letting out a chuffing roar and reaching out its oversized hands straight toward her.

As she walked, Janis wondered at Sylvie/Angel's words. What had he meant about living her own life? She'd never been in charge of her own

7

Night fell as Sylvie and Jay wandered through crowds of city dwellers, coming or going from dinner, making their way home from work or out to drink. Janis' trail grew thicker as they walked, building hope within Jay. If she had been taken far away by something the trail would be thinning, not growing stronger.

"Not much farther," Jay called back to Sylvie over his shoulder, excited.

She gave a thin smile. Dark circles hugged under her eyes and Jay made a promise to himself to find a place to sleep as soon as they found Janis.

The golden trail bloomed around the corner of a sleepy department store and he hurried to follow it, ducking off to the side in a narrow space between two large buildings. The trail ended in the shadows, light swallowed by the dark. Jay released the rest of his power and Janis' trail faded from sight. Sylvie caught up with him, doubt etched into her face. He held a finger to his lips, just in case.

"Here?" she whispered in question.

Noise came from the shadows. Sylvie clung to the side of the building, worried as the noise sounded again; a low, grating noise of stone rubbing against stone. As Jay's eyes adjusted to the darkness he saw the slope of a huge back of something emerging in the dim light. The thing was larger than a dumpster. Its back ended in a small head, the top of which was as tall as first floor windows in the nearby building.

"Janis?" Jay whispered into the narrow opening. The large thing moved, stiff muscles rotating under gray skin covered in a dark moss.

"Jay?" Sylvie hissed. "What is that?"

The creature straightened, listening with small, swiveling ears before shaking its head and returning to whatever entertainment held its focus. Jay waved a hand behind him for Sylvie to wait and started to sneak up on the big creature.

"Janis?" he said again, louder this time.

From around the body of the hulking figure a shrill voice answered. Jay halted in his progress when he heard the voice call out, "Tell this thing to leave me alone!"

"Janis!" Sylvie called in elation from her spot back toward the main street. The creature heard her. It shook itself and uttered a sound like a lowing cow crossed with a falling boulder.

Jay stumbled backward, recognizing the creature. "Oh, shit!"

"What?" Sylvie's voice had changed from happy relief back to uncertain fear.

"It's a troll." The stone being staggered to its feet.

Though still huge, this troll was small and stunted unlike its larger, and more violent brethren in northern climes. What this poor thing was doing this far south and in a city mystified Jay. He was getting tired of the feeling. Nothing was following the rules, nothing was as it should, and Jay had yet to find a reason why.

"Sylvie, quick, come here, it has to see us." He beckoned to the psychic without taking his eyes from the troll.

"Are you kidding?" she shouted. "No way in hell."

Jay turned and looked at her with a smile he couldn't hide, giddy that he had found Janis.

"Why are you smiling? Stop that."

"Trolls don't like humans. If it smells our bodies it will run off."

Gulping, Sylvie took a step forward, hesitating at first but walking faster with encouragement from Jay. The troll sniffed wetly, small hippo-like ears swiveling and tiny black eyes flicking about. When it caught the scent of Sylvie and Jay it stiffened and whined, shrinking back against the wall of the building, stone skin screaming as it rubbed up against the concrete. Janis appeared when the creature shifted its weight aside, the ghost looking no worse for wear aside from an angry expression and hands over her ears blocking out the grating noises from the troll.

Emboldened, Sylvie took another step toward the creature, walking past Jay.

"Go away!" she yelled up to it.

The thing hesitated until Sylvie raised her arms and waved them. The troll hauled its bulk to its feet and took off deeper into the alley at a stumbling run, a rocky landslide in the darkness.

Cold slammed into Jay.

"You found me," Janis said, her words muffled.

He lifted his arm to twist around and look at her, his heart warm with relief and happiness.

"Are you alright? What happened?"

The ghost released Jay and stood back, tugging down the hem of her skirt and smoothing out her shirt. "No idea. I thought we had all jumped together but when I opened my eyes, I was alone in the alley. That's when I went looking for you. Where did you guys end up?"

Janis smiled at Sylvie who was walking over.

"The Chattahoochee."

Janis' mouth dropped open, the grin gone from her face. "Does that mean your Porsche...?"

Sylvie patted the ghost's shoulder to dismiss the rest of her words.

"We're alive, we found each other. That's what matters." The words came out clipped.

Janis looked apologetic. "How did you guys get into the city?"

"Can we take this conversation off the street?" Jay told the two women, peering over his shoulder in the direction the troll fled.

Sylvie was glaring at Jay. "We walked."

"The whole way?" Janis stood aghast.

Jay broke into their conversation. "We need to leave before the troll comes back or worse."

"That's what it was? I couldn't jump away from it."

"After jumping all the way to Georgia with us in tow? I should think not. You won't be able to jump again for a few hours yet."

"Well, if I can't jump and we don't have a car, what do we do now?" Janis asked.

"We're going to speak to Rowan at Edge. It's a bar and he's a green thumb and he'll know how we can get this sorted out."

Standing in the humid night air, damp and foul with the smells of a muggy city, Jay allowed himself a cigarette. He inhaled a huge breath and let it out with a loud, smoky, sigh. He was exhausted. The lack of stamina he possessed as a human was perpetually aggravating. Reapers didn't grow tired just as ghosts didn't sleep. The first days on Earth as Delilah, the first body, she hadn't slept, not realizing she needed it. On the sixth day without sleep, she had collapsed on a street corner in downtown Johannesburg. She had awoken much later in a hospital bed.

Keeping a regular sleeping schedule after that hadn't been difficult, not when she learned to recognize exhaustion for what it was. Despite understanding the need, sleeping every day was an aggravating exercise. Even stopping to rest after any tiring activity was more than annoying. Now, his knees ached and his legs felt like liquid but he would have to push this mortal body a bit further before stopping to rest. Besides, he had a feeling he was about to get some real answers.

First, he had to make it to Edge.

NINETEEN

Tensith was more than unhappy. He had been banished from the Hill without the proper judicial proceedings and he was no closer to an answer for any of the questions swirling around his mind. It was also raining.

He had found his way back to Richmond after observing the reaper in the alley when a mountain troll had almost flattened him against the side of a concrete building as it rushed past. He had been doing as Friend suggested, scenting around the city looking for the reaper when he picked up the smell of troll instead. The creature had been young, underdeveloped, and frightened by being so far from home. Trolls were considered of substandard intelligence and, while magical, they had never been invited to make their home within either of the courts. Instead, they were left to backwater caves that held no appeal to curious spelunkers. They were reclusive and skittish creatures who avoided humans and many other creatures at any cost.

Tensith had revealed himself from the shadows to try and calm the beast when the wind had shifted. Peering down the narrow corridor, he saw the reaper. He could make out two other figures at the mouth of the alley, but the reaper was staring into the darkness, trying to discern Tensith's form. Friend's scent had also come to Tensith then, a latent aroma from the reaper's clothing. Well, that cleared him from needing to complete Friend's directive to find the reaper and send it to the den. He had given a small laugh when he realized part of the scent lingering from the demon was desire.

The concentration of the reaper was broken as his companions dragged him away. Tensith had debated revealing himself but there was no glory with the lone reaper and the girl who was already dead. What he wanted was the whole affair to be his alone to unravel before the courts, before his people. Then they would bow to him like they used to his mother. He would have their utmost respect. So instead, he had held himself still until the reaper left. Then he had turned his attention to the troll.

To find such a creature in an alley at the center of the city had Tensith mystified until he had seen the broken collar and leash. The broken remains of the restraints had been in a tattered mess near a rotted out dumpster with flaking rust. Much of the rust had been removed, leaving behind the raw metal edge. The troll had used the sharpened side of the dumpster to saw off his collar. Tensith had sniffed at the items and reared back.

Demons.

That had grabbed his interest. This particular troll was being kept as an exotic pet by whatever local demon had been struck by the fancy to do so.

It took a lot of power to subdue a troll. They were more trouble than they were worth. Being able to subjugate one denoted a lot of power. Not unusual for a demon, but they avoided having to work hard at anything they didn't need to. Tensith had pawed at the collar and the ruined leather flopped over, revealing fae runes of binding etched into the inside of the material. This troll had been a gift. Fae gold on demons, fae craft on a strange pet for a demon, Tensith's mind whirled. It was clear the fae and demons were working together. But in what capacity and for what purpose, he strained to comprehend.

Finding no more answers in the alley, Tensith had left Atlanta. He followed the trail of the ghost and the reaper in reverse for many miles all the way back to Virginia. No further clues came to him but he knew it paid to be thorough. He even went back to Maeren's park to sniff around, and let her know he had been banished, but all he got was a stale trail and an earful of admonishment from his worried sister.

Despite the torrential late summer rainstorm, he was now sniffing around the OCME trying to find a way into the building. The back door reeked of the reaper and cigarettes, even through the rain. Tensith sneezed more than a few times as he prodded around for an opening. The entire building was protected by mortal locks and cameras along with a magical barrier that smelled of the demigod living in the house close to Maeren's park.

As if summoned by thought alone, a sweeping sound of wings startled Tensith into releasing his fox glamour. He whirled on his two feet and stood before the exact being he had been avoiding. Thunder rolled in the distance.

"This building is shut," the demigod said. His wings of solid ink were splayed behind him in a display of dominance, contrasting with the stark white of his coat. The rain was beginning to darken the fabric.

Tensith bared his teeth. "I am looking for you, not to disturb this...place." He wasn't sure what mortals called such mortuary temples.

"What do you want, fox?"

"My name is Tensith and I come on behalf of the reaper," he said, sweeping into a shallow bow. The effect was lost a bit due to the water soaking him from head to toe. That partial-truth was enough to get the demigod to lower his wings. His glamour was one of an older mortal man, short and round but with strong arms and strong countenance. He had let his wings slip through the disguise in a show of force but they wavered and began to fade as Tensith spoke. At his breast was blue stitching and the fae sharpened his eyes to read the small words. "I believe he is in grave danger, Anat."

Anat glowered through the rain. "Your kind caused harm to a pair of witches not two days ago and yet you come skulking around here talking of a reaper?"

"I am not my kin," Tensith protested, wiping water from his brow. The acrid taste of contaminated city rain coated his tongue. "I have been banished from the Hill for trying to find the truth."

"Speak, fox, and fast," Anat warned. The demigod's arms remained crossed but his wings had faded to be hidden by his glamour once more.

"I know you are aware of the sheefrah that travels with the reaper. I bargained with her parents sixteen years ago and yet she died early and without a ferryman to attend her. The council knows that sheefrahs are being snuck into our deals but they are hiding something bigger, something worse than breaking the law and creating sheefrahs again. Right now, they are after the reaper and they want the girl to tie up loose ends."

The demigod regarded the fae as thunder rolled in the distance and rain soaked through his clothing.

"Why are you making this my problem?"

Tensith bristled. "I should think it is all our problems. Dying reapers, ferrymen missing souls, and demons hoarding fae gold. Something is not right. You have seen such troubles," he said, pouncing on the flicker of recognition he had seen in Anat's eyes.

The rain pounded onto the pavement of the parking lot between them. Anat's brows were furrowed against the downpour.

"I have seen nothing," he maintained.

"That is not true," Tensith argued. He had seen the depths in Anat's eyes and seen the doubt that flickered there. "I know it is not true."

"Fae, I don't know you. I don't trust you, and I won't betray my standing by divulging secrets to you."

"Our kinds used to be allies at one point," Tensith groused.

"That was a different time, fox. One you weren't even alive to experience."

Looking skyward for patience, Tensith shook himself, flinging water from his fur.

"Can I not persuade you at all, demigod? Let us find shelter and I can tell you more of what I know, so that you may trust me."

As if on cue, the distant thunder rumbled again, louder this time as the storm moved closer.

"How is my cousin?"

"The reaper is well. The ghost too. They are in Atlanta."

"Why there?" Anat asked, startled.

"There is a demon there that is...occasionally helpful. They were supposed to connect, I believe."

As if waiting for this precise moment, harsh laughter came from the trees lining the back of the parking lot.

"You were followed?" Anat snapped a glance at Tensith.

Tensith drew his glamour around himself, shifting into a fox. *Not that*

I was aware.

"What do they want?"

To tear us apart. This will not be pleasant.

The demigod shed his white lab coat and left it on the stairs at the back of the brick building. Stretching his neck, he released his glamour and became an olive skinned warrior of old. Wings of shining solid black stretched out behind him.

"I will not wait until they come. I meet my enemies head on."

He strode off across the pavement, avoiding cars and vans, heading toward the field at the parking lot's edge. Shaking himself in the rain, Tensith followed.

We will meet them together, he said when he caught up to the demigod's long strides.

"So be it. What weapons will they have?"

Knives, swords, pikes, anything sharp and dangerous.

"Wonderful," Anat muttered.

Do not worry, demigod. I have some tricks up my sleeve.

Tensith shook himself again, not to rid his fur of the rain, but to begin the shift. His whole body shuddered as he accessed the magic laced into his very veins. Letting loose a snarling screech, Tensith's body rippled and began to swell. His dark muzzle lengthened and snapped at the air as it grew, canines lengthening to the size of a man's forearms. The scent of embers at the end of a dying fire blew around them and in a green flash, Tensith was a new creature. Now the size of one of the sedans in the parking lot, the fox was huge and hulking. Thick ropes of muscles bunched beneath his fur as he walked. Behind him and waving as if to fan the air, were several thick tails of deepest red and black.

"You are a nine-tails?" There was awe in Anat's voice.

Not as majestic as my mother's kitsune ancestors but yes, I can be one when I wish.

"Allow me to follow suit," Anat said, and reached into a pocket of Sideways. Out came a long wooden spear, far taller than him and made so to extend his reach. It was tipped in a flat spade of iron as long as his forearm. "Normally, I would prefer to use my bronze weapons, but when dealing with the fae, one has to be practical."

Agreed, Tensith said through bared teeth.

Armor materialized on Anat's body; an iron breastplate lined with linen and iron greaves to guard his shins. A light but strong circular wooden shield ringed with iron appeared on his left arm as his right fist enclosed a double-edged short sword. A leather scabbard settled upon his hips.

Not bad, Tensith said at his comrade's visage, the picture of ancient might.

Anat nodded once and when he righted his head, it was clad in an iron helm. "We do this right or not at all."

The pair entered the line of trees in tandem, wet pine needles and decaying leaves squelching beneath Anat's sandaled feet and Tensith's oversized paws. Beneath the light canopy of trees, the rain lessened a bit, though everything still smelled musty and damp. In a clearing past the bramble, stood a fae troop of elven warriors, the elite of fae fighters. Elves were strong and quick, predisposed to fighting in defense of their kind. Tensith counted their enemies with a hardening heart. There were over thirty of them.

The soldiers were clad in matching Western medieval style armor made from calcified wood. The effect was stunning, Tensith had to admit, as the minerals running through the wood shone even beneath the rain coating their surface. At the seams of the harder plates of armor, their green and gold skin was covered by interlocking pieces of hardened leather.

One of the elves standing next to a flag bearer stepped forward. He removed his helmet revealing long silky black hair and sallow, milky green skin. He inclined his head in the shallowest of nods to Tensith. He ignored Anat outright.

"We have come to remedy a mistake," the elf announced.

Gloven, Tensith said with a growl. *You rarely leave the Hill these days.*

The elf named Gloven smirked. "I am an instrument of the council. Their will is mine. As such, I go where they wish."

The rest of the soldiers' armor and weapons creaked as they adjusted their stances, uncomfortable with the rain soaking through the joints in their protective coverings. Tensith noted he had been correct, all the warriors were armed with swords at their hips and other melee weapons useful for close-quarter combat.

No laws have been broken here, Tensith said. *Your services are not required.*

"Then why are you dressed for battle?" Gloven taunted, gesturing to Tensith's expanded form. He then acknowledged Anat. "And you are keeping odd company, are you not?"

"I keep my own company, elf," Anat said in a low voice, inky wings flaring. A few of the elves took a step back at the movement. "We do not want this fight."

"Again, it seems as if your attire betrays your true intentions."

Tensith snapped his jaws. *Leave this place and go in peace.*

"Our orders are sound. We must cut the infection out before it spreads." Gloven's gaze flicked to Anat. "You too, demigod."

Before Tensith or Anat could react, the elves charged with their weapons raised and battle cries on their lips. Anat flapped his wings and used the force of the wind to knock over two elves who reached him first. Hovering in mid air, he soared over the first line of soldiers and landed behind the squadron, brandishing his spear in challenge.

Tensith broke left and dodged the oncoming elves with the easy grace of a predator. At his size, a single swipe of his paw brought several challengers to their knees. His claws caught at their armor, the tips catching just beneath a seam and ripping it free. The elves screamed their pain as the slashes revealed dark, sap-like blood.

"Get up, you worthless maggots. Defend yourselves!" Gloven had dropped his helmet at some point and was red-faced as he screamed orders to his soldiers.

The distant storm had blown directly overhead. Rain lashed down on them all, the canopy of trees doing nothing to staunch the onslaught of water. Anat ripped his own helm from his head and threw it at an advancing elf. The metal hit her on the side of her own helmet and she went down with a shout, stunned. Thunder boomed, following a sharp crack of lightning that lit up the conflict in sharp relief. Tensith twisted, his tails fanning out in a half circle before he snapped them down in a violent wave. A burst of energy caused the nearest elves to launch in the air as if they had stepped on a landmine.

For a moment, it felt like they were winning. Anat speared an elf through a soft spot in his armor and turned to face the next opponent. Tensith ripped at the soldiers with his claws and down they fell, dark blood staining the ground where rainwater had pooled within their footprints, the water cloudy with the substance. Gloven brandished his sword at Anat who descended upon him from the air, wings spread at his back.

"You are nothing," the elf seethed. "A forgotten relic."

Anat landed hard on his feet, spear at the ready.

"I have been death for many," he said as he circled Gloven, keeping an eye out for other elves willing to charge him while distracted. "I will be yours, too."

Anat lunged and Gloven parried, the speed of the elves revealed in the movements. Spinning on a single foot, Gloven slashed at Anat's spear and cut through the wood with a blade of fae forged steel. The staff splintered and the flat iron spade spun away into the darkness at the force of the cut, disappearing under the bramble. Tossing away the broken staff, Anat unsheathed his sword, the iron point illuminated by another flash of lighting. He slashed at Gloven, the elf meeting his strike with his own sword, the metals clanging but the noise lost to the wind now howling through the trees. The storm was picking up.

"Fox!" Anat called, swiveling and unbalanced on the pulpy forest floor.

Gloven managed to slide his weapon free and jab through Anat's shoulder, puncturing his wing. Anat bellowed in pain as the elf yanked the sword out of the wound. Tensith leapt over a line of fae and rushed to the demigod, nine tails thrashing to keep his balance. His fur was dark with blood, both elven and his own from the many cuts across his back. Anat sagged against Tensith's rump, the two keeping an eye on the remaining elves who had formed a loose ring around the two.

More come, demigod, Tensith panted. *The blood calls.* As soon as he said the words, two more troops of elven warriors materialized between the wet trees.

"Then we are lost," Anat said.

Not yet. We fight for something greater. Allow that to give you strength.

"I have strength left," Anat protested. "Just nothing else. Fight with me, fox, and we'll be able to hold them off."

Together they launched forward, dividing what remained of Gloven's troupe. The elf leader screamed to the new soldiers to join the fray. Anat battled four elves at a time, wings working hard to keep him balanced as the spun on the balls of his feet, parrying and stabbing out his weapon. Tensith was all teeth and claws as he withstood the advances of the rest. He and the demigod found themselves back to back once more as the fae watching from the trees rushed to join the fight.

"Not long now!" Anat cried out as he sank his sword into the side of an elf. She screamed through a thunder clap and collapsed to the ground. Across the clearing, Gloven picked up a discarded bow. Tensith barked a warning before a rogue arrow whistled through the air and embedded itself into Anat's side.

Hold, demigod, Tensith encouraged Anat as he grunted and ripped the arrow from his muscle. *Your time is through,* Tensith told Gloven and he ripped through his armor and chest with a quick swipe of his paw.

"There will be no justice for you!" Gloven screeched from where he sagged against a tree. A gash ran from the elf's chin to his stomach and was not shallow. He cupped both hands around his belly. "You have betrayed the Hill!"

I seek to save it! Tensith snarled. Gloven did nothing but slump over, dead. More soldiers rushed toward them, a never-ending stream. Tensith's paws stumbled over several bodies of fallen elves and the fresh warriors seized the opportunity to grab him. There were too many. Other elves grabbed Anat's injured wing and forced him to the wet ground. Anat spat out the mud but could not move from his position.

"Fox!" he called out for help but Tensith was surrounded in his own right.

"Stay still, you insect," an elf with his knees pushed into Anat's back crooned. Anat thrashed, wings pumping in a fruitless effort. Two more soldiers fell upon him and cut through the leather straps securing his armor. They ripped it away with a noise of disgust at the iron metal.

Anat! Tensith yelled.

"Shoo fly," the same elf said before hacking at Anat's wings.

Tensith shifted on the ground, his claws digging deep into the mud to find purchase to leap for where Anat was. Lightning flashed, drowning the world in a moment of pure, white light. In another breath, the wings were cut from the demigod's back. Sound crashed around the forest as thunder rolled and Anat screamed with agony.

Something built within Tensith, a foreign sensation he had never experienced. It gathered in his tails and they grew heavy, drooping and dragging on the forest floor. Mud and blood was everywhere and he limped from a spear that was stuck in his front leg. Anat's horrible cries echoed around Tensith as his tails grew even heavier. The urge to flick away the weight came to his thoughts and he choked on a breath. His ancestors had such a power but he never thought it had come to him. In all his testing of his nine-tails form, he had never been in a situation such as this, his life or other's had never been in danger during training. He vaulted over a line of elves and crashed into the soldiers holding Anat to the ground. He snapped his jaws around them and tore at their flesh. The fae drew closer to the demigod and the fox, recovering from their surprise at Tensith's sudden move. Tensith stood over Anat, teeth bared at the advancing soldiers. Instinct took over and he raised his tails as one.

One of the elves was smart enough to recognize what was about to happen. "Retreat!" she cried to the others. "Fall back!"

But it was too late.

The gathered power within his tails was unleashed upon them all when Tensith slammed all nine to the ground with a bray of fury. A blast of energy radiated outward and flung the elves into the air. Lightning flashed and in the brief flare, everything appeared suspended in time. Another wave of power undulated from Tensith and when the lightning dimmed, the fae disintegrated into nothing more than dust that was washed away by the falling rain.

Tensith's body spasmed. He felt empty, depleted, and his eyelids drooped as his form shrank to become the size of a fox one more.

In another breath, Tensith collapsed next to Anat and slipped into unconsciousness.

Miles away, in a park filled with dogwood trees, Maeren felt her brother fall and keened her heartache.

TWENTY

"**D**O YOU HAVE SOMETHING against taxis?" Janis asked as Jay let a fourth one drive by, horn honking in unanswered question.

Jay flicked his finished cigarette into a street gutter.

"I wish to go into Sideways," he stated. Silence greeted his plea and he could hear the sounds of Janis and Sylvie fidgeting as they waited for something to happen.

"I don't think it's working," Janis stated flatly. "Raise your arm."

A horn sounded in the distance. The noise startled them all, the note lingering on, worming its way deep into the mind and reverberating there until it turned flat and sour. Jaundiced headlights grew fat and round as the strange car approached.

"What is that?" Sylvie whispered at the vehicle pulled up beside the trio.

What stood before them was styled as a turn of the century carriage car, with the wheels operating on a system closer to a steam engine train than an automobile. The facade of the vehicle was made in the skin of what could be a boar and completely covered in coarse, dark brown hair. At the front, near where a grill would be, a piggish snout snuffled wetly, picking its way through traffic by smell rather than by sight of a driver. Tinted completely black, the windows stared and Janis and Sylvie dropped their eyes awkwardly. One of the headlights went out and back on as the car winked at Jay.

"This is a wild taxi. It will take us into Sideways as I can't bring you both with me on my own right now."

A back door materialized on the side and popped open in front of Sylvie.

She shook her head. "I'm not getting in first."

Jay stepped around her and slid into the taxi, putting the feeling of the seats out of his mind. They were made of dark leather, but the material was warm to the touch and moved, adapting to the weight of its passengers. Janis climbed in next, looking around at the interior of the car in interest. As a ghost, she did not feel the strangeness of the seats. Sylvie entered and sat, the tension in her face obvious as she clenched her teeth tightly together in her discomfort.

"We're going to Edge, please," Jay instructed the empty space before the seats. The inside was smaller than it looked to be from the outside with room for only one row of seats. Where a fiberglass barrier would normally be in taxis humans drove was nothing but a wall of darkness, giving the impression of a black hole. The effect was nauseating if stared at too long. The empty air absorbed Jay's words and the taxi jolted forward.

Sylvie yelped and grabbed onto Janis who shook the other woman off of her solid arm.

"What was that?" exclaimed Sylvie, now desperately holding onto the side door handle of the car and sliding down in her seat. She felt as if her insides were moving faster than her body sitting in the strange vehicle was.

"We're moving into Sideways. If your ears get clogged, open your mouth and move your jaw around. It helps," Jay instructed. He felt giddy. He was entering Sideways with human emotions and they were getting the better of him. There was always a sense of homecoming and belonging when he went to Sideways before but now Jay felt the overwhelming senses of relief and comfort.

"What's wrong with you?" Janis whispered to Jay, trying to keep Sylvie out of the conversation. The woman was on the verge of a panic attack and Janis didn't want to alarm her further.

Jay spoke to the ghost through a wide smile. "I don't know. I feel like I'm coming home after a long trip."

Janis considered his expression. "Yeah, an acid trip. Calm down."

"I can't. The feelings are too strong. Do mortals always feel this when you return to a place you like after a while?"

"I wouldn't know, but sure." Janis glanced at Sylvie who was holding the knot on her necklace and praying under her breath. Janis had only traveled into Sideways with Jay but she empathized with the woman; her own trip to this place had been more than frightening.

"Are we there yet?" Janis asked Jay out of the corner of her mouth. "She's not doing so well."

Jay looked over Janis to see Sylvie with her eyes closed, necklace between her palms. Before he could say anything, all three of them jerked forward as the wild taxi came to an abrupt stop.

The door sprang open and Sylvie was the first to leap out, her whole body giving a shudder as she turned her back on the wild taxi. Janis slid over to exit without rushing, watching Jay stick his hand into the black void and pull it out again, rubbing his wrist.

"Go on," he nudged the ghost gently. The fare was a week added onto his human life, a small sum to pay in the face of his five hundred year sentence. The new week still hurt as the contract burned onto Jay's bones was updated, the markings within his body shifting to accommodate the new addendum. The stinging sensation passed quickly and Jay thanked the wild taxi which just gave a wave of its door once Jay stood outside on the pavement and drove off with a loud snort, fading into thin air.

The night was cool and pleasant in Sideways, unlike the Atlanta it mimicked, this place never grew too hot or too cool. The pale moon at zenith above them was watery, as if seen through a film. The air smelled of rosemary and summer rain on concrete and there was a faint sound of an ever blowing wind whistling in the background. Jay surveyed his surroundings and wondered why it wasn't more crowded. Sideways was the primary residence for most paranormal beings who were no longer welcome on the human plane or who were unable to find a small, undisturbed corner to call their own. This place, Edge, a bar for those living on the fringes should have been abuzz with activity, hosting things of Jay's ilk and otherwise. Jay took note and added this matter to his running mental list of things that troubled him.

A sound of retching came to Jay's ears and he saw Sylvie bent over retching with Janis holding her hair back. The ghost was uttering soothing words and using her other hand to pat the woman's back. He turned away, wanting to afford Sylvie privacy.

"It's okay," he heard the ghost say. "Everyone throws up sometimes."

The city in Sideways didn't look like any city in the human world, rather all of them pushed together. Buildings were built as if vying for space, newer structures built on top of or in between older ones, their materials varying wildly from traditional brick, wood, and stone, to sleek buildings made entirely of steel or concrete, to ones covered in flower wallpaper or bed linens. Snatches of different places came through on the street where they stood. Two large skyscrapers stood before them with a low, brick and wood bar spanning the distance between them. A laser-cut metal sign screwed into the brick wall of the building directly in front of the small group read "EDGE" in capital, stencil-shaped letters. The door was black with a silver knob in the exact center, making it seem trendier than Jay knew the inside looked. Sylvie stumbled up to stand next to Jay, wiping at her eyes.

"Where did you take me?"

"I didn't, the wild taxi did. We're in Sideways."

"Where is everybody?"

"I don't know."

Sylvie shivered.

"We're going in there?" Janis asked, interest piqued.

Jay supposed he didn't have time for a cigarette. "I don't know what's going to be in there. If you stay near me, it shouldn't be a problem. Edge is supposed to be neutral territory, but I'm not sure about anything right now. Follow me."

Janis and Sylvie exchanged a frown as Jay started up the short wooden steps and forced the sticky door open with his shoulder. The smell of mildew and stale beer engulfed them in a pungent welcome.

The dim, dusty white lights above the free-standing rectangular bar at the center of the room illuminated a handful of patrons. Directly across from the entrance sat two figures with skin made from the space between dusk and nightfall. A lone golem huddled at a table behind the pair of star-beings. Jay wasn't totally sure, not with one of the four large support beams built into the corners of the bar blocking his perspective, but sitting in the far corner was a figure that looked suspiciously like Bastet. Jay was fond of the goddess and wished he had time for a greeting or a short visit. Tending bar was a pale dhampir, standing in the space behind the counter, leaning up against one of the round corner pillars, idly picking at her nails.

A jukebox played softly from a corner and the worn wood beneath their feet was sticky with a patina of spilled drinks and other liquids from over the decades. Inside, the architecture was an amalgamation of styles from across the years, from saloon to speakeasy to modern corporate bar, the walls changed in material every few feet and the rest of the space was put together in a patchwork of chairs and tables and decor from various periods of the bar's life.

"We're here to see Rowan. Where is he?" Jay leaned an elbow on the surface of the bar. He felt Sylvie and Janis come up to stand on either side of him, following his instructions to stay close. Janis ran a finger over the wood grain of the bar and flicked a stray peanut onto the floor.

The part vampire did not look up from her cuticle care. "He retired."

Jay straightened, shocked. "I didn't know."

"There was a memo." The dhampir flicked away a bit of skin, finally raising her eyes to see to whom she was speaking. Her eyes went wide when she saw Jay. "I guess you wouldn't have gotten it."

"I guess." Jay studied the dhampir, scorn upon his face. The legacy of the extinct vampires lived on in their strange half-human progeny. It was more like quarter and eighth by this point, the human bloodlines diluting the race, but they still were able to digest blood and many of them craved it as strongly as their ancestors had. The neutrality of the dhampir now had never sat well with Jay. What they did in the shadows was their own business but their questionable activities had long gone overlooked.

Jay felt unsteady on his feet, unsure of his next move. Rowan had been his only contact in Atlanta in touch with the roots of the world and the green thumb was gone. Sylvie and Janis looked up at him expectantly.

"Do you want something to drink?" asked the dhampir, sounding as if she'd rather go back to cleaning her nails.

"I can't drink," Janis said with a sad smile.

"You can consume other things, if you want." The dhampir's lips split into a slow, sinister smile.

"I can?" Janis looked to Jay for clarification but he was glowering at the dhampir.

"She's not thirsty," said Jay in a dangerously low voice. The half-vampire held up her hands in submission and left to check up on the star-beings at the opposite end of the bar.

Janis tugged on Jay's shirt sleeve. "What did she mean, 'consume'?"

Jay ran a hand through his hair that was in desperate need of a wash. "She meant drugs. Highly addictive ones like dead man's blood or ash tree powder. You'd forget who you were and then your brain would leak out of your ears as ectoplasm and you'd be trapped here forever."

Janis dropped her hand from his arm.

"If your friend isn't here," began Sylvie, "does that mean we're going home?"

Jay leaned his back against the bar, looking out at the front of Edge.

"Not..." he trailed off as he saw what sat at a table in the corner near the door, hidden in dim bar lighting. The hair on the back of his neck stood on end. It was an archangel. "...yet." Jay finished his sentence in a whoosh of breath.

"What is that?" Janis almost tripped over herself to hide behind Sylvie. Her ghostly form flickered with fear. Jay cleared his sight to peer behind the glamour to see what Janis saw.

Countless overlapping, concentric circular bands traveled in a steady rotation and orbited on unseen axes. Embedded into the rings were innumerable repeating organic holes that looked sunken into flesh. Many were black pockets of emptiness, but others held blank, staring eyes. Some were recognizable, a cat's eye, a goat's, some sort of reptile, and human ones, but they were all different. As the bands moved, they warped as if on some geometrically impossible path, and the eyes blinked in unison, controlled by the same intelligence.

The whole being floated in mid-air. In the middle of the gleaming rings of light, where the source of brightness originated, was a golden spinal column. Loose vines of a central circulatory system was still attached to the spine, golden veins and arteries dripping molten yellow metal. No drops of the stuff landed on the floor below the thing, instead, they abandoned gravity and joined with the bands, glittering like tears in the corners of the many eyes. Several pairs of wings sprouted from the nothing space next to the spine, all vying for a place to spread out fully to display pristine white feathers tipped in gold.

"Stay back," he told Janis who looked only too happy to comply. The ghost tugged at Sylvie to stand with her.

Holding his breath, Jay approached the small table. The archangel shifted. Heaving a massive sigh, he moved his wings slightly, allowing Jay to see his light blue-gray skin and the side of his face. He was wearing the traditional glamour of the mal'akim.

Raphael had never been to Edge before, not in all of his existence. His two massive, golden feathered wings sprouted out of his back and swooped up in a gentle curve to crest at the carpal joint. The top peaks of the folded wings stood high over his head, the height of them in their semi-tucked state about five feet taller than Jay's body. Several small and fluffy axillary feathers lay on the ground around him. Janis picked one up and pocketed it when she thought no one was looking.

The archangel's wings drooped heavily down the back of his chair and rested, partially unfurled, in a relaxed semi-circle around the table, creating a wall of wings around the archangel. His thirty-eight foot wingspan occluded the path toward his table and Sylvie and Jay had to pick their way around, giving the feathered appendages a wide berth. Raphael sat close to one corner of the bar, his secondary and primary flight feathers brushing up against the wooden walls. The tables and chairs nearest to him were in a jumble, either having been shoved aside or knocked over when he first entered and settled onto his chair. Jay righted one of the chairs, removing the obstacle from his path.

"Don't bother," Raphael spoke in a low voice, slurred with drink but still drenched in otherworldliness. His head was bent, head propped up by his right hand, his left clutched around a glass cup of dark amber liquid. As Jay grasped another chair and set it upright, Raphael moved his left wing, drawing the pinion back from its half extended position around his body and folding it completely behind his back. He moved it at a slithering pace, dragging his feathers along the dirty bar floor. Janis and Sylvie remained behind Jay, clumped together in nervousness

One wing tucked away, Jay saw Raphael in full and stared at the pitiful sight. The angel was wearing nothing except for a pair of black athletic shorts, the same favored by basketball players, and was barefoot. Though, glancing down at his disheveled appearance, Jay knew he wasn't looking much better. Jay cleared his throat to address him.

"Raphael," he used the archangel's most common name. "Your Lord keep your health."

Raphael snorted a laugh. Lifting up his left hand, the angel gave a toast. "I keep my own."

Raphael drank deeply from the glass, emptying it in a single swallow and following it with a belch. Looking over his shoulder, Jay saw Sylvie nodding for him to try again. Jay took a deep breath and used a different approach.

"Healer, Helper, will you not hear my plea?"

The archangel sat up fully at the words, wings sweeping open as his back straightened, causing Jay and then Sylvie to back quickly out of the way. Janis forgot too late she wasn't able to jump. Now that she was a fully formed ghost, the massive wing didn't pass through her. Instead, she was knocked to the ground and pinned. Yelping, the ghost wriggled helplessly under the weight. Raphael, in no hurry, let her struggle for several long moments before lifting the wing. Janis scrambled to her feet, rushing to stand beside Sylvie and adjusting her clothing, glaring at Raphael.

"That's an angel? People would be so disappointed," she spat.

"They aren't all like this. And they are never, ever, drunk," Jay said.

The rusty, metallic sound of Raphael's laughter followed Jay's words. Inebriation did not suit the angel, it pulled a veil over his handsome, androgynous face. A filmy cloud had formed over his piercing, violet gaze and the liquor had turned his luminous red-brown hair to a dull sheen of brown and gray. His usually healthy black fingernails were now a deep crimson, the color making Jay's stomach turn. The human invention, not healthy for the men and women of the earth, was especially poisonous to most immortals, their bodies taking much longer to metabolize the drink.

"Drop the formality, reaper. We're alone in this place and," Raphael dropped his voice to a dramatic, slurred stage whisper, "I promise I will not tell anyone."

He twitched his wrist, fingers passing over the top of his glass which refilled instantly. It was being siphoned off magically from other bottles at the bar where the dhampir noted each volume decent with a tick of a black marker upon the glass.

Jay shifted his weight from foot to foot. "Let the record show I tried."

The archangel inclined his head from behind his drink, a hum of bored agreement echoing at the bottom of the glass. Jay curled his hands into fists, frustrated.

"My brethren lay slain by a joint force of demons and corrupt fae and it must stop. Will you help us?"

"Why?" Raphael put down his glass and swirled a finger around the inside rim before licking the digit.

"Because it's wrong, because it's against the order of things. Raphael, surely you must see this."

The angel fixed Jay with a long, heavy stare. "I do see it and I don't care."

"You don't mean that."

"Did you ever stop and think that it is for the best? That it's happening for a reason?" Raphael took a gulp of the dark liquor.

Jay closed his mouth, aware that it was hanging open. "What are you doing here, Raphael?"

The angel ignored the question and jerked his head toward the jukebox. It started playing some country tune Jay did not recognize. Exasperated, he faced Sylvie and Janis with a heavy sadness upon his shoulders.

"Let's go."

Sylvie looked at Raphael. "But we didn't find anything out. He didn't help us at all."

"We're going," he said firmly. "Janis!"

The ghost jerked from where she stood, staring mesmerized at the angel's form and trotted to catch up.

"But..." Sylvie protested again.

Raphael stood up, knocking over his chair. His wings stretched to fill the space behind him, bowling over more tables and chairs. The tip of his left wing brushed up against the bar, knocking over containers with lime and lemon slices and causing the dhampir to stop cleaning her nails and glare. His wingspan was so large that even in Edge with more than enough space to house patrons of various sizes he was unable to extend his wings fully.

"Good to see you again, Your Grace." Raphael's words were directed at Sylvie.

The woman didn't acknowledge the greeting as she stood before the archangel's full earthly form, more than overwhelmed. Jay saw her stop breathing, the true nature of what Raphael was shorting out her neurons. Jay leapt to cover her eyes. Even while intoxicated, the body of the archangel at full power would be too much for a human.

"Raphael! You know better!" With Jay's hands protecting her eyes, Sylvie started to breathe again. "A human cannot bear such majesty!"

"That, reaper," he said in a gravelly voice, folding his wings away, "is no human."

Jay took his hands from Sylvie. She stared up at him in fear and confusion.

"Sylvie?" A green color bloomed in her irises before fading back to their regular brown color. "What?" Jay trailed off weakly. His mind felt like it had just hiccuped. Behind the bar the dhampir was laughing darkly.

"What's your problem?" Janis snapped at the part-vampire who answered only with a sinister smile. She mimed holding up a phone to her ear with one hand and then hanging it up on an invisible cradle.

"Click," the dhampir said, grinning and showing sharp teeth.

Jay's hearing faded into a ringing tone and his stomach fell to his toes. "No." His voice sounded like cotton had been stuffed into his throat. There was a shift in the room and the smell of wet moss floated in on some unseen breeze.

The star-beings had left and the golem cowered in the corner curled up in a clay ball. Bastet, if she ever had been there, was gone. Cold pressed against Jay as Janis huddled next to him.

"What's happening?"

"Sylvie, who are you? What's coming?" Jay grabbed Sylvie's shoulders with both hands and shook her, wanting to shake the dazed look off her face. Her gaze was unfocused, like she struck her head upon something hard. With slow, foggy movements, she reached up and grabbed for the iron knot at her neck.

"Sylvie, I am Sylvie..."

Her eyes were deep pools, inhuman. It was impossible. Jay shook her again, harder this time.

"Tell me!" he shouted, not caring if he caused her injury. It was his job to protect Janis and he was failing at it once again.

Janis tugged at Jay's elbow. "Stop it, Jay!"

Jay gave Sylvie another rough rattle. Raphael laughed and drained his drink, shifting his wings, feathers rippling. The archangel dropped his glass, body disappearing in a quiet flutter of feathers before the glass hit the surface of the table and shattered.

"Just Sylvie..." the woman muttered blankly.

One hand supporting the back of her neck, Jay pushed her bangs back from her forehead and squinted into her eyes.

"Tell me who you are!" he commanded, forcing power into his words. She released the Celtic knot, red marks remaining pressed into her palm.

Tell us who you are, his reaper power repeated.

Sylvie wrapped her hands around Jay's arms, nails scraping against his skin and pushing back with strength he was astonished to find she possessed. "I'm Sylvie Rachel Cottor, leave me alone!"

A rush of green light smacked into Jay's eyes. Purple spots bloomed in his vision and he released the woman, staggering backward and hitting the bar with a thump. The dhampir's laughter came close to his ear as she wrapped her arms around Jay and held him fast to the counter.

"Just Sylvie..." The woman fell to the ground in a faint.

Jay struggled against his captor.

"You have stepped in it now, reaper," the dhampir crooned, lips grazing his jawline and earlobe. Dread pooled into his gut. His gaze flicked back to Janis whose face was etched with fear.

"Jay?" the ghost asked, her voice quaking.

In the distance, Jay heard the peal of mischievous laughter and smelled wet, slippery forest leaves.

"They come," the dhampir whispered again.

"It's okay, Janis." Jay focused on the ghost, holding out a hand. Something inside his chest squeezed hard. The smell of damp and rotting leaves grew stronger.

"No," she said flatly. Janis' expression shifted at the tone of his voice.

"Oh, yes," the dhampir crooned. Jay writhed against her arms but she held fast, superhuman in her strength.

"I will come for you, I promise."

"No," Janis repeated, standing dumbfounded.

The squeezing sensation moved up to the back of Jay's throat, constricting his words. Tears pricked at his eyes. She was only a child. She deserved none of this.

"I found you before, remember? Back in the alley?"

Janis trembled.

"Remember?" he demanded an answer.

Janis barely squeaked out a yes.

"If I found you then, I'll find you now."

Harsh laughter filled the room with a loud, ringing echo, a wind rising up within the bar smelling of thick, overripe vegetation. Janis screamed, the sound filled with pain, as she grabbed at her stomach, doubling over from the invisible force now wrapping around her middle. Jay was helpless, trapped in the dhampir's preternaturally strong arms. Janis screamed again as the invisible force tugged her backward a few feet, her heels sliding across the wooden floor. She lifted her head with some difficulty to stare at Jay.

"I will find you again," he promised her. At those words, and to his great surprise, a tear slid down his cheek.

The wind rose to howl, kicking up dust and dirt from the bar floor.

"Jay!" Janis cried out as the force dragged her backward with increasing speed, pulling her fast toward the far wall. Before she collided with it, a dark green hole of empty space ringed with moss opened up on the wood and sucked Janis through. Deep green light bloomed from the portal as it closed with the sound of wood striking wood.

Janis was gone.

TWENTY-ONE

H ERE WAS ANOTHER NEW emotion.

Rage.

Jay felt it clench at the pit of his stomach, deep and hot. It waved through his body in fiery ripples, carrying his good sense with it. It felt good to let his mind go free, to let it wash away into the oblivion of wrath. It was almost calming. Jay's body stilled at the sensation and, with the portal closed, the dhampir released him from her vice grip.

Immediately, Jay turned, swiveling on his feet, using the momentum to punch the half-vampire hard on the cheek. Pain erupted on his knuckles and he shook out the hand, biting back a cry.

The dhampir fell to the ground clutching at her face. Jay pushed himself up onto the bar and swung his legs over, coming down hard on the other side and walking deliberately toward the part-vampire who scrambled away. The rage that filled him urged him to use his fists again. Grabbing at the front of her shirt he struck her face using a short, jabbing punch that broke her nose. The dhampir cried out as black blood gushed from her nostrils.

"Where did they take her?" Jay growled.

"It's not my fault," she whined.

"You made the call!" Jay yelled as he wound up his arm and hit her with the back of his hand.

"I'm not the one who took her away. Ow! Stop it!" Jay had hit her again. "What the fuck do you want with a ghost anyway? She is not yours, not in your state, she never was. Mind your own business and keep your head down."

He shook the dhampir who cried out in agony. "What do you know?

Tell me!" She regarded him in solemn discomfort, choosing her next words carefully. In her silence, Jay heard the cartilage in her nose resetting as it healed. "I will break your nose again," he warned when she did not speak fast enough for his liking.

"She was a deal! Her parents bargained for a baby and it looks like the time came for the debt to be paid."

"I know that already," Jay growled. "She's a sheefrah deal, so what?"

"That's all I know."

Jay let go of the dhampir, rocking back onto his heels. She scrambled farther away from Jay muttering profanities and gingerly touching her nose.

"It was standard. A sixteen year deal. People do it all the time, I don't know why you're so worked up about it. The contract is binding."

His head rose. "What did you say?"

The dhampir wiped at the blood under her nose. "That it's a contract, terms and conditions, all of it legal, above board. Reapers like that sort of thing."

"No, before that."

The dhampir sucked on her fingers, licking at her own blood, outer lips ringed in crusty black.

"Standard deal?" she suggested. "You get a baby for sixteen years and then they collect. Everyone knows that. Even that faerie with you knows that. Take it up with her kind, not with me."

The dread that had pooled into Jay's gut before spread outward in a cold wave of growing trepidation.

"She was fifteen," he whispered, staring at the floor, feeling dizzy. "It's not legal if she died before her sixteenth birthday."

"Hmm?" the dhampir hummed, distracted by the taste of her own blood.

Jay lifted his chin and glared.

"Janis Lyn Pereda was only fifteen."

The dhampir watched as he stood up, shaking with fury. Power flooded to the surface without him needing to call for it. Jay flexed all the muscles in his body. Wood exploded away from him with a loud crunching noise, creating a broken gap in the bar behind him. Glass bottles of alcohol shattered or tipped and fell to the ground, breaking open upon the floor and spilling out their pungent contents.

"It's just a ghost. One little soul no one cares about."

The cold feeling spread from his chest across his whole body. Turning swiftly, he grabbed a piece of jagged wood and threw it at the dhampir, the motion laced with his power. The crude stave shot through her neck and embedded itself deep into the wood at her back, severing head from body. The light went out from her eyes. The bones on her face and the front of her body collapsed inward, skin and muscle deteriorating into a brackish sludge that dripped off of broken peaks of molten fulvous bone.

Jay staggered under a heavy weight crashing down on him as twenty five more years were added to his sentence, the penalty for taking a life in his human form. Agony slammed into Jay, making him slip and come down hard on the ground, wood and glass slicing the palm he threw out for balance. Blood pooled beneath his hand and Jay cried out, not at the cut, but because the writing etched deep into his bones began to move.

The week added before by the wild taxi was small, a single book finding a place on a crowded bookshelf. Twenty five new years surged into him demanding space. They forced their way onto his bones, branding him inside with new marks. Jay trembled, sure he would break in two from the excruciating pain. At the culmination of the stabbing, throbbing torture, the binding chirography shifted and settled into place. Jay was left breathless and panting on the floor of the bar while the hot smell of his sizzling flesh curled into the air.

He opened his eyes onto the dead dhampir and his shoulders slumped with the weight of his mistake. As he remembered the fear in Janis's eyes, Jay knew he would gladly take a hundred more years if it would help him find her. Then, a hard knot of cold realization slammed into his gut and a wordless sob echoed out of his mouth.

He had taken a life.

With his emotions so new and volatile, the ramifications of what he did came rushing in all at once and Jay couldn't process them fast enough. Tears fell from his cheeks as he couldn't contain the frustration and rage. Killing the dhampir had been rash and regret flowed heavily into him next. Jay had been too focused on his emotions around Janis to stop himself and curb his rage. Breathing heavily, Jay sat back onto his heels.

"Is this what it's like?" he asked the air around him in a cracking voice. The dhampir's corpse reflected back to Jay the horror of his actions. "I'm sorry," he told her.

He felt as if there was a sea within him, an ocean of human feelings filling him and lapping around the space content with their new surroundings. Frustrated tears sprang to his eyes as he watched the rapidly decaying dhampir. It was unbearable, all of the emotions. He felt so tired, so human. Holding his injured hand to his chest, Jay struggled to his feet and walked to where Sylvie lay upon the floor, regarding the woman coolly. He nudged her calf with a foot.

"Wake up," he said.

A loud crash came from behind him and Jay whirled, readying for another fight. It was the golem, running at a clumsy gait toward the door. Jay's attention went back to Sylvie and he poked at her again, harder.

"Get up."

"What happened?" she asked, struggling to sit up. She clutched at her head with a groan. Blinking, she looked around the bar. "Where's Janis?"

"She's gone." Jay turned his head, throat tightening. He could feel tears start to gather again. He blinked rapidly.

Sylvie dropped her hands to her side, distress upon her face. "Gone? Who took her?"

Jay didn't want to explain. He shook his head, tucking his chin away from Sylvie so she wouldn't see him cry. He wanted to shout at her, at the only person around who would hear his cries of misery and confusion. Struggling to remain in control, he clenched his jaw and swallowed against the words of rage he wished he could violently expel. Calmly, he explained with a sniff, "You're not a psychic."

"What's going on?" She moved to stand, and the iron Celtic knot swung out from the neckline of her shirt and hung heavily on its chain, waving back and forth in small moments. The shine of it caught in the dim bar light and flashed, catching Jay's eye.

Despite his turmoil, a sense of detached calm settled around his body, stemming from the feeling of realization at the end of a long puzzle. *Iron-bound,* Jay thought with unfeeling interest. It was so obvious, how had he not guessed it before? He had walked in her mind and not detected anything amiss. The work done to Sylvie to hide her true nature was flawless. Jay was impressed in spite of himself.

"I think I have a concussion," Sylvie said, straightening from her bent-over position and oblivious to Jay's churning mind.

"Who took Janis?"

"Who...?" Her face was earnest and her confusion was plain on her face but Jay brushed this aside, too upset to spare her feelings. "Jay, I don't know."

"Who are you? From which part of the Hill do you hail?"

"Hill? What are you talking about?"

Jay thrust his injured fist out to the side, clipping the top of a nearby chair and sending it toppling over with a loud crash. Sylvie jumped, her eyes flicking toward the noise then back to Jay filled with trepidation as he yelled, "Raphael called you 'Your Grace', Janis' parents made a deal with the fae to bring her into this world, when I looked into your eyes before I did not see a human staring back at me! So, if you please, 'Your Grace', who are you?"

"Sylvie!" she shouted, her own anger rising, words filling the bar.

"That's not going to cut it!" Jay roared back. "Which Court? Seelie or Unseelie?"

"What are you talking about?" Her face was arranged in utter bewilderment.

"Seelie or Unseelie, damn you!" Jay screamed into her face. She began to cry. "Don't you dare! Tears of the fae are as false as they come!"

"I don't know what you're talking about!" Sylvie bawled, her voice choked with sobs. "Jay, I grew up in Missouri, in Springfield. There was a tree in my backyard and my mother died of a brain tumor when I was twelve. What the fuck do you want me to say? I'm telling you the truth! First you tell me I'm a psychic and then you say I'm something else, why don't you just stop trying to tell me who I am!"

Before Sylvie could control her impulse, she darted a fist out and punched Jay in the chest. The force wasn't great; the action was more shocking than painful. Jay rubbed his chest, surprise cutting through the width of his anger.

"I'm sorry," Sylvie said, chastened, holding the hand that had punched Jay with her other, covering the fingers in shame and twisting them nervously.

"I'm sorry," Jay echoed, feeling tired. His strong human emotions had run him hard and he felt used up. All that was left was exhaustion. He reached out to a nearby chair, groping until he clasped it in the fingers of his good hand, and pulled it towards him. Sitting down heavily, he kept his injury elevated, propping his elbow up on a nearby table. "I should have known. It was too easy to convince you to leave your home and come with us, to make you leave with two complete strangers. You feel no attachment to your human life. The memories you have, of the tree, of your mother, of your name, they're all false. They have been pressed into your mind so hard you believe them."

"I'm not Sylvie?" The end of her question cracked into a whisper.

"No."

Jay couldn't bring himself to look at her. Instead, he watched the gash on his palm slow in its bleeding to a slow ooze of congealed blood. The magic binding a reaper to a human body worked steadily to correct the non-fatal wound.

Sylvie grabbed a chair and dragged it across the floor, scraping the legs across the short distance to Jay's table. She plopped herself down on the seat, glowering at Jay. "I don't believe you."

"It doesn't matter."

Sylvie's frown deepened. She had been expecting more of an argument. The pent up energy expelled itself with her saying, "Oh."

Jay glanced around at the decimated bar, unaware of Sylvie's deflating. "There is nothing more for us in Atlanta."

"You're just going to sit here, then?"

"I don't know what else to do." There was a lump in his throat and, while he swallowed against it, his voice was still thick when he spoke. "I don't know what to do."

"What about Janis?"

"What about her?" Jay growled.

"I didn't do this," she said, voice soft but firm. "You cannot blame me for a people I don't even know, didn't know I belonged to." Sylvie cleared her throat. "That I don't belong to."

She was interrupted from speaking further by a deep hooting sound from outside Edge. The noise floated into the bar past the door, left ajar by the quickly egressing golem. It sounded again and sparked the urgency in Jay back to life. He crossed the bar to the door, peeking out, before beckoning Sylvie to join him.

"Our ride is here."

Perplexed, Sylvie stood and followed. Jay stood next to a wild taxi whose side door had just materialized in the side and popped open of its own accord.

"We didn't call you," he said, bent over to speak in through the open door. The whole car seemed to shrug and then the door gave a little wave, hinges squeaking, beckoning them inside.

Sylvie squinted at the vehicle. "How normal is it for those things to just drive by? Like, in your world."

They were both interrupted by the impatient honk of the wild taxi who waved its door again. The honk was followed by a hissing and crackling, ending in a pop, the noise of an old radio starting up. The scratching, whining sound of a dial searching for purchase with a nearby signal came next and breezed through the clamor of several stations — static, arguing voices, the snippet of a gospel song, then back to static — before settling on a voice that was familiar to Jay even with the diminished audio quality.

"...you hear me? Reaper! Can you hear me?" The voice of Anat wasn't a recording, it was streaming live from beyond where they were in Sideways, from all the way back in Virginia.

Jay stumbled and caught himself against the wild taxi, unnerved. "Anat?" He coughed to clear his throat, his voice had cracked and the word hadn't come out very loud.

Through warbling static, the voice of Anat spoke again. "Reaper...in trouble...after me." The poor connection cut through Anat's words. "...warning. Don't...Richmond."

"What?" Jay called out, straining to hear. A harsh electronic whine flared up and abruptly the message cut out, leaving the pair listening on the sidewalk next to the wild taxi in astonished silence. Jay recovered first. He poked his head inside the car door, speaking to the black wall that separated the passenger side from whatever it was on the other.

"Did he send you? Was it Anat?"

The taxi honked once affirmatively in response.

"Take us to Friend's den," Jay instructed the vehicle as he slid inside. When Sylvie didn't follow, Jay poked his head out from inside the car. "Get in, please? I need to help them."

Jay's voice was heavy with fatigue. The seats squished down, accommodating Sylvie's weight as she slid inside.

Inside the wild taxi was cool and quiet, allowing Jay to assemble his thoughts. He couldn't guess what was driving the fae to create sheefrahs and to trap them into faulty bargains that ended with a demon killing them before their time. The power found in any soul taken before their time was immense. Jay could only imagine the amount found in a human soul mixed with fae magic.

Jay looked over at Sylvie, now sleeping, head lolling forward on her chest. How had he missed that she was a faerie? All that iron in her, pinning her down, it should have been obvious. Sylvie sighed and muttered something in her sleep. Jay felt helpless. He needed to help Anat, to find Janis, and to stop the reaper killings. Jay wished They would tell him what to do. He raised his eyes upward.

"Why is this all happening?" he whispered to the fleshy ceiling of the wild taxi. Tears fell unbidden down his cheeks, waves of emotions taking over. Jay closed his eyes in helpless frustration.

A deep, whistling voice floated out from the dark space in front of the backseats.

"Do not give up hope."

Jay jerked his head down and stared openmouthed at the blackness. He had never heard a wild taxi speak before. No one had.

"I..." he stuttered.

The wild taxi interrupted with a sharp, rattling inhale. "The path you walk upon is true. Stay on it, reaper. There are those who watch and wish you well."

Stunned, Jay sat in silence as the car drove them out of Sideways and back to Atlanta. His head was a jumbled mess of thoughts and feelings. He thought he had grown used to them by now, the new sensations of shame and guilt. But there was another, stronger emotion lurking in the depths of him.

Jay blanched.

Sorrow.

He looked around the inside of the taxi, as if something would pop out and ridicule his thoughts. He was experiencing what he dared think would be beautiful all the way back in the Richmond morgue. Wretched anguish. How could he have ever thought this might be exquisite? It was awful.

The foul feeling crept up his spine with fingers of greasy frost, at once chastising him for his idiocy in breaking the barrier and filling him with blame and misery at the pain he caused the ghost. Janis was innocent in all this, that's what broke his heart the most. She was caught in the middle without any say. Ironically, Janis had just been in the wrong place at the wrong time, when she stumbled into him at the OCME. No one had chosen her as their opponent or to represent a larger group. Yet, here she was, singled out by the shadowy enemy for a crime she could not defend herself against.

The anguish climbed Jay's throat, pinching at the muscles there and demanding a physical reaction to the sorrow. A reaper full of regret. He knew, distinctly understood, that he would never be the same. For no reaper was ever made to hold an emotion this complex and survive it.

Early morning light peeked out over the top of the city. In the pre-dawn, no one was around to see the wild taxi stopped and idling outside a used bookstore. It came to Jay then that he had forgotten what day of the week it was. He kept staring at the dark void before him as he sat on the seats. They eventually rippled with impatience and a door popped open on the side. Shaking himself out of his thoughts, Jay extended his hand into the dark black for payment. Nothing happened. He jiggled his wrist. Something caught his hand then, a force holding onto him and giving the feeling like he was stuck in the sucking hose of a vacuum cleaner. It wasn't painful, just odd. In the black, something squeezed at his wrist and then released his hand. There was no sting of an added week settling into him, the vehicle hasn't asked for payment. Jay held his arm close to his chest, rubbing the skin.

"Right," he said, turning to pull at Sylvie, rousing her just enough from sleep so she could slide out of the cab and exit the vehicle. They stood, Sylvie leaning into the crook of Jay's shoulder with her head against his chest. Jay watched as the door closed and the wild taxi's engine rumbled as it pulled away, red taillights fading into the air.

TWENTY-TWO

J AY EXTRACTED HIMSELF FROM Sylvie with a shrug of his shoulders. The woman groaned in protest but stood on her own, detangling herself from Jay and rubbing her eyes with a huge yawn.

"What is this place? Have we been here before?" She gave a little shudder and turned to walk away, the den's glamour working.

Jay lunged out and grabbed her elbow, hauling her back before she got too far. He pulled her close and drew a hand down over her eyes, brushing across her skin with the side of his palm and smallest finger

"What the fuck are you doing?" Sylvie protested, trying to bend backwards away from his touch.

Jay dragged up the smallest amount of his power to push it over her eyes. "I'm trying to get you to see."

"I can already see, damn it!"

"To see properly," he amended. Keeping his hand parallel to the ground, Jay pushed at the air as it gathered beneath his hand, magic thickening and increasing in pressure as he drew the glamour away from her. He gave one final push and it dissipated. Jay removed his hand. "Sorry."

"Maybe if you didn't do so many stupid things you wouldn't have to apologize so much," Sylvie snapped. Then, she blinked, looking at the bookstore front of the demon den. "What was that?"

"Do you feel like you've left the stove on somewhere?"

She blinked several more times. "No."

Jay continued down the stairs realizing too late he wanted a cigarette. He pushed against the itch, he'd have to smoke one later, he promised himself. The humidity in the early morning was already oppressive and the clean shirt he had used his powers to acquire several hours earlier had already spoiled against the night's activities and the sweat that had started to roll off him. He grit his teeth against the sour feeling. He threw Sylvie a glance over his shoulder and watched as she hesitantly took the stairs. Jay reached out to open the door to the demon's den for a second time.

The putrid stink of the corruption hit them in a wave. Jay felt a sharp tugging on his arm as Sylvie clung to him as she doubled over, dry-heaving. Breathing through her nose, she stood, pale and shaky. "Oh my..." Jay cut her off with a hand over her mouth.

"Don't say that name in here. Don't even think it."

She jutted her chin out and Jay dropped his hand.

"I get it," she whispered. They walked forward together in the short hallway staying close together. "We're not going through that curtain are we?"

Sylvie nodded her head to indicate the black curtain with the red arrow painted on it at the end of the hall. The fabric waved lazily in and out to an unfelt wind and with each flap came the cloying smells of a dangerous kind of rot. They both tried to breathe through their noses but the evil in the place permeated in more ways than just smell. The air itself was heavy with fecund malevolence.

You are back, the darkness beyond the waving curtain exhaled to Jay. A shiver crawled down his spine and Jay tugged on Sylvie, moving her to his right so he stood between her and the curtain. The curtain uttered a disappointed sigh and music seeped out from beyond the fabric. It was a welcome change from the chorus of screaming children from the other day.

"I know that song," Sylvie said, head tilting. She scrunched up her face, listening. "Is that *Crossroad Blues*?"

The song by Robert Johnson filled the hall and Jay snorted at the self indulgence. The curtain waved in a way that suggested it shrugged.

"Tickets?" They were standing before the ticket booth built into the side of the hallway halfway down. Friend's face fell when she saw Jay, black-painted lips tugging downward. "Reaper," she said, bright, cat eyes flicking around, checking to see if they had company. "What are you doing back here?"

"We need to use the Quick."

Friend shook her head, locs whipping around. "No," she hissed. "I'll not compromise my position. Find another one."

"This is the only one for miles and you know it. Just let us use it." Jay failed to keep the desperation out of his voice. He had to get back to Anat, he had to find Janis. Friend was shaking her head again.

"No."

Jay felt a calm fury settle over him. Anat was his family, whether they acted it or not, they were beings of the same purpose. And Janis. It was his fault she was lost. He had brought her to the graveyard to face Tick and he had exposed her to the dangers in Edge. He promised he'd find her and he would, he had to. Jay leaned forward over the counter of the ticket booth, voice a low growl.

"Are you fucking kidding me, Friend? Have you just forgotten our history all of a sudden because I would be delighted to remind you and let everyone else in this disgusting place know what—"

"Friend?" A new voice oozed out from behind Jay and Sylvie, interrupting the proceedings. Jay stiffened and stood from his bent position over the counter, refusing to look around. Sylvie started to sneak a peek before Jay clamped a hand on the back of her neck, forcing her to keep her gaze forward. Squeaking in alarm, Sylvie's eyes were round from the small glance and her fists were clenched tight. "Friend, what is this?"

Lost for words, Jay stared at Friend whose eyes were as wide as Sylvie's. In a flash, Friend darted out a hand and knocked her knuckles against the glass in a square shape. When the material disappeared, Friend snatched at Sylvie's throat. With surprising strength, Friend dragged Sylvie up and over the partition, ignoring Sylvie's scrabbling hands. Once Sylvie's heels were clear of the counter, the glass returned.

"You brought me a little surprise," Friend purred, nothing but insidious intent etched upon her face. "And here I thought you didn't care." She ran a single finger down the side of Sylvie's face, which was turning red from lack of oxygen.

Playing along, Jay adopted what he thought was a relaxed stance. "A small token of good faith," he improvised. Sylvie's eyes rolled in their sockets as she stared at Jay.

Friend continued to pat Sylvie's face, dragging the woman close to her side while keeping a vice grip on her throat. Sylvie sputtered a coughing protest, words lost in the choke.

"Friend?" the voice behind Jay came again in question. The evil, grating voice dripped over them all, making even Friend shiver. The cat demon licked Sylvie's cheek and then smiled sweetly over Jay's shoulder.

"A present for me," Friend said. "Nothing of concern."

Sylvie wriggled under Friend's grip but the demon shook the woman into stillness. Jay noticed that by shaking Sylvie, Friend was keeping the woman from looking at the creature in the hall.

"I was already hungry but this one is working up my appetite." Friend shook Sylvie again and in a final dramatic gesture, flung the woman to the far end of the small ticket booth room. "Just one today?" she asked the thing behind Jay.

"I already paid for the week," it reminded Friend who smiled, though the grin didn't reach her eyes.

"Of course, my mistake." She reached a hand up to grab a handle above the ticket window. She nodded at Jay. "Thanks for the offering."

Friend pulled down a sheet metal door down over the window indicating the ticket booth was closed. The metal divide clicked shut in a final slam and left Jay alone in the hall with the thing.

"Reaper," it said in its low, wet and gravelly voice. Rotating on his heels, Jay nodded his head in acknowledgment to the lich. It was tall, skeletal, and terrifying. The flesh was shrunken from existing across centuries. Its skin was mottled and dehydrated and showed every turn of bone beneath. This one was wearing ō-yoroi, the leather and metal armor rotting and rusty with age. In its prime, the samurai armor would have been impressive, now it was covered with a film of green algae growing over the surface. The black of the lich's eyes filled the sockets with the colored nothingness surrounding a single pinprick of deep red light at the core, swiveling as its gaze roved over Jay. Jay suppressed a shudder. Even as a reaper, he gave the things a wide berth. "Kind of you to think of Friend in these uncertain times."

"Indeed," was all Jay could manage.

The lich stayed silent, studying Jay under its unsettling gaze. Its eyes moved to focus on a spot near the curtain as it walked away.

"Enjoy your show," Jay called out, fear making him talkative.

The lich glided through the curtain to a fresh wave of the blues song before disappearing into the black behind the fabric. A scraping sound of a latch came from the ticket booth and Jay whirled. The whole door to the booth swung open inward and Jay needed no urging to slip inside. Friend was holding open the door and locked it behind Jay.

"You are an idiot," she hissed at him as he walked by.

Ignoring her, Jay moved to Sylvie's side. She was still slumped on the ground where Friend had thrown her, but there was now a small round pillow behind her back. It was clear that Sylvie had been crying, tear tracks still wet upon her cheeks. Every now and then she gave a guttural cough, the sound ragged in her throat. The skin on her neck was red and raw and Jay ached to see it.

"I'm so sorry," he told her and was answered by a glare. Sylvie was holding a small plastic donut to the back of her head. "Friend gave you an ice pack?"

"I hate you both!" Sylvie tried to scream but it came out in a hoarse, cracking squeak.

Friend arched an eyebrow. "I just saved your life, human. If you had looked at the lich you would have died."

"She's not human," Jay said, standing and offering a hand to Sylvie who turned up her nose at it. Friend snorted at the action. "She probably wouldn't have died."

Friend scratched at a nearby wall with her clawed nails to sharpen them, interested but determined not to show it. "Are we done here? Because I'm not going to compromise my position here further. That was too close with the lich." The demon's voice was calm but she looked furious.

At the mention, Jay was reminded of what happened. "In the hall, the lich said something odd." Friend blinked at Jay but her pupils had gone wide with interest. "It seemed to think that we're all living in troubled times."

"Their brains are all full of rot," Friend purred.

Jay sighed, exasperated. "Even your kind feels it, Friend. There is something wrong with the order of things."

She picked at her yellow nails, chipping the polish and sending tiny bits sailing to the floor. "Whatever do you mean, dearest?"

From her place on the ground, Sylvie gurgled in frustration. Jay put a hand out to tell her to wait.

"Reapers are dying. They are being slaughtered and for no other reason than they are doing their jobs." Friend continued to look bored but she had stopped picking at her nails. Jay took another breath. "And I think I know who's behind it."

Friend's head snapped up, pupils circular and dark. "Who?"

"The fae."

At the words, Friend hissed, her pupils tight lines. "They wouldn't dare. They know where they stand with me and mine."

"We just came from Edge. Raphael himself was drinking as if the world was going to end."

"It didn't," Friend pointed out.

"It's not just..." Jay pushed at his hairline in frustration, ignoring his body's growing craving for a cigarette. "Everything's screwed up and people keep getting hurt. Damn it!" He slapped his hand against a nearby wall in frustration. Friend raised a thick brow and Jay struggled to calm himself. He sighed. "It's a long story."

Friend returned to picking at her nails. "You got this far, you might as well say it all." She grinned up at him, pleased she would get to kiss him once more.

Jay hesitated, thinking hard. "Fine," he said after a moment and held his hands up, palms facing the demon. "Take my memories."

Friend's skin shifted as she walked toward Jay, twisting into patchy fur and back again. Sylvie made a gagging noise of disgust. Close now, the demon brushed his hands away and leaned into his chest. Jay lurched back, forgetting to combat his human sensibilities that were repelled by Friend. She grinned when she saw his expression.

"You're so fun in this form."

"I should apologize, it's making me very rude."

She grabbed the back of Jay's neck, forcing his head down. Jay closed his eyes when Friend's lips met his. The demon leaned into the kiss, flashes of Jay's second human life coming to her mind so fast it pulled at her. Jay felt his stomach lurch and he grabbed out for Friend. He held on with his arms wrapped around her torso, pulling her close to steady them.

Sylvie cleared her throat.

Ignoring the woman, Friend tightened her arms around Jay, tangling her fingers in his hair, nails scraping against his scalp. She saw the last three years he had lived in his current body in jumbled snatches. Jay was unable to reign back the intensity of the onslaught, his powers too much out of his control. Friend kissed him deeper and he kissed back with building intensity, both intoxicated by the open flowing of Jay's enhanced power. He felt warmth bloom in his lower belly. Friend made a little noise in the back of her throat when she felt him start to press hard into her leg. Jay felt faint at the noise. Before, when they had kissed, his power hadn't been involved. This was now so much more.

"How long is this going to take?" Sylvie asked in a bland voice. "Not that watching you two make out isn't fascinating."

Gathering more strength than Jay thought the situation should call for, he pulled back and broke the kiss. Friend's eyes were still closed, her lips parted as she panted, trying to get her breath back. Jay wanted to cover her mouth with his again and he bent, his forehead touching hers. With great pain, he turned his head, shivering when her lips grazed his jawline. It was hard to push her away, his body screaming at him to pull her back, his movements slow and dream-like. Jay struggled through to hold Friend at arm's length, looking down at the demon.

"Friend, I'm so sorry. I can't control my powers anymore."

Her eyes fluttered open and her pupils were blown wide. "That was unexpected. But don't be sorry." She smiled mischievously up at him. Jay shook his head.

"I should know better." He bit his bottom lip, mouth still remembering the feeling of hers. "My body is now more in control of me than I am." He stepped away, disentangling himself from her arms.

Friend licked her lips with a frown. Her eyes grew foggy, darting back and forth as she chased the lingering memories Jay gave over to her. "Those weren't our hounds." She looked up, eyes flashing. "And what you said to the dhampir, she was fifteen?" Jay nodded. "Then the contract..."

"Would be void," he finished for the demon who looked more than angry.

"The fae have bitten off more than they can chew. I'm insulted that they think they can get away with this. It needs to be reported."

Jay sucked in a sharp breath. "You think he doesn't know?" Demons acting of their own accord without permission never ended well.

Friend gave a noncommittal gesture. "His attention is spread thin, he relies on his council to keep him informed of such things. And who knows how heavy their pockets are."

"Who is he?" Friend and Jay turned at Sylvie's voice, the woman was now standing, leaning against the wall with the ice pack still on the back of her head. The look on Friend's face stated that she had forgotten Sylvie was in the room.

"My sugar daddy," the demon retorted. Sylvie looked at Jay to clarify. "Lucifer."

Sylvie's eyes popped open wide and she drew back. "The Devil? Is real?"

Friend chuckled at the woman's fear and turned back to Jay, ready to ignore Sylvie again.

"I'll go to him, if this is so important to you." Friend sniffed, trying to sound indifferent. "I suppose it might matter to me sometime down the road. I can't promise I'll be granted an audience but if I am, your plea will be heard. I can be quite persuasive." The demon hacked a deep, wet cough and spat out a hairball that sizzled on the ground, acid smoking against the wooden floor.

"I bet," Sylvie said, holding a hand over her mouth and looking green.

Friend glared at Jay. "You're going to owe me so much when this is over."

"You're sure you'll be okay, reporting all this? Won't you get in trouble?"

The demon's face split into a mischievous grin. "Oh, yes, I love playing tattle-tale."

"And your den? It will be alright without you?" Jay jerked his head in the general direction of the curtain.

"I've got a good staff. They'll remind those who need reminding who's boss if it comes to that. Besides, you can't take souls, I don't care how much dirty money is running around. Souls are not property and the fae need to learn this lesson again, it would seem." She rounded on Sylvie and looked the woman up and down. The demon sauntered over and tapped a long, yellow fingernail twice on the Celtic knot around Sylvie's neck. "Whatever you are, Jay's right, it isn't human. Someone did a nice job on you. An iron seal, to keep you in your place. I bet you don't remember a day without this bit of jewelry. You couldn't take it off if you tried."

Sylvie froze, shoulders hunched up against Friend's words.

"Friend," Jay distracted the demon away from Sylvie who was now trying to take off the necklace to no avail. "Which court is in power? My years have gotten mixed up and I wasn't tracking their elections before I was exiled."

"The Seelie is what I last heard. Strange that they should want to sully their good names with us despicable demons."

Jay rubbed at his temples. "I hate politics," he mumbled under his breath.

"Do you still want to use the Quick or do you want to stand around some more? I've a long journey of my own, you know."

"Yes, I need to find Anat. The fae have him." Jay squinted at Friend. "You're sure you'll be able to find the Morningstar? You know where he is?"

Friend pulled a face. "Let me worry about my boss. I don't worry about yours. How is Four, by the way?"

Jay looked away. "I wouldn't know."

"Aww," purred Friend, sarcastic in her sympathy. "Little reaper all alone." Jay jerked his head to glare at the demon who looked him up and down. "Not so little though, in this body. How can you stand being so...tall?" Her grin flashed as she fixated upon his lap.

Jay rolled his eyes, the gesture making him feel very much like Janis.

"Friend." The demon met his gaze and her face fell when she saw his expression.

"No."

"I haven't said anything yet."

"You want to ask me another favor, I can tell."

"Friend, please."

Friend grunted out an exasperated moan. "Fine! What do you want?"

"Your feline form."

Friend narrowed her eyes with a hiss. "Why?"

"After you speak with the Morningstar, I need you to find Janis."

Friend looked disgusted. "The little human is in the Hill."

"And you can sneak in, get to her before I can." Jay's gaze was heavy on the demon, imploring. "Please, Friend. She's lost and alone and won't know what to do."

"All this sentimentality is bad for my complexion."

Jay took two big strides forward and his power collected around him without him knowing. Clasping her hands in his, Jay tugged Friend close again.

"Friend, I'm begging you. Janis needs someone. You know what the Hill is like and it's even more unsettling for a human. Do this and I'll give you ten years of me once my sentence is over. Go to her, see that she is safe, then come back to me."

The demon was short of breath. Jay had dragged up his power to show her what he was feeling but, unaccustomed to how strong he now was, he had taken too much. The residual spilled over giving him a gravitational pull of charisma. His human emotions swirled around the demon, full of complexity and depth. Demons, unlike reapers, were no strangers to emotions, but anything this profound would be overwhelming for anyone.

"Reaper, stop," she choked out, tears spilling over her cheeks. "I don't want those feelings."

Jay pulled his power back but kept her hands in his own. "Will you help me?"

Friend looked up into Jay's deep brown eyes. He felt her fall into the whirling depths. He tried to shield her from it but, as she stared, he realized she could see the shades of death he once had been and feel his ache to return to that form as if it were her own burning desire.

"Yes," she choked out.

Jay gathered her into a hug, pinning her arms to her side and smothering her face against his shoulder."Thank you, Friend. Thank you."

The demon squirmed and pushed him away.

"If you're not going to kiss me, don't bother touching me. I don't hug," she said with admonishment, though he thought he saw a flash of satisfaction rush across her features. "I'll go find the little human, don't worry. I haven't visited the Hill in ages, anyway. I think I'm due."

"Thank you, Friend."

"You'll come straight to me after your years are through. We'll have fun." She gave him a nasty grin.

"Once you're back from the Hill, come find me and we'll have some fun now," Jay said with a genuine smile back, confusing Friend enough for her to turn away, cheeks red with a blush.

The demon moved to the wall at the far end of the small room. With a single fingernail, Friend searched across the wall until her nail found the crack she was looking for. Like a box cutter, Friend dug her nail into the seam and drew it across and then down, revealing the outline of a door. Digging her fingers into the crack, she pulled, and opened the door to reveal the Quick.

It was an awful sight. The hole was less a circular shape and more like a slash of a wound on bloated pink skin, the orifice infected with black crust and oozing a yellowish slime. Beyond the opening, a blueish sort of darkness beckoned, breathing in, then out, pushing its fetid smell into the small room.

"Jesus Christ," Sylvie swore.

Friend's body shifted to look more feline than human. "Jay!" she hissed. "Control her! I do not tolerate such filth in this establishment."

"Sorry," Sylvie said to Friend who had shifted back into the shape of a woman and was smoothing her dress.

The demon waited, staring at the pair. "Are you going or not?"

Jay looked at Sylvie. "This is quite safe. I've used one before."

The woman's expression was doubtful. "Do they all look like that?"

Jay eyed the monstrous hole. "Never mind, don't answer."

Jay extended a hand. Reluctantly, after considering the gaping maw once more, Sylvie dropped the doughnut-shaped ice pack on the ground and grabbed hold.

"Now or never, kiddies," Friend purred.

Hot, yellow pus dripped from the bottom lip as if in anticipation. Jay closed his eyes, stepped forward, and pulled Sylvie in after.

TWENTY-THREE

IT IS THE ABSENCE of things that exist in the void.

The void is life without life and death without death.

A world of empty things.

There are no names in the void.

Those once with names break apart and come together before splintering again, shifting and knitting into shapes that do not exist.

There is no life in the void.

The journey is timeless. Time long ago left places such as this.

If there was pain in the void it would consume all it touched, searing like fire and burning like icy wind. Agony ripping over and over again in an onslaught bordering upon pleasure.

There is no release from this pain.

What once was life is in this empty place.

Nowhere exists and it is here.

TWENTY-FOUR

S YLVIE AND JAY WERE falling.

Was that what it was called? The name for the sensation was hard for Jay to remember. His mind was jumbled, returning to earth out of the Quick. *Yes, falling.* Falling toward the ground.

A field rushed up to meet them and in a flash Jay twisted, grabbing Sylvie as he tried to turn them around, hoping to hit the ground on their backs. There wasn't time and they landed hard on their sides. Jay's shoulder rolled threateningly in its socket and Sylvie cried out as her hip took most of the force. They kept still after their abrupt landing, letting the shock of re-entering the world fade from their bodies.

The air was summer-sweet, clean after a rainstorm, and felt like home. Jay studied the surroundings as his vision cleared and he saw woods ringing a clearing through the tall wild dew covered grass of a meadow. Movement came above him and his eyes snapped up to watch a tiny, white butterfly dart through the air.

Sylvie groaned. "I'll put up with one of those weird taxis next time. I'm never doing that again."

"A wild taxi could not have taken us so far even in Sideways."

Sylvie sat up and clutched at her head. "At least it would have been faster. How long were we in there?"

"We weren't. We arrived at the exact same moment we left. That's why they're called Quicks."

Her mouth dropped open.

In the silence of her astonishment, Jay twisted his body to push himself up to his feet, standing in shaking movements. Blood rushing around in his head, he surveyed the field, still wet from an overnight rainstorm.

"Not that I wish to experience that twice, but if these holes exist, why waste time with my Porsche earlier?"

Jay's eyes watered against the morning sunshine as he peered into the boundary of trees surrounding them. His paranoia had increased over the past few days. He heard the grass rustle as Sylvie climbed to her feet beside him.

"Quicks are hard to find and well-guarded. I didn't think we were in as much danger before—I didn't know you had brought your phone."

Sylvie gave a short, embarrassed cough at the accusation. Jay stopped his surveillance, satisfied they were alone in the field. Sylvie was dusting off the seat of her pants. The damp dirt smudged over the fabric instead of flaking off.

"Now I know." She looked up and squinted into the distance over Jay's shoulder. "What's that?"

Humming with alert energy, Jay turned on the spot. "Where?"

At the far end of the field there was movement coming from the ring of trees. It was a figure, waving frantically to them and calling out with a voice made faint from the distance. The being held up another, supporting the weight with an arm under a shoulder.

"Don't tell me we have to run again."

"Wait," Jay instructed, squinting harder at the figure, waiting. His body was balanced on the balls of his feet, muscles bunched and ready to run. The pair of figures drew closer and Jay rocked back onto his heels when he saw who it was. "Anat!" Jay rushed forward. He was being held up by a strange female, a forest nymph by the look of her, one Jay did not know. Sylvie hurried after Jay. The reedy stalks whipped out at their legs as they pushed through the grass, stinging through the fabric of their pants.

The nymph cried out as Anat stumbled and fell from her arms, something he cradled within his own weighing him down. Jay fell to his knees when he reached Anat, sliding in the muddy dirt when he hit the ground hard. He grabbed for his injured friend, pulling him off the ground and supporting his back. To his horror, Anat's wings were gone. Bloody stumps were the only remnants of his once great pinions. An unmoving fox was cradled close in Anat's arms, the animal limp and lifeless.

"Please help," the dryad begged. "The fox is my brother. Your friend told me you could assist us."

Jay pushed hair back from Anat's face. He was not the same as the old man heading up the OCME. Gone were the wrinkles and aged complexion. Anat was now young and naked save for a skirt tied at his waist. The fabric was a simple, white linen folded into pleats that circled the whole of his hips with a tie knotted at front. Reddened and scratched knees from his tumultuous entrance peeked out from the tumbled hemline tossed around his muscled thighs. His rich golden skin shone with sweat, an effect of his exertion and injuries.

"Help Tensith," Anat coughed. "He saved my life."

"There is a creek nearby," the beautiful nymph said. "It is free from pollution and I already have permission from the water sprites to use it."

"Can you carry the fox?" Jay asked and the nymph nodded. He cast about for Sylvie. "Help me with Anat." They shouldered his weight as best they could and trudged through the trees at the edge of the field to find a small brook with cool, clear water running over stones. With effort, Jay and Sylvie eased Anat into the babbling water, who shuddered in relief at the contact.

"I had to fight in my true form," Anat coughed. The demigod closed his eyes against the pain of memory. "I have to start over, reaper. I reset the clock."

Jay tried to hush his friend and assure him that they would think of it later but Anat shook his head, needing to press on.

"They tore away what little I had left. My wings..."

"Don't think of such things now," Jay soothed. "They will grow back."

Anat shook his head. "Where is the fox?"

The dryad sat in the stream with the fox in her lap, long fingers massaging clean the bloody fur in gentle motions. "He will not wake," she whispered, looking to Jay.

"He is a kitsune, a nine-tails," Anat said. "I felt you come out the Quick and came here with Maeren when Tensith would not stir."

"If you felt us, there are others who must have as well."

Anat struggled to give a shallow nod. "You cannot stay long. All the holes are being watched. I told you not to come back to Richmond."

"I had to," Jay whispered to the demigod reclining in the stream. He placed a hand on Anat's shoulder. "Let the water do the work, I don't sense death on you yet."

Anat scoffed but nodded and closed his eyes, relaxing into the creek. Jay waded to where Maeren held the fox in her arms.

"I don't sense it on him either," he said to the nymph.

"You are very strange," she told him, angling her head and appraising him. "What are you? You appear human and speak like one and yet, I can tell you contain the depth of time within your bones."

Jay thought of Janis, who would keep him honest. "I was a reaper," he said, though he resented using the past tense. Maeren leaned forward and held his gaze.

"A human reaper," she whispered in amazement. "I have never seen the like."

"Tell me about it," he grumbled. Maeren tilted her head in the other direction at the sentiment that was foreign to her. Jay put a hand on Tensith's side that rose and fell in a steady rhythm, a good sign. "He's strong, merely recovering from his exertion of power."

Relief washed over the dryad as she slumped in the stream. "I am unfamiliar with this side of him," she admitted. "I do not even think he is well acquainted with all of his gifts."

Jay nodded. "Let him rest, he should be fine."

"Thank you," Maeren said, petting her brother and watching over him.

With another nod, Jay moved to help Anat sit up, freeing his already growing wings from the water. Anat grabbed Jay's arm, squeezing with urgency to reveal what Tensith had told him before the fight.

"When have you known the fae to work with the Turned?"

So it was true.

"A friend is helping with that as we speak. We can hope the Morningstar will respond."

Anat nodded and released Jay's arm, comforted for the moment.

"It's worse than that. We saw Raphael," Jay said in a soft voice, wishing he didn't have to add to Anat's misery.

"Raphael? What did he want?"

"Nothing, but he strongly implied the City knows of the plight of the reapers and does not care."

Anat's new wings rippled as if they meant to whisk him away to safety, to a place where things made sense. "It is not possible. What of Them? They must be..."

"I don't know." Jay closed his eyes, the pain of sorrow heavy in his heart. "Of that, Raphael had nothing to say."

"Are you going to be okay?" It was Sylvie who had spoken, her voice full of concern, as she looked upon Anat.

"The fae are quite nasty fighters," he told her. She looked away.

"Did they say anything?" Jay questioned.

Anat groaned as his now juvenile wings began to itch, their growth aided by the water flowing around where he sat. "Plenty, but it seemed they were more concerned with the fox."

They wanted to cut out the infection, said a new voice.

Maeren cried out in relief and Anat twisted to try and see Tensith. Jay forced Anat to remain still, wings still growing.

It seems I discovered too much about the contract violations.

With tender movements, Maeren set Tensith on his feet before he eased his body to lay in the stream.

"The ghost was taken before her time," Jay informed Anat. "The Peredas, her parents, made a deal to have a child for sixteen years. Harm came to her a few days before her birthday, breaching the terms of her contract."

"Tensith told me," Anat blew out a breath. "What happened when you brought her to a ferryman?"

"She wasn't on any of their lists. We came across Tick but he didn't want to take her into the next place, he wanted to sell her."

"You were right, fox," Anat said, raising his voice so Tensith would hear him over the flowing water. "Killing reapers ensures one will not be there to intervene in an early death. The fae can kill whomever they wish. Including sheefrahs. All that untapped potential... It would render those souls very powerful. The ferrymen of the damned must be on their side too."

"I cannot believe the Seelie court would do such a thing," Maeren gasped, though Tensith tried to calm her. "Do not tell me to hush. Harnessing the power of souls is too great for anyone to bear."

Tensith swished his tail in silent comment, water flowing over his hunched shoulders.

"In either case, we need to leave before we're found," Jay announced. He peered at Anat's still flightless wings. "You'll have to use some of my power to heal faster so we can move quicker. Stay still."

Anat closed his eyes, face screwed up in anticipation. "I remember how it works."

"Works?" Sylvie asked in a nervous voice. "How what works?"

Maeren, he nudged his sister. *What do you see of the female?*

"Nothing past her iron bindings," Maeren said, squinting.

Sylvie heard their words and shook her head with a sigh. "Not you too," she moaned.

Jay placed his hands on Anat's clammy shoulders and closed his eyes. Up from the well within him, he called his power.

"Do not mess this up, reaper," Anat's voice trembled.

Life, Jay's power growled from deep inside.

"Yes," he told the power, "give it to him."

It rushed out, rocking him forward to press down hard on Anat's shoulders. The force shoved the injured demigod back into the stream. He cried out at the impact but Jay kept his hands upon Anat's skin. A hot rush surged out of Jay in a giant wave, slamming into Anat and flowing into his body. When the scream of pain reached Jay's ears the sound was dampened, as if coming from very far away.

Life, his power repeated. His power was a burning, fierce thing inside him, bubbling up and demanding to be used. He had given Anat too much, he had dug so inside himself for the sake of saving his friend he hadn't seen to curb his efforts.

"Pull back!" Jay commanded.

The power reluctantly retreated.

Gasping for air, Jay sat back onto his heels, water splashing, and opened his eyes. Two black handprints remained on Anat's shoulders, charred skin smoking.

"What did you do?" Sylvie yelled.

Maeren and the fox abandoned the brook and backed up several paces from the scene. They gestured for Sylvie to stand with them, which she ignored.

Anat writhed in pain, wings flapping in the shallow stream and body spasming as the lingering power stitched him back together from the inside out. The smoldering handprints were the last to heal. The scorch marks collapsed in on themselves as new skin rushed to fold over the burns.

"Shit," Jay muttered.

The demigod opened his eyes and white light flared like two search-lights, flickering when he blinked. His wings started to flap, beating against the creek and spraying water as he made a desperate attempt to fly. Jay scrambled from the stream and Sylvie retreated to hide behind a nearby tree.

Anat was rising to his feet by the sheer speed of his moving wings, water droplets showering them all. The underdeveloped things did not take him far but they allowed him to hover close to the ground.

"*Reaper, what have you given me?*" Anat's voice boomed out. The deep bass pitch echoed across the field.

Sylvie cowered at the strength in his voice but Jay was transfixed. He had heard that voice before. It was his own.

"Let it drain, Anat!" Jay yelled up at the hovering demigod, struggling to be heard over the loud humming of his wings. "I gave you too much, I'm sorry!"

Anat tipped his head back. The white light spilled skyward, rushing to escape from his eyes and nose and mouth. The light steamed up from the pores on his face and curled away into the air. More light spilled out from the cracks around his nails, at his fingers and his toes, leaking from anyplace it could find.

"Reaper!" Anat's voice was mixed with the voice of Jay's power as it started to settle into his body, absorbed by the confines of the demigod. When the light faded, Anat sank to the bank of the stream, wings slowing to a halt and dropping behind him. Anat looked up, breathless. "What did you do to me?"

Jay struggled to sit up, bending to help Anat to his feet. "I didn't mean to."

The demigod winced, shrinking away from Jay. Maeren and Tensith approached with wide eyes and hesitant steps.

"This tastes of humanity." The demigod swayed once before steadying himself. Anat surveyed Jay with a cool stare. "That is not the power allotted to the banished."

Jay closed his eyes against a headache beginning to form at his temples. "The emotional barrier between this human body and my reaper essence broke."

Anat shook his head. "Our kind are never supposed to feel human emotions."

"There is nothing I can do," Jay snapped. "What I can do is find Janis wherever she is in the Hill and put a stop to all this. Fox, can you help?"

I am called Tensith and I have been barred entry. Tensith sat on his haunches. *Besides, my sister has been away from her heart tree too long.*

Maeren frowned at her brother who gave her the smallest shake of his head. The nymph sighed out a puff of pollen. "I am sorry that we cannot offer you more help," Maeren said to Jay. "But we must take our leave."

Jay nodded. "I understand. Thank you for saving Anat."

With a small wave from the nymph, Tensith and Maeren turned and walked into the woods.

"They're leaving?" Sylvie asked, following the path of the fox and dryad with a disbelieving gaze.

Anat drew up his eyes to meet Jay's in a steady, telling stare. "We need a portal."

"The Howe Caverns in New York have the closest portal," Jay said. "But they'll be heavily guarded. We need time and distance to hide our trail so we aren't followed. The next portal is in the Ice Caves."

"Shoshone? But that's all the way in Idaho!" Sylvie's voice was tinged with worry. "And aren't they a huge tourist attraction?"

"The main caverns, yes." Jay pushed his hair back from his forehead. "Anat, she is right. They are miles away. We must fly together."

"No." Anat shook his head.

"There is no other way."

"I would not risk it," Anat argued.

"Nor would I, given another choice!" he roared in frustration, startling both his companions. "This is the eleventh hour, Anat! Will you not help me or not?"

"I know you have seen what the eleventh hour will be, reaper, and it is not this." The demigod contemplated Jay with a heavy gaze. He smoothed out a wrinkle in the fabric of his wrapped skirt and sniffed. "If this is our only option."

"I need to help Janis. I don't know what I'd do if something happened to her."

"Stop, with the emotion, reaper. I will help you."

Jay released a relieved breath. "Thank you."

"Are you ready?"

Jay nodded, steeling himself. "Sylvie, take a few steps back."

Anat lunged forward and clasped Jay's forearms with his hands and tugged, drawing out another surging of Jay's power and pulling Jay along with it. The air around the pair wavered, the molecules beginning to vibrate, rising to an angry hum from the sudden influx of power saturating the air. With a noise like a grindstone churning in water, Anat opened his body and drew Jay inside.

TWENTY-FIVE

J ANIS WOKE UP COLD on the ground. She breathed in, then out. Blinking several times, she realized she couldn't see anything. Sitting up in a stage of shock, Janis stopped and groaned. Her entire body was stiff and sore and felt like she had just run a marathon. Smells filtered in through her nose and she choked on the forgotten sensation. The air around her was thick with mildew, someplace dark that had never seen the sun. Jay had told her as a ghost, she was unable to touch, smell, and taste. But now, she felt so alive. Janis shivered as she felt real, cold stone beneath her fingertips.

She looked down at her hands and moved them, sifting the loose layer of dirt that covered the stones. How was it possible? With a start she saw her hands were colored blue and thought she was changed for one wild moment. Instead, the blue light was coming from the ceiling. Janis craned her neck up at it and squinted at the relative brightness, eyes pinching in pain as her pupils retracted at the sight. The light rippled across the ceiling, covering the stone in a layer of organic illumination that looked to be like the undersurface of a pool.

Janis tried to sit, using her hands to support her, and slipped. Her body crashed down, arms crumpling under the weight. Her body was heavy, so heavy. Gingerly, Janis flexed her palms against the cool stone floor and pushed to sit upright. She shouldn't be feeling anything, she was a ghost and had lost all sensations. Janis patted the stone ground and small bits of dirt rubbed at her palm, sticking to her skin when she picked her hand up to inspect it.

Where was she?

Shifting to study the wall next to her, Janis concentrated and tried to poke her hand through the stone. She swallowed a cry of pain when the fingers jammed up against the material. Cradling the hand, a thought came to her. She sat up straighter, ignoring the muscle pain in her back, instead relishing in the humanity of the sensation. She was alive again!

"What are you smiling about, human child?"

Janis jumped as a heavy, gravel-filled voice startled her from the darkness.

"Um," she said, stalling for time and peering hard into the shadows. "What?"

The sound of a low, scaled stomach dragging across stone came to her ears.

"You better wipe that grin off your face before any of them see it."

Crawling into the dim, blue light of wherever Janis was, came a lizard-like creature. It was as long as Janis was tall and looked like some sort of crocodile crossed with a frog. The beading of scales upon its back was tarnished copper, light green as if they haven't been cleaned in years. Two bold, black stripes formed at the base of the thing's nostrils and crested up over its head and ran down its back, parallel, until coming together at the tip of the tail. Four bowed reptilian legs worked to haul itself closer to Janis who screamed and rushed to the far side of her cell, falling hard onto the floor, unsteady on her legs.

"Get away from me!" she yelled at the creature, looking around for a rock to throw. She found a small pebble and chucked it, the small rock bouncing off the nose of the animal. Janis watched the pebble roll away into the shadows. The creature stopped moving and exhaled its version of an affronted huff, a lick of hot flame shooting out of its mouth. Janis screamed again. "Don't hurt me!"

"I am not going to hurt you. Calm down, you foolish thing, and be quiet."

Gulping, Janis did as she was told, sagging a little against the corner of the small room but not moving out of her crouch. The creature flicked out a purple tongue from its wide, flat head.

"You are going to be quiet now?"

Janis nodded and the tongue flicked out again.

"I can taste your lie. Say you will be quiet and behave."

Janis said nothing but kept the creature in a stony gaze.

The creature flicked out its tongue again. "What is your name?"

"Janis. What's yours?"

"Byst."

Byst's tail waved back and forth, brushing against the stones, the noise echoing against the walls.

Janis shuddered at the strange noise.

"I told you not to be afraid."

She closed her eyes. "It's kind of hard to not be afraid of a big lizard that talks."

The creature drew himself up as best he could on such stubby legs. "I am not a lizard, I am a salamander."

Janis cracked open one eye. "Like the kind in little ponds and stuff?" The salamander inclined its head.

"You are speaking of my mortal brethren. They are much smaller than I am and do not possess magic."

"You can do magic?" Janis relaxed further, opening both her eyes and letting her shoulders drop from their protective hunch, curious.

"Yes. However, it might draw the attention of our captors."

Despite her fear, Janis yawned. She hadn't slept since before she died. It was odd to feel exhaustion again. "Captors?"

Byst fixed her with one black eye. "You are in the dungeons, human child."

"Whose dungeons?" The salamander flicked out his tongue.

"The dungeons under the Hill."

"Where?"

A loud bang sounded in the distance and Byst turned to drag himself away into the shadows, low belly whisking over the stones.

"Hey!" Janis called out to his retreating tail. "Don't leave me!"

From outside the cell was a voice, speaking what sounded like a poem in a sing-song and growing louder as the speaker drew near, words echoing off the odd acoustics of the stone walls.

"I see drowsy water rats." Janis's heart pounded in her chest hearing the strange voice. A sharp giggle came from outside the bars at the front of Janis's cell. "Hello, you wild thing. Just look at those eyes."

Janis froze when she saw the face at the bars. It was a woman, of a sort, strange and short and plump, with deep crimson skin and bright blue eyes. Her head peaked at the back, skull elongated and ending in a sharp point. Black beetle wings fanned out and were tucking away behind her, settling out of sight. Decorating her shoulders were oversized epaulets made of curling birch tree bark. The ornamental shoulder pieces were sewn onto a shapeless knee-length wrap tunic made from a strange type of leather. Bark lined the rest of the strange woman's outfit, overlapping like scales. She raked a long finger across the bars of the cell, bone against metal, smiling at Janis who was having none of it.

"Are you going to tell me where I am or just keep saying stupid nonsense?"

"You are under the Hill, little soul." The faerie woman's voice was a dull croak and full of malice. "Rejoice and be merry, for you are home."

"This isn't my home," Janis threw out in defiance. "Why am I in a dungeon? You can't hold me without official charges."

The woman smiled, showing hundreds of small, pointed teeth. Janis drew back in fear and the stranger's smile widened. Janis bit her lip and gathered her courage back around her.

"My friends are coming for me!"

The woman laughed, throwing back her pointed head and exposing a throat with golden tattoos inked into the red skin made to look like the pattern of wood grain. "No one cares that you are here, little soul." Her smile shifted into a condescending grin. "Get comfortable, no one can help you now." With that, the guard left, chuckling until out of earshot.

Janis slumped down, body sliding down against the stones, ordering herself not to cry. Despite her thoughts, tears pricked at her eyes. She put a finger to her cheek and stared at the water with a frown.

"Ghosts don't have tears," she said out loud. The sound of a flicking tongue came from her left.

"You do in the Hill, human child. Things work differently down here." The salamander emerged out of the darkness.

"I'm alive?" Her voice cracked.

Byst waggled its head. "No."

She started to hiccup, failing to hold onto her already fragile composure. Janis tried to speak between the halting gulps of air, her words punctuated by whimpers. "I just can't deal with this anymore," she cried, trying not to hyperventilate too much. "I don't want to be dead again."

"You are neither dead nor are you alive. You are a fetch."

"What's a fetch?" Janis wiped at her streaming eyes, gulping. She started to calm, focusing on the strangeness of Byst's answer.

"An apparition of your living self."

Janis sniffed. "So, I'm a ghost again?"

Byst waggled his head. "Ghosts cannot exist in the lands of the fae. Here you are a fetch. It is different but similar, yes."

"That doesn't make sense." Janis turned her head to wipe her nose on the shoulder of her shirt.

"Nothing does here," Byst said in a terse voice. "This is the Hill, your laws of physical do not apply."

Janis gave a short chuckle, still sounding more like a sob. "Do you mean 'physics'?"

The salamander looked as annoyed as a salamander could. "Respect your betters, human child!"

"Last time I checked, we're in the same cell."

Byst muttered to himself before raising his voice for Janis to hear him. "All the same, the rules of your world do not work here."

"What do you mean?"

"While I can do magic in your world, should I wish, here is where my power flows strongest." To demonstrate, the salamander waddled into a better position and drew a symbol in the dirt floor with the tip of his tail. The writing flashed a bright, moss green and turned into a delicate plant stem, sprouting through the dirt to bloom into a white rose before bending over to die and crumble away into dust. Janis was impressed in spite of herself. "The rules are different. Magic is everywhere down here, available to all who have the need."

Janis nodded to the cell door. "Bust us out."

The salamander blinked. "Of course, measures can be taken to prevent certain magics from being used in specified places."

"Figures," Janis grumbled. "That woman was a faerie? And you're a faerie?"

"No."

"But you can do magic."

"That has no bearing upon who I am. I am fae but not a faerie. We are under the Hill where there are many faeries and other magical creatures who are all fae. Understand?"

"Sure," she mumbled, not wanting Byst to know she was confused. She scratched at the floor next to her feet, lifting her pointer finger to inspect the dirt now under her nail. It didn't feel like special faerie dirt but she still hated the alien quality to this place and felt tears threaten to start back up again. Janis broke the quiet. "My friends will come for me."

Byst flicked his purple tongue.

"They will. Why does no one believe me?"

"Seeing is believing, human child, and there has yet to be someone in the land of the fae that the fae did not invite."

"I wasn't invited. I was stolen away. And I still don't know why, I might add."

"Sadly, that happens too."

"I don't think 'sadly' covers it. You can't just take people against their will."

Byst flicked out his tongue. "Your kind, human child, does it all the time."

Janis sat staring at the salamander. "It's still wrong. Why am I in the dungeons? I didn't break any laws."

"That you know of. Faerie laws are very tricky."

"What did you do?"

"I? I did nothing but serve my people faithfully for hundreds of years and this is how I am thanked for it." Thin tendrils of smoke curled up from Byst's nostrils.

Janis was confused. "You got chucked in jail because you were doing your job?"

The salamander spoke through his memories, as if he had forgotten Janis had asked him a question. "I thought I was going to be fine, exempt even, but it did not matter. They came for everyone in the Seelie court. Enslaving some but killing most of us. I was one of those lucky enough to be put in the dungeons." He croaked a laugh. "Others were erased and exiled. Perhaps that fate is worse."

"What are you talking about?"

"The Autumn Detente, human child, the bloody revolt of the Unseelie court."

Janis stared. "If it was a revolt why is it called a detente?"

"That is what they call it," Byst spat. "It was not a resolution between the courts, it was a revolution. But the Unseelie have their propaganda and we all have to listen to their lies."

"When did it happen?" Janis was still lost, wishing this had been a chapter in one of her history books.

"Forty two years ago."

Janis' mouth hung open. "And you've been down here that whole time?" Byst nodded. "Jesus," Janis swore, pity in her gaze. "What was the revolution about?"

"What they always are about, human child. Power." A loud bang came from outside the cell, causing Janis to jump and Byst to hiss and back away from the front of the cell, belly scraping the ground.

"Where are you going?" Janis twisted around to watch as Byst disappeared into the shadows at the far corner of the cell.

"Get away from the bars!"

"Why?"

Another loud bang sounded from down the hall and Janis jumped, pressing her face up against the bars to try and see what was happening. She heard a loud scraping sound of a heavy door opening up onto the tail end of terse orders.

"...and move the new batch out to processing."

The command was followed by stomping footsteps. From her position at the bars, Janis could see movement down the hall. Several faeries of all shapes and colors came into view and passed by her cell.

"Let me out!" Janis yelled as they walked by.

One of them stopped to sneer at Janis. He was good looking, in a way Janis thought was a bit too handsome. He had golden yellow hair and a strong jaw and greenish tinged skin but when he smiled his gums were pitch black and dripping tar. Janis pulled in her breath and take a step back from the bars.

"We'll let you out soon enough," the faerie said. His small flightless wings of black iridescence and red veins running through them buzzed behind his back. He leaned in and reached through the bars to try and touch Janis with a gentle caress. Janis stepped back and fell, landing hard on her backside and the air rushed out of her lungs.

"Get the fuck away from me," she wheezed out.

The faerie's face fell in mock distress. "Don't want out anymore? Very bad, human child. Always changing your mind."

He slashed out his fingers and raked the air in front of Janis' head causing her to crash down on her back. With a cackling laugh, the faerie withdrew his arm from her cell and moved on with his fellow guards. Janis supposed they must be guards as they all wore a similar colored uniform and all carried thick wooden clubs.

The procession trooped down the dungeon hall and Janis propped herself up on her elbows, breathing hard.

"These ones are ripe and ready," came the whooping cry of one of the guards, now out of sight from where Janis was. She crawled as fast as she could over to the right corner of the cell and smushed her face against the bars trying to see as far to the left as she could. From where she couldn't see came the sounds of jangling keys and cell doors being dragged open followed by howls of protest from prisoners dragged out of their cells.

"Grab his legs!" came the voice of another guard.

Janis heard the pleading sobs of the prisoner. "Please! Let me go! I haven't done anything!" Her heart pounded in her chest as she heard the sickening sound of a meaty thump followed by cruel laughter from the guards.

"Chain them up and move out, we don't have time for this," barked a harsh voice, silencing the laughter from the guards. "Get that door open."

The rattling of sliding metal came to Janis' ears. She heard the scuffling noises of a fight and the muffled protestations of the prisoner. His voice escalated down the hallway, shouting, "...know who I am?"

"A rose is a rose, my pet," came the voice of the guard. "Calm down and let us collect your petals."

There came a thump of something hard hitting something soft and a cry of pain that made Janis wince. Chains clinked and locked, echoing down to where Janis held herself frozen in horror, before another faerie voice shouted a command for them all to move out. The rhythm of many feet walking at once accented by the jangle of metal reached Janis' ears before she saw the chain gang of shuffling prisoners escorted by their faerie guards. She shuddered when they came into view and shrank back away from the cell door. The faerie who had taunted her earlier was escorting the prisoners on the far side, away from Janis, but he gave her a hearty wink and a lick of the lips as he went by. Janis resisted the urge to shudder and instead glowered at him, trying to look braver than she felt. Everyone tied up was human, as far as Janis could tell, and all of them looked beaten and very ill treated. At the front of a line walked a child, a twelve year old girl, with a thick line of dried blood running from her nose to her chin, crusted and dried on her skin. The child was in a hospital gown and was shivering in the cold damp air of the dungeon.

The prisoner at the back of the line, the one who insisted by his name he was exempt from the tortures placed upon him, was causing a new commotion. She saw him for the first time as the line of prisoners were prodded forward. He was old and bald and reminded her of some politician she had noticed in passing the news when her parents watched.

"Let me go! Do you know who I am?" the man roared, white face turning red, what wispy gray hairs left on his head jerking along with his movements. "Do you know who you're dealing with?"

"Don't care, don't care," one of the fae guards chanted with a malicious smile.

The man's face turned a deeper shade of red. "Let go of me now!"

The shouted protestations echoed down the hall as the line of chained prisoners moved out of Janis' sight. She heard a door slam open down the hall and the jangling of chains fade away with the dying wails of the prisoners. The unseen door at the end of the hall slammed shut leaving Janis and the rest of the dungeon in silence.

The slithering sound of Byst approaching came from the shadows of the cells. Janis stood in shock, backing away from the bars. "Who were all those people?"

Byst hesitated. "I do not pretend to know what unsavory business the Unseelie deal in."

"I have to get out of here," Janis announced to the air around her.

"Would that you could."

Janis frowned down at the salamander. A strange noise came out of the darkness behind Janis. She twisted around.

"Did you hear that?" she asked, listening hard. It came again and Janis recognized it as the sound of a cat's meow. Out of the darkness came a tortoiseshell feline slinking toward Janis, yellow lamp-like eyes fixed on her. It got close to Janis and flopped down onto its side, tucking in its legs and begging to be pet.

"Where did you come from?" Janis asked, kneeling down with a smile and obliging the animal by petting the soft underbelly fur. The cat had an odd pattern, black and brown and then this light pinkish color that looked pretty but didn't quite seem to mesh with the other shades. It chirped a quiet meow of satisfaction at being stroked and scratched. A mouser in the dungeon, Janis didn't imagine the cat got a lot of positive attention, at least not in this horrid place. Janis had a cat growing up, when she was younger, it died before she could form a more adult attachment with it, but she still had pleasant, but hazy, memories of a fuzzy white companion who loved his chin scratched and who slept curled up on her second pillow at night. "What a pretty cat you are."

"You are not supposed to be here," said Byst with a snarl, surprising Janis into looking up from the cat, though she continued petting.

"I know, we've been over this."

"Not you, that thing you are touching."

Janis looked around to the tortoiseshell in confusion, hand stilling. It gave a small, chirping meow. "The cat? It's harmless."

"She is not a cat. That is a demon."

Janis yanked her hand back from the cat's stomach. "What?"

"I come and go where I please," said the cat, flipping over and extending her front paws in a stretch.

Janis jumped back, scrabbling away on her hands and heels, kicking

273

up dust as she scooted across the ground. It didn't quite sound like words, more like cat noises that were understandable.

The cat gave her an appraising look. "Don't scream."

Dumbfounded, Janis said the first thing that came to her mind. "Byst said you can only get here by invitation."

The cat shook her head and said, "Yes, but I'm a cat," as if that was answer enough.

The salamander dragged itself away from the demon but keeping his back turned as if facing down a predator. "You cannot be here, leave now!"

Unimpressed, the cat licked a paw.

The salamander flicked his tongue in warning. "You cannot remain!"

The cat was eyeing Byst, keeping him in her sight even as he began to circle. When he drew too near, the cat rippled, tripling in size. She arched her back, fur on end and bunching her muscles together, ready to spring. "You will not win this fight, fae."

Byst wagged his head in annoyance. "You are on the wrong lands, demon."

The cat extended all her claws. "I've not come here to deal with lowly worms."

"Worm?" Byst drew himself up in his indigence. "How dare you!"

The salamander lunged, striking out with his long purple tongue. The tortoiseshell leapt up into the air, landing to the side. She swiped out with sharp claws and tore out a chunk of the fae's eye ridge. Byst howled in pain, retracting his tongue and hooting his injustice. The cat backed away, fur still on end and back arched.

"I am stronger," panted the cat. Blood leaked from Byst's wound, the blue-black substance splashing upon the ground. Janis watched in horror as the blood soaked into the dirt floor. Wailing and with his tail thrashing, Byst heaved the bulk of his body in retreat and slumped in a far corner, hidden by shadows, a trail of blood splatters in his wake.

"What a fun waste of time," said the cat.

Janis looked around in astonishment and was shocked to see the tortoiseshell was back to a normal size and was washing her paws free of blood.

"What was that about?" Janis squeaked before clearing her throat and repeating her question at a lower pitch.

The feline gave her a shrewd look. "Don't pay attention to Byst. He's old and senile. He's been in these dungeons too long. The fae aren't meant to survive behind bars. Too bad they're not iron; it would be a better deterrent."

"You know him? Who are you?"

Her tail swished. "The reaper sent me."

"Jay?"

The cat nodded and resumed cleaning her paw.

Janis turned to look triumphantly in the direction of Byst. "I told him Jay'd come for me but he didn't believe me."

"Not yet, small human. He's got to find a way into the Hill all his own and they don't make it easy."

"He'll find me, I know it." The relief flooding through Janis made her deaf to the warning.

The cat blinked at Janis before returning to washing her paws.

"Um, what's your name?" asked Janis, feeling self-conscious asking that question of a cat.

"Friend," the cat purred, pink tongue licking up and over her nose.

"I'm Janis." Friend sat back, reached a hind leg up, and bent to clean between her legs as an answer. Janis looked politely away. "I hope you have an idea on how to get out of here because from what I can tell this is pretty much a dead end."

Friend dropped her hind leg and sat down looking like a furry sphinx, tail extended behind her. "Plenty of ideas."

When the cat wasn't forthcoming, Janis spoke again. "Care to elaborate?"

"No."

"Why the hell not?"

"The reaper said for me to find you so you were not alone. He didn't mention anything about getting you out."

With a groan of frustration, Janis wondered if all demons were so contrary. "Fine, be unhelpful."

Friend just yawned again and closed her eyes until they were narrow slits.

Janis decided to get up and walk around the cell. It was pretty big, from what she had seen on TV and in the movies, she wondered why it wasn't smaller. Although, with her and Byst sharing one, Janis bet their captors were doubling up. Stepping around Friend, who opened one eye to make sure her tail wasn't trodden upon, Janis started at the back corner where she had awoken. She paced around the cell at the perimeter, keeping track of the number of steps she took.

"Under the Hill," she muttered as she walked, remembering what Byst had told her. What was this Hill? Was the whole place a Hill or was the dungeon itself beneath one? Stone gave way to metal bars as Janis crossed in front of the mouth of her cell. The door wasn't that long, the captive space longer than it was wide, and Janis soon came to the corner where Byst was hiding. The injured salamander was curled up into a ball, long tail tucked in around him. Janis knelt. "Byst, are you okay?"

The fae didn't move but let out a croaking grunt.

"He's fine," meowed Friend from across the cell. Janis pursed her lips but stood and walked around Byst to trace the rest of the space through the last corner and back around to where she started.

"Now what?" she asked the cat who sat up, looking annoyed that she wasn't going to be able to nap.

Stretching, Friend meowed, "Now I leave to find my reaper. I have to tell him I have completed the task he set for me." After a pause, the cat added, "And to tell him that you are alright."

Janis' face fell and panic began to gnaw at the edges of her mind. "You're leaving? But how do I get out of this place?"

Friend sauntered closer to Janis, tail curling under her chin. "You'll figure it out. My reaper said you're smart and that you don't give up."

"Your reaper, huh?"

The cat's fur stood up on end all over her body and Janis wondered if that was her way of blushing. As if in confirmation, the cat began to purr.

"I will tell the reaper where you are but you can't stay in this cell. The reaper will meet you in these lands. Escape, find a hiding place." With another flick of her tail, Friend trotted out of the cell between the bars and vanished into the gloom.

TWENTY-SIX

I T WAS DARK INSIDE the demigod at first.

Jay tumbled about in the black ocean of Anat's core and couldn't figure out which way was up. Testing, he prodded around until he felt for the spaces and he righted himself. He aligned his body with Anat's, slipping his fingers into fingers like gloves, toes inside toes. Arching his back, Jay released his wings, flapping them in jerking movements until he could slide them into the confines of Anat's wings, skeletal ones inside dark velvet ones. They flexed together, moving their flying muscles, testing. Jay took a deep breath, chest pushing at Anat's so it rose and fell. Together, they opened their eyes. Inside, Jay gasped.

He had grown accustomed to seeing through human eyes, with their three color receptors. In the body of a demigod, Jay was more than overwhelmed. The colors burst in his mind, filling his head with a riotous display that left a cacophonous din ringing at the back of his eyes. Viewing the world through the demigod's twenty eight photoreceptors introduced Jay to a world filled by an alien rainbow. Anat turned to look at Sylvie and Jay was forced to follow his line of sight.

Her hair was no longer just red with brown and gold highlights mixed in. There were shades of blue and yellow and orange and colors Jay couldn't describe. The sea of hues was so multitudinous his brain had to offload the visual processing to his other senses. He was amazed to hear the shadows under her jawline and to smell the complicated hazel of her irises.

The synesthesia is too strong for me, Jay choked out inside their layered minds. *Close it off! Please!*

Anat shifted in mild annoyance to the request. The colors faded and Jay was left with a muted version of Anat's sight, although shades of ultraviolet and the deepest reds remained. The pain in his mind retreated with the colors and he could focus better upon his other companion.

Sylvie stood frozen under Anat's gaze. "Do not worry, faerie," he told her. "The reaper is within me." He then patted his chest.

"Uh," Sylvie's face rippled through the emotions of doubt and fear.

Explain yourself better, Jay urged Anat.

"Jay's still alive?" she asked before Anat could speak again.

He nodded. "I had to take the reaper within me to use its power. I cannot fly without its strength and it cannot fly without the right form," Anat said.

"We're flying to Idaho." Sylvie's statement was flat and without emotion or question.

Anat nodded and Jay's head nodded along inside.

"Great," she muttered.

"This is not flying as you think of. It will be quite a different sensation."

"No," she said as a response. "I'm sorry, I'm not going."

"I can't do this alone," said Anat, speaking with Jay's strong emotional words. "I need your help to find Janis. And we can't enter the Hill without the proper escort."

"I'm not a faerie, damn it! Please, let me go home."

"That is not an option," Anat said, his voice hard and even as he shook free of the vestiges of Jay's emotion. "My cousin doesn't know how to ask this of you, so I will. I chose this life, a mortal one, after centuries of tending to humans. I wanted what they had: a chance to live and then to die a peaceful death."

Sylvie stood silent.

"A spell has been cast over you to keep you here as one of them. You live in exile like us but are unaware of your predicament, and for that I envy you. You exist in blissful ignorance. You are free to live and love as you so choose. When I was attacked by *your* kind I was forced to assume my old form once more. I was eighty-three years away from remaining human. Now, I have to start back at the beginning and wait for another thousand years to pass before I may become human."

"But I—"

"Silence!" Anat roared, showing his anger for the first time. "You are iron-bound and that connects you to the fae. You will take us into the Hill, you will solve this problem, and then you will gift me back the years I lost at the hands of your kind. Faerie magic is the most powerful in this world. And if you don't help Jay, I will put you to sleep until you make it to the portal."

"How dare you threaten to knock me out just for your little road trip. I had nothing to do with your attack and I'm sorry you lost all those years but I have no magic, I can't give them back to you. Jay, please, make him understand."

Anat strode forward and was upon her before Sylvie had time to react.

"You are iron-bound," he said before grabbing at the Celtic knot on her neck. He lifted it off her skin and concealed it in his fist, dampening the power it held over Sylvie. "Now do you see, faerie?"

Sylvie stumbled, breathless, her knees buckling and legs weak. She stared up at Anat, eyes unfocused and far away.

"Under the Hill," she mumbled.

Enough, Jay sternly told Anat from inside and the demigod dropped the necklace back onto Sylvie's skin.

Her gaze snapped to attention. "Don't ever touch me again."

Sensing she had reached a decision, Anat held out a hand from an appropriate distance away and waited. Sylvie clenched her jaw and hesitated a moment before placing her hand in Anat's. He held her palm in a tight grip and Sylvie closed her eyes.

"Just tell me when we're there."

"You will know," said Anat and pulled her close to his side.

Jay searched for his power. It flooded into him without a word, flowing out of his back and into each little hollow wing bone igniting them with such a strength he should not have. Anat's wings convulsed as their meshed bodies moved with the new flooding of magic.

Go! yelled Jay and as one they moved their wings.

The entire world shifted but the tiny group remained stationary, as if their feet stood on solid ground. Jay was thankful Sylvie's eyes remained closed for the journey as emptiness rolled beneath her feet. If she was surprised into letting go, she would be thrown into a white abyss of motion to be lost forever, trapped in the gaps between places on the Earth.

Jay and Anat's wings beat in sync, building to top speed as Jay eased into the full breadth of his power. The force of his magic filled him with a leaping joy; he hadn't flown since his banishment. The emotions it brought to him surged into his heart and he pushed his wings to go faster.

Do not lose control, Reaper! Anat warned in a tense voice.

Jay shook the words away, enjoying the loud sound of wings thumping in his ears. He counted off where they were by modern day states and counties they fly by.

Almost there, Jay said in a distracted voice, still keeping track of the townships.

Slow the pace, Anat urged.

Wing muscles screeching in protest, Jay slowed to a controlled stop. The world around them changed from a blur to a smudge to defined objects.

"Faerie, we have arrived," Anat informed Sylvie who nodded. To Jay, he added, *Well done, Reaper.*

"Oh, God," she swore, holding a hand to cover her forehead. Back on ground no longer rotating beneath them, Anat released Sylvie's hands and she swayed, feet unsteady.

"Do not worry if you are feeling dizzy," Anat told her. "Flying with our kind can be unsettling."

"You fucking think?" Sylvie moved her hand to cover her eyes.

Turning his focus away from the distressed woman, Anat addressed Jay. *It is time for you to leave my body.*

Jay concentrated on himself as a separate being, his own entity. He wiggled in the glutinous cavity of the demigod. The work to free himself was tough and progress slow. Jay shimmied his body in sinuous movements, using his elbows to drag his body forward.

White light shone through a gossamer film of skin above Jay. It was so thin he could see the sky. Palms together, Jay pushed his hands forward and ruptured the delicate tissue with the points of his fingers. Warm summer air rushed in and he heard birds in the trees. His eyes pinched with contracting pupils in the growing dawn light.

Jay braced himself against Anat, one hand on his shoulder, the other scrabbling at his midsection. Grunting, he hauled himself out, extracting his body in a long and sticky movement. Struggling and twisting in violent jerks, Jay emerged from Anat's left side and had to stop to rest halfway. A horrified scream shrieked out from Sylvie's direction.

"I'm going to be sick," she said, turning from the grotesque sight, gagging.

Gathering strength, Jay took a deep breath and engaged all his muscles, pulling himself from the demigod an inch at a time. There was enough of his body free for gravity to take over and Jay pitched forward to the ground, throwing his hands out to catch his fall. Jay sprawled on his back panting and grateful that the wet slime of Anat's viscera could not follow him and linger on his clothes and skin.

A complaining yowl sounded from the distance and they all looked toward where the noise had emanated from among the trees. Dashing toward them out of the underbrush scurried a tortoiseshell cat. Jay could not keep the smile from his face as the demon ran closer to them, shifting in mid-leap into her second form right before she drew too close.

"You didn't tell me how far you would be going," Friend panted, standing before them. "I had to run all the way from the Hill to catch up with you." As if to demonstrate how put out she was, Friend made a show of adjusting her dress and hair.

"I'm glad you did," Jay answered, feeling a warmth envelop his heart as he looked at her. Friend pursed her lips but her cheeks sported the faintest of a pink blush. "How is Janis?"

Friend smirked. "She's fine, she's in a holding cell in the dungeons. I like her, for a human."

Jay could only hope that she would stay safe for now. Not even Friend could help her other than provide scant protection. "How did you manage to find us?"

"Never mind about that," she stated, but her blush deepened.

"If she found us, others can too," Sylvie said with concern.

Anat frowned in agreement.

"No one's following you," Friend said, tucking a loose loc back into the hair tie holding her bun in place.

"Then how did you find us?" Sylvie asked, hand on a hip.

With a loud huff, Friend admitted, "I can track the reaper's scent." She blinked at Jay several times. "I took a tracer from you when we last...spoke."

"They would still be able to follow me," Anat said with a darkening expression. "My trail moves from Richmond to here. I will head off and lead them away."

"We don't know if we're being followed," Jay said, trying to keep worriment out of his voice. "If something happens to me, you have to help Friend look after Janis. I know we're more kin than friends, but if I could ask this of you now, as a friend, I would."

Anat turned and took a few swift steps to close the distance between him and the reaper. His wings stretched to encircle their bodies as Anat closed his arms around Jay, hugging him close. Anat's hands cupped the back of Jay's neck and pulled him to bend down. Their foreheads met in a lingering gesture.

"You have never been without my friendship, reaper," Anat said when he pulled back. "Or my support. I shall stay."

Jay dipped his head in a shallow bow. "Thank you."

Friend sniffed. "Where to next?"

Jay looked up. "Into the Hill. Follow me."

As far as Friend could tell, they were moving north. August in this Idaho place was still warm but it wasn't anything to compare to the stifling humidity of the South. A small breeze gathered and blew across her skin and, despite the lack of moisture in the air, Friend allowed herself to enjoy the sensation. Her poor reaper, however, was suffering. She smirked at the back of his shirt, soaking with sweat. Friend was used to heat but the reaper was not. He had promised a short walk and it hadn't yet been twenty minutes, but he was already a sweaty mess.

Her eyes traveled down the wide expanse of Jay's back and settled on his tapered waist and firm backside. The demon's smile spread. She would have to grow used to using pronouns and calling him a name, but it wouldn't take long for her to get used to him having a body. Friend's eyes grew foggy as she descended into her imagination of all the potential enjoyment of their future.

The smells of summer, grass, trees, and the hot morning sun shining on wildflowers surrounded the little troupe as they followed their leader in a somewhat straight line. Friend had never visited this place before, though she knew many demons loved the main city in the state. Far outside of the metropolitan area, she was enjoying the natural sur-roundings.

Her eyes flicked to the reaper, her fingers pressed to her lips, Friend remembered the last kiss she and the reaper shared back in her den. His power had been overwhelming, burning into her with an intensity she had never before felt. What would it mean for a reaper to join with humanity by way of his emotions? Friend swallowed. What would it mean for a demon to taste the fallout of such actions? The reaper's power was stronger, more commanding than anything Friend had come across in her long life. It called to her, pulling her forward. Even just thinking of it, she almost stumbled. She shivered. Something within her wanted to answer that call, to follow the path the reaper now walked, straight into humanity.

"Here!" Jay called over his shoulder, interrupting her thoughts. "It's just down this hill."

An expansive parking lot before a visitor's center greeted them as they emerged from the trees off the side of the drive.

"What time do the caves open?" Sylvie asked Jay.

He shrugged. "I haven't visited before."

Sylvie arched an eyebrow. "Sure wish I had an iPhone."

Jay ignored her last remark and brought them over to a grouping of picnic tables where he could sit and rest his weary knees. Anat sharpened his eyes and looked toward the door of the visitor center.

"In about two hours," he said.

There were already some vans and RVs in the parking lot, along with the cars filling up the employee section. Anat pulled a glamour around his body and shifted into the body of the older male he had been before his form was ruined by the fae.

"It might be busy today, cousin."

"There's nothing we can do about that. We'll rest here for now."

Friend was grateful to take a seat next to Jay on the bench. She wasn't tired, but her mind didn't feel clear. A warm hand touched her back in a gentle caress. She looked at Jay sidelong.

"Reaper..." she purred, unable to help the unconscious rumble.

He smiled at her. "Are you okay?" Jay asked.

She wrinkled her nose but nodded. A few of her locs had come loose from her hair tie and he brushed them back to tuck behind her ear. The moment was so tender, Friend almost shifted to her cat form and scratched him.

"I'm well," she told him, sliding down the bench seat to put space between them. "I'm not used to...hiking." She managed to make the word sound offensive.

Jay chuckled. "Not in those shoes."

Friend considered her footwear. They weren't ruined yet, but they would be. "I didn't have time to grab anything else."

"Speaking of footwear," Sylvie started, "can one of you put a magic spell on me so I don't look so raggedy? I can't go inside looking like this."

Across the other side of the picnic table, Anat tipped back his head and laughed but Jay nodded. Sylvie moved to stand before Jay where he sat at the picnic table.

"Try to stay still." He rubbed his hands together for a few seconds before snapping them apart and placing his palms flat against Sylvie's thighs, near her pants pockets. The cleansing breeze fluffed the denim material and the cotton of her shirt and when the fabric settled, they were as if just bought from the store.

"Thank you," Sylvie sighed in happy relief.

Friend shifted into her cat form, unwilling to let Jay see the territorial anger that flashed across her face when he touched the other woman. Ridiculous, all of it, Friend had no time for such feelings. As she watched him with slitted eyes, she did halfway wish he would pet her.

7

The caverns opened with little fuss, though when they wandered inside the visitor center, there were plenty of mortals for them all to blend with the crowd. Most visitors were families on vacation or the occasional curious local. Jay thought they would stand out but even Friend, no longer a cat, in her strapless dress and fancy platform shoes, didn't cause anyone to blink an eye. Jay saw another tourist wearing something just as out of place and felt himself relax.

"Since you were too afraid to break in after-hours, what's your plan?" Friend smirked.

"I don't know the way in these caverns, I didn't want to waste more time by getting lost." Jay pointed over in the direction of several booths with glass in front of them. "We need tickets to gain access to the caves. The tour is how we can slip away at the back of the group."

Anat grunted, stepping to the end of one of the ticket lines. "The closer portal would have been one back east."

"I know," Jay said. "But I didn't want to chance using a different one."

"You know who guards this entrance," Anat added in a quiet voice.

Jay dipped his chin. "I do."

Sylvie perked up. "What now?"

"Aosen," Friend purred with a grin. "A dragon."

"A what?" Sylvie's eyes went wide. "How does no one know about dragons living here?"

"Because," Jay whispered back. "They're very careful."

"That's not a real answer."

"It's not my job to know about the routine of dragons. All I know is, contrary to popular belief, they don't eat a lot."

Sylvie let out a sort of hysterical sounding snort of a laugh as they took their place at the back of the ticket line. "Popular belief? Jay, it's not like people think dragons are real!"

The woman behind the counter interrupted the conversation with a smile. "How many tickets?"

"Four," Anat rumbled while Friend snapped down a credit card. She winked at Jay.

"Head out that door and across the lawn to the cave entrance. You can't miss it. Enjoy your tour!" she chirped, dismissing them with a smile, her eyes already sliding to the next group in line.

Following the directions, they walked outside, blinking in the sunlight. Jay again took the lead across a short gravel pathway to another building where the entrance to the caves was housed. About a dozen other people were already in the building waiting for the tour to start.

"All ticket holders for the eleven o'clock tour please gather over here!" an employee shouted to the room. Everyone turned and shuffled as one, young children squeezing past legs and giggling.

The man who spoke was dressed in a uniformed jacket and faded, very broken-in jeans. His beard was scruffy and grew over his entire face, circling around his chin and cheeks and ending at his wild curly hair. The jacket displayed the Dowe Caverns logo across the back in large embroidery with a matching, smaller emblem sewn onto the front breast. He waited for most of the tour group to gather around him before speaking again, a smile breaking across his tanned skin.

"I'm Alejandro, and I'll be your tour guide through the Dowe Caverns!" Alejandro turned to a door behind him as another cave tour guide held the entrance open. He ushered the crowd toward an elevator at the far end of the room behind the door. As the elevator descended, several children shouted out in their excitement, watching the rock rushing past them through the open metal cage of the lift.

At the bottom, Alejandro led the tour into a large, cavernous gallery filled with limestone deposits and water dripping down from the ceiling onto other types of sedimentary rocks. Around the group came noises of admiration and wonder. "This way to the river," Alejandro instructed.

The pathway led to a rushing river with a long wooden dock stretching along the side of the bank. Bobbing in the current lashed to the moorings, were several wide and shallow boats, lined with bumper buoys around the sides. Each boat had flat bench seats made of metal, perforated down the middle.

One at a time, Alejandro helped the tour into the boat, running through a speech on safety. Grabbing two long poles, he pushed away from the dock. While they floated, Alejandro spoke on the history of the caves, from their forming millions of years ago to Arthur Dowe's discovery. The boat followed the underground river around twists and bends of rock. The light was dim but not gloomy, electric light built into the corner where the curving, natural rock walls met the cave roof.

After about ten minutes on the river, Alejandro steered to the side, bumping up against a natural dock cut out of a slab of light colored rock. "We'll make our way deeper into the caves." The boat pitched as he disembarked and helped the tour from the boats. Alejandro arrived at the last row and helped Friend out first. "Having fun?" he asked.

"Oh, yes," Friend answered adamantly, bobbing her head up and down. Anat stifled a laugh.

Alejandro tied up the boat and laid the poles across the empty seats for the return journey. Another boat bobbed up and down in front of the one they rode in on. Farther down to the left, before the river disappeared around a bend carved into the rock, a net was set up to stop untethered boats from being swept away by the chugging current.

Alejandro walked to the head of the crowd, drawing them together in a tight group with the gesture of his outstretched arms. "Alright, follow me and we'll make our way further into the caves."

The tour started to move, following the leader, while Jay, Anat, and Friend hesitated at the back. Sylvie began to follow the group when Jay spoke.

"Sylvie," he instructed out of the corner of his mouth. "Your shoe's untied."

"What? No it's..." She stopped walking, eyes round with comprehension, and bent to attend to her shoe, pantomiming tying laces on her sandal.

Taking advantage of the moment, Friend blew a kiss at the tour group, sending a wave of forgetfulness toward them. When the kiss settled, anyone with a memory of seeing the four would be forgotten. Alejandro, and the rest of the tour group, rounded a corner, their voices fading in the deepness of the cave.

"What now?" the demon asked.

Anat was already walking back toward the water. "Back to the boats, we have to continue down the river," he said.

Jay chose one of the boats roped to the farthest end of the natural dock, near the net.

"Get in," he said, picking up the long steering poles. He waited until Anat and Sylvie boarded and then handed one of the long poles to Friend when she was settled. "I'll be at the front."

He untied the boat from its mooring and hopped onto the prow. Right before their boat collided with the net, Jay took his pole out of the water and tapped out a wet, counterclockwise square on the netting. The braided nylon disappeared and they glided past where the partition used to be. As soon as the stern of the boat cleared the space, the net popped back into being with a soft pop.

Electric wiring and lights hung in a line at the top of the cave ceiling, although at a lesser frequency than the main part of the caves. This section of the caves were roped off to tours for their lack of sightseeing appeal but were still open to staff.

The current picked up around a bend and Friend and Jay found themselves trying to keep the boat from bumping up against the walls of the cave. The river twisted them around until the color of the water turned from a milk teal to a deep green.

"Here!" Anat shouted, wings flaring out from under his glamour over the sides of the boat, helping to keep them balanced. He pointed at a docking station on the bank before the river ended in a tumble of a waterfall coursing under a low rock.

Sylvie jumped out of the boat, causing it to rock and the bow to dip down with Jay's weight on the front.

"Grab the rope," Anat instructed, tossing it to Sylvie. His wings beat a few times as Friend climbed from the boat and checked her shoes once she was on solid ground again. Jay was the last to leave, dropping his pole on the ground and leaving the boat moored to the dock.

They delved into the cave for over an hour, careful not to disturb too many loose stones or to lose each other in the darkness. At some point, Friend abandoned trying to navigate her way forward while wearing high heels and shifted into a cat, darting around their feet as they walked.

They picked along for many more minutes, finding their way by touch alone. When light again came to their eyes, it took them a moment to realize they could see. Coming from no particular direction, the light filled the space. It was dull and soft; embers at the bottom of a dying fire. It gave enough illumination so they no longer had to caress the walls for support. The air turned dry, sucking up all the moisture from the air like a winter tundra. Jay licked at his lips.

"I'm thirsty," Sylvie muttered to no one in particular as the baked air sank into their throats.

Friend meowed, "We are close."

At their feet, pebbles shifted, the slightest movement of rocks rolling away from the space in front of them. A noise comes at the four, pitched so low it is impossible to discern distance or location. A wave of fevered air blew around them, drawing sweat from Jay's pores and wicking the moisture away at the same moment.

"Dragon," Anat whispered, voice low and hoarse from the arid atmosphere of the cave. The party inched forward, keeping to one wall and following it as the narrow passage curved and opened in a quick turn to the left.

"Fuck me," Sylvie croaked.

The space before them was enormous. The sweeping cavern descended into blackness leaving them on a natural ridge. The ceiling was somewhere in the dark above, echoing back the sounds of tiny stones rolling down slopes or water dripping from stalactites before hissing away into steam in the hot air. To their left, the source of the dim light came from a dent in the wall, twice as tall as Jay and wide enough to fit a car, an alcove containing dragonflame. It was an ever-burning yellow and orange fire, a reflection of the power held within a dragon's belly.

Smells of time and memory circled, pungent but impossible to describe, the redolence of forgotten places remembered by maps lost to history. It was cloying, as the thick air was far removed from any chance of ventilation.

The lair of a dragon.

Jay cleared his throat and tried to summon enough saliva to swallow the nerves stuck at the back of his mouth.

"Good afternoon, Aosen" he called out into the large space. The words bounced away, fading into the places the dragonflame did not touch.

There was silence after the last of the echoes dispersed. Then, the low, rumbling noise from before sounds again. Now that they were closer, Jay recognized it as scales moving over stone.

"Reaper," an answering voice purred, the word elongated in a rolling cadence, the speech of a huge being. "You woke me up. I thought your kind knew better than that."

A huge, reptilian talon rose up out of the dark and grabbed a cluster of rock near the ledge, using the stalagmite formation as support. Causing the ground far below to shake, Aosen adjusted from laying to sitting. At least, Jay assumed this was so, the parts of the beast visible in the flickering firelight was only the claw circled around the rocks at eye level.

Aosen's pebbled skin was colored somewhere between gray and black, but there were other unnamed, unseen colors that made up the hide. With the limits of how far into the color spectrum human eyes could see, Jay's descriptions fell short.

The dragon was enormous, beyond enormous. Wind whistled in the dark and an object whipped past them. Somewhere high above it stopped, and had a feeling that its neck was not extended to its full length. Two oblong shapes of the dragon's deep orange eyes peered from the gloom. The smoldering light disappeared into darkness when the gargantuan beast blinked.

Dragons were similar to lobsters; leave them alone and they would continue to grow. There was no sense to this, Jay thought, eyeing what parts of the dragon he could see. Nothing had to be this big. His human body stood a few inches over six feet but he was only as large as the smallest scale on the dragon's knuckle.

"Do not be afraid, Your Grace. You and I are kin. It is this Angel of Death who is out of place here." When Aosen spoke, scorching blue light filtered out through the negative space around its teeth, waving hot against the dark air and warping the space like a desert mirage. "Two Angels of Death, if I am not mistaken."

Anat dipped his head in respect, "Aosen."

"And a...*friend*," the dragon purred.

Friend chirped, sounding as if she were nothing more than a normal cat tracking a bird.

Sylvie leaned over to Jay. "Should I curtsy?" she asked out the side of her mouth.

If boulders were covered in velvet and dropped into boiling water, it would sound like the dragon's laughter. "No, Your Grace, you needn't curtsy to me, although the gesture of respect is much appreciated."

"Why?" Sylvie asked.

"It would seem she has lost her memory," Jay hurried to explain, lest the dragon take Sylvie's words for an insult. "That's why we're here, to seek passage into the Hill and to find answers."

Hot wind slammed into them as Aosen sighed. Friend darted behind Anat's legs as the demigod flared his wings out for balance. Jay rocked on his heels, feeling his cheeks tighten as the skin dried out.

"So, you have come to me. What do you promise?"

"She doesn't know what she can offer, without her memory she has no knowledge of procedures such as this," Jay answered for her.

The dragon shifted its weight. "But you do, reaper. You remember."

Jay nodded before darting a glance at Anat. The demigod shook his head but Jay's fists clenched.

"I offer you the stars." Jay held his breath, licking his lips in a fruitless attempt to wet them. At his ankles, Friend had moved to wend around his feet, showing her support.

"You would offer this?"

"I would."

A small puff of dragonflame burned blue out of the nostrils, illuminating the Aosen's head for a second before the flame cooled red and died out.

"How desperate is this quest, reaper?"

"They took our friend," Sylvie called out, voice thick. "Will you let us through?"

The dark pupils in the orange eyes swiveled to consider Sylvie. The copper pools grew larger as the dragon moved its head closer to the ledge. It sniffed at them, Sylvie's bangs and the loose fabric of her shirt pulling upward in the vacuum of air.

"This is a strange story, even if you do not believe it yourself, Your Grace." Aosen pulled back, eyes regarding them once more from afar. "No one may pass into the Hill unbidden. Why waste your time and come here?"

Jay gestured to Sylvie who stood frozen in shock at being smelled by a dragon. "She has the power to grant the invitation, we just need to find the portal."

The leathery sound of adjusting wings bounced around the cave.

"Amusing," he said, as quietly as a dragon could. "The stars—you can promise this? How is it this power is within one who is banished?"

Swallowing, Jay closed his eyes, calling his power.

Banished and released, a gateway through a human soul, it said, lifting out of Jay's body with ease.

Aosen was startled, body bumping into stone far below and causing a jumble of rocks to fall with a grinding crash.

"Impossible," he accused. "You cannot merge with your mortal shell." He turned its head to the side and considered Jay with one eye. "How have you done this, reaper? Tell me you cannot feel their emotions?"

"Unfortunately, he can," Anat grumbled from behind Jay.

The dragon made a noise that almost sounded like a snort. "You were never made to feel what they feel. However, if this gives you the power to send me home..." he trailed off, voice shifting to what sounded like hope. Wings adjusting echoed through the cavernous space again. "I accept your offer." His eyes fixed on Sylvie. "Stand still, Your Grace."

Before Sylvie had time to panic, Aosen opened its mouth wide, the blue fire held deeper within his body illuminating the ridges inside his mouth. Steam billowed toward the ledge and Sylvie flinched.

"I can only give back what was erased," Aosen said, voice mingling with the magic air flowing around Sylvie. "I do not have the authority to reinstate your powers. That vault," he added, "is shut very tight."

The cold steam tightened around Sylvie's body, thickening to obscure her in a sort of cocoon. A knot of the steam thickened around the Celtic knot upon her chest and flared bright, burning the necklace away, severing what anchored her fae essence in her human body.

They all watched as the opaque air rotating around Sylvie sank against her, coating her body like a second skin. It slowed to a stop, flashing a bright light of a deep green, shining into the cave and forcing Jay to shut his eyes against it. When he opened them a moment later, a different Sylvie stood before him.

Human no longer, the fae that remained was beautiful and alien. Her hair was a brighter shock of red with loose curls tumbling down her back to end at the top of her hip. Leaves and small twigs with growing green berries attached were tucked into the strands. Her brown eyes were gone, replaced to now shine amber and set at an odd angle, larger in their sockets than a human's ever could be.

"Sylvie?" Jay asked with caution.

The faerie cocked her head and a lock of hair moved to reveal a pointed ear. Her large eyes blinked and pink lips that faded to a healthy, yew green color at the corners, parted into a mischievous smile.

"Reaper," she stated in a voice sounding as if it did not belong to a world where sports cars and cell phones existed.

"Your Grace," Aosen said in a respectful voice, "welcome back."

Sylvie's eyes flicked up to the dragon and her smile widened. "I have not seen you in many years, Aosen. I will not forget this deed."

The dragon's eyes disappeared into darkness, bowing his head.

"What am I dressed in?" Sylvie kicked off her sandals and flexed her bare toes. Her long, nimble fingers tore the shirt fabric as if it was little more than paper tissue, ripping the garment to shreds and depositing it away from her on the ground like trash. She tore free of the jeans and underwear and stood before them naked. "Disgusting human rags."

Wings fluttered out from her back, the delicate things floating in the air before settling behind her. They were a deep, natural yellow, the membranous material stretched between supporting veins of green. The silky texture of her wings faded from the muted yellow to a greenish orange, ending in ragged edges colored in red as autumnal as her hair. They appeared as a cross between a maple leaf and a butterfly. She laughed gaily when she saw the dragonflame, wings brushing the ground behind her like a train.

"I invite you into the world of the fae," she said to Friend, Anat, and

Jay.

Jay glanced back at the dragon. "That's where the portal is?"

Aosen's voice rumbled deep in its throat. "You will come back for me, Angel of Death, when you are no longer trapped in mortal form and I will see my home once more."

The huge beast moved through the shroud of darkness and disappeared in a gust of burning air back into the shadows of the pit below.

"I will not forget," Jay promised to the dark. Turning to the dragonflame he walked behind Sylvie, careful not to step on the tips of her wings. "After you."

Without waiting to see if they would follow, Sylive stepped into the fire and disappeared.

TWENTY-SEVEN

JANIS SPENT THE NEXT few hours trying to think of a way out of the cell.

Of course Jay would send the most unhelpful demon, she groused to herself. Though, she was thankful that he had sent anyone at all. And, she supposed, if he had told Friend to find her in the dungeons, it must mean he was safe enough somewhere to make a plan.

Friend had told her Jay would meet her in Faerie but she hadn't said where. She had to get somewhere safe to hide and wait. She eyed the solid metal bars blocking her egress. Easier said than done.

"Byst?" she asked as a sudden thought came to her. The salamander was still in his corner, curled up in the shadows. "It's safe to come out."

The fae unfurled himself and dragged his body so he could see Janis.

"What do you want, human child?"

"Why are we in the same cell?" She nodded her head to the door, indicating the greater dungeon beyond. "Why aren't I with the rest of the people?"

Smoke curled from his nostrils. Dried blood from his injured eye ridge remained on his face like a new stripe upon his rough skin.

"The Unseelie have brought in so many souls," the fae said. "There are many to process."

Janis sniffed. "I heard it's illegal to take souls."

Another puff of smoke came out of the salamander's nostrils. The creature was laughing at Janis's words.

"You think that stopped this court? They knew what they wanted long before they won the last election. No sooner were they sworn into power than they began collecting souls to stay in power."

"You can't just take people's souls and you can't take people against their will. People do not belong to anyone but themselves."

"While that is a nice sentiment, the Unseelie do not care."

"That's disgusting," Janis snapped.

"And yet, that is what they have been doing."

Janis stood up, pacing the length of the small cell. "Someone should do something about this, we should do something."

"Sit down, you will tire yourself out," Byst swished his tail.

"Is anyone doing anything?" The salamander sighed. "What? Tell me."

"When the Unseelie Court won the election over the Seelie, they made sure they would never be challenged again. They banished most of the Seelie Court to the human world, erasing their memories and locking away their powers. It was a takeover, turning our democratic council into a dictatorship." Janis stared at the creature. "Do not blame me, I voted for the Seelie."

Janis shook her head. "No, that's not... Elections?"

"Once every fifty years. Well, it is *supposed* to be every fifty years. The Unseelie have changed all that."

"Who's left to disagree with all this?"

The salamander gave his own version of a shrug, "When the Unseelie Court won, the Seelie Court was banished and their staunchest supporters were thrown in jail. There was not even a vote." Seeing the confused look on Janis's face, Byst elaborated, "It was not supposed to happen, remember."

Glaring, Janis crossed her arms. "I still don't understand why faeries need slaves if they have magic."

"The Unseelie Court cannot take souls as slaves but they can harness their energy. Souls have power, human child."

"Are they killing people?"

"Unfortunately, yes," his tongue flicked in the air around Janis. "The human soul is beautiful, the purest form of energy existing on this world. Mixed together. The Unseelie wish to stay in power so they have found a way to take that power and use it to their advantage."

"Murder," Janis stated. "At least tell me what the reapers have to do with it."

The salamander let out another smoke-filled laugh, "They do not have anything to do with it."

Janis frowned at the fae. "Yes, they do, Jay and I found out they are being murdered, too. He's one of the reapers that's alive and knows about it."

"Come again?" If the salamander had fur it would have stood on end. Janis watched with some concern as a ripple passed over his pebbled flesh.

"My friend Jay is a reaper."

"You did not arrive here right after you died?" Byst demanded, quaking.

"No, Jay was trying to help me look for a ferryman and I was..." Janis never got to finish.

In a swift motion, Byst lept toward Janis, slamming her back into the dirt and landing his heavy weight upon her chest.

"Get off!" Janis cried as best she could beneath the salamander. "You're hurting me!"

"There is one way this works, sheefrah," Byst spat, "and you are not supposed to have time to dally with a reaper." Byst moved off her chest and scuttled to the bars at the front of the cell to croak out a loud, clamorous call into the quiet of the dungeon.

"What are you doing?" Janis gasped out, relieved of his weight bearing down on her lungs. Byst croaked again.

As if on cue, the red faerie who had teased Janis swept out from the shadowy air, materializing in front of the cell bars.

"Come out, come out, wherever you are," the red fae woman sang in a sickening tone.

Byst shook himself and his body warped, skin shifting and bones bubbling up under his skin until he became a rotund little man. His form started to vibrate, gaining momentum and peaking at a speed that made Janis' stomach flip, forcing her to look away. When she dared look again, Byst was on the other side of the bars, glaring up at the woman.

"I need to go to the council."

"No," Janis whispered, jaw dropping.

"Why?" The red faerie's voice had a petulant whine to it.

Byst flicked a tongue out between his now semi-human lips. "We are not so secure in our new position of soul collection that we can afford to ignore the possibility we have drawn the attention of a reaper. I do not know what they are doing out there but they should have been keeping this under better control. One reaper, it seems, is aware of the others who have died."

"Did the human child tell you that? You know all humans lie," the other faerie rolled her eyes, dismissing his concern.

Byst slammed his hand up to the fae woman's neck and squeezed, "It is a good thing I hide away in these dungeons to do this spying job or we may have never known what danger could be coming our way. I have to report this to the council." He released her and she stumbled back a few paces, massaging her neck.

"Oh, please," the red faerie croaked out, her tone remaining skeptical but her black beetle wings twitching against her back.

"I take no chances if reapers are involved. Or when one of our ferrymen miss picking up an entire soul. I have been down here long enough," Byst turned to look at Janis. "I am sorry, human child. I will not see you again."

A curious sort of rage grasped Janis by the shoulders and she sprang to her feet, rushing to the bars and reaching out between the gaps to strangle the evil thing before her.

"I hate you!" she screamed as Byst and the woman laughed at her efforts. "I swear to God I am going to burn this whole fucking place to the ground."

Incensing Janis further, the red faerie reached through the cell bars and patted her twice on the head before Janis could jerk away.

"There are no gods here, sweetling. They have no authority in the Hill." Still giggling, the fae woman moved off with Byst who croaked out a command in his loud voice for other guards to join him in the barracks.

Janis stopped breathing for a moment, entire body going still. Sucking in a deep gasp of air, she forced herself to feel calm. In a steady rhythm, she released her breath through her mouth. Her mind focused on what Byst had said earlier, that magic in faerie was available to anyone who had a need. She certainly needed it now. But what to do? She couldn't just create a trapdoor or other way out of the cell, that magic was sure to be blocked as Byst had said earlier. What else could she do?

Iron. Friend had dropped her a clue after all. If the demon was to be believed, fae were deterred by iron. Janis bent on her knees and cleared a space in the dirt, creating a work surface. With her pointer finger, she drew a simple knife in the dirt floor but made it large, the blade almost as long as her forearm. It was a childish rendering of a weapon but Janis imagined the intent mattered more than any details. When a knife didn't appear in midair as had Byst's flower, Janis sat back on her heels in defeat.

She couldn't do it. Maybe if Jay were here, he could instruct her on how to wield magic and then...

"And then what?" she snapped out loud to herself. No matter how hard she wished for something different, she was on her own. Janis took a deep breath, trying to force her pounding heart to calm. She traced the details of the blade in the dirt with her finger.

Why hadn't the magic worked for her? Janis thought back to everything Jay had told her about sheefrahs and faeries. Her mind raced through past conversations, seeking a clue to something, anything. Was she too human to do magic? Thoughts swirled in her head, making her dizzy. She wasn't all human, she didn't have a ferryman, and she couldn't do magic now. Janis felt an ache begin behind her eyes and thump all the way down in her heart.

She felt like she did when she was little, when her mother would make her sit on the kitchen stool and hold one hand over one eye, then the other, demanding she read from the eye chart taped to the fridge. Her mother had told her, over and over again, that she was different because of her eyes, that she would just have to accept the differences and live with the bullying because it wasn't going to get any easier.

Janis didn't know when her mother's obsession began, but she had been dragged to countless doctors offices in her childhood. None seemed to be too concerned about her vision or her eyes. Even her mother lost interest in them for a few months after those appointments, but then, as if it were a growing itch, Janis would catch her mother staring and frowning.

Janis sat up straighter.

She was alone, she was confused and lost, but she wasn't helpless. She was different, but it wasn't bad.

Janis slammed her fist down on the impacted dirt floor and smoothed away her original drawing. This time, she ripped her finger through the surface, cutting out the shape of a knife with slashing strokes of her nail, breaking it in the process.

She scraped away at the dirt, drawing the most realistic dagger she could manage without any trained artistic skill. As she drew, she imagined the glinting metal of the iron blade, the sound of it slicing through the air, the smell of the leather wrapping around the hilt for the best grip, a natural animal hide that would give her the upper hand when it came to fighting. With a final slash of her finger, the drawing was complete. Janis sat back on her heels to admire her work.

"Now, that's a fucking dagger," she swore into the empty cell, reveling in freedom to choose her own words and speak them however she wanted. Fading into brightness, the outline she created glowed green, a pulsing green light rose up from the floor.

"No way," Janis breathed, believing that even the slightest wind might disturb the apparition.

The light began to bleed inward from the original lines, filling in the gaps she created with her drawing. Her eyes were wide, taking in the magic, her magic, with awe. The light spilled over the small bumps in the dirt and connected with itself at the center of the dagger, tendrils of green knitting together with itself and merging into a solid form. The green light flared and brightened to white.

A loud scraping of metal erupted from somewhere down the hall of the dungeons. Chattering voices followed the screeching noise and Janis knew she was out of time.

"Come on, come on," she urged, casting a worried glance over her shoulder. The voices grew closer. It was either now or they would spot what she was doing and stop her before the knife was complete.

Iron, iron, iron, she chanted in her mind. She closed her eyes and knelt over her creation, hands on either side forehead almost pressing into the ground.

"Please," she whispered.

The bright white light she could still make out from behind her eyelids guttered and went out. Janis' eyes flew open and she wanted to scream in triumph. Steaming in the dirt floor beneath her was a newly forged iron dagger. She jumped and scrambled to hide the weapon behind her back as the bars of her cell slid open with a loud rattle.

"Stand up," came an order. It was a new guard, not the red fae woman from before. This faerie was tall and reminded Janis of a stick bug.

Remaining in a crouch, Janis considered his movements, wondering if they would be fast or slow.

"No," she told the stick faerie.

"Stand up," he said again, an amused expression on his face. His voice was thick with spite and he raised a baton in warning. "Don't make me hit you. Even though I want to hit you."

Janis groped in the dirt behind her heels and found the handle to her weapon.

"Fuck you!" she screamed out, the words ending in an absurd war cry as she sprang up and rushed the faerie, brandishing her weapon and slashing wildly. The dagger connected with the lanky body of the strange creature and sizzled on impact. Triumphant, Janis slashed again and struck off a delicate arm, the one holding the baton.

The faerie fell to the ground next to his arm, writhing in agony. The arm twitched in the dirt before curling up in jerky movements, the skin turning black as it formed into a grotesque, twisted shape.

"Iron!" the fallen guard shrieked out in furious pain.

Janis remained in a crouch, weight balanced on the balls of her feet and ready to run.

"That's right," she threw out in a reckless taunt. Another guard moved to enter the cell, their blue body in the shape of an ant.

Thrusting her weapon out before her, Janis struck the ant faerie across the chest, drawing a shallow, jagged cut across the exoskeleton. The faerie cried out and toppled over as it backed away from Janis and her iron. Taking her chance, Janis dashed out of the cell, darting around a chain gang of human prisoners and brandishing her weapon at anyone who looked fae.

"Stay back!" she screamed as she ran, following blind faith that she

302

chose the right direction.

"She has iron!" Janis heard one of the wounded faeries warn. "Don't touch her!"

Feeling giddy, Janis bounded up a set of stairs, running with her long dagger out in front, slashing at the air as if to clear a path through invisible reeds. She rounded a corner, hoping left was the correct direction and sprinted over the slippery stones. She came upon an open door and laughed with abandon as she saw Byst in a small room with several other guards.

"What?" the fae croaked, confused.

She flashed her dagger, then reached for the door handle and slammed it shut. A surge of adrenaline coursed through her body as she heard the door to the guard room lock. Spinning, Janis checked to see no one was following her before turning back to the hallway and breaking into a run again, moving fast and far away from the dungeons. Her skirt bunched around her legs and migrated up and away from any sort of modesty, but Janis did not pause and fix it.

She came upon stairs, narrow passageways, twisting tunnels, and more stairs. Refusing to slow down even for a moment, Janis pursued her path forward with abandon, but was emboldened by the feeling of gradual ascension to a higher level within the structure. The instinctual need to find higher ground filled her lungs and drove her muscles. A dull, resonating alarm bell clanged somewhere behind her and Janis raised her weapon in victory. She was alive and free. The alarm sounded again and she tucked her arm back into a running stance.

The narrow, tapered toes of the cowboy boots pinched and the tight bridge of the shoes rubbed causing blisters to begin forming but Janis ran on. The low heel made her back ache and the arch of her feet tingle, but she pushed herself even faster. Sweat trickled down her back and she felt a blister on her right ankle burst and bleed. Instead of worrying, she found herself smiling.

Blood, sweat, and tears, she chanted to herself as her boots pounded against the stones. Byst had told her she still wasn't alive in the dungeon, but she sure felt like she was.

I am human, human, human.

The corridors grew brighter, some sort of dancing rows of lights replacing wall torches, while the sound of murmuring voices in conversation came to her ears. Janis slowed, her body shaking with the effort of her prolonged run and fading adrenaline. She began to dart and duck, slipping around corners and up spiraling stairs cautiously. She saw a few faeries, wandering through the passageways with business of their own. Janis wondered where she was, guessing it might be in the bowels of some sort of castle, if the ancient masonry and dusty tapestries sagging on their wall hangings was any clue.

Janis slipped around a large pillar, peeking out from behind the curve and gasping when she saw a small procession of fae marching in formation. She jerked her body back behind the pillar and forced herself to think fast. She could hear their conversation continue and relaxed when she realized they had not seen her. Carefully, she edged around the squat column as the crowd came closer, timing her movements with the sound of their passing voices, keeping the stone support between the group and her position. Once on the far side of the pillar, Janis dashed away from her cover and into a small hallway splintering off from the main corridor.

She came to an unbalanced stop in front of a small storage room and yanked open the wooden door, bolting into the room and easing the wood closed behind her. Panting, she rushed to the small window set high into the back wall of the room and peered out. Grass and dirt greeted her vision. She was at ground level. Frustration boiled in her veins as fitting out the window will be impossible. Picking her way to move behind a shelf stacked with cleaning supplies, books, and two small hay bales, Janis settled down into the narrow space between the shelving and the wall to rest.

Twirling the iron dagger in her hand, Janis let her breathing calm and tried to force her heartbeat to stop thumping loudly in her ears. She began to cry in silence then, tears spilling over her cheeks as she hit a wall in her mind, unable to come up with any ideas of what she should do next.

"Jay," she whispered in a silent prayer. She sniffed and wiped her nose, mindful of the dagger she held. "Please come find me, I can't hide forever."

Janis cried until her eyelids drooped. She jerked her head up once, then twice, desperate to refuse the inevitable sleep of exhaustion that finally overtook her before her head could jerk up a third time.

TWENTY-EIGHT

A COOL DRAFT PRESSED against the exposed skin of Janis's back. She stirred, uncomfortable and aware of sleep leaving her. Drowsy, she lifted her head and looked around, smacking dry lips and wishing for water. Her tongue was heavy in her mouth and it took a few swallows to get her saliva flowing again. A painful spasm jolted through her lower back and she choked back a groan. Janis unfurled her body with care, unaccustomed to sleeping in such a cramped position. Something heavy was in her palm.

Her memories flooded back and Janis gripped the handle of the dagger anew, mind alert once more and heightened in fear. Her heart rate jumped, body flooding her system with hot, fast-moving blood, ready to run. The muscles in her legs bunched in response, tingling as blood flow was restored, and Janis bit back a noise of protest. Her entire body was sore. She didn't even want to venture a guess at what her poor hair looked like after a night without a protective silk wrap. Her feet stung and her skin was caked with dried sweat and Janis thought that even if she had to run now, she couldn't.

Despair hit her. There was nowhere for her to go. Janis looked around the small storage room and willed herself not to cry again. Lost. The word settled hard into her chest. She closed her eyes again and wished for sleep to reclaim her but it was no use. She opened her eyes and glared at the stone wall before her.

Janis weighed her options. The protection of this tiny room wouldn't last so long. She wasn't sure how long she had been asleep. If no one ended up finding her here, she bet Jay wouldn't either. Still, it was stupid, not wanting to move from her position of safety. Janis had seen too many

306

movies when she was alive to want to head back out into an unfamiliar place with enemies all around. She fingered the sharp edge of her iron weapon in thought. The blade slipped and sliced a narrow cut in her thumb but Janis smiled, unaffected by the minor injury.

Magic.

I need a door, she thought. *One that opens to a place of safety*

Staying behind the shelving unit, Janis leaned forward and began to scratch into the stone with the tip of her dagger, drawing a crude square. With the outline of the shape complete, Janis added a round circle off to one side as the handle. Pulling the iron blade back from the wall, she waited. Green light blossomed out from the primitive markings she scraped, following the trail of first the square then the small circular handle. The light faded and left behind a door.

"Perfect," Janis breathed, awed by the magic before her. The door handle seemed to wiggle, as if happy with the praise. Janis gripped it and twisted, pulling at the door before she gave herself time to consider how odd its movements were. A rush of wind swept into the small storeroom, sending stray bits of hay from the bales to the floor and making Janis squint. The wind died down as the pressure between the storage room and what lay beyond the new door adjusted. The air smelled sweet and inviting, a fresh and salty scent wafting up from the square hole. Poking her head through first, Janis blinked when she saw a stretch of sand spread out before her.

"A beach?" She drew her head back and glanced at the small storage room, trying to orient herself. This was where the magic thought was a safe place? The sound of the ocean drifted up from the square door, waves breaking and surf bubbling back and forth. Ducking, she side-stepped through the opening, boot sinking as it met sand. She hesitated there, one foot on stone, the other on the beach. It was an odd feeling, in and out, between one space and another, liminal.

From the side of the storage room Janis heard the alarm heralding her escape start up again. In surprise, she jerked and hit her head on the lintel between the two worlds. She tried to steady herself but the ankle on the side with the beach twisted in the soft sand and tipped her weight away from the room and into the new place. Janis fell upon the beach with a heavy thump and watched as the door, set above her in the air, closed from the other side and vanished.

Janis lay on the ground, a sick feeling of unease passing over her even as happy sunlight beamed from above and gulls cawed in the distance. The beach was picturesque. Janis had never been to a tropical location but she imagined this is what the most popular destinations were like. Fine, white sand, palm trees studding the coastline, and aqua blue water lapping at the shore.

Coconuts sat dropped in the sand, two of them nearby her landing place. Seeing them, her stomach growled. With her dagger, Janis dug into the husk, notching a small cut into the skin. The blade was sharp, sharp enough to make quick work of a coconut's tough exterior. Using both the tool and her hands, she peeled at the outer layer from the break in the skin.

She worked on the large seed until the pieces of the discarded husk littered the ground around her. Janis studied the coconut when she finished. It wasn't perfect but she knew she could cut a hole in the top to get to the edible core. With a good amount of force, she exposed a small opening at the top with the knifepoint. The silky sweet smell of coconut milk and meat wafted to her nose and she sucked at the hole, drawing out the milk into her empty stomach. The liquid dribbled down her chin and she wiped her mouth when the milk ran dry.

Sitting in the sand on this strange beach covered in coconut milk, Janis felt an absurd amount of guilt and regret. She was no longer sure, when this was all over, that she would remain anything other than a ghost. Nothing had gone according to either her or Jay's plans, and Janis was beginning to think it was futile. Would she be able to stay in the Hill as a fetch? Would she want to? At least she would be able to eat and drink again.

Her stomach growled once more, invigorated by the milk and protesting for more food. Janis picked up another coconut and set it tight between her feet, using the sturdy heels of her cowboy boots as braces. Wanting to save the knife for use as a weapon, she decided to try something else to avoid dulling the blade. Lifting the peeled and drained coconut over her head, she slammed it down onto the unopened one.

A hairline crack appeared, ringing the inner shell of the peeled coconut until it split in two, revealing tender white meat.

As she pulled chunks of coconut from the shell, she kicked off her boots, shedding them from her injured feet. Mouth full of fruit, she sat back in the sand, relaxing and wiggling her toes, stretching them out in the cool breeze blowing off the ocean. She heaved a sigh.

This place isn't so bad.

A dark shape passed overhead and Janis twisted, dropping the coconut and holding the dagger at the ready. The shadow came from a large beetle that landed a few feet away in the sand, wings buzzing to a halt and standing upright upon its back. When the beetle moved, a blinding flash of gold reflected off the back of the insect. Wiping at her watering eyes, Janis tried to make out the markings on its back. Before she could decipher the pattern, the beetle's wings started up again and it took off into the air, zipping toward Janis at a high speed.

Janis screamed, scrambling to her bare feet before the beetle could collide with her body. She watched the beetle land.

"What the hell?" Janis murmured, squinting at the bug.

As if in response, the insect started to shake, its whole body trembling as bits of it punched out from the inside, forcing the exoskeleton to duplicate and then triplicate, growing bigger and bigger. Janis screamed again at the awful sight of the growing beetle before turning and running away, wanting as much space between her and the monstrous thing as possible. With her shoes left behind, Janis forced herself into a flat sprint, holding the dagger in her hands and crossing the hot sand barefoot.

Unsure if she was making progress, Janis tossed a look over her shoulder at the insect. At that moment, the beach gave way to hard rock and, with her head turned, a jagged stone clipped at her toes and sent her sprawling. Landing on the rocks face first, the breath was knocked from her lungs and she bit down on her tongue when her chin smacked against the hard slab.

Gasping for air, Janis rolled onto her side and clutched at her mouth, knife abandoned beside her.

"Ow, fuck," she swore with an injured lisp.

A tiny buzz of laughter sounded nearby and Janis lunged on her stomach for her dagger, twisting to try and see where the sound came from. She was alone on the beach aside from the beetle who was perched on the trunk of a palm tree some feet away, back to its original size.

"Shut up," Janis told the bug, her throbbing tongue forcing her speech to sound thick and labored.

She didn't think the beetle had been the one to laugh but after the last several days, she wasn't sure. Janis held the dagger out at the beetle as she climbed to her feet. She wheezed as she moved, diaphragm sore from her fall. Knife in hand, she considered the round, fat beetle clinging to the trunk of the palm tree.

"Just stay there," she demanded as she began to slink closer. "Good little bug," she said, crossing one foot over the other, one eye on the uneven and rocky ground. "Stay small."

Just before she was close enough to spear it with her weapon, the beetle took to the air and buzzed out of reach. She groaned in frustration, slashing around with her iron blade. With a soft, organic thud of metal hitting plant matter, the dagger embedded deep into the trunk of a palm tree. She tugged at the handle of the iron dagger to no avail. She pulled at it again, wrestling with the weapon in several different directions. The trunk of the palm held fast to the iron. Janis gave it the finger after several more moments of her fruitless game of tug-of-war.

"Want some help?"

Janis screamed and whirled, searching for the unknown voice.

"Up," the voice said again.

Janis looked skyward and saw the fat beetle floating in the hot ocean breeze. "Who said that?" she asked, not knowing what to expect.

"Me." It was the insect. It flew over her head and landed on the handle of the blade sticking out of the palm tree. It clicked its wings. "I'm not going to attack you," the beetle said in a dry tone. "I'm trying to help you."

Janis wiped at the sweat trickling down from her forehead into her eyes. "Why?"

"I was told to."

"No offense, but the last faerie I trusted did not help me." Janis took a step back as the beetle rushed to the end of the dagger handle.

"I am not fae!" the little thing shouted. It backed up a few paces on spindly legs and clacked its wings once. "I am a scarab."

Janis raised an eyebrow. "How do I know you won't turn into an evil faerie?" She couldn't be sure but she thought she heard the scarab utter a sigh.

"I don't care if you believe me. I am a messenger and I am here to do my duty."

"What duty?"

The round insect flicked its wings again and the gold writing etched upon them flared. "My master Khepri bids you good morning."

Janis waited in silence for more. When nothing came, she shifted her weight and scratched at her neck. "Now what?"

The scarab shook itself and emitted a soft buzz. "Tactless," it muttered. Louder, it continued, "You are not alone on this island, mortal, but you are the only human. As such, you will follow me to the Place Between the Stones."

Janis pulled a face. "No thanks. I was just looking for a safe spot to wait for my friends."

"I assure you, there is no safer spot than the Place Between the Stones."

"Right," Janis hummed in mock agreement. "I bet your stones are great but I'm just going to stay here and wait for my friends."

The scarab remained silent and Janis cleared her throat feeling awkward.

"But thank you so much for the invitation."

Without another word, the scarab turned in a circle and vanished.

Alone again, Janis set back to work at the dagger stuck in the palm tree. The thing would not budge. Peering closer, Janis cried out in dismay when she realized the wood of the palm had started to grow around the blade, as if the knife had remained in place for a century or more. Angry and confused, Janis grasped the handle and dragged on it with all her weight.

"That does not make sense!" she yelled out to the tree in between her grunts of effort. "Where the fuck am I?"

311

"If she will not come to us, we will come to her," a voice boomed, deep and metallic and filling the air as if to replace every molecule.

Janis threw her hands over her ears but the words could not be drowned out. Sunlight flared and washed the world away into white, forcing Janis to shut her eyes and fall to her knees, face down on the sandy stones. The ground shook and behind her there were thumps of coconuts falling and smashing open upon the ground. It was over before Janis could register any pain. In the new, very much appreciated, quiet, she sat up and yelped at the sight before her.

Men, women, animals, and beings in the shape of things she can not describe stood before her.

"Holy shit," Janis breathed, unable to stop herself.

A woman with dark brown skin and long, curling black hair that fell to her ankles stepped forward, approaching a figure made of fire. "She is just a mortal! How dare you move us all at once to stand before her. She should have come to us!"

The fire-being held out a hand and the woman stopped in her advance. "Sito, calm yourself. It is done."

The woman spoke again in a loud, harsh tone. "I do not care!"

Janis hid her face away from the voice. It sounded like fields of wheat moving in the wind, of skin sliding against skin, of love whispered from a mother to a new baby. All facets of the voice crush down upon Janis forcing her lower and lower to the ground.

"Stop!" another voice cried out, making the image of dark red clay come to Janis' mind. "You are hurting the child."

The overwhelming sensation that came from the woman's voice lessened and Janis was able to raise her head to peek out from under her arms she had thrown across face. The speaker who had come to her aid was a bearded man with skin colored a deep red, naked and holding a long spear. His black beard was long and pointed, curling down his chin in an ancient fashion. He smiled at Janis but she shrank back, shivering. Even though the man was smiling at her, Janis could see his kindness was a shadow of what would exist in a human. His gaze was void of true empathy. It was then she knew for sure, when she saw what lay behind the man's dark eyes, that she was in the presence of gods

"Are you alright?" he asked Janis who closed her eyes and moved her forehead back to face the ground.

"You scared her, too," the woman said. "This will get us nowhere."

Behind eyes shut tight, Janis could see another flash of bright light but heard silence when it faded. Taking steady breaths, she waited several long moments before daring to move again. Tilting her chin, she squinted one eye open and closed it when she saw a small, wrinkled old woman sitting on folded legs in the sand before her. Janis continued to breathe and waited for many more minutes in her curled position before a cramp in her left hamstring forced her to move.

Stretching and shaking out the muscle, Janis scooted backward to put even more distance between herself and the lone figure seated upon the sand. She massaged the back of her thigh as she watched the woman, waiting to see if she would move.

The woman was naked, her brown skin in a shade Janis did not recognize, although flashes of familiar skin tones lurked in the dips and crevices of the woman's wrinkles. White hair grew from her head and fell around her body like a thick, white cape. The hair faded away first to silver, then to a deep, shiny black at the ends. It was so long that the locks rested on the ground, ringing around the woman in a circle twice. Janis had a feeling that if the woman stood up, she would not be above four feet tall.

"Hello, Janis," the woman said, her eyes and mouth remaining closed. Janis jumped in surprise and moved backward even further. "You know what we are."

"I don't know you," she said, voice trembling.

"I am First Mother," the god replied in a simple statement. "We thought it best that I approach you. This form is reassuring."

Janis didn't feel reassured but she wasn't filled with quite as much fear from before. "I don't recognize your name. Where do you come from?"

"I was before. I am First Mother. I was yours before the Great Ice." The god's mouth never moved but Janis felt the warm shadow of a grin hang in the air between them.

Janis' mouth dropped open. How many hundreds of thousands of years ago was that?

"Do not think of time. I am First Mother. I do not need your understanding."

"Okay," Janis said, feeling very tired. She put a hand across her brow, as if it could stop this strange and ancient god from interpreting her thoughts. If this was the land of gods, or beach of the gods, or wherever, how was this any better than being in a dungeon?

"You are safe here. No fae can reach you now. I am First Mother."

Janis frowned at the god's speech habit and her ability to read minds. *All I want are answers, plain and simple.* Janis fell back onto her heels when the god shifted her form and morphed into the shape of Kate Pereda.

"Mom?" Janis choked out, knowing it was impossible but not caring at all.

"I missed you, baby girl," Kate said and held out her arms, opening her eyes to smile at her daughter.

Her voice was the same. Her eyes were the same. Janis stood, tripping to her feet and stumbling forward in her rush to hug her mother. She collapsed in Kate's arms and began to cry, letting the comfort of her mother's embrace wash over her.

"It wasn't my fault," she choked out between sobs. "I was different because the fae made me that way. I'm better now. You have to tell dad, please."

Janis broke back into tears, letting Kate rock her and shush her, rubbing her back and feeling so real. When Janis began to calm, Kate kissed her forehead.

"Janis, this place isn't for you. It is the place of forgotten gods, of deities no longer worshiped. You do not belong here."

Janis nestled her face into the crook of her mother's arm.

"I was trapped, I was in the faerie dungeons and I needed a place to escape. I don't know how to get back." Janis' voice cracked, threatening to let her emotion spill out again.

"Hush, baby. They'll help you get back, don't you worry."

"But I don't want to go back, my soul will be harvested for energy." Janis frowned, trying to remember what Byst had told her. "Something like that. I have to wait for Jay to come get me. He'll know what to do."

Kate put a hand on Janis' forehead and made her daughter look up. Kate smiled, expression full of sadness. "You know what to do. You must not wait for the reaper. You can't stay here, baby. They have to send you back."

"Fine, then send me back to the real world, not back to the place with all the faeries." Janis sat up, moving away from the embrace of her mother's arms. "Don't send me back there, not without Jay."

Kate's form shuddered and twisted, sliding back into the shape of First Mother. Janis recoiled and moved away from the god in the sand.

"I am First Mother. The path forward is the same as the path behind."

"You can't put me back there!" Janis didn't bother to keep her voice from growing louder. "You're a god, you can do what you want!"

First Mother shook her head. "We are not all we once were. There are limits. I am First Mother."

Janis pounded open palms on the sand. "If you're First Mother, do something!"

The god remained quiet, her brown, wrinkled face unmoving.

"Please," Janis begged. "They'll take my soul."

The god tilted her head from one side to the other. Her closed eyes and mouth remain passive, betraying no emotion. "The labyrinth. I am First Mother. You can go that way."

Janis hesitated. "Where? Which labyrinth?"

"The only one there ever was. The only one there will ever be. I am First Mother." The god opened her eyes and Janis gasped. Pockets of rich darkness filled the wide sockets, white lights dancing in the depths. The universe was in First Mother's eyes. The god reached up and plucked a hair from the top of her head. Reverently, she passed it to Janis. "Take my hair. Find your way. I am First Mother."

Accepting the single strand of hair, Janis held it close to her chest.

"Where is the labyrinth?" she asked again, confused.

The god leaned forward and smiled wide, showing pink gums and a handful of yellow teeth. "*Here.*"

Janis looked into the god's eyes. The darkness of the space held within pushed outward, spilling and covering the face of the First Mother. It filled the edges of Janis' vision. Leaning forward, Janis was swallowed by the stars, drawn inside the god and pushed on to a place far away from the strange beach of forgotten deities.

TWENTY-NINE

ARKNESS GRIPPED JANIS, HOLDING her somewhere around her middle. She floated, for what felt like days, in a world filled with color. Distant swirls of space cloud formations hung in the starry emptiness like a captured snapshot of milk poured in coffee. Pinpricks of light dotted the background of everywhere she looked: uncountable suns burning away. A planet loomed behind her and when Janis twisted to see the gargantuan thing, she felt sick. It was not familiar, not a planet from her home solar system. The orb was ringed with many circles of red rocks and black dust, making it appear sinister. The quiet and the vastness of it all made Janis close her eyes against the frightening beauty.

You will go to the labyrinth, daughter, the voice of First Mother told Janis, speaking from a place beyond the nebulas and winking suns but sounding as if whispered from just nearby. *I am First Mother. Do not let loose my hair.*

Janis looked down and felt the strand of hair fluttering in her hands against an unknown breeze. Having forgotten all about it, Janis clenched her fists tight, holding fast to the gift.

Get ready, the god's voice came again. *I am First Mother. You are almost there.*

Janis wanted to ask where but found her voice gone when she tried to speak. Panic began to set in as she opened and closed her mouth trying to find her voice. Her heart rate climbed higher and higher, building on itself. Stars whirled around, the points of light circling faster and faster until Janis had to close her eyes against the sickening sight. She lurched forward and felt solid ground.

Opening her eyes onto a hard-packed dirt floor, Janis closed them

317

again as her stomach rolled, experiencing gravity after floating without it for so long. The crude floor was cool beneath her bare feet and Janis shivered. Wherever she was, it was underground and cold.

Stone walls arched so far up over her head they disappeared into darkness. Janis was at a junction of five hallways splitting off from the center. Peering down each passage she could see torches posted high up on the walls illuminating the corridors of stone and dirt in flickering light.

"Shit," she said, remembering with the swear that she could speak again. "Shit, shit."

Her words came echoing back to her, bounding from a place deeper in the tunnels, where the dim light did not allow her to see. Janis squinted, peering into the tapering dark, and a feeling of deep apprehension settled around her shoulders.

The strand of First Mother's hair wriggled in her grasp and she held fast, eyes darting to the mouth of each hallway on high alert. The strand moved again and Janis connected its movement to when she turned and faced a certain passage. She approached the mouth of the tunnel to her left and entered, hoping there would be no monsters within this maze.

Janis walked within the tunnels for what seemed like hours. She had no way of telling the time and she gave up counting the seconds almost as soon as she'd had the idea. The corridors were endless and just as Janis thought the hair was tugging her in one direction, it would stop, backtrack, and point her to take a different road. Trusting the thin strand was becoming a more difficult task.

She wished the hair she had been given was her mother's hair instead. Kate's form the First Mother took was ice piercing Janis' heart. It was an unfair reminder that while at the time was comforting, only served to distract her thoughts now. In her hands, the strand of hair vibrated and Janis stopped mid-step. There was no fork in the tunnels or any bend to slip around. Janis looked over her shoulder. Should she go back? The hair remained humming but increased past the movements it made to communicate directions.

With wide eyes, Janis stared. The thin strand on her open palm was vibrating so rapidly it appeared as a black shadow across her hand.

Janis blinked. No, the color was black. She peered at it. The color had changed. With a sudden snap, the strand coiled into a length of curl and stilled. Janis knew in an instant it was her mother's hair.

"Thank you," she whispered to the First Mother, holding the strand close to her chest. The little bit of her mother, in whatever capacity, buzzed in encouragement to continue forward. But Janis didn't move. She remained standing in the middle of the tunnel with her eyes closed, searching for memories of her mother.

Janis did not weep but her heart hung heavy with all the regret it carried. She knew her behavior in life had not been her fault but the urge to want to fix it was a lit fire in her soul. If she could explain to her mother why she hadn't cared for her music or wanted to bake cupcakes together, she would be satisfied. Janis no longer cared about living or even solving her murder, all she wanted was one last chance to explain to both her parents that she had loved them all along. Nothing in this world or another could take that away from her.

With a gentle squeeze, the strand of hair shivered and morphed back into what the First Mother had given her. Janis rubbed at her eyes though she had shed no tears. Living was easier, she decided. Being dead came with too many unanswered questions and unfulfilled promises. The hair wrapped around her hand in comfort and encouragement, taking her in the direction of another tunnel.

Turning to the right, Janis heard a splashing noise and felt a cool, fresh rush of air hit her face. Invigorated, she rushed forward and found a small pool at the base of an underground waterfall. The water was black in the unsteady torchlight but it didn't feel sinister. The falling water was a welcome sight from the monotony of the maze walls of stone. Settling down at the edge of the small pool, Janis made herself comfortable and dropped a handful of dirt from the ground into the water, testing it out. When nothing happened, she dipped a toe into the cool liquid and eased the rest of her feet into the water, relaxing onto her hands, one palm still over the line of the god's hair, just in case.

She was careful not to splash too much and made as little noise as possible. Even with her precaution, Janis couldn't help but to let a smile spread across her face as the water soothed her sore feet. A small wave lapped at her ankles coming from a part of the pool that the waterfall did not touch. Janis froze, retracting her feet from the water with slow movements.

From behind the ruinous tumble of rocks at the back of the pool came another wave. Janis stood, gathering up the god's hair. She thought the broken rocks jutting out of the water were a geological accident, not a hiding place for anything sinister.

"This is what you get, Janis," she whispered to herself.

Movement came from behind the rock. A small gasp escaped Janis' lips as two black eyes peered out at her. The dark water rippled again and the head of a woman poked through the surface. She swam toward another pile of rocks in the pool closer to Janis. Reaching the small island, hands grasped at the stone and the woman pulled herself out of the water, balancing her body on the surface.

Janis stared, unable to blink. The woman was beautiful, her light brown skin shining as water beaded off it, black curls of her hair sticking to her naked body. Her nipples were jet black, raised points on two large, sagging breasts. The creature's eyes were the same color as the pool of underground water, reflecting the bare minimum of light from the torches mounted on the wall behind Janis. The woman studied Janis who closed her mouth, not wanting to appear rude.

"I'm sorry," Janis called to the woman across the water.

The stranger flinched, startled by the loud noise.

"Sorry," Janis said in a softer voice. "I wasn't..." she trailed off, watching as the woman tilted her head, one pointed ear sticking out of her wet hair. "Can you understand me? Sorry I put my feet in your pool," Janis said, speaking slowly.

"Sorry I put my feet in your pool," the woman repeated, her words sounding as if spoken underwater.

Janis perked up. "You can understand me?"

The woman in the water tilted her head the other direction. "You can understand me?"

"Oh," Janis said.

"Oh," the woman repeated.

Janis picked up a foot and wiggled her toes, gesturing from her foot to the pool of water, miming asking for permission. The woman nodded. Janis smiled.

"Thank you," she said, easing her sore feet back into the water.

"You're welcome," the woman said.

Janis yelped, ripples breaking the surface of the water from her submerged feet and calves.

"Don't yell," the woman instructed, holding her hands with black webbing between her fingers, to cover her ears. No longer holding onto the rocks, the woman slipped into the water and vanished under the inky blue surface. She reappeared next to Janis and pulled herself out of the water to sit next to the girl on the dirt floor. Janis held herself still, fear and confusion beating in her chest. "It's so loud when you yell."

Janis feared the worst, but the woman smiled and adopted the same stance, feet in the pool, weight balanced on her arms behind her.

"Okay," Janis breathed out, keeping her voice even and soft. "No yelling."

"Why are you in the labyrinth?"

"I was brought here by a god when I escaped the faerie dungeons."

Keeping the god's hair held in one hand, Janis offered another part of the strand to the woman who grabbed it and drew it close to her black eyes.

"First Mother," she muttered. "Hair of a god." She dropped the strand and slipped back into the pool, wetting her entire body before breaking the surface again and climbing out to sit next to Janis.

"Are you a god like First Mother?" Janis hedged.

Her new companion shook her head, water droplets landing on Janis' cheek.

"I am a naiad."

Janis thought the word was pretty though she had never heard it before. "I don't know what that means. Are you a faerie?"

"I suppose."

Janis' brows pinched. "Are you...an Unseelie?" she asked with hesitation, remembering the quick history lesson from Byst in the dungeon cell.

The naiad tilted her head.

"I belong to no court," she said with a surprising vehemence. "I gave myself to the labyrinth long ago. I am a nymph of no name."

Janis nodded along with her words. "That's cool," she offered, unable to come up with another platitude for the naiad.

"Where are you going in the labyrinth?" asked the naiad.

Janis let out a breath. "Believe it or not, I'm trying to get back into the land of faeries, just not the dungeons again."

She shuddered. Never again.

"I would come with you if I could." The nymph smiled. "It seems like you are on a great adventure."

"It's not so great. It's more scary than adventuresome."

"Even so," the woman mimicked the shrug, trying it out. Deciding she liked it, she repeated it several more times. "Even so, even so."

"Am I on the right path into the Hill?" Janis couldn't tell if the hair beneath her hand twitched or not.

The nymph nodded. "Don't let go of the guide."

"The what?"

"The guide, the guide!" the nymph urged, flapping her webbed hands at the hair still held in Janis' grasp.

"Oh, yes, I won't." Janis turned away.

"Wait." The naiad stopped, tugging on Janis' hand until Janis had to bend at her waist to hear the whisper of the nymph. "The feather in your pocket. Forget nothing with the angel feather."

She released her hold on Janis and sank into the water, gone from sight.

❧

Tensith was sure he had just heard voices. The fox held still and listened, ears pricked forward toward the sound. There it was again. He heard the movement of water and a shout of surprise echoing to him down the tangled corridors. Scenting the air but unable to discern anything, he broke into a run following his ears.

He hadn't wanted to journey into the labyrinth, the risk of getting lost was so great, but it was a way into the Hill he knew of that would not be monitored. No one paid attention to the old entrances. Once the portals had been created, the rest of the fae had no use for minotaur lairs, bunyip swamps, or rusalka tree roots for gateways. It was so much easier to dip into one of the many portals that did not have creatures guarding them who wished to fight or ask endless riddles.

After dragging Maeren away from Anat, Jay, and the strange iron-bound female, Tensith had told her of his plan.

I make for the Hill through the labyrinth, it is the entrance I remember how to navigate best. I want you to stay with your heart tree for that is where you are safest.

"What are you going to do?" Maeren had asked, dogwood flowers dropping in her wake. She was nervous.

He shifted into his two-legged form and clasped her hands in his.

"I wish for the deference once given to our mother," he told her. "I want our lives to mean something great again. I will find this girl in Faerie and show the truth to the council."

"Why does a life have to mean something great to be worthy of respect?"

Tensith released her hands and gathered his glamour around him. *You do not understand,* he said.

"You are right, brother. I do not."

With those words, she turned and melded into her heart tree, disappearing into the bark.

Annoyed that he could not have the last word, Tensith bared his teeth at his sister's tree and left for the labyrinth. He had been surprised at how well he remembered the way, even the stop halfway to the center at the naiads pool. The gurgling of her underground waterfall came to Tensith as he rounded a corner. He darted behind a rock before he was seen and watched as a nymph sank back into the pool and remained beneath the water. Janis was sitting on the edge, her feet dangling in the water. There was one way to the center of the maze and the girl had found it. He jumped onto a nearby stone and let pebbles and dirt fall from under his paws so the sound would attract attention without scaring the girl.

Janis whirled, one hand by her side in a fist with a strand of hair wrapped around her palm and one hand in the pocket of her skirt clasped around something. Something in her demeanor relaxed. Although she had been startled by the noise, she wasn't surprised to see a fox. Tensith supposed he hadn't been all that inconspicuous over the years after all.

Hello, Janis.

"What do you want?"

Do not be afraid, child. I am here as a friend.

"Are you a Seelie?"

His body puffed up, fur standing on end. *I align myself with the Unseelie,* he said in a wavering voice.

Janis' brow creased in a worried frown. "The ones who revolted against the Seelie?"

I... Tensith blinked. *What?*

"The Unseelie who fought to take power away from the Seelie."

The fox held her gaze with his black eyes. *No, child, you have it all wrong. Will you walk with me? We have many miles to go yet.*

Janis stood from the pool and held out her fist but then stopped. "How do I know I can trust you?"

I know the reaper, Tensith huffed. Janis raised her brows. *And I have looked out for you since you were very small.*

"That was you?" Janis was astonished.

My name is Tensith.

"It's nice to meet you," she said, painting her words with politeness that pleased Tensith.

Come, he said. *We must hurry.*

At a trot, he took off down the tunnels with Janis at his heels.

"When I was in the dungeons," Janis explained once she had caught up, "a fae told me about the Autumn Detente, that the Unseelie court was hungry for power and took it from the Seelie."

I was still in my youth then, Tensith began. *My sister Maeren and I were content as all fae are in early years, making merry and cavorting without a care in the world. But something was changing. The wind blew sharper and the moon grew dimmer and the Seelie attacked.*

"Not your court?" Janis asked.

He shook his head. *It was the Seelie with their bloated arrogance and never-ending sense of entitlement on how to govern the Hill. They promised peace, they promised a beautiful future for us all, but when their speeches turned radical, trouble came to all our hearths. My court stood up to them, of course. The Unseelie council protested their new self-righteous philosophies. How could they decide what was right for all fae when there was no cooperation between the courts, no opportunity for the voices of our people to be heard in all aspects of the government?*

"I heard a very different story, you know," Janis said, gripping the tendril of hair afresh.

I am sure you did, Tensith told her, darkly. *The Seelie have an uncanny ability for delusion. They have retold the story so often with them in a positive light they have forgotten the truth. They destroyed the Unseelie leaders,* he said in a rough voice. *My mother sat on that council and she was taken in the attack.*

"I'm so sorry."

There were others who opposed the action within the Seelie court. Anyone who spoke out was banished, doomed to live in the human world with no memories of the Hill. A fate I do not envy. He shuddered at his words.

"You survived," Janis pointed out. "What happened to the rest of the Unseelie court?"

Many were killed, some were enslaved or banished to forgotten corners of the dungeon and left to decay. I had to pledge neutrality in order to survive but still I work every day to prove I am not a threat to the Seelie rule. Until now. He sat back on his haunches and tilted his head upward. *Until you.*

Janis took a step back. "Me? I didn't even know about the fae until a few days ago."

The fox put a paw over one of her bare feet. *I was there, sixteen years ago, in Arizona.*

Surprise flickered across Janis' features.

Your parents made a deal with me for you. They wanted a child and would do anything to get one. Standard bargains produce a changeling that remains with them for sixteen years. By then, the child is strong enough to return to the Hill and bless the land with their essence.

"I don't know what that means," Janis said, voice wavering.

Changelings are not meant for life, the fox explained. *They return to this world in a dissemination of being. They bless the flowers, the milk, and every tree with their energy when they disperse. It is our way of things.*

"My parents bargained for me just so I could disintegrate into some plant?" Janis cried out.

You would not do such a thing. You are a sheefrah, Tensith explained. He began to walk again and Janis waited for several long beats before following. His ears swiveled back to capture her footsteps and he could hear her ragged breathing. *It is not so bad, being what you are. You are special, not many of your kind exist.*

"I don't exist," Janis growled. "I'm dead."

Ah, Tensith answered. *I understand you may feel that way but in the Hill, you exist. The part of you from the Hill lives on.*

"Are we in the Hill now?"

No, but we are close. When we arrive, you will have to help me across the border. I was cast out for reporting the problem with the deals and cannot find my way back on my own.

"What problem?"

That sheefrahs are snuck into the bargains instead of a changeling. It was subtle, even I did not begin to suspect what you were until years had passed.

"I'm still trying to wrap my head around the fact that my parents had to bargain for my existence."

It was my understanding that they struggled to conceive a child of their own. This is where the fae step in to help in such matters. A faerie born and raised under the Hill holds no great power. But place that same fae child in the arms of a human? They return to us strong and ready to bestow their power back to the land.

"Why are they stronger when they're raised by humans?" Janis stopped walking.

Tensith circled back to her. *There are many theories, but no one knows.*

"What does any of this have to do with me?"

The creation of sheefrahs has been outlawed among the fae for years. That you exist is testimony to the corruption in the Seelie court. You were not supposed to have died when you did, but two days later.

Janis struggled to speak. "Did my parents know I would die when they bargained with you?"

Tensith hesitated. There was so much more to the bargaining magic. They knew, but they had also been ensorcelled to look upon the deal with favor. *Yes,* he admitted.

Softness drifted through Janis' mind. The absurdity of receiving closure that she wasn't supposed to die when she did was overshadowed by the fact that she would have still died no matter what. What a colossal cosmic joke.

She existed because her parents were desperate enough for a kid they were willing to look anywhere to find one. Janis' thoughts were swirling into a storm. They knew, they fucking knew she would be alive for a short sixteen years and they still went through with it.

Rage gathered within her. How could they be so selfish? How dare they force her into existence that was nothing more than a failed attempt at copying true humanity? Her entire life had been a half-assed approximation envisioned by these stupid fae who had no real understanding of the mortal world.

Her parents had cursed her. Janis trembled at the thought. They agreed to the creation of something they didn't understand and then were upset by her differences when she wasn't perfect like the other children, a good little girl they could look at with pride.

There was too much inside her, too much boiling within. It hurt. It was too painful to keep to herself. Janis tipped her head back and let out a ragged scream so loud, Tensith flattened his ears. It tore from her throat, ripping away from her as if she didn't expel it, but something had reached inside and pulled. Echoes of her cry bounced down the labyrinth's tunneled halls until the sound dissipated around corners.

It was bullshit. It was all too big for her. She was furious, with her parents, with the fae, with the world, and even Jay. She was done, done with all of it. It wasn't fair that she didn't have access to her true self because her parents had wanted their own child so much. She had no other purpose for existing besides that her parents wanted her.

She shed no tears, she didn't have any left.

What she did have was a strand of hair from a god, an angel feather, and newfound rippling rage that thundered beneath her surface. Janis turned to the fox. "What's your name again?"

Tensith.

"Tensith," she took a shuddering breath. "Take me to those responsible for this. Now, please."

"We're here." The fox had slowed to a stop in a small chamber.

"What is this?" she asked.

The fae's entire body twitched as he drew a glamour around himself and appeared before Janis now on two legs. "This is the center of the maze."

Janis didn't have time to acknowledge his nudity; she was too shocked by his pronouncement. "This entire time we've been walking to the middle and not to the exit?" She restrained herself from shrieking.

Tensith circled the room, fox fur patterned skin a dull shine in the torchlight. "This is the exit." He extended his hand. "We have work to do yet, child."

She took it with reluctance and as soon as she did, the hair in her hands disintegrated into the air. There was no going back now, she would be lost forever if she stayed.

"Invite me to join you under the Hill with my name," Tensith instructed.

Gathering a breath to her, Janis said, "Tensith, I invite you to join me under the Hill."

A breathtaking flash of green light bloomed around them and when it faded, the center chamber of the labyrinth stood empty and silent once again.

THIRTY

I T WAS COOL IN the portal to the Hill, the air damp, like a forest coated in morning dew. There was no plant life in the gray emptiness of the portal, yet unseen branches slapped at Jay's arms, invisible cobwebs broke over Anat's wings, and the crunch of moss and fallen leaves sounded beneath Friend's cat feet. Sylvie walked before them all. Her wings trailed down her back and Jay had to remain vigilant as not to step on the long train of their ends. Her long hair rested between her wings and swayed as she walked.

Jay stumbled against an unseen rock and Sylvie half turned, cocking a pointed ear to see if he would fall. When he did not lose his balance, she returned to walking. "We are almost there, reaper. Control yourself."

He glared at her back. "I'm in control," he grumbled. "Where does this portal lead?"

Sylvie's wings fluttered as she flexed them. "This is a back door, it will take a while to get to where we are going."

A large, wet leaf Jay couldn't see slapped him full in the face. He pushed at it angrily. "At least can you let me see where we're going?"

"Reaper, you dragged me all over Earth without explanation. This is how I felt."

As the troupe continued to walk, bits and pieces of their surroundings faded into sight. A veritable forest materialized under their feet and Jay skirted around the trunk of a tree just in time, some of the bark crumbling off as he brushed by. Branches and tall grasses moved aside for Sylvie, sprang back into place to tangle Jay and Anat. Friend navigated the vegetation with grace and yowled in annoyance when her paw landed on something squishy and wet.

"Can you tell us," Jay grunted as he ducked away from almost cracking his head open on a low-hanging branch, "if we're almost there..." He was cut off by a loud popping noise and the forest surroundings gave way to an interior.

"We're here," Sylvie said to them all with a grin, her entire demeanor mischievous. She peeked around the room and smiled again. "No one is home."

The quarters were lavishly decorated, a seat of great wealth. The chambers were a set of connected rooms splitting off from a central atrium containing a large desk pushed to one side and a small pond of water set into the center of the grass floor. Under the shallow water, rocks were covered in green slime. Though the blossoms weren't visible, the entire apartment smelled of lilacs.

Above, a chandelier covered with pinned butterflies twinkled. Hanging between each doorway were long, gauzy curtains made of a light blue material. Dotting the corners of each room at the meeting between the grassy floors and the light stone walls grew many varied succulents, like an organic baseboard.

"Hmm," Sylvie mused, walking through the rooms and touching various objects. "Whomever they are, they did not redecorate." She gave the other three an impish look. "I am pleased at that."

Anat walked around a marble stand supporting a wooden lute strung with gold. It hummed with Anat's approach. When he side-stepped away from it, the instrument quieted.

"From now on you will refer to me as 'Your Grace'. I am Sylvie no longer."

The faerie moved through one of the many doors into a different room. It had a round table in the center made out of a trunk of a cut tree. The stump remained with its roots buried deep into the grass floor, its many rings proclaiming its venerable age. Sprawled across the flat top was a generous spread of fruit and cheese and bread. Friend leapt onto the surface and sniffed at a grape.

"Yes, Your Grace. What's your real name?" Jay asked, shooing Friend away from the grape.

The faerie blinked. Her eyes flicked back and forth as she searched her memories. A darkness passed over her expression.

"I cannot remember." Her gaze met Jay's and the intensity of her stare made him take a step back. "The name of a fae is sacred, tied to our powers. You know this."

He nodded. "Find your powers and we find your name."

"Or the other way around," Anat added.

The anger dripped away from Sylvie's face, replaced with a wolfish grin. "Indeed. Meanwhile, I shall explore my old closet to find myself some clothes. And maybe a new necklace too."

Anat's wing brushed against the side of Jay's shoulder as the demigod bent to his ear. "We have to find the sheefrah," Anat said in a quiet murmur. His eyes flicked in the direction of where the faerie had walked. "She no longer has the capacity to care about a singular human as she did when she was mortal."

Worry buzzed around Jay's skin like an electric charge. He hadn't thought of that.

"That's why I don't like the fae," meowed Friend as she pushed a golden cup from the mouth-watering spread closer to the edge of the table with a paw. "They love nothing but themselves."

Jay tried not to roll his eyes, now almost a habit from Janis rubbing off on him.

"And what are demons?" he asked. "Or any other kind that walks this Earth if not creatures of self-concern to the point of survival?"

Friend leveled an even, golden stare at Jay. "We don't have time for your philosophizing. Anat is right. She is a faerie once more and will not care about your little ghost."

"Then we find her on our own," Jay said.

"No need," came the faerie's voice from the other room. "I will help for I believe I will find answers of my own betrayal following the trail of the sheefrah."

Friend pushed the cup off the table and it crashed to the ground. The faerie swept around the corner back into view.

"I would appreciate it, demon, if you respect your surroundings even if you do not feel the same about me."

Friend gave a small hiss but stopped when she saw the faerie. She was wearing a gown of icy lavender made out of moonbeams and spider silk. The fabric floated around her body like a second skin padded on top of a gap of air to allow for movement. It was cut in an ancient silhouette, delicate interlocking twigs holding the style together at her shoulders and in a looping belt slung low across her hips. At one end hung a gold medallion with some sort of seal stamped into the metal, a twelve pointed star. The exquisite dress was translucent, and her body shone through on display as if it were another thing of beauty she owned and wished to exhibit.

"I respect your fashion," Friend said with a snap of her jaws before leaping off the table and shifting to her human form. "I want one."

"No, Friend," Jay warned. "We don't have time."

Friend turned her pout to Jay. "I just want to look pretty for you."

Anat coughed and the faerie smiled.

"We have time for this, don't we, reaper?" Friend cajoled.

Jay shook his head but the faerie had already looped arms with Friend and tugged the demon with her into the back rooms to find another dress.

"We shall be quick," she promised.

"Self-absorbed indeed," Anat commented.

Jay rubbed at the bridge of his nose. "Can you locate Janis?"

"My powers are quite obfuscated here, cousin. You know the fae do not like others using their gifts in their lands. Their magic dampens my own. I can fight, but nothing more."

"Then I can't think of a way to reach her," Jay said with a sinking heart. "I had Friend tell her to get out of the dungeons and hide but if I know Janis, she'll want to retain forward momentum. She might be anywhere."

"She might have found help," Anat offered. Jay shook his head.

"We'll have to rely on the grace of the fae."

"Perhaps not the best move for us."

"Reaper," said Friend as she came back into the main room from the closet. Jay turned and flushed an immediate dark red. The demon was dressed in the fae style, with little modesty and all attention on craftsmanship. Her gown was opalescent and shimmered as she moved. Opal stones cascaded from her shoulders and dripped down as if poured across the front of the dress, obscuring her breasts from view. The rest of the gown was opaque, but with enough translucence for Friend's brown skin to add a level of depth to the glinting fabric that set Jay's heart racing.

"That's... I mean it looks great," Jay choked out.

Friend smiled, delighted by his discomfort. He cleared his throat.

"Your Grace, can you take us to the dungeons where Janis was kept?"

Picking at a peeled tangerine on the table, the faerie frowned at the fruit.

"I have none of my powers yet," she said as if it were nothing more than a momentary thought passing through her head. "We shall have to be most clever in our movements." She studied the group before her. "You will not pass as fae," she informed Friend who changed to her cat form.

"I'll stay out of sight," she promised.

"Very good, but you two..." The faerie shook her head as she looked Jay and Anat up and down. She whisked away into the back room and reemerged carrying two cloaks. "This is the best we can do. They are enchanted to turn a curious eye from the wearer but the magic will not work on those with a more scrupulous view of vigilance." She handed a cloak to Anat and Jay, the former struggling to don the garment over his large wings.

"This isn't going to work," Friend meowed from her place at the faerie's feet.

"Hush," she commanded. "Believe in it or it will surely fail before we start."

Friend licked at the ruff on her chest in response. Without another word, the faerie led them to the back entrance they had taken to find her quarters.

"There will be guards outside my door, no doubt sleeping on the job with them thinking there is no one within, but I do not wish to sound the alarm sooner than necessary. Follow me."

Ducking behind a large tree growing between two stone walls, the faerie disappeared. With a sullen meow, Friend followed.

Jay grabbed Anat's arm. "You're right, I don't trust her," he whispered.

"As I said, she has one goal now, to find her name and her power. I will watch her too," Anat said with assurance. With that, the two entered the hidden passageway.

This tunnel was different from the portal into the Hill, though it was damp and covered in lush undergrowth of a forest. They walked over spongy mushrooms and dew covered rocks, guided by the light of bioluminescence from various creeping vines and carpet moss. Anat struggled to keep his cloak covering his head and his wings at the same time, the flapping fabric snagging on thorny branches. He cursed and was chided by the faerie.

"We are almost to the dungeons, demigod," she said.

Jay tried to remain quiet when he tripped over a root instead of calling out the pain of a stubbed toe.

The soft, natural light of the tunnel's landscape gave way to torchlight. The faerie removed a torch from its metal sconce and held it aloft. Friend shook out a back leg, a wet leaf stuck to her paw.

"I sense unease here," Anat whispered to no one in particular.

"The dungeons," the faerie said, pushing at a boulder. The large rock swung open with deceptive ease for its bulk, revealing a slim crack of light from the space beyond. "Stay close," she commanded before passing through the doorway.

Mildew and rust met their noses as they arrived at the large antechamber before the gateway to the dungeons. The lighting was odd, flickering torches on the walls competed with soft blue light running along the ceiling from an unseen source. The gates were an archway of veined granite stone with two guards on either side of the opening, another standing in the middle with deep blue skin and milk white insect wings. The guard shot a quick look to the seal hanging from the faerie's belt and snapped to standing at attention.

"Your Grace!" the blue faerie squeaked, pausing in her examination of the guards at the gates. She was holding a ream of parchment and a quill. "We were not expecting..." the guard trailed off, frowning. The soldiers on either side of the dungeon entrance exchanged looks with one another. The blue faerie tilted her head. "You were ex-" Before the guard could finish her sentence, Friend spat a burning clump of acid at the guard's feet and Anat broke into a quick run toward the guard on the left, cloak falling off his ink-dark wings. In an instant, he relieved the soldier of his sword. The demigod spun, cracking the butt of the weapon on the side of the guard's helmet and sending him to the ground, unconscious.

Fight, Jay's power demanded.

It was there, ready and waiting for him and Jay almost stumbled back in surprise.

"You're here," he said.

We are here, it answered. The voice had a new note to it, a new musicality it never before possessed. *Human*, it rumbled, a sort of satisfaction surrounding the words.

"Help first, then we talk," Jay told it.

He dipped into his merged human and reaper power. It reared up, lurching out to blast the last guard in the chest, causing her to fly backward and crash into the stone threshold of the dungeon entrance. How he had managed to access his power in the Hill, he had no idea.

"Are you going to help?" Friend called out as she clung to the first guard's shoulders, scratching at her face.

"I have no magic," the faerie who was once Sylvie retorted.

Anat leapt to Friend's defense and kicked at the guard's middle, colliding with the bark armor in a loud splintering of wood. Unbalanced, Friend jumped from the faerie guard and sailed through the air until Jay caught her in his arms.

"Careful!" he chided the cat who snuggled into his grasp.

"I saw you use your power, reaper," she purred. "Quite impressive."

"Intriguing," the faerie said in a bored tone as she swept past him.

Jay followed the faerie into the dungeons still holding Friend, who was now refusing to walk.

"How?" Anat asked him, head bent to stifle the conversation from being overheard.

"The question is how you don't feel it," Friend interjected. "His humanity gives strength to his powers. It's nice. He's warm now instead of cold." She nestled herself further in his arms.

Jay and Anat exchanged a look over the cat.

They walked past the guard room and caught sight of a fae that looked like a fish with legs grab hold of a conch and speak into it.

"She returns!" the fae shouted into the shell.

Jay felt Friend shift in his arms and he lunged into the room, releasing her.

"Enryah is back!" the fish fae managed to get out before Friend landed on his scaly face, claws first. He fell to the ground swearing and screaming.

Anat's eyes flicked to the faerie who was standing still outside the guard room.

"Your Grace?" he questioned.

She exploded in a flash of green light, blinding Anat and streaming into the guard room where Friend hissed at the sudden brightness and Jay threw an arm over his eyes. The fish fae howled with pain as the green light surrounded him and shot him across the floor until his head hit the back wall and he fell silent.

"I am Enryah Sylphian," a voice from inside the burning green light spoke with a fierce intensity. "I am returned."

The light faded, revealing the faerie floating in the air with a subtle smile on her lips. The lavender dress swirled around her body, as if she had been turning in the air and the fabric was slowing a beat after her movements stopped. Slippered feet touched the ground and her wings settled around her.

Movement came from behind as a group of fae guards raced down the dungeon hallway, spears leveled at her back. Enryah waved a single hand at them and they froze between one step and the next before their wooden armor and helmets splintered inward, collapsing in on itself and crushing their rib cages and skulls.

"The dungeons," Enryah said without a second glance at the carnage. "Come."

Anat followed a beat later, stepping over the dead. Friend, also ignoring the bodies, meowed at Jay's legs until he bent to pick her up.

"I'm not going to carry you around forever," Jay told the demon, trying not to look at the mess.

"Yes you will," Friend purred.

Jay couldn't resist and he scratched at her delicate head behind her ears.

Shouts from further in the dungeon echoed against the stone walls and Jay ran to catch up. Enryah had pinned the guards against the ceiling of the cave-like dungeons with her magic and they struggled there, backs illuminated by the blue light. Several terrified prisoners peered out from behind bars.

"There are souls in here that should not be," she growled up to the restrained fae. "They are demon deals, are they not?"

One of the trapped guards, a yellow-haired elf, tried to speak, Enryah's magic crushing his windpipe.

"Yes," the guard squeezed out, turning a deep red.

Friend sniffed the air.

"I don't smell anything," she told Jay, sounding miffed that she had overlooked this detail.

"I learned of this treachery before my exile," Enryah snarled loud enough for all to hear. "The keeping of souls owed to the Turned hidden away in the Hill to escape the notice of the Morningstar. All to line the pockets of demons greedy enough to risk not paying tithe to their devilish master. A trade for demons helping the fae gain the energy sheefrahs possess when killed before their contracts come due." With a clenching of her fist, the necks of the fae held against the ceiling all snapped at once and their bodies fell to the ground with grotesque sounds.

Friend sprang from Jay's arms and streaked away into the darkness of the dungeons with a yowling cry that sounded like she would "be right back".

"This betrayal runs deep." Enryah's eyes flashed in anger as she turned to look at her companions. "We head for the council."

Janis was in a world of color. She hadn't seen anything of the Hill except for the dungeons and was surprised to find the rest of this world was a pleasant and beautiful one. Flowers of every color released their pungent sweet perfume and trees with trunks wider than she was tall waved in a warm breeze. It was a hot summer back on Earth but here it was a perfect spring day. Tensith sighed next to her, content to be home.

"This is where I come from?" Janis asked in awe. The sunlight was mild and beneath her feet was a crush of soft moss that soothed her skin. Some distance away, a deep blue lake sparkled like a sapphire gem nestled in green velvet.

"You never lived here. You were made from the essence of your mother and father mixed together with the magic of the Hill."

"Mixing?"

Tensith angled his head, not quite understanding her need for clarification. "They signed the contract."

She sagged against a nearby tree, relief flooding through her.

"He wasn't sure," she babbled. "Jay wasn't sure if they were my true parents but they are!" She smiled with abandon at Tensith. "I'm theirs."

The fae plucked a strand of rowan berries from a bush. "They were always yours, child. Even if you hadn't been made, they would have been your family." He crossed the short distance between them. "Tuck these away, they will help you from being ensorcelled by another fae."

"Where can I hide so Jay will find me? Friend told me I had to stay hidden and wait." Janis tucked the berry bunch in her skirt pocket.

Tensith glanced at her. "You spoke with Friend?"

"In the dungeons. Why?"

"And they say the fae are the tricksters," Tensith muttered to himself.

Janis examined a fallen oak to see if she could crawl inside to conceal herself.

"We are not waiting in the bramble for trouble to come to us," he announced, cutting short her examination of the log. "I shall bring you to the council where we will plead your case."

Janis paled. "I can't go back there! I just escaped from the castle."

"It is called the Hallow and you must. There is no one else to hear of this treachery." The fae shifted back to his fox form. *You are the proof, child, and you must stand up for what is right.*

"This shouldn't be my job," she grumbled.

The fox flicked his tail and started trotting down the forest path.

The woodlands around them were verdant and stunning. It was, Janis supposed, how forests were supposed to be. There were no buildings in the distance, no parking lots or the honking of car horns or trash tangled in the bushes. It was peaceful here, just the quiet contemplation of things growing in the sunlight and animals existing among the foliage. Birds of every kind flew in and out of the tall trees and Janis saw several rabbits dash away once they spotted the fox.

"Are these creatures faeries, too?" Janis asked of Tensith who shook his head.

They are as they are in your world, though perhaps they are better off here.

"I'll bet," she said. "It's so beautiful here."

Janis imagined herself living in this gorgeous world, frolicking through the pine and maple trees and eating from the land whenever the fancy struck. It would be idyllic and she guessed that she would want for nothing.

It is, Tensith agreed. *That is why I seek to help it. You can never know the allegiance to this land as one born here does.*

"What would have happened to me, if a ferryman had come?"

Tensith turned his wet nose up to her and was quiet for a moment.

I do not yet know for sure, but if you were a sheefrah, your existence was meant to be secret. I imagine your power would be siphoned off somehow. Given to those behind this plot.

Janis shook. "You have got to be kidding," she said, voice low and dangerous.

The forest didn't look quite so beautiful anymore. The path they were on began to slope upward to a hill covered in a thick growth of trees. At the top, stood a crumbling stone palace that seemed to loom out over the high ground and glare down at Janis.

We will find out soon enough, Tensith said. *Welcome to the Hallow.*

THIRTY-ONE

NRYAH STRODE FROM THE dungeons as Anat and Jay trailed at her heels. With bursts of her green magic, she trapped any hapless fae they came across in a wrapping of thorny vines and leaves gagging their mouths. Her wings trembled with her anger, buzzing at her back as they made their way to the upper levels of the Hallows.

They reached polished double doors beneath an archway of twisting birch trees. Enrayah stared at the doors, inlaid with intricate golden patterns depicting stars in the heavens. The faerie seemed to be steeling herself, but against what Jay did not know. He found he missed the human she once was. He could relate more to her as a mortal than to her now as fae. Years ago, Jay knew his feelings would have been the opposite. Now, with human emotions coursing through him, his opinions were much changed.

With both hands, Enryah pushed open the double doors. It was a large theater, more so than a courtroom or any other place of government Jay had known. The chambers were huge, with a curving gallery for spectators that spread out in a half circle from a wide central aisle bisecting the two sides. Above, there was a second level to the gallery, a mezzanine with even more seating. It was the old throne room, updated to suit modern fae life. Hundreds could sit in the space with an unobstructed view of the thirteen seats arranged in an arch behind a wood bar that was topped with a slab of rough cut quartz. The mineral seemed to still be growing, crystals forming at the edges of the wood. Set onto the quartz bar were numerous pillar candles of all different sizes, their drippings melted together into a waterfall of wax seeping over the edge.

Twelve seats were carved from obsidian except for the last, placed in the middle, which was more of a throne. Its form was simple, a bent and twisted tree with a seat carved into the wood, but it had been transmuted from bark into solid gold. It was the throne of the old fae, an heirloom to the past.

"It should be mine," Enryah muttered, as if in answer to the royal set itself.

The floor before the bar of thirteen council seats was an exquisite parquet floor, the decorative white oak and cypress darkened with age laid out in a diagonal mesh pattern within larger framed squares. At the center was a circle of many different colors of wood framing an elaborate twelve pointed star made from maple. The wood was worn with age but well cared for and beloved.

The council chambers were empty but that didn't stop Enryah. She walked to the center of the floor and held out a hand. Green light formed at her palm and flowed up to her elbow.

"I am chancellor Enryah Sylphian and I hereby declare this council session begun!"

Enryah held her hand up and the light shone from her fingertips to the ceiling in a bolt where it broke apart, skittering across a mural of an ancient battle that was painted there. The candles on the bar lit as one, black smoke rising from the wicks. Her loud words did not echo through the empty space but instead were swallowed by the green magic before it dissipated into the air.

"What should we expect, Your Grace?" Anat asked, shifting on the parquet floor.

Enryah gave him a sly grin. "They will listen before they fight. Us fae love nothing more than some tawdry entertainment where others are humiliated."

The doors opened and several fae in long, sweeping black robes made their way down the aisle, staring at the trio on the main floor. The last of the faeries was a tall gray skinned kelpie with silky black hair braided down his back.

"You cannot call a council," he told Enryah, baring two rows of shark-like teeth. "You were banished."

"Sit down, Sailis, and for once in your life keep quiet."

The kelpie stared at Enryah until a tiny flying fae with a chestnut horse head and lanky male body flitted close to his ear on wings made from basil leaves.

"Your Grace, Lady Enryah is correct. It is in the bylaws that any chancellor, past or present, may call a council meeting to order."

"Very well," the kelpie said stiffly. "We shall proceed."

He, along with other members of the council, took their seats with Sailis settling onto the golden throne in the middle. No sooner had the last of the councilors finished adjusting their black robes around them did the doors swing open once more, admitting a cavalcade of fae all wishing to witness the proceedings. The benches in the gallery both on the ground level and in the mezzanine filled. Smaller fae and those in animal form, took up space in the aisle or stacked on top of one another, using each other's backs as support. Some faeries with wings clung to the decorative wooden corbels at the ceiling or hung in the air, wings beating. Still more fae pressed together at the doors to the council chambers, craning their necks to get a look at the banished senator who dared to come back and call a meeting to order. They wanted a show.

The kelpie gnashed his many teeth in displeasure at the large audience. "This meeting of the council is a closed matter..." His words were drowned out by the loud jeering and complaining of the crowd.

"You cannot keep us out!" a fae adorned in hanging moss called from her seat near the front. Sailis glared at her but more yelled their displeasure. Enryah tossed her head in thinly veiled delight at the chaos the kelpie was unable to control. High up on the balcony a fox sat beside a cloaked figure who fidgeted, uncomfortable amidst the cacophony.

A chenoo from the back rumbled, "Get on with it!"

"Where is it written that any council meeting is private?" shrieked another faerie, vying to be heard above the crowd. The horse headed sprite hovered around Sailis' ears again, speaking fast. The high chancellor was forced to hold up his hands to placate the gathering.

"If you will all be still," Sailis' voice boomed with magic, "we will begin."

He nodded at the sprite who dipped his pinkish horse nose in acknowledgment. The sprite unrolled parchment from his belt and began to read; thin voice amplified by the lingering kelpie magic.

"Fae all, new and wise, come and seek the knowledge of the council herein the eighth month of the year seventeen thousand sixty-one. We commence this meeting with High Chancellor Sailis Kelorn presiding."

With a flourish, the sprite tucked away the parchment and sketched a bow to the kelpie while hovering in midair. Sailis nodded to the faerie and gathered his attention around Enryah, ignoring Anat and Jay.

"You return to this court uninvited, Enryah Sylphian," the kelpie announced with solemn tones, intentionally dropping her honorific. Titters splashed through the crowd at the declaration of her name. "How have you broken your iron seal?"

"Dragonflame," she said, lifting her chin. Her answer elicited more whispers within the gallery. "For no binding can remain when burned free by the truth." She turned to address the captive audience. "I was wrongfully sentenced to a mortal life for wanting to help all fae. My own Seelie court exiled me because I discovered the truth."

Some of the crowd who were already in agreement with Enryah whooped and cheered for her to continue. Sailis' gray complexion had turned waxen. A gorgeous blonde faerie with pinkish skin and white hair two seats to the right leaned across the bar. "This court does not recognize..." she tried to say.

Enryah spread her glittering wings, calling all eyes back to her. "The fine Folk of the Hill know nothing of this, but for a select few. Those who were so hungry for power and wished to keep the Seelie in control they were willing to forfeit the elections."

"Bring back the elections!" an unseen fae in the crowd called out, others gnashed their teeth at the declaration and guards at the back of the massive room had to stop more than a few blows.

"Did you not wonder why the Seelie were able to hold onto their positions?" Enryah swept out an arm to encompass all of the council. "Did you not wonder why they have been blessed with enhanced magic?" She turned, glaring at the white-haired faerie and lowering her voice to speak directly to her. "Do I not wonder how Vilena Soren sits in my seat?" The faerie in question squirmed on her chair. "They have snuck sheefrahs into changeling bargains and steal their power when demons kill them before their time. In exchange for our gold and something more it seems... I have seen it with my own eyes, a dungeon full of souls belonging to the Turned!"

A hush settled over the gathered fae at her words. A few council members motioned to their attendants and spoke in hurried whispers before the subordinates dashed off to elsewhere. Enryah remained gazing into the crowd, meeting the eyes of any who opposed her pronouncement. In the second floor gallery, the hooded figure turned and muttered to the fox who shook his head.

"I am a peaceful guest within these lands," Jay started formally. "I mean to add to this truth. My kind, reapers, are butchered when they discover this treachery."

"Ah!" Sailis cried, standing from his chair. "You cannot escape this lie for reapers cannot be killed."

"The power gained by placing sheefrahs in the changeling contracts and killing them before their time affords great power to those receiving it. Enough power to kill death," said Enryah before Jay got a chance to answer. "You're paying the demons to hold back the ferrymen who would find out the truth and to do your dirty work of murdering the sheefrahs."

"Or paying off the ferrymen directly. Those of lesser scruples are in on it too, such as the ferryman Tick," Jay added.

Sailis and the rest of the council stared at the trio before them as the crowd raged in the galleries. Fights broke out and guards were dispatched to stifle the offenders and haul them away. Anat's wings flared in answer to the growing volume of the spectators and the guards spaced along the walls of the ancient throne room changed the way they stood.

"What proof do you have of this?" Sailis managed to be heard above the noise.

Enryah faltered as the crowd did, each fae listening intently for the answer. Anat and Jay kept silent. The kelpie smiled in triumph.

"I thought as much," he said with a dismissive wave of a hand.

344

The hush that had fallen reverberated all the way to the mezzanine where Janis and Tensith sat. The quiet sank deep into Janis and hammered in her bones. She trembled with the rage she felt burning in her stomach. She was here all because some faerie wanted power.

Jay stood in the middle of the floor, head held high in spite of the lack of concrete evidence he was presenting to the fae council. His fists clenched as he stared straight ahead. Inky wings of black shifted next to Jay as Anat adjusted his stance, readying for anything. Friend was nowhere to be seen. After another moment of silence, Jay's chin dipped in defeat and Janis felt herself stand without knowing.

Tensith tugged at her sleeve.

"Sit, child," he implored.

"I am the proof," Janis announced in a clear voice.

She surprised herself with how steady her speech was despite the nerves causing her whole body to tremble. Angry shouts and cries of uproar came from the assembly. Everyone in the audience craned to see who had spoken. Determined, Janis tugged the hood off and let the cloak fall to the floor.

"Janis!" Jay shouted from the center of the floor. "Don't!"

"My name is Janis Lyn Pereda and I am a sheefrah born of a bargain." Her voice gathered strength as she spoke, the words rolling off her tongue, her truth spoken at last. "I was killed by a demon before my contract was up." She was shouting now, straining with the desire to lay out all the facts, to communicate the injustice of her wasted and stolen life.

"If we are no longer concerned about being inconspicuous..." Tensith grumbled before leaning into the side of Janis' legs, amplifying her voice.

"One of the ferrymen that you've been paying off forgot to get me and bring me down to your dungeons to await slaughter! You will remedy the false language added to the bargain contracts and you will let my friends go!"

The assembly roared in response, each fae clamoring to have their own opinions heard. Janis could tell some were against her as they shook their fists at where she stood, faces twisted in rage. Others still seemed to be on her side. Janis' shoulder was jostled in camaraderie and support by a faerie that stood behind her on the balcony.

"The Seelie must be held accountable!" bellowed another supportive fae from the lower gallery. His neighbors turned on him and pushed him to the ground, falling upon him with fists or swinging tails.

Janis remained standing, braced against the waves of judgment. Jay's back was to the council and his eyes were locked on Janis.

"Are you okay?" he mouthed.

She nodded once.

Those with wings were taking flight, bringing their arguing into the air. The head of the council stood from his elevated seat and held both hands aloft, trying to calm the gathered.

"This court does not acknowledge these unfounded allegations!" Sailis cried out, demanding to be heard. He banged his fist on the wooden bar to call for order. "We do not concede to the validity of such libel! Sit down," he yelled. "Sit down and all will be well."

The crowd, for the most part, settled, though some had taken their seats again and ceased arguing with their neighbors, waiting to see what would happen next. Most wore pleased expressions, thrilled that this drama was playing out before them.

"Stay there," Jay enunciated, making sure Janis could read his lips. "Stay with the fox."

Janis slid her eyes from Jay to the grinning beautiful faerie woman who had first spoken. Enryah, Janis thought she had said her name was. With a jolt, Janis realized that the faerie woman was Sylvie. She looked like an enhanced version of the woman, but her eyes... They were like her own now. Overlarge and inhuman. Whatever happened while she was parted from them, it must have been big. Janis didn't know why, but she felt a stab of grief for the human Sylvie.

Sailis was consulting with the guards at his back when Anat spread his wings.

"They will not listen, Your Grace," he said. "You must end this now."

"Death has no place in the Hill," Enryah snapped. "You and the reaper will do as I say and wait for the right moment."

"Guards," the kelpie said, growing tense and Enryah's words. He jerked his head toward the middle of the floor.

A dozen armed warriors flooded the pit and fell upon Jay and Anat, twisting their hands behind their backs before they caught up with the surprise. Metal rattled as chains were placed around both their wrists.

With a placid look on her face, Enryah blocked all advances with a shroud of green light. She and Sailis locked eyes with one another and the high councilor shook his head. Enryah bared her teeth. A few of the council members had the gall to smirk down at them.

"You are no longer welcome here, Lady Enryah," an elven councilor with skin as dark as a new moon sneered.

The crowd remained agitated, calling for free elections and for the council to tell the truth, in whatever form, but they had ceased their fighting, waiting to see what would happen.

"Get the fetch!" Sailis yelled to the guards on the balcony.

"Let me go!" Janis shouted as she was shoved forward by two guards at her back, both her arms captured by their tight grips and heels slipping as they dragged her to the stairs at the back of the mezzanine.

Tensith was nowhere to be seen and she wondered if she had made a mistake in trusting the fox. Janis was transported roughly to the ground floor of the grand chambers. Steel manacles were clasped around her wrists behind her back before she was pushed into the pit, stumbling across the polished wood floors.

"Trapped once again," Janis muttered when she regained her footing next to Jay. "You were supposed to prevent all of this, you know."

Without a word, Jay bent to place his forehead against hers. Janis squeaked in surprise at the reaper sign of affection.

"I was so worried about you," he said, straightening. "What happened?"

"You don't want to know," she said, tartly.

Jay tipped his head back to laugh and earned a jab from a butt of a guard's spear in the side. He doubled over and chains clinked as Anat moved to help, blocked by a circle of spear tips.

"Stay where you are," warned a guard.

"This is all very dramatic," Enryah said in a bored voice to the council.

"There remains no proof," Vilena argued with Enryah who didn't look too worried about being surrounded by soldiers holding their weapons

347

steady in her direction. "How do we know if this fetch is what she says she is?"

"Look at her, you fool," Anat growled, chains clattering as he adjusted his arms.

"Looks can be deceiving," Sailis sniffed.

Shouts came from the back of the room as Tensith darted through the crowd in his human form, pushing at those who did not move out of his way.

"I have the contract!" he panted as he drew near. "I have the exact bargain I gave her parents sixteen years ago."

Sailis snatched the rolled parchment from his hands.

"All this proves is that you are to blame for creating a sheefrah. This mess is on you, fox."

Tensith snarled but had no answer.

A cat landed upon the council bar and faced the center of the floor, stopping all conversation in its tracks.

"Luci is waiting for an opening," Friend informed them without preamble. "Find a mirror."

"Demon!" Sailis screamed to the guards. "Capture her!"

Friend scrambled to hide between Jay's legs.

Without waiting for the soldiers to move in on the cat, Sailis let loose a bolt of power aimed at Jay's legs. Friend shifted, using her human form to yank Jay free of the blast. They toppled over, knocking Janis to the ground as they went. Before she hit the wood, Friend was a cat once more, landing on her feet, spitting.

"Get a fucking mirror," she snapped at Janis as she and Jay helped each other to their feet.

Friend tripled in size as she had in the dungeons with Janis and turned toward the nearest fae and slashed with her claws. The guard stumbled back in surprise and Friend streaked away, disappearing into the shadows.

Sailis stood behind the bar and slapped a gray hand on the quartz bar top. "You will be banished again, Enryah, for disturbing the peace. Your companions will be sent to the dungeons. And I want that demon!"

Enryah stood at the very center of the floor, feet planted atop the twelve-pointed star in the wood. "The truth will burn you, Sailis," she told the kelpie. With a sweeping motion, she pointed a palm at Janis and tugged the air between them.

With a yelp, Janis was pulled across the floor. She hung suspended, toes skimming the ground, Enryah's palm at her chest.

"No one has collected the energy from you yet," she told Janis. "I am sorry for this."

Before anyone could act, Enryah pumped Janis' chest once, causing the girl's back to arch and bright green light to spill from her core. Janis screamed in pain as Enryah siphoned off her sheefrah energy, made powerful by her humanity. Jay launched himself at the faerie but bounced off an unseen wall. He fell to the ground, clutching his shoulder.

Janis could not stop screaming. As the magic flowed into Enryah from her body, she cried in agony. The faerie pulled at something that could not come undone, that did not want to be extracted. Whatever it was inside, it had grown with Janis for years. It was entangled with her very essence and it longed to remain. Her back arched further as Enryah commanded it, ordering it to come forth. Janis no longer had air in her lungs to scream, her mouth open but silent. The root of what it was would not loosen, it was tied tight around her soul.

"You'll be taken with it, Janis!" Jay called out to her. "Let it go!"

She wept for this strange thing inside, this remnant of what ruled her in life. It was her, who she was. It had always been there, guiding her through everything she did. What would happen to her once it was gone, once she was free of it? Who would she be? Pain seared her insides, worse than she had ever felt. She was terrified, not of the pain, but who she might become alone in the world with nothing to stand in her way.

"Give it to me," Enryah demanded through clenched teeth. "You are making this harder than it needs..." She never finished her words. A blast of power shot from Janis, pulsing into Enryah and leaving Janis to slump to the floor in a dead faint.

7

"Janis!" Jay ran to her side, knees sliding on the wood floor. He was unable to turn her over with his hands behind his back. To his relief, she groaned and tipped onto her back on her own. Janis blinked her eyes open and Jay sucked in a breath. Her eyes were a honey brown and now fit her human face.

"What happened," she croaked, throat raw.

"For fuck's sake, remove these chains!" Jay shouted at Enryah who raised a brow but snapped her fingers, releasing the metal. Jay cradled Janis in his arms. "How do you feel?"

"I don't know... Lighter, maybe?" She tried to sit up but Jay held her in place.

"Don't move, yet," he instructed. Tensith came to his side as a fox

Her energy is drained, reaper. She is a fetch no longer. They have drained the life force from her completely. Whatever faerie power was lingering deep inside her is now gone.

Janis shook her head. "But I feel fine now, just a bit dizzy. I should be okay soon."

Tensith bared his fox teeth. *She will fade into nothing, as all mortals who die in the Hill do. She will not last the night.*

Jay wanted to rip Enryah apart but when Janis looked up at him with her beautiful brown eyes, he saw more bravery there instead of fear. His heart splintered.

"It's okay," Janis told him, pushing him away so she could sit. "We technically solved my crime, right?" She tried to smirk but the grin faltered on her lips. "I was going to die anyway, just a day later. And this time, I'll get a ferryman."

Not if you remain in the Hill, Tensith added. *You have to leave this place soon.*

"This isn't over," Jay whispered through a throat so tight it burned.

Enryah was holding out her arms, looking at her hands as if her new power was collected there. "The power is immense. Is this what you all feel like?" she asked Sailis who stared in shock. Next to him, Vilena stood from her stone chair.

"You have violated fae law, blatantly flouting it before the entire council," Vilena said, a sneaky smile on her face.

The dark elf on the other side stood as well, exchanging a look with Vilena. "The punishment is death. All in favor, speak now."

A chorus of "ayes" rose from the rest of the councilors. Sailis turned his malicious yellow eyes on Enryah.

"We are in accord. You and your companions will be put to death at once."

THIRTY-TWO

T HE GALLERY ERUPTED. SOME called for their deaths and others screamed for the truth. Enryah remained in the center of the floor, seething, as she looked at Sailis who wore a triumphant look.

"You are rotten to the core," she told him. "I have just done as you have and taken sheefrah power!"

"Yes, but we are more subtle about it," Sailis said, keeping his voice low enough so the crowd wouldn't overhear.

Anat moved to Jay's side as he stood, Janis following. "We need that mirror, cousin."

"Why are you guys so obsessed with this mirror?" Janis asked.

"Lucifer can only move in the space between two reflective surfaces facing one another from one who would invite him. It doesn't much matter although the more reflective the two surfaces are, the easier it is for him. So, mirrors work best," Jay explained. "And no one can enter the Hill who isn't invited. Not even the Morningstar."

"Not like we can ask them," Janis said, jerking a nod over her shoulder at the frenzied audience.

Fae had begun attacking members of opposing courts or opinions. Some tried to leave the council room while others pushed into the space, wanting a piece of the action. The guards were outnumbered, though they remained fighting for control.

Sailis had lost all authority over the crowd. He spread his hands and a green wall of light formed around the council bar and the main floor, blocking off any spectators from rushing the bench. To the guards that remained within the blockade, now a mere shimmer in the air, Sailis ordered, "Take them to the dungeons. Immediately."

Touch me and die, Tensith growled to nearby guards who were approaching his rippling fox form.

His body pulsed and grew until he was ten times his size and nine tails waved behind him. One of the fae councilors called for Tensith's immediate execution for showing his kitsune form in the council chambers. As if in answer, Tensith's large jaws clamped down over a soldier's head and crunched. Janis looked away, stomach rolling.

Using her newfound, stolen power, Enryah threw a bolt of magic at the council bench, though it fizzled away against their unseen protective spells. Jay ducked a ricochet of power thrown in retaliation by a wizened-looking council member.

"You all will pay for your lunacy!" screamed Enryah as she threw more power at the fae council, their unseen protective barrier shaking from the force.

In the mess, Janis crouched on the ground away from the center of the floor. Tensith and Anat held off most of the guards from reaching her and Jay now huddled together crouched on the floor, avoiding flashes of magic. Janis glanced up at the bar and saw a full pitcher before one of the council fae, now screaming at their private guards to do something.

"I have an idea." She lunged for the pitcher. The fae councilor who sat behind the water jug gaped at Janis open-mouthed as she grabbed the handle of the pitcher and yanked it off the bar, hurrying back to Jay. She poured the water out on the wood and bent over the puddle.

"What are you doing?"

"We can use the reflection of my eyes in the water for the, um, the, uh..." She could not bring herself to say Lucifer's name or one of his many epithets.

"No, Janis! Do you know how painful that will be for you?"

In a blink, Friend reappeared, shifting into her human form to hold Jay back when he rushed to Janis' side.

"It's too late, reaper," the demon said. "She already created a bridge. I told you, he was ready to move."

Jay shook out of Friend's grip. "I can't let her do this! We'll think of another way."

"Luci is the only being strong enough to combat fae magic, reaper. It's this or nothing."

The surface of the puddle moved a little when Janis spoke, her breath causing minute ripples in the water. She held her eyes wide.

"It's the one idea we have and it needs to happen now and you've got nothing else."

"Pull her into a pocket of Sideways," Friend instructed before punching an approaching fae in the face. "She needs quiet."

"We're in the Hill. I can't access my powers here," he complained to Friend's back guarding the two of them around the pool of water along with Tensith and Anat.

"Just try it, you stubborn reaper," Friend snarled. "It worked in the dungeons."

Biting his tongue, Jay closed his eyes and called his power to him. Janis felt a familiar tugging sensation behind her navel and an uncomfortable urge to pop her ears. She tried to remain focused on the little puddle on the ground before her as she was folded into Sideways with Jay and Friend.

"Janis..." Jay panted when the space around them shuddered to a stop.

"She's fine," Friend put a hand on Jay's shoulder. "She's very brave."

"But she shouldn't have to be," he said, monitoring Janis' activity in dismay.

Friend morphed back into a cat and twined herself around Janis' ankles.

"Hold still," she advised the girl, rubbing her tiny head on Janis' leg. "The more you move, the more painful it will be."

Janis took a deep breath. "Okay," she said in a small voice.

"I'll be here," Friend said and sat beside her. Jay crouched on her other side in the quiet of Sideways.

The little puddle was so shallow, larger clumps of dirt broke through the top of the water. This close, Janis could see all the details in the mud, the variation of colors and even tiny bubbles floating upward from where she had breathed air into the water as she spoke. She stared into her own eyes, the brown irises murky in the dim light of Sideways. Her eyes that had been such a burden for everyone in her life except her. Eyes she didn't know she should have hated. Eyes that kept her apart. Eyes that were so different until now. Janis kept looking into her reflection as if she would fall into it, as if the small pool of water would widen and swallow her whole and tuck her away from this world and her own. She would fall without end as she had within First Mother and her life would be about liminal space.

There was movement. A shadow in the background of her mind. It moved again, taking the form of a person.

"There's someone else. In the reflection, standing right behind me," Janis choked. She began to tremble and Jay threw his hands over her shoulders.

"Don't move," he urged.

A cool trickle of discomfort dripped over her forehead. It didn't feel like anything more than a cold finger had been dragged down her skin at first. The figure inside his eyes drew closer. Janis' teeth began to chatter. The pain across her temple expanded into a throbbing torture as whatever she saw in her eyes through the water reflection was seeking a way out. The figure moved to her right side, drawing ever closer but not taking shape. In the moment between one blink and another, she realized she couldn't breathe.

"Jay," she gasped, unable to draw in more air. Her throat felt thick and something squeezed at the sides. Janis moved her mouth open and shut to try and breathe but she could only exhale. In short bursts, she released the remaining air from her lungs until they were hollowed out. Her tongue swelled against the back of her mouth, cutting off the airway.

She was going to die. Again. With the horrifying feeling of not being able to breathe, Janis remembered she'd had breath the entire time she was in the Hill and now she was about to lose it again. Could a fetch die? She pondered the question as the edges of her vision blackened.

A hand slammed up against the puddle.

Choking, a single tear fell from Janis and landed on the surface of the little pool. As the ripples ringed around where her tear had fallen, Janis was released. She fell backward, supported by Jay. Friend darted away, lest she get crushed. Janis gasped for air and scooted away from the puddle where a huge, bloated eye was now roving around the space, looking for a way out. In an instant, the eye disappeared as the figure drew back, a shapeless shadow once more.

"Get away from the water," Friend said from behind them.

Jay helped Janis to her feet and Friend seemed to materialize into the shadows of the pocket of Sideways around them.

Whispers and echoes of strange voices swirled around the small space. They seemed to have weight to them, as if they were not just infinitesimal sound waves but instead a strong gust of wind blowing in from the north. Snippets of words sung and spoken reverberated past where Janis knelt as if she were nothing more than a stone in a river of sound. Friend hissed into the darkness.

"He comes," she purred, adding to the breathy voices. The utterance was snatched up and drawn into the stirring current, her words joining with the others.

"He comes, he comes, he comes, he comes," echoed in the air, overlapping at first and then joining together into a rising chant.

"Friend?" Jay whispered. The sound of a wheezing laugh answered him.

"Brace yourself, reaper. The Devil walks this night."

Jay shuddered at Friend's words. Despite his occupation and existence, Jay had not dealt with this leader of demons. Lucifer wasn't the only one, but he was by far the most significant.

The chanting peaked in a gathering of air, sounding like an explosion was about to happen. But it hung there, suspended between one second and the next. Detonation never came. Instead, a connective folding between two planes of existence slid through the air, incomprehensible to the eye. Lucifer Morningstar arrived in the expanse joining a drawn breath and its release, arriving into the space as if he had always been there.

"Get up from the dirt, little one. You don't belong there."

Janis flinched as a cool hand landed on her shoulder.

"Don't be afraid, you have done nothing wrong." The voice was velvety smooth and confident like each word was paired with an upward turn of the lips. It was what lay beneath the sound that wasn't right. All those gathered whispers chased after each word he spoke, seeking something within the syllables that was imperceptible.

Janis rose on trembling legs. She didn't know if she should look at him or not. She was far past the edge of her understanding. She kept her chin tucked and her eyes on the ground until she felt that cool hand cup her cheek and tilt her head up.

Janis met Lucifer's gaze head on, her new brown eyes wide but unwavering. His were an icy gray and stood out against dark lashes and rich golden brown skin. His black hair was short but made of large, loose curls that lay tousled atop his head looking windswept. A strong, regal nose sat above a wide, full mouth framed by heavy laugh lines. All he wore were some type of dark pants and a simple black shirt that covered his arms and clung to a broad chest. He was the most beautiful person Janis had ever seen, even in movies.

"You look amazing," she blurted and Lucifer smiled, teeth straight and even.

Faint echoes of laughing voices accompanied his smile and floated to Janis. She cocked her head, not sure if she imagined the sound.

"You are very kind," Lucifer told her, releasing her cheek and addressing Jay before he turned to face him. "You, reaper, are almost human."

"I couldn't stop it," Jay admitted. "I care too much about humans."

Lucifer smiled again. "I know what you mean," he said. Whispers of love and wonder and understanding trailed after his words. "Where are we, Friend?" His attention moved around the space as if it were a wild thing.

"Sideways, my lord," she answered without hesitation. "In the council chamber in the Hallow."

"They have just called for our execution," Jay said.

Lucifer's eyes roved to the reaper, his face even and serene.

Janis had sidled next to Jay and tugged on his sleeve to whisper in his ear, "Why is he so nice?"

A smooth chuckle broke from Lucifer as he grinned at Janis.

"Bad rep, I guess," Lucifer drawled, his words ending in a whisper that echoed around them all. "There are souls here, Friend."

"I told you," she gloated, cleaning a paw.

Lucifer ignored her attitude.

"Interesting," he murmured. The word duplicated when it left his lips, bouncing around the pocket of Sideways. Then, he gave a shallow nod. "Come with me now."

Sideways dripped away and in its place formed the council room.

The uproar of arguing voices ceased.

"Right on time, Your Highness," Enryah said, her voice slicing through the silence. "We were just about to call a vote for the new head of council."

"How dare you!" screamed Sailis. "He has no rights on these lands!"

Anger simmered in Lucifer's eyes, over his entire body, a wave of heat warping his outline like a desert mirage.

"I have every right," he said, dangerously soft. "You broke that agreement when you began to treat with my demons. The souls they were supposed to bring to me linger in your dungeons, do they not?"

The assembled fae cowered from the sight of Lucifer.

Sailis stumbled over his words. "Ah, n-not to my knowledge." Lucifer's stare bored into Sailis until the kelpie swallowed once and added, "Your Majesty."

Lucifer's eyes slid to other's on the fae council. He took them in one by one, whispers and murmurs of unintelligible words drifted around him, as if he were instead made from ideas and tones instead of flesh and bone.

The whispers gathered to a climax of overlapping voices and Lucifer's body pulsed, the very air around him warping its reality as he changed. Beautiful golden wings, three stacked atop each other on either side of him flared, as long as the whole council chamber, the tips of each feather smoldering in a banking fire. Glowing cinders and flakes of curling embers floated to the ground and soon a pile of ash gathered beneath his wings. Flames enveloped a ring of horns growing in a perfect circle from his temples and meeting at the crown of his head. His body was broken and deformed, a grotesque mockery of his once beautiful glamour. His skin looked like it was boiling from within, blackened in places as if he walked from a fire. The rubbery, sappy scent of tar and sweet stench of burnt flesh filled the space and coated every surface.

"I am the Fallen," Lucifer spoke and deep in his mouth, magma rippled beyond his tongue. Red-hot molten tears slid down his cheeks, burning his skin anew in their wake. "Any souls bargained for by my demons belong to me. They are not to be kept secret from my court in your dungeons."

Janis trembled next to Jay, huddling against the reaper to hide from this being of fire and pain. Every bone in his body was broken and set at the wrong angle and his movements were jerky and inhuman.

Sailis stood his ground behind the bar, though many of his fellow council members trembled at the sight and hid behind the wood and quartz.

"Begone, you foul thing," the kelpie said, gaining courage as he spoke. "The land of the Hill and beyond does not welcome such an abomination. You and your Father have no jurisdiction here."

Lucifer raised one muscular arm, veins of fire shining through his bloated and pink scarred skin. Howls arose throughout the great hall as souls rose through the parquet floor, clawing at invisible hands that grasped their necks. Janis clamped her hands over her ears at the awful sound but she was unable to block out the penetrating wails. Lucifer raised another arm and clenched a fist of broken fingers. All around the chamber, demons appeared.

Bobby materialized in a far corner, trembling and looking terrified. His dark curls quaked as he shivered in fear.

"You son of a bitch!" Janis screamed at him before she could stop herself. Jay held her at the waist to keep her from running across the room. "You fucking murdered me! I'll kill you!"

Bobby took a moment from his cowering to sneer at her. Janis screamed in wordless outrage.

"These are my betrayers," Lucifer was saying in his white-hot voice. "My loyal subjects, working against me all for what? Fae gold?" Some of the demons fell to their knees in apology but Lucifer ignored them, turning his blazing eyes to Sailis. "You let them keep these souls here in exchange for the killing of sheefrahs, didn't you? All so they didn't have to share with me."

Friend shifted into her human form and motioned for Janis and Jay to start backing away. Most of the fae in the gallery were mesmerized by the events, frozen and watching to see what would happen next. Anat put a hand on Jay's shoulder and looked pointedly at Tensith for the nine-tails to join them.

"I loved you!" Lucifer screamed out, raising each of the demons into the air. "You reach beyond your station and glut yourself on souls kept secret from the family!"

With another twist of his gnarled fingers, the demons melted like scorched wax and fell into puddles on the wooden floor, shrieking in agony until the last, viscous drop fell. Janis kept her eyes locked on Bobby's as his face melted away into nothingness, a sour feeling turning in her heart. As the demons disarticulated, Lucifer pulled his hand into his chest, dragging the souls toward and into him, forcing them into his being, a white light blazing as each soul sank into his skin.

"My lord!" the musical voice of Enryah cried out to Lucifer. "You have dispensed justice upon your betrayers but with your business dispatched, you must leave these lands to the fae."

Lucifer's molten eyes met Enryah's. "The matter is not settled," he told her in his unwavering voice, words coated by the magma in his throat. Tears continued to fall across his cheeks and Janis realized with a start that he was in constant pain. All that fire was hurting him.

The fae in the audience, held back by the magical barrier, began to clamor at the barricade, calling for the dissolving of the Seelie Court's monopoly on their government. The air in the council chambers began to gather together, pulling into a growing wind that circled the large room like a prowling beast. Lucifer began to glow from within. He rose into the air and white light spilled out from his unblinking eyes. The light streamed down and pinned Sailis as if under a spotlight. In response, the council stood as one, chanting in their own strange and secret languages, gathering their powers to them. The stolen power from forgotten, murdered sheefrahs.

The wind built around Lucifer as he warred with the magic of the fae. It lashed around Janis, forcing her to squint her eyes against the growing strength of the howling air. The barrier holding back the crowd from the main floor and the council bench shattered, green light flaring for a moment. Smaller fae were sucked into the swirling vortex and were carried around the room as others began to scramble out of the chambers. Green light burst in sparks as flying fae were dashed against the walls and their lives snuffed out.

"We need to leave before we get caught in the cross-fire," yowled Friend over the noise, still a cat. "This isn't going to be pretty."

"We cannot leave," Anat bit out. "The kelpie's magic is too strong. Only another fae may break it."

Jay's eyes met Janis' at the same time.

"I'm fae," Janis announced. "Or, at least I was. That has to count for something."

Tensith's nine-tails whipped behind him in the raging tempest. *It does not. Enryah took the last of your sheefrah essence when she siphoned the power from you.*

Janis' mind raced. "No," she said before repeating herself. "No. I have magic here. I don't need to be fae to use it. 'Magic is available to all who have the need', that's what Byst said."

That old salamander? Tensith questioned.

"I can still do magic!" Janis called out, triumphant.

You do not have the power.

Janis nodded to Jay. "But he does."

Shocked, Tensith shrank back to his normal size. *You do not know what havoc that would cause.*

"Who cares? We need to leave and I have the means to help us do it." Janis tugged on Jay's hand. "Do it."

Jay looked to Anat who held a pained expression. "There will be no return from this, reaper," the demigod warned over the sound of the whistling wind. "You will have to give her all your power. Your body-"

"It's fine," Jay cut him off as he clasped Janis' hand tighter. "Prepare yourself."

Leave me behind, child, Tensith told Janis who nodded once. *My glory will have to wait for another day.*

"Focus on me, Janis," Jay said in a hoarse voice. "Let me give you the power."

"What did Anat mean, there will be no return from this?" she asked in a voice that trembled.

Jay smiled. "I fear this body has carried me as far as it can. This will be the last act I do as Jay."

"I don't want that to happen," she told him. "We're...we've done so much, been through so much..." Her words faltered and died.

Jay smiled. "If I told you a week ago you'd say that, I'd be dead."

Janis shook her head, unable to laugh.

Across the room, Lucifer roared. The sound shook the very foundation of the Hallow. The line of councilors wavered, some of the fae taking a momentary step back from the noise. Sailis screeched at them to stay where they were. Tensith remained fighting what guards were left standing despite the winds and Enryah added her magic to the light of Lucifer.

"It's time, Janis!" Jay cried, gripping her hands anew and looking inward, gathering all of his essence.

All the power, it roared before flooding Janis.

Jay's body cracked, something inside breaking. There was a change within, a sudden ache, and he collapsed.

A searing energy rolled through Janis. She felt on the verge of tumbling over a hill or swooping low from a great height. And there it was.

Power.

Janis climbed to her feet, flexing muscles and marveling at how all this could be contained by her body. And it was her body. Not her parents, not the fae's, not even a mixing of worlds she never asked for. She was individual from anything else but her own self. Without another thought, she lifted a hand and pointed at the kelpie.

"It's over," she said in a voice that sounded both like her own mixed with Jay's. With a great crack, pure energy flowed from Janis, breaking Sailis' body and the barricade around the council chambers. A piercing shriek echoed her shot of power and she knew then they were free.

"The barrier is gone!" Friend called out, shifting to her human form and bending to support Jay, lifting his torso from the ground. "Get us out of here!"

Anat scooped Jay's other side and together the demon and the demigod supported his weight between them. Janis nodded and closed her eyes, remembering what it was like to jump when she was a ghost. The power within her was warm, a living thing. Or was that just her, now? She smiled at the easy comfort of the magic racing through her veins. It was Jay, who he was, all around her as if he was standing at her side, waiting and encouraging her to make the next move.

And she did.

THIRTY-THREE

I T WAS WINDY, WHERE they stood.

The green grass was in need of a mowing and the long tips waved in the breeze. The trees rustled above them and the sun was bright and summery. Janis looked around. The power within her was gone, used up in their escape from the Hill, though she didn't feel empty at the loss.

"I knew you could do it," Jay's voice was behind her, and she pivoted. Anat and Friend set Jay down on the grass, leaning him against a stone.

Rough dirt was piled beneath her feet, still bare after the loss of her boots. It was a fresh grave. They were before Janis' gravestone in a small cemetery in Petersburg. She looked at the words carved into the stone.

Janis Lyn Pereda. Our beautiful daughter. You will be forever cherished.

Janis knelt at Jay's side. "Did I hurt you when we jumped here?"

"No," Jay coughed, voice cracking. "This is from giving you power."

Friend shifted into a cat and rubbed against Jay until she could squirm under his arm and wiggle onto his lap. She sat there, purring, while Jay tried to stroke her head with a trembling hand.

"What can I do?" Janis asked, head bowed.

"Let's just sit here for a while. It's a nice day out," Jay answered with another cough.

"Lu still has some loose ends to tie up," Friend said between yawns.

On the other side of Jay, Anat settled into the grass and leaned back so their shoulders touched.

It *was* a nice day. The sky was a rich, painted blue and what clouds there were looked like blown glass set into the air. Janis wished she could feel the wind that brushed the tops of the trees and fluttering the green and yellow leaves but, outside of the Hill, she was a ghost once more.

It didn't feel so awful now, being dead.

Where she knelt before her grave, she could see them all at once; Jay with Friend on his lap and Anat next to him, leaning against her headstone. It no longer felt abnormal to not be alive. This was what felt normal. Being around Jay and their friends.

But what would come next?

"He's here," meowed Friend, moving from Jay's lap and shifting back to her human form, ruined faerie dress and all.

A gathering of whispers grew behind them and Lucifer appeared, wearing his beautiful glamour once more. He stood tall with his eyes closed and his face tipped up to the sun.

"All set, boss?" Friend asked, bobbing an ironic curtsey.

The fallen angel kept his eyes closed.

"There is a new council in place, headed by Enryah and Tensith. Representatives from both courts, working as one." With graceful movements, Lucifer opened his eyes and looked at Janis. "I am to give you a choice, little one."

Janis blew out a steadying breath. "I think I've had enough of being a ghost, thank you."

She stepped back when Lucifer smiled, his beauty was so arresting.

"You are a little different than other souls, don't you think?"

She blushed and ducked her head. "If you say so."

Whispers of laughter danced around Lucifer as he continued to smile at her. "I do." He nodded to the others. "I require three witnesses."

Friend and Anat nodded to Lucifer while Jay closed his eyes and tipped his head back to rest on Janis' gravestone.

"Janis, I offer you this gift: to pass on into peace and eternity or to return to life."

"Are you serious?" she gasped.

Lucifer blinked, waiting for her answer.

Janis' mouth hung open. This was everything she wanted, everything she had hoped for since she first opened her eyes in the OCME as a ghost.

"Tell her the rest," Jay croaked.

Lucifer tilted his head. "You would live, but without any memories of what has transpired."

Her heart lurched. Her eyes shot to Jay, who was grinning crookedly at her.

"I wouldn't get to see you again?" Janis asked in a small voice.

Jay shook his head. "You wouldn't see me in this body anyway."

"That's not the point," she said. "I wouldn't remember you. Any of you."

Anat looked away and Friend plucked at the ruined fabric of her faerie dress. With a pang, Janis wished to see Siroun and Sylvie one more time. She wondered if she would go on to meet other strange and wonderful people on her own. What would her life be if she forgot all of this?

Tears gathered in her eyes. She could go back to the world with her parents and school and places without faeries and demons and strange creatures. But she would have to leave them all behind. She would have to leave Jay behind.

"There's no other way?" she asked Lucifer. He cupped a hand around her cheek but remained silent.

"Live, Janis," Jay said from his spot on the ground. "See your parents again. I promised that would happen, didn't I? I was very right."

Janis gave a watery laugh. "Please don't make jokes right now, you suck at them."

Something in the air changed. Janis felt an adjustment of the world around her, like she had missed a step at the top of a staircase. Jay hissed in a breath and Anat and Friend had gone still.

"I knew They weren't lost," Jay said in hushed relief.

"Of course not. They have seasons of presence and absence just as we all do. They will remain when I and all this are long gone." Lucifer's voice was a thousand whispers. "Decide, little one, for They come and I must leave."

"Janis," Jay pleaded, eyes bright with urging. She ducked her head.

"Fine," she said, shoving her hands in her pockets and curling her fingers around the rowan berries from Tensith and the discarded angel feather she had picked up from Raphael all the way back in Edge. It was soft and downy as she ran a thumb over it.

"Are you sure this is what you want, child?" Lucifer asked. His voice was so beautiful, a song of longing and love.

"I'm sure."

Lucifer bent to kiss her brow. A cool breeze burst across her skin and tightened around her like a film.

"You have five minutes, little one," he said before he vanished with the softest of whispers.

"Five minutes for what?" Janis asked, whirling about, hands clasped into fists. The juice of the crushed rowan berries spilled from her clenched hand and the angel feather crumpled in the other.

"They're on Their way," the demon said, body shivering and fur rippling across her entire form. She looked down at the reaper. "Time for me to check back in on my den and my cats."

Jay nodded.

"I'll find you again," Friend told him in a promise. She bent and caught Jay's lips in a ferocious kiss that made Janis blush. The demon straightened, winking at Janis. "Bye, kid."

Friend morphed into a cat and took off like a dart across the grave-yard, angling for the nearby bramble to disappear beneath.

Anat stood his ground next to Jay, though his ink black wings trembled. "Get behind the stone, Janis," he instructed as the air pressure around them shifted.

Janis scrambled to obey. She heard a popping sound, like an uncork-ing of a bottle but when she peered around the headstone, she saw nothing. She couldn't feel a change, but she noticed Anat and Jay staring at something a few feet in the air. They spoke in hushed reverent tones Janis could not make out.

Insects buzzed in the distance, reveling in the late summer heat.

"Anat?" Janis whispered. He ignored her.

"I do," he said after another minute of silence. Then, he bowed his head. "Thank You."

Jay reached for Anat and clasped his hand. "I'm happy for you," Jay said. "Death has always been your dream."

Anat smiled, bending to bring his forehead to Jay's. The two held still for a moment, remaining silent while wind blew over the graveyard grass. Anat stood, gaze unfocused and far away. "Goodbye, my friend." He took two steps forward, to where Jay stared at something Janis couldn't see, and before he could take a third step, Anat was gone.

Janis gasped, her heart turning over.

"Yes, I know," Jay told the empty air. "I understand."

"No!" Janis shouted, running around her grave marker and barreling into Jay's arms, hugging him. Behind his back, her fingers were curled into fists so tight her nails left half-moon impressions in her palms. She was probably getting rowan berry juice all over him. "They're taking you away, aren't They? Into a new body?"

She felt him nod.

"You and I will both be gone in a moment," Jay told her, squeezing her in return. "I've never known anyone like you, Janis. You are the best human I know."

Janis protested. "I'm like the only human you know."

"And what a human indeed."

Janis wiped at her cheeks. He couldn't leave, not yet. Not when she was about to live again. "Jay, I..." she said, voice cracking as words failed her.

Janis felt a hand on her shoulder, though it could have just been the light summer breeze, and she separated from Jay.

With renewed energy, Jay got to his feet.

Panic bloomed in Janis' chest. She had so much to say to him, so much to talk about, that she felt short of breath.

"I won't ever forget you!" she called out in a rush.

Jay turned with a smile. "You will. Do something great with your life, okay?" He took a step, then another, and was gone.

Somewhere, across the burial grounds, a bird called out its song, the sound mixing with the thrumming insects. The wind blew across the treetops again and Janis was alone. She looked back to her gravestone and startled. It was gone. The mound of tilled earth was replaced with grass and a few scattered weeds. Janis felt the sudden urge to close her eyes. Before she did, she brought her closed fists to her heart, clasping her hands together before she drifted away.

SEATTLE

Twenty Years Later

THE HOSPICE WING OF the Swedish Medical Centre was quiet. The usual coughing and quiet mutterings and phones ringing in the distance were nothing but pleasant white noise. After fourteen years as a hospice nurse, Kana knew this floor, and all the sounds that came with it on an intimate level.

Room 403 was empty and Kana, after leaving the family in the hands of the grief counselor, had returned to the room to straighten it up a bit. She set a box down on the bed, the empty cardboard resting on the fresh linens next to her clipboard. Kana circled the room, placing photographs, cards, and small trinkets of memorabilia into the box as she went.

There was a scarf on the ground behind the chair on the corner, forgotten when it had slipped off the plastic covered seat cushion and landed upon the linoleum. She bent and had to try three times before her fingers successfully pinched at the thin, silky fabric. Shaking it out, Kana put it in the box with the rest.

Puttering around the rest of the room, Kana thought back to the name of the woman who had just been taken away down to the hospital morgue.

Still bad with names, she thought to herself. *And to think, you knew this woman for three weeks.* She wracked her mind, not wanting to give into reading the clipboard.

Mrs. Blythe O'Connor. The name came back to Kana and she smiled to the room feeling satisfied. She took a vase of almost-dead flowers from the windowsill and moved to the ensuite bathroom, closing the door behind her out of habit.

370

Grabbing a fistful of stems before tipping the vase over, Kana wrinkled her nose as brackish water poured out. The brown liquid circled the drain for a moment and gurgled away, leaving a stray leaf at the grate. She picked up the shriveled thing and flicked it into the trash before depositing the rest of the wilting blossoms into the basin with a dull thud. She looked up into the mirror above the sink and fixed her sagging ponytail by grabbing two bunches of hair and pulling.

Before leaving the room, she used the toilet. Sitting on the seat and thinking still, after all these years, she would never get used to this part of being a human. Not that it was so awful; she had seen worse. It was strange to her, a necessity of living without any trace of romanticism. A neat, businesslike behavior. She flushed the toilet and washed her hands, grabbing the vase and opening the door.

A tall, Black woman stood at the foot of the vacated bed, reading Kana's clipboard.

"Sorry," the stranger said. "I was just checking something." She turned and Kana felt the breath go out of her lungs all at once. "I'm doing my hospice segment this month and I got my rooms mixed up."

"No trouble," Kana said, struggling to keep her breathing even.

It couldn't be.

The woman was still thin, but her limbs held no trace of the lanky awkwardness of her teenage years. Her dimpled chin was as strong a feature as ever, though her arched brows, decorated beneath with a subtle swipe of dark eyeshadow, softened her expression. She had laugh lines now. They framed her glossed lips, a sign of the joy that had finally found a place for itself in her life.

She held out her hand, keeping the clipboard in the other. "I'm Dr. Pereda."

Kana hesitated, then switched the vase to hold it cradled in her other arm before shaking the doctor's hand. "Kana Minami, hospice nurse." She hoped she wouldn't feel how sweaty her palms were.

Dr. Pereda smiled. "Nice to meet you, I'm sure we'll bump into each other again."

Kana smiled in echo, unsure of what to say. She couldn't believe it. Kana felt her heart swell with pride as she looked at Janis. She had grown into a fine woman, secure and capable, and Kana could see the deep intelligence sparkling in her now normal, but still beautiful, brown eyes. Kana's human emotions swirled around her now, though she felt comforted by them instead of disconcerted. She felt everything with a depth and familiarity she never could before she changed, before she integrated with her humanity. There were so many facets to the regret, admiration, joy she felt now, it was still fascinating.

"Do you own a cat?" Janis asked, interrupting Kana's thoughts.

"What?"

Janis pointed at something near Kana's feet. Kana looked and let out a small laugh when she saw some cat hairs at the cuff of her scrubs.

"Oh, yeah. She sheds so much, it's impossible to remove all of it."

Janis chuckled. "I better get back to work," she said. "This is yours, I believe." She remained smiling as she handed over Kana's clipboard.

"Thank you," Kana said to Janis' back as she walked out of the room. Kana's shoulders slumped as she tucked the vase into the box. It would have been impossible, but nice to be recognized. Putting the clipboard in the box for the time being, Kana hoisted the effects of the late Mrs. O'Connor and balanced it on her hip when she flicked off the light. Finding her way down to the elevator to change floors, Kana lost herself in memory.

Handing off the box to the patient liaison office and informing them to which patient it belonged, Kana grabbed the clipboard and trudged back to her desk on the fourth floor.

Dropping into her chair in the nurse's station, Kana ignored the bittersweet feeling, now fresh in her mind.

I wish I could tell her everything, she thought to herself.

She moved her computer mouse and the machine brightened from sleep mode. Had Janis ever mentioned wanting to come to Seattle? To become a doctor?

"I can't remember if she told me that," Kana muttered out loud, private thoughts invading her speech.

"What?" a fellow nurse at the next desk asked.

Kana swiveled in her chair and smiled. "Sorry, just thinking out loud." The other nurse returned her attention back to the phone pinched between her cheek and shoulder.

Rotating back, Kana clicked through a few screens on the electronic health records software. She stopped at one page and dragged the clipboard toward her, scanning the information on the paper and making sure it was correctly reflected on the computer. Kana tapped on the keyboard a few times, striking keys in sharp motions as she edited small pieces of information.

She palmed the top of the clipboard, pushing against the spring loaded clip to remove the top sheet of paper and flipped it over to the other side. Kana froze.

At the bottom of the paper was a note, scrawled in the messy, hand-written style of a doctor. Taped to the back was a yellowed feather that had seen much better days. Looking up and around, Kana made sure no one was watching before bending over to read the words, staring at them, making sure not to miss a single letter.

Hey, reaper. Long time no see.

Heart beating fast, Kana sat back in her chair and started to smile.

7

Acknowledgements

It is such a pleasure to be able to write my first acknowledgements page. I have wanted to write a book since I was eight years old and, due to the large number of years since then, I have amassed a lot of people to thank. This is going to be so fun!

Thank you first and foremost to my family. Mom, Dad, you knew I was going to do this a long time ago and didn't say "boo" to me going full liberal arts in college while financially supporting me. Thank you, Nevin, for acting out my first stories with me on the fireplace "stage". Thank you also to Andrea for cheering me on from all the way across the country.

Thank you so much to my editor, Taylor Johnson, I could do nothing without you and that includes staying sane throughout the entire process. Thank you for not only providing excellent and quality edits, but for holding my hand during late night anxiety attacks, answering my every annoying question right away, and discussing the deeper points of music with me (Taylor's Version).

To my first editor, Whitney Saunders, thank you for getting me started and for only cheering me on when Spellbound snapped me up.

Speaking of Spellbound, thank you for being not just my publisher but my champion in my literary endeavors. From the moment you believed in my manuscript to seeing it transformed into a tangible book, the experience has been surreal and exhilarating. Your team's support, from editorial guidance to marketing efforts, has been instrumental in bringing this dream to fruition. It's an honor to have worked with professionals who are as committed to my story as I am. What a special and rewarding relationship this has been, and I can't wait to see where this partnership takes us in the future.

For the use of her name, thank you to my friend Archer. It is such a good name, and it fit into the story perfectly. And thank you for being one of my first guinea pigs back in the 2010s reading the first scraps of what I wrote. And thank you for reading it again when it was a little better.

To my other guinea pigs, Alanna and Chelsea, thank you for patiently accepting the odd bits and pieces I fed you over the years without complaint.

I wouldn't be who I am today without my friends Caroline and Annikka. Thank you for always being available to text, despite the time change.

Thank you to my original beta readers, especially Emerson, and my sensitivity readers, Tia and Yvonne, Jennifer and Taiya, who made my story better even at the very end. Thank you to everyone on my ARC and PR teams for reading and reviewing. Each and every star is a win in my book.

Thank you to Anna Harmon for the most delightful and beautiful book cover. You 100% knocked it out of the park.

My writing groups Book Babes, Grubstreet, and everyone in The Chat have been pivotal in helping me develop this book. Thank you for working so hard for absolutely no money.

Thank you to Michael Marano for reading the original chapters and shaking me out of my bad habit of using mirrors to describe characters.

Finally, thank you to Alex. I love you more than I have room here and I am so grateful you're on this journey with me. I hope you're ready for many more adventures.

ABOUT THE AUTHOR

Nikki M. Griggs is a lifelong writer with a degree in Creative Writing and a deep love for all things fantastical. A marketing executive by day, Nikki writes from her home in Seattle. When on "just a quick break" from writing, Nikki can be found playing video games with her husband and on long, rainy walks with her pup. *Janis and the Reaper* is her debut novel.

FOLLOW NIKKI'S WRITING JOURNEY!

author@nikkimgriggs.com
Nikki M. Griggs on Amazon
www.goodreads.com/nikkimgriggs
@nikkimgriggswrites on all social media platforms

Printed in the USA
CPSIA information can be obtained
at www.ICGtesting.com
JSHW03021001023
49312JS00008B/31

9 798891 230040